THE FLANAGAN OPTION

THE FLANAGAN OPTION

A Novel

BRUCE A. BOWMAN

SHIRES
PRESS

4869 Main Street
P.O. Box 2200
Manchester Center, VT 05255
www.northshire.com/printondemand.php

THE FLANAGAN OPTION

Copyright © 2009 by Bruce A. Bowman

ISBN Number: 978-1-60571-052-5
Library of Congress Number: 2009913737

Building Community, One Book at a Time
*This book was printed at the Northshire Bookstore, a family-owned, independent bookstore
in Manchester Ctr., Vermont, since 1976. We are committed to excellence in bookselling.
The Northshire Bookstore's mission is to serve as a resource for information,
ideas, and entertainment while honoring the needs of customers, staff, and community.*

*Printed in the United States of America
using an Espresso Book Machine from On Demand Books*

ACKNOWLEDGMENTS

I am grateful to my family and friends for giving their time to edit my manuscript and for sharing their comments.

First and foremost, I am, once again, indebted to my wonderful wife, Leslie, for lovingly and enthusiastically encouraging me to write and publish this novel. Many thanks, also, go to my two sons, Gregory and Douglas, for their thoughts after listening to me read my manuscript aloud.

My good friends remained a constant source of encouragement. My thanks go to Jack and Letha Sawyer whose opinions, as veteran readers of countless novels, I treasure. I wish to thank Paul Viollis, a distinguished security expert for his advice. The Reverend David Campbell proved to be a wealth of knowledge on Rome and religion. I wish to thank my newfound friend and fellow Christian brother Tony Piscitelli for his assistance and strong encouragement. Thank you to Laura Odell, always a good friend and advisor, for her critical insights.

*"Non nobis, Domine, non nobis,
sed Nomini Tuo da gloriam"*

*"Not unto us, Oh Lord, not unto us,
but to Thy Name be given glory."*

**Psalm 115, verse 1
The Holy Bible**

THE
FLANAGAN
OPTION

CHAPTER ONE

Could you truly kill Satan?

Imagine having a loaded pistol in your hand with Satan sitting unawares in the adjoining room.

Would your hand be steady and your aim true?

Could you muster the courage to pull the trigger?

Was it possible to do?

Let's state that it is possible and that you could muster the willpower. Would a regular lead bullet penetrate Satan's armor or would you need a silver bullet? Perhaps, a titanium bullet of super strength?

What caliber would you need? Surely, a .45 caliber round would suffice, wouldn't it?

Where should you aim? Does Satan have a heart to target? Would a clean head shot be enough?

Regardless, why even bother to try? Isn't Satan immortal until God claims victory at the end of time?

Who are you to dictate the terms for Satan's demise?

We all have odd thoughts coursing through our minds, don't we? Our sense of reality differs enormously from person to person and from culture to culture, doesn't it?

Odd thoughts, indeed, were distracting Marco Spitini at a most unfortunate time. He desperately needed to remain focused for he was about to slay Satan. Or, at the very least, one of the devil's deputies.

Thankfully, Marco had something better than a pistol. His arsenal was infinitely more sophisticated.

Marco Spitini opened a small, white plastic bottle and poured out a red gel capsule that he placed among a colorful assortment of medicinal pills in a diminutive silver cup. Closing the bottle, he dropped it into his pants pocket. Next, he opened a bottle of seltzer water and filled a crystal glass engraved with an ancient coat of arms.

Battling the distractions of a stressed mind, he paused to review the plan's details. Spitini could think of no critical omission. In true form, he had left nothing to chance. This last minute loss of focus surely was nothing more than the inherent weakness of the unpredictable human mind, yes?

If he was to vanquish Satan's principal lieutenant, Spitini needed to assume his usual cold, aloof frame of mind. There could be no trace of any crime whatsoever. His victim had to appear to die a natural, although untimely, death. Anything less would place his cause in great danger for the target's death would produce intense worldwide scrutiny.

Happily, modern technology afforded perfect weapons for the perfect crime.

The red gel capsule looked identical to that prescribed by a physician. Even the white print markings matched; but, this capsule contained no medicine. Instead, it held powerful, lethal bio-regulators.

Marco Spitini did not understand modern biological science, but he had learned that bio-regulators were by far better than any poison. Whereas poisons are plant extracts or artificial products, a bio-regulator is very similar to biological substances naturally found in humans for regulating normal physiological processes. Bio-regulators were, therefore, 'clean' weapons that would go undetected by any autopsy whereas the simplest of autopsies would reveal a poison. And, he reminded himself, the amount needed to produce death was miniscule compared to a poison.

Spitini marveled at the scientific ingenuity behind this biological weapon. The former Soviet Union had taken warfare to an entirely new level during the Cold War. Legions of Soviet scientists working in complete secrecy genetically engineered these clever weapons. However, the disintegration of the Soviet empire left the scientific geniuses destitute and scrambling for funding. Many sold themselves to new state sponsors who were quick to come to their rescue. Indeed, Spitini's benefactors had hired some of the best scientists to replicate and improve upon their former Soviet work. The red gel capsule lying in front of Spitini was the product of one such research effort.

The capsule that Marco Spitini so carefully placed on the silver tray contained not just one, but two bio-regulators. One, publicly known within academic circles as Substance P, would lower the victim's blood pressure thereby producing unconsciousness. The second bio-regulator, unknown to the rest of the world, would complete the deadly bio-regulator cocktail and cause the victim's immune system to attack itself. Death was sure to rapidly ensue within a matter of hours while the victim lay unconscious, unable to call for help.

The medical community would be confused, but inevitably would attribute death to immunological complications associated with the victim's poor health.

Distracted once more, Spitini gazed out the open window onto the square below. The sheer white curtains parted in the slight breeze to reveal an amalgam of international tourists and locals feting another unusually warm, sultry July evening in the square below.

The din of motor cars and vespas in the distance and the backdrop of spectacular city lights reminded him that Rome never slept, even at this late hour of nearly eleven o'clock.

Incredibly, Rome had survived millennia despite mankind's sustained mischief. Rome was the place to be if you wanted to carouse with intense passion in Nero's shadows. This ancient city had witnessed every sort of human scandal, conspiracy, crime, combat, political maneuvering, love affair, and murder.

Times may change, actors may come and go, and governments may rotate, but, in the end, Spitini soberly reflected, history does repeat itself in so many ways. How would history remember him?

The sudden shouts of young people in the square below broke his wandering thoughts. Marco, feeling his pulse racing as the moment of assassination approached, realized that he needed to calm himself. And so he began to pray. Silently, without uttering a word aloud, he prayed.

"Grant me peace and calmness of mind, standing firm in your name … grant me the courage and clarity of vision to do your will, …."

In the weeks leading up to this final act of treachery, Marco wrestled with his faith. Could he justify murder in God's name?

" … give me the strength to fight enemies in dark places, to vanquish the evil tyrants who curse your faithful servants, and to stand victorious at the threshold of a new age …."

Marco was intent on dealing Satan a severe blow.

"… accept me as your faithful servant able to do Your Will, not mine, to my final breath …."

If needed, Marco Spitini was prepared to be a martyr. Anything for the greater cause.

" ... may this cup liberate my peoples from Western dominion so that they may carry Your Word to the four ends of the world. Allah, all praise is yours. You brought all into existence. May the peace and blessings of Allah be upon the noble prophet Mohammed and upon all who follow in his footsteps until the Day of Judgment. In the name of Allah the merciful and the master of the day of judgment, I pray for strength and courage."

With a renewed sense of focus, Spitini looked into the adjoining room. And then, with perfect calmness, Monsignor Marco Spitini, the principal assistant to the Papal Secretary of the Holy Roman Catholic Church, picked up the silver platter, turned on his heels, and strode into the adjoining room to battle Satan.

CHAPTER TWO

Pope John Paul III, deep in thought, sat at his desk with his head bowed. Not aware of Monsignor Marco Spitini's entrance, the pontiff stared relentlessly at the papers arrayed on his desk as if through sheer strength of mind the answers would come to him. Too much was at stake to permit fatigue to overcome him.

He was finding it difficult to sustain his high workload. The bout with bronchitis had sapped his energy and, ever a poor patient, he was terribly annoyed with the imposition of physician visits, medical tests, and medications. The loss of sound sleep during the warm summer nights further intensified his discomfort.

The nightly glass of port on his desk was meant to relax him for a good night's rest, but even that customary remedy was failing him. This morning, for example, he had awakened from another of several troubling dreams.

In one dream, he found himself trudging along in a desert. He was weary and thirsty. He remembered seeing a passing caravan of Middle Eastern nomads in robes and turbans noisily jabbering aboard camels and taking no notice of him despite his pleas for water. The heat was unbearable and he was growing thirstier. Finding no sign of an oasis, he took the tall Papal Staff and struck a boulder, but, instead of seeing water spring forth, bright red blood spewed onto the desert floor. Surprised, he stepped back and clumsily dropped his Staff which was then crushed by the boulder.

The night before, John Paul III was deeply shaken by another dream wherein an angel appeared to him at the foot of his bed. John Paul remembered his futile attempts to speak with the angel in John Paul's native French language, then Latin, and, finally, Greek. The angel, wearing a pure white robe, did not reply, but, instead, raised his right arm to point toward the ground by the pontiff's bed. Suddenly a shaft of brilliant white light shot from the angel's outstretched arm and pierced the floor to illuminate hell beneath. John Paul remembered leaning over his bedside to be taken aback by a repulsive drama unfolding below him. Men and women in tattered clothes were tearing at each other in anguish and in physical pain to climb slimy, snake infested walls in vain attempts to escape hell. Leaning too far, the Pope felt himself falling off his bed towards hell, but at the last instant, the angel rescued him and rose heavenwards with John Paul in his arms.

Awakening from these troubling dreams, he felt vulnerable and frighteningly mortal. Who could blame John Paul? These dreams were unwelcome intruders on his peace of mind.

A good night of sleep with peaceful dreams would be such a tremendous relief.

Perhaps, he should heed his physician's advice to retire to his summer residence south of Rome in the peaceful, small town of Castel Gandolfo. The 17th century Papal Palace situated high above Lake Albano, had an absolutely stunning view of the Italian countryside that would lift his spirits. The clear, cool air and the serenity of the vast gardens would provide much needed respite from the stifling Roman heat and the never-ending hustle and bustle of the city. It might just restore his sleep. Unfortunately, he felt compelled to attend to critical matters of state that required the full resources of his Vatican staff. In particular, John Paul needed to reassess his ecumenical outreach programs.

As the Pope for over three years, he had actively sought to bridge the growing gap between Christians and Muslims. Many of his fellow French citizens' worries that Islam was now second to Catholicism in France had sparked a growing confrontation between Christians and Muslims. Although greatly troubled by this, he had to admit that affairs between the two camps were never very amicable. Particularly in France where Islamic terror groups had operated for decades to undermine France's efforts to buoy up the Algerian government.

It was no secret that there was a lot of bad blood between Islamic fundamentalists and Frenchmen. In more recent times, Islamic fundamentalists subjected Paris to a wave of bombings in 1986 and, again, in 1995. It was a grisly matter with rescuers having to amputate victims' limbs in order to extricate them from the metro subway cars. The bombs, built of propane tanks filled with nails and bolts, were designed to inflict maximum human carnage.

Not immune to terror threats, the Catholic Church was often targeted, too. Muslim terrorists slit the throats of seven French priests whom they had kidnapped. Pope John Paul III had even lost a good friend and mentor in French Bishop Pierre Claverie whom the Muslim terrorists assassinated to protest the French Foreign Minister's 1996 arrival in Algiers.

The confrontations continued into the 21st century. As the senior French Cardinal, Pope John Paul III mediated the passionate dispute arising from Muslim students wearing the traditional 'hedjab' veil to their French schools. Barred by school administrators from entering their schools, the protesting students drew international attention. He, additionally, witnessed the turmoil of violent street demonstrations protesting the Muslim immigrants' squalid Parisian living conditions where poorly maintained apartment buildings were prone to burn.

In seeking solutions to these Christian-Muslim confrontations, Pope John Paul III was the very model of France's program of assimilation. On the international front, he joined the majority of his fellow Frenchmen in opposing the American-led invasion of Iraq. He organized the French dioceses in collecting food and medicine for shipment to Iraq following the capture of Bagdhad. He found the monies to sponsor Catholic health care teams in the Mideast, too.

Upon election as Pope, he assumed the name of John Paul to announce his very public, international activism in the name of religious reconciliation. Taking his cue from Polish John Paul II who had staunchly supported ecumenical outreach, French John Paul III was determined to reach out to the world's Muslims in order to counter fundamentalist Islamic aggression and Western bigotry.

After all, John Paul II, had made surprisingly successful advances to Islam. He was the first Pope to enter a Muslim mosque and he even went so far as to kiss a copy of the Qur'an much to the consternation of ultra-conservative Catholics. He appealed to Muslims to end "the chain of hatred and terrorism which threatens the orderly development of the human family."

John Paul II was also a master of finding common ground between the Christian and Muslim camps. "Your god and ours is the same God, and we are brothers and sisters in the faith of Abraham," he declared. Believing that Jews, Christians, and Muslims accepted God's attribute of peace, Pope John Paul II spoke ardently of building a multi-religious community of believers patiently "inaugurating a new era of justice and peace." And ever a skillful diplomat, John Paul II distanced himself from the American war in Iraq thereby circumventing radicals' attempts to link Islam to the East and Christianity to the West in a new East-West conflict.

The next Pope, Benedict XVI, also sought to find the common ground between Christian and Muslim faiths. Acknowledging their common heritage in Abraham, the German Pope urged the two communities to recognize the Ten Commandments as shared, universal moral imperatives for opposing cruel terrorism.

John Paul III prayed that God would permit him to continue this ecumenical outreach in order to quell the Christian-Muslim conflagration before it reached the proportions of a religious inspired world war.

Unfortunately, according to the reports from his far-flung dioceses that lay on his desk, that task was proving more and more difficult. He was finding it increasingly difficult as Pope to bridge the growing chasm between the two religious communities.

His fingers tapped impatiently on his ornate desk. Made of the finest mahogany it was adorned with intricate carvings of angels, the Apostles, and, at each corner, a gargoyle. It stood tall and proud atop graceful legs with curved arches rising to support the table and anchored by bold lion paws.

Atop its highly polished surface stood a desk lamp illuminating a hand carved wood cross from the idyllic Bavarian town of Oberammergau and a small, brass incense burner in the shape of an altar. Off to the right was a polished silver-plated paperweight in the shape of the symbolic Christian fish. John Paul III sat at the center and head of the two columns with the papers stretching out in precise rows with the most noteworthy papers closest to him. He had read each of them at least twice, carefully taking into account the veracity of each source and painstakingly cross-referencing reports. He was forming an exceptionally troubling assessment.

Those papers closest to him in both columns had red borders denoting their extreme sensitivity and urgency. They had arrived from the Church's worldwide dioceses over the course of the last week in wax-sealed envelopes placed within diplomatic pouches.

If this were a national ministry of defense, these papers would be stamped top secret in red ink and tightly controlled within a special-access program.

He marveled over the Catholic Church's global access to information. The vast collection of confidential reports that the Catholic faithful gathered and passed along to the Vatican for evaluation regarding governments, national leaders, political revolutionaries, trade issues, and competing religious activities was one of the world's best kept secrets. Catholic priests, monks, nuns, and parishioners were virtually everywhere. They had tremendous access to people at all levels, all ages, and all faiths. The CIA was surely envious.

This extensive human intelligence network permitted the Pope to undertake extraordinary action even in fairly recent times. In 1978, Papal intervention in South American diplomacy prevented a major war between Chile and Argentina by mediating a territorial dispute over Patagonia. Pope John Paul II was known the world over for intervening in Polish affairs to defeat the communist government. The Pope's ardent advocacy for humanitarian aid had served to undermine many a ruthless government's oppression of its citizens. Furthermore, the Vatican, to this day, has a representative at the United Nations and has a voice in many key international organizations.

The Catholic Church's human intelligence network truly rivaled that of any of the major national spy agencies. Who would have guessed?

Intelligence was essential. As the world likes to say, knowledge is power. The Catholic Church had mastered that lesson long ago. But, the Church augmented that with unswerving loyalty and inspiring faith to guide it where knowledge trails off.

Whereas people in the modern information age demand every conceivable bit and byte of data in their quest for material advantage and control, they remain bedeviled by imperfect knowledge. Or overwhelmed by a deluge of raw data. In the end, good leaders rely on their gut feeling. A decision is, ultimately, an act of faith – either in oneself or in God.

The Church had learned to train men to act with certainty on limited information. Through faith, these men could comprehend the unknown and extract information for action.

The Catholic Church had been blessed with great men and women of faith serving God to restore hope, to counter the devil with force wherever necessary, and to support the downtrodden. Indeed, God had rewarded the Church's faith throughout the centuries with seemingly miraculous results. But, where the Church saw God's hand in motion providing miracle after miracle, the world only saw the exercise of the Church's powerful influence and wealth. No wonder the world often dismissed miracles as mere coincidences. However, the faithful, always cognizant of God's ultimate power, recognized God's right to intrude upon mankind whenever God wanted. Hence, a miracle was nothing more than God shouting at us, "Listen up! I have something to say!" And listen the Church did.

Yet, even the Church failed from time to time. Humans are fallible and, so, a congregation of humans embodied by a church could not hope to be infallible. Nevertheless, John Paul was certain that this was not a time for failure. Indeed, as he gazed incessantly at the reports on his desk, he had to admit that a miracle would be most welcome now. The Catholic Church was under attack and time was running out to counter an imminent threat.

John Paul's confidential files mirrored international media reports that have long confirmed a worldwide assault on

Christians. Saudi Arabia oppresses over a half million Christian guest workers by forbidding Christian services, churches, and Holy Bibles. Infractions often lead to arrests, or, in the case of a Muslim who has converted to Christianity, to death sentences. Pakistanis effectively use their Muslim blasphemy laws to threaten Pakistan's two million Christians with imprisonment. In Indonesia, uniformed militia forced Christians to convert to Islam at gunpoint. The Egyptian government finances mosques, but denies renovation permits for Christian churches. Chinese communists are jailing lay Christian leaders, priests, and Bishops.

Even in formerly tolerant nations, government customs officials are removing Bibles from entering missionaries and outlawing Christian preaching. In France's former Algerian colony, only twenty empty Catholic churches remained after the Muslim government converted many to mosques and nationalized all of the Roman Catholic schools and hospitals.

The virulent level of violence astounded John Paul. He could not miss the irony of the hostility directed towards Christians preaching world peace. Muslim gunmen of the Moro Islamic Liberation Front fighting for a Muslim homeland murdered a Catholic priest in the Philippines. Elsewhere in the Philippines, the Abu Sayyaf Islamic group kidnapped a Catholic priest along with seventy-five children and teachers from the Claretian Catholic School. After demanding that all church crosses be removed, the terrorists executed the priest when he refused to save his life by reciting Muslim prayers. Teenage students attending a private Christian high school in Poso Kota, Indonesia, were ambushed by Muslims and decapitated. Elsewhere in Indonesia, Muslim militants attacked a Catholic school with a disabled children's center in order to convert the compound to a military base for attacking the adjoining Christian neighborhoods. In Nigeria where Muslims have put bounties on the heads of all priests, a mob pulled Father Bello from his car, gouged out his eyes, and murdered him in cold blood. Protestant and Catholic clergy have been tortured and killed in war torn Sudan. Egyptian mobs destroyed over a hundred Christian-owned businesses and killed twenty Christians. Priests were gunned down in African civil wars.

John Paul had earlier reviewed a thick report outlining the ideology of hatred taught in mainstream Muslim schoolbooks used in Saudi Arabia and Saudi academies worldwide. Beginning in their first year of school and reinforced each year thereafter, Arabic children are taught that every religion other than Islam is false and that Muslims will triumph over the 'Jewish apes' and the 'Christian swine.' John Paul was particularly struck by the admonition to school children that the Muslim greeting 'Peace be upon you' is only for faithful Muslims, never for non-believers. Chillingly, the Muslim textbooks reminded John Paul of early twentieth century European school books warning young, impressionable children of evil Jews thereby fueling the fires of the holocaust.

In 2005, a Saudi school teacher made the grave mistake of countering these textbooks with positive remarks about the Holy Bible, Christians, and Jews. He was summarily fired and condemned to prison after suffering a flogging. He was pardoned only after international protests.

The Church was under attack from within, too. Adversaries had successfully infiltrated the Church undermining its vitality, worldwide appeal, and diplomatic influence. Priests were sodomizing young children, questioning papal authority, and deviating from sound theology. In the end, the Church was ridiculed as old-fashioned, mismanaged, and corrupt. The media's over-sensationalism had not helped.

His fingers stopped tapping. Shifting his weight, Pope John Paul III drew his hands in close and clasped them against his chest. Speaking softly to himself, John Paul III prayed, "Lord God, I beseech you as your humble and obedient servant to grant me wisdom and the power of discernment to counter the forces of evil besetting your Holy Church. In the name of your son, Jesus Christ, amen."

He let out a slow, deep breath. His mind cleared and sensing that the Holy Spirit was reassuring him, he refocused what little energy he had at this late hour on the reports. These red-bordered reports indicated that another kind of adversary had infiltrated the Catholic Church. This was an insidious adversary who was hell-bent on destroying the Catholic Church and, perhaps, other Christian churches. For whatever reason, this adversary had planted one or more moles in the Roman Catholic Church. The reports detailed worrisome indicators that this enemy was preparing to execute a strategic plan to undermine the Roman Catholic Church and, later, the major Protestant churches.

John Paul wasn't totally convinced by the reports. Muslim terrorists had clearly targeted western economies; but, after all, no one had flown an airplane into a church.

Nevertheless, Muslim militants clearly sought to destroy Judaism and Christianity in order to supplant them with Islamic law. Surely, a covert onslaught against the Roman Catholic Church, the mother church of Christianity, made indisputable sense?

Eventually, Islam would have to confront its rival religions. Little did he know that the first shot of a protracted war against the Roman Catholic Church and its fellow Christian religions was aimed squarely at him.

"Your Holiness, I have your medications for you. Is there anything else you wish before I retire? Spitini inquired, interrupting the Pope's thoughts.

"Oh, ah, thank you, Marco." The Pope glanced up at Spitini and waved him forward.

Spitini nodded and stepped towards the Pope placing the silver tray on the Pope's desk. "Will Your Holiness be working more this evening? Are you absolutely sure that you do not wish anything further?"

Spitini had become accustomed to seeing John Paul neglect the physician's orders to curtail his work schedule.

"Oh, ah, you are very kind to keep asking, but, thank you, no. I will be just fine." Then, looking at his watch, John Paul realized how late the hour had become. "Oh, my. It is late. I must put these reports aside and go to bed or Doctor Terzini will be terribly upset with me." Looking back up at Monsignor Spitini, John Paul continued, "You should go to bed, too. You are very kind to check in on me every night."

Despite the warm words, the Pope looked up at Spitini with some irritation. The Pope had never taken to Spitini, but had grown to respect Spitini's painstaking attention to the smallest of details and ability to work long hours. Spitini was almost too perfect – highly intelligent, well spoken, perfectly groomed and slim, exceptionally attentive, and a master of the Church bureaucracy. Thankfully for Spitini the Church had use for men despite their total lack of potential for pastoral duties.

The Pope also knew that the dour, black-haired Spitini was not well liked by much of the Papal staff for Spitini was seen as arrogant and aloof to anyone of lesser rank while fawning over anyone of senior rank. He almost did not accept Spitini for the post of principal assistant to the Papal Secretary for those very reasons, but a key Cardinal had highly recommended Spitini to assist John Paul in his effort to bridge the Christian-Muslim conflict. John Paul had to admit that he needed someone like Spitini because Spitini had a tremendous understanding of Islam. Monsignor Spitini's years serving the Roman Catholic Church in difficult Muslim countries proved invaluable to John Paul's ecumenical initiatives. A European priest who had navigated, much less survived, several deeply Muslim cultures and who spoke Arabic and Farsi was a rare asset at the Vatican.

John Paul often sought Spitini's assistance in communicating and visiting with Muslim leaders as well as in corroborating key elements of the reports now lying on his desk.

Nevertheless, John Paul kept the threat of a cunning adversary and mole to himself. No need to mention it to anyone until further substantiated, he reasoned.

Pope John Paul III glanced at the cup of medications and frowned. "I wish I didn't need to take any more of these pills. I'm tired of pills. I'm tired of doctors. I'm tired of being sick."

Pope John Paul then had to laugh. "Listen to me, Marco! I'm beginning to sound like a young child whining to his parents." Reluctantly, he then reached for the medications and glass of water, but drew back.

"Marco, the seeming impasse with the Muslim community vexes me. Perhaps, my approach is wrong. Rather than proclaiming a Church initiative led by the Pope himself, I should follow modern business practices and decentralize. That is, step out of the spotlight and reinforce grassroots initiatives. Give the Bishops more resources and decision-making authority."

He paused and studied Spitini's reaction, but there was none. John Paul reached for the tray and picked up the glass of water. He took a sip and added, "If I do, you are likely more valuable to the Church out there than here at the Vatican. Think it over and let me know where you would like to serve."

"Your Holiness, I am comfortable here, but I will gladly serve the Church wherever you deem it best."

"Give it some thought. In the meantime, I am thankful for your service here." John Paul then reached for the red gel capsule and swallowed it and his other pills, one by one.

Seeing John Paul re-focusing his attention on the papers before him, a relieved Spitini prepared to exit.

"Very well then, Your Holiness. I hope that you do not work much longer tonight. I will see you in the morning," Spitini replied knowing that while he would see the Pope, the Pope would not see him.

Dead men can't see.

CHAPTER THREE

Monsignor Marco Spitini left the Papal apartment at a measured pace. Bypassing the elevator to use the marble stairway, he headed for the ground floor. At the exit he nodded to the Swiss Guards and wished them a good night knowing that his time of departure would be noted.

Stepping outside into the warm, humid air, Spitini headed for his apartment in the Vatican compound assured that he had completed his mission. Yet, he walked briskly with quiet confidence and no outward sign of jubilance. He had completed his mission thanks to Allah. The world would awaken to find the Pope dead. Praise Allah.

He had every reason to feel pride. Spitini fancied himself as the new and improved version of the papal assassin. After all, a fellow Muslim, Mehmet Ali Agca, had been unsuccessful in his attempt to assassinate a pope, John Paul II, in 1981. The West, in its quest to finish off communism, had successfully pinned the failed assassination plot on Bulgarian intelligence operatives and the communist order suffered great shame. Spitini could not help but wonder about the validity of the west's claims. Was Agca really a Bulgarian instrument or were the Bulgarians merely an instrument for the west to attack the east? If the Bulgarians did not send Agca, who did?

Marco Spitini was satisfied that he had, in fact, successfully assassinated John Paul III. The red gel capsule was sure to work. It simply had to. Come tomorrow, the name John Paul would surely be the unluckiest of all papal names. John Paul I had unexpectedly died from a heart infarction after only thirty-three days as pope. Conspiracy theorists, to this day, suspect foul play. The succeeding pontiff, John Paul II, had survived Agca's assassination attempt, but the after-effects weakened him and appeared to hasten the onset of Parkinson's Syndrome. And now, John Paul III was as good as dead.

There was no doubt in Spitini's calculated thinking that John Paul III had to go. Only then could the concerted campaign to undermine Christianity begin. John Paul had been far more successful in his ecumenical outreach to Islam than he gave himself credit for. Relations with a great many Sunni clerics had improved and there were signs of moderation in anti-Christian sentiment. For instance, Pakistan was considering a revision of its blasphemy law that was responsible for much oppression of Christians. These advances greatly concerned Spitini and his Shi'ite mentors who were sensitive to their Sunni counterparts' ongoing persecution of the smaller Shi'ite sect.

Spitini had had high hopes for John Paul's professed ecumenical interests after suffering through the preceding pontiff's ill-advised policies. In Spitini's biased mind, John Paul's predecessor, Benedict XVI, had embarked on an internal witch hunt targeting bishops who were deemed too sympathetic to the plight of Palestinians and Muslims in the Middle East. Most of these bishops were replaced by bishops noted for their open support of Israel. Marco Spitini ruefully had to admit that even he had subsequently fallen victim to this purge when his newly assigned bishop dismissed him from Lebanon.

It was in Lebanon where Spitini had first encountered Islam and where he grew disillusioned with the Catholic Church. He discovered a religious Shi'ite community that rivaled Catholicism in its passion for ritual, mysticism, and charismatic movements. Yet, he was increasingly disturbed by overt western oppression of the Muslims. For reasons he traced back to his father, Spitini was struck by the seeming hypocrisy of the west and its puppet, Israel. Sympathetic to the Muslim plight Spitini spent much of his time assisting and educating Muslims. His reassignment from Lebanon back to Bolivia, after four years in Beirut, startled him and, many years later, was still a bitter memory for him.

The Catholic Church had subsequently embarked on a program that Spitini could only call a massive Islamophobic crusade. Influential Italian cardinals publicly called for the closing of mosques throughout Italy, for laws banning Muslim immigration, and for the elimination of Islamic religious education in Italian schools. The Italians were joined by an international chorus of cardinals and bishops who sharply focused on Islamic terrorism and the perceived Muslim refusal to be assimilated. To Spitini's horror, they even went so far as to pronounce that Islam violently opposed pluralistic society and modernism.

Despite his early admiration for John Paul's outreach efforts to Muslim leaders, Spitini's view of the pontiff quickly soured. So much so that Spitini was now firmly convinced that, despite his early overtures to Islam, Pope John Paul III was simply another manifestation of Pope Benedict's ill-fated policies. But, with a thin ecumenical veneer to shield the pontiff's true aims of blunting Islam's advance. There was little reservation in Spitini's mind that the Catholic Church was moving on a path of confrontation with Islam.

For instance, the Pope preached ecumenical reconciliation between the religions on one hand, but on the other hand the

Pope was all too happy to win converts from Islam. Spitini now believed that ecumenism was nothing more than an underhanded move to win Muslim converts to Catholicism. The proof was in the pontiff's published edicts that proclaimed that only Catholic churches were true churches and that only Catholicism could lead mankind to divine salvation. Spitini noted that this tack unmistakably implied that all others were bound for eternal damnation.

Nor was the Pope content to rely on edicts and proclamations. His ambitious new missionary programs deployed hundreds of young, overzealous Catholic lay leaders worldwide to proclaim the Catholic message, distribute Holy Bibles, and win converts. Western medical teams openly wore crucifixes before their Muslim patients. Bishops increasingly refused communion to Catholic politicians who accommodated overly liberal policies. Lastly, the Church's radio broadcast its Christian message globally, much like the United States beamed Radio Free Europe into communist Eastern Europe.

The Pope's audiences in Rome were all too often granted to western political leaders. Indeed, in seemingly bowing to the growing number of European Islamophobes, John Paul had even entertained one of Europe's most divisive, outspoken authors of anti-Muslim immigration last winter. Whom did Pope John Paul III think he was kidding?

John Paul III had, also, embarked on a vigorous internal program of reform to shore up the Church's management, ideological loyalty, and finances. Early results were positive. The loss of parishioners in America and Europe continued, but at a reduced rate. Donations to the Catholic Church were up and the Vatican was enlarging its worldwide missionary initiatives.

In Spitini's view, this was not a Church seeking mere ecumenical rapprochement with Islam. Frankly, Spitini sourly viewed Pope John Paul's reign as more reminiscent of the Catholic Church's response to the Protestant Reformation centuries ago. Faced with the schism between northern and southern Europe following Martin Luther's denouncement of Catholic Church practices, the Catholics went on the offensive in establishing the Jesuit Order, an extremely ideological, supremely organized, evangelically aggressive Catholic Order that squared off against protestant reformers. Jesuits fanned out over the world to challenge Protestant evangelism, to proselytize in the far reaches of the newly discovered Americas, and to establish renowned universities. Spitini vowed that this history would not repeat itself and thereby bedevil Islam's victory. If anybody was aggressively to convert infidels and defend the faith, it would be the Shi'ite Muslims.

Happily for Islam, Spitini predicted that John Paul's death would weaken the Catholic Church. He leveraged his position at the very highest level of the Catholic Church to understand its future direction. Painstaking, covert research, direct interaction with Church leaders, and access to confidential documents provided great insight into the political workings of the organization and the motivations of key individuals.

Marco Spitini's analysis indicated that a large contingent of influential cardinals believed that the Church was suffering from a profound crisis. They believed that the sins associated with modernism had weakened the Church. Liberal theology and a watering down of doctrine permitted too much subjectivism to reign.

These same cardinals had grown weary of John Paul's costly international agenda. They regarded John Paul's ecumenical outreach as a costly failure. They reasoned that the Church's limited funds were of more value in reforming the Church. They were, therefore, poised to turn the church from outreach towards internal restructuring and education.

Spitini's analysis also indicated that under new leadership the Catholic Church would re-establish its Euro-centric focus in order to cut off Europe's retreat from

Christianity. A European, and very likely an Italian, would be selected as the next pontiff in order to signal Catholicism's return to its roots.

This was good news for Islam. It was poised to advance and to occupy the voids left behind by the withdrawing Catholic missionaries. Simultaneously, Islamic terrorists would covertly work to undermine the Catholic Church in Europe and elsewhere. This would serve two purposes: first, to weaken the Catholic Church for Islam's final assault and, second, to protect the millions of Muslims living in the West.

Of course, Islam also needed to turn its sights on the remaining Christian religions. Protestantism in northern Europe and England, the Greek Orthodox Church, and the Russian Orthodox Church needed to be simultaneously weakened for Islam to prevail. It would be a protracted, complex campaign; but, it was necessary and inevitable.

Reaching the door of his Vatican apartment, Monsignor Marco Spitini crossed the threshold and refocused on the days ahead. This was no time for overt jubilation. He could ill afford to let down his guard. As the last person to see Pope John Paul III alive, he was all too aware of the intense scrutiny coming his way. Spitini needed to organize his thoughts in order to play the critical part of a shocked, grieving priest.

Upon entering his apartment, Spitini flicked the light switch to illuminate the main room. He hurriedly crossed the room dodging a brown leather chair with a deft hip movement at the last moment and, as always upon returning at night, opened a large window. However, on this occasion he only opened one wooden window shutter. Not wishing to have an electronic signal or phone call intercepted, Spitini's handler had instructed him to use an unobtrusive signal, such as opening one shutter, instead of the usual two shutters, to signal mission accomplishment.

Pausing a moment, his gaze followed the shaft of light onto the cobble stone courtyard below. Surprised by the opening shutter, a black cat scurried under a dark bush before it could assault a smaller, white cat. Peering into the deep shadows was futile, but he thought he saw a darkening shadow move. Spitini wondered if that person, a secret comrade in arms, felt as elated as he did. Taking a deep breath of the aromatic, warm air, Spitini turned back into the room and, heading for the bathroom, began to prepare for bed, as he always did. The nightly ritual would last exactly ten minutes. He could lie in bed thereafter to mentally steel himself for the morning. Sleep, he admitted, would likely be difficult anyway.

Indeed, Spitini lay fully awake in bed for nearly two hours thinking and rethinking his actions and words for the following day. In his typically fastidious fashion, he coolly examined everything step by step to ensure that he committed no errors. However, as he confirmed in his mind that he was prepared for the coming day's events, his mind began to wander before dropping off to sleep.

His dreams drifted towards his family. His father had been an Iranian expatriate who ran afoul of the Shah. He fled Iran for Europe where he met Marco's mother, a young southern Italian beauty. After a short courtship, they married and within a year had their first and only child, Marco. Marco's father, who had adopted the Italian Spitini name, was adamant about blending into the native Italian community so he outwardly converted to Catholicism and established himself as a trustworthy accountant and, eventually, a member of the parish council in the small Italian farming community.

Growing up among the hearty, outgoing farm families, the introverted and agonizingly quiet Marco had few friends except for the characters in his books. He was the one that everyone knew would succeed elsewhere. Indeed, Marco's mother had always had high hopes that her scholarly son would one day honor the family by taking the vows of a Catholic priest.

Nevertheless, during those special moments alone with his father that all young boys treasure, Marco's father would talk of his life in Iran. As a youngster, Marco was fascinated by his father's retelling of the epic tales of Mohammed, the Islamic defeat of the Byzantine Empire, the valiant battles against the Crusaders, the Moors' conquest of northern Africa and Spain, and the Arabs' gallant desert combat against Germany and the Ottoman Empire. Along the way, Marco's father would also privately share with his son the religious faith of Islam as well as teach Marco a bit of his native Farsi language.

Following his father's tragic death in a car accident in 1980, Marco Spitini gave up his engineering career and, to his mother's delight, entered a Catholic Seminary at age 28. A mature and disciplined student, Marco graduated with high marks and was ordained a Catholic priest. Recognizing Marco's aptitude for engineering the Catholic Church, at first, dispatched him to Central and South America where he busied himself with small construction projects: small chapels, rural schools, and municipal water and sewage projects. He returned to Italy where he served in Venice and then at the Vatican.

The Church then sent him to help the Lebanese Christians rebuild. After four glorious years there, Spitini returned unhappily to South America. Fortunately, he was able to leverage old favors from his days at the Vatican in order to obtain a new assignment back to the Islamic region. Spitini found himself ministering to the small, persecuted Christian community in Pakistan. However, once again, he found himself identifying more and more with the Muslims. Still resentful over his banishment from Lebanon, Spitini progressively grew more and more disenfranchised from the Catholic Church. He nearly left Catholicism, but fate intervened. He let himself be recruited as a mole for Islam.

Masoud Sadeqi smiled to himself when word of Spitini's success reached him. Masoud had endured a year of intense planning and coordination to reach this night. His patient recruiting of Spitini for Iran's secret war against the West had paid off. Now he only had to wait for the morning news to announce the pontiff's passing before proclaiming victory and offering prayers of thanks to Allah.

Masoud recruited Marco Spitini nearly four years ago in Pakistan. On sabbatical from his Italian university in Florence where he taught mathematics, Masoud noticed Spitini's fervor in supplying Shi'ite farmers in a small town with foodstuffs. Always a good reader of people, Masoud instantly recognized Spitini's cynical disappointment with the Catholic Church. Pretending to befriend Marco, Masoud soon discovered Spitini's Iranian heritage and mounting fondness for Islam.

Not wishing to press too fast, Masoud patiently steered Spitini closer and closer to Islam. Then, on the night before Masoud was due to return to Italy, he answered his door to find Spitini in an extremely agitated frame of mind. To Masoud's delight, Spitini excitedly began talking of his wish to convert to Islam. It was then that Masoud proposed an alternative to his new student, Spitini.

The overthrow of the pro-Western Shah and the ensuing Iranian occupation of the U. S. embassy clearly did not endear Iran to the United States and its western allies. The Iranian mullahs correctly predicted that the West, through the United Nations, would mark their regime for sanctions and isolation. A growing confrontation between the Islamic East and the Judeo-Christian West was certain to replace the former Cold War pitting the communist East against the capitalist West. Therefore, Iran embarked on a secret war to lay the foundation for ultimate Islamic victory. So, rather than welcome all expatriates back to

Iran, the mullahs encouraged selected patriots to remain abroad in Iran's service.

Masoud, a graduate student at France's Sorbonne University, was persuaded to remain in Europe to covertly further Iran's cause. Within five years, Masoud had assembled a small band of Iranian graduate students and guest workers to serve as Iran's eyes and ears. The group had grown into a network of spies with Masoud secretly at its pinnacle. But, it was Marco Spitini who was Masoud's crowning recruit.

Marco was a perfect recruit. Marco's youth, intelligence, and Islamic fervor endeared him to the Iranian professor who, much like the Red Brigade terrorist faction, taught at day and plotted at night. Masoud early on recognized the Catholic Church's prominent role in Western influence and had always been awestruck by the Church's immense capabilities to collect and use information. He, therefore, persuaded Marco to remain in the Catholic Church. Ever since, the professor served as Marco's mentor. And handler.

Marco was a superb Iranian mole within the Catholic Church. For much of that time, he did not have much useful information to pass along, but Iran could afford to patiently bide its time. Marco's surprising ascendancy to the post of principal assistant to the Papal Secretary working in the very heart of the Vatican was the turning point. Monsignor Spitini now had access to the Church's most sensitive cables as well as admission into the innermost circle of the Catholic Church's leaders.

Iran grew increasingly alarmed over the vigorous reform initiatives of Pope John Paul III. Within a short time, Iran's secret forces had determined that the Catholic Church needed to be silenced and reduced in power. To that end, the Pope was targeted and Marco was covertly trained to be the assassin. The perpetrators were encouraged by Marco's reports that the small group of leading contenders to replace John Paul III were very aged, largely unknown Cardinals who shared little interest with the Pope in undertaking a public, activist position in international affairs. So far so good. It was time to take action.

Masoud had grown confident in his assessment that Islam had to strike at the heart of the devil if Islam was to fulfill God's plan of worldly dominion. It had to strike at the very heart of western civilization, namely, the Judeo-Christian foundation of western thought, culture, and values. Islam must defeat Christianity in all of its forms. Where better to start than the mother church founded by Saint Peter himself?

With the Catholic Church consenting to the rising tide of Islamophobic attacks on European Muslims, it was all the more important to silence the Catholic Church. Europeans were increasingly prone to jeopardize the rights of the continent's millions of Muslims and to throw up barriers to further Muslim immigration. Even the European Union had had significant second thoughts about admitting Muslim Turkey.

Indeed, the Catholic Church was gradually more and more a critical translator of Islamic practices and beliefs to Europe. Although Europe was now deeply secular and many a Catholic parish wasn't much more than a senior citizens' club, much of secular Europe still held the Catholic Church in high esteem. This was exceptionally troubling to Masoud.

Masoud was struck by the irony of a Catholic Church that was highly authoritarian, yet ardently championed democratization. In Masoud's estimation, the West would be wise to critically examine the immense power vested in a single, self-proclaimed infallible pontiff.

Masoud reflected that, in contrast, the community of Shi'ite believers resembled the New England Congregationalist movement. No one single Imam led Islam and the debate among different groups of Muslims was, in Masoud's experience, far more egalitarian than any Catholic deliberation.

The Catholic Church must be shown to be the sham it is – a weak, privileged male society with self-serving secrets and double-standards. Catholicism had hoodwinked the world for two millennia into falsely worshipping the dead prophet Jesus Christ.

This was a war for the world's souls and it would be fought on many fronts. First and foremost, it had been fought on the economic front. The planes hitting the World Trade Center were proof of that. However, if Islam was to supplant the world's religions, the war was destined to be fought on the spiritual front. Finally, Masoud knew it would be won on the military battlefields. Praise Allah for delivering the nuclear bomb to Iran so that Islam might achieve final victory.

Masoud bristled under his collar whenever he recalled Western injustices. Iran was destined to forever reverse Islam's recent embarrassing losses to the West and Israel. Muslims needed to reclaim their holy sites from invading infidels and reassert their ownership over their oilfields. Masoud fervently believed that under a resurgent Iran, Muslims no longer would have to submit to past tragedies played out under European rule, such as, having to helplessly watch as Muslim women are raped in Bosnia or soldiers trampled under advancing American tanks.

Masoud trusted that with the rise of Islam the West would no longer regard Muslims as uneducated Arabic nomads atop camels herding sheep across barren deserts before returning to their harems. Or as irrational, over-emotional, and belligerent religious fanatics seeking to impose anti-modern and oppressive cultural rules. Masoud remained convinced that the world would soon awaken to the glory and might of Iran, his benevolent patron and financier, at the forefront of the Muslim vanguard.

Although a majority in over fifty nations, Muslims lacked a unifying leader. A resurgent Islamic Iran would be the charismatic leader destined to restore Islamic supremacy and to counter globalization's 'westoxification' of their culture.

The assassination of the Catholic pontiff was Masoud's proudest contribution to the Iranian cause. More glory remained to be earned.

CHAPTER FOUR

"The Pope is dead. Details at the top of the hour."

"We interrupt the regularly scheduled programming to bring you news of the Catholic Pope's death."

""Now to our correspondent in Rome to learn more of the shocking news out of the Vatican."

America, five hours behind Europe, was awakening to media reports on the sudden and heartbreaking death of Pope John Paul III. Without prior warning of any Papal health problems or medical visits, the major news networks were caught flatfooted. Scrambling to put anyone or anything on the air, NBC, CBS, and ABC were airing past footage of the Pope and of the official statement read by a Papal spokesman on their morning shows. By eight o'clock they would be relaying the 'official' reaction from the White House where the flag had already been lowered to half-mast. With its worldwide reach, CNN was able to broadcast live analysis by its Rome-based correspondents standing in St. Peter's Square beginning to fill with mourners. Despite their evident physical proximity to the news sources, none of them were any wiser regarding the facts and circumstances. Fox News was first to begin airing 'live' interviews with European political leaders while BBC countered with 'live' interviews of two Catholic Cardinals, official statements from Buckingham Palace and 10 Downing Street, and analysis from an English physician. Not to be outdone, the internet blogs and news sites were abuzz with commentary, conjecture, and conspiracy theories.

Cardinal Sean Murphy had already declined nine interview requests by seven o'clock that morning. The truth of the matter was that he did not know anything more than the hapless media. The official email from the Vatican had merely stated, "The Pope is dead. Come to Rome."

Cardinal Murphy, awakened at half past three that morning, was predictably still in a foggy state of shock in his office adjoining St. Patrick's Cathedral in midtown Manhattan. With no appetite for breakfast, he had earlier retired to a small chapel in his residence for prayer. In the meantime, his staff had composed an official statement from the Archdiocese of New York and had notified the Catholic prelates in New York to initiate the appropriate plans for mourning and prayer. The archdiocese was exceptionally occupied and industrious despite heavy hearts and tears.

Now standing in his office at eight o'clock, Cardinal Murphy was dictating instructions to his executive assistant. He needed flight reservations, a limousine and an escort at the Leonardo da Vinci Airport in Rome, appointments at the Vatican, diplomatic credentials and passport, an assortment of documents, and more. A small staff delegation needed to be assembled for accompanying him to Rome, too. Appointments for the next several weeks had to be cancelled. There was much to do.

"Does that do it, your Excellency?" his executive assistant inquired.

"Yes, yes. That will do for now. I'm sure that a thousand additional items will pop into my head, but let's get going," he replied. "Oh! I almost forgot! Please, get my friend Ernie Flanagan on the phone."

As his assistant left the office, Cardinal Murphy glanced at his computer terminal to note that there were far too many emails arriving in his in-box, but none from Rome. Sitting down, he clicked on his internet Explorer icon to check a couple of bookmarked news sites, but he was disappointed to find no new details from the Vatican.

The phone buzzed and he picked up the receiver. "Hi, Ernie. Look, you've no doubt heard the news of the Pope's death."

"Yes, that's right. I am most grieved. We all are."

"No, I don't know very much about the situation. I am totally surprised and in the dark on the details. I thought John Paul was in good health, although we had some indication that he was having some sort of a lingering cold. But, then again, you know the old Roman saying that the Pope isn't sick until he's dead. The Curial staff may have been protecting his privacy and authority."

"Yes, that's right. I'll be heading to the mother Church in Rome."

"When? Oh, tomorrow. Tomorrow afternoon from JFK. So I won't be able to make our usual lunch. Please forgive me Ernie, but I know that you understand."

"Thank you for your prayers and thoughts, Ernie. I'll see you when I get back, but it could be September for all I know. The pontiff's funeral will likely be in a week and a half. Then, a week or so later, the cardinals will assemble in a conclave to elect our new pope. No one goes home until a pontiff is announced and installed. I've got no idea how long that will take. This is a first for me."

"Look, my friend, I've got to go. May the Lord's blessings be with you. Talk to you later."

He hung up the phone and, taking off his reading glasses and rubbing his temples, Cardinal Murphy leaned back into his high-backed office chair. In the morning turmoil, he hadn't realized just how weary he was until now. He closed his eyes, rested his arms on his lap, and began to reflect on the coming burial rites and his first conclave to elect a Pope.

Cardinal Murphy was not a contender for the Papacy, nor was he the senior Cardinal from the United States. The short list of papal contenders surely included a small group of other, more senior Cardinals. Indeed, it was Pope John Paul III who had placed the scarlet red cap marking Sean Murphy as a Cardinal of the Holy Roman Catholic Church on his head just two years ago. However, Cardinal Murphy did entertain hopes that an American would be elected Pope in the near future. But, he never imagined that the near future would arrive so quickly.

The American Catholic Church was beset by a host of problems that it must overcome before any American would be earnestly considered for the Papacy. Child molestation cases had drawn the public ire and the ensuing settlements had appreciably drained the coffers. The Catholic Church's positions on abortion, pre-marital celibacy, homosexuality, and female priests were poorly supported by Americans, much less the liberal northeastern Catholic seminaries. And with the increasing conservative tilt of the Church, far too many American Cardinals were perceived by their fellow Cardinals as too liberal and modernist.

No, he reluctantly had to acknowledge that a growing gulf between Rome and the United States must be bridged before any American could hope to win a papal election in a future conclave.

Cardinal Murphy could not have been more wrong. True, his analysis was absolutely correct. The facts spoke for themselves. The Church's direction was clear. However, surprising events would soon transform apparent reality. Indeed, in the coming weeks he would play a pivotal part in an unfolding, high stakes drama at the Vatican. An American would be at the center of the furor and Cardinal Murphy would have to decide whether the events were mere coincidences or a series of divinely-inspired miracles.

This morning, however, Cardinal Murphy was exhausted. Finding himself at the center of the Church's papal election was the last thing on his mind. With his eyes still closed, it wasn't long before the Cardinal drifted off to sleep for what would become a short fifteen minute nap. It would be one of those deep slumbers from which one feels totally refreshed. Remarkably, he would also recall every vivid detail of his dream.

Cardinal Murphy found himself in a helicopter that was flying north over the Verrazano Narrows Bridge connecting Staten and Long Islands. Evidently, it was now autumn for the trees were a mix of yellows and reds. It was a brilliant, clear morning with every feature of the Manhattan skyline ahead clearly visible. Every few days, a high pressure front carrying crisp, cool air clears out the Manhattan smog to reveal a beautiful, magnificent sight. This was one such morning.

The helicopter veered slightly to its left and headed towards the mouth of the Hudson River. Peering ahead, Cardinal Murphy saw the gaping void where the twin towers of the World Trade Center had once stood. He was expecting to see the tall steel skeleton of the long-delayed World Trade Center Memorial, but, to his bewilderment he couldn't see anything but the glaring reflection of the sunlight from a cluster of small buildings on the site.

After motioning the pilot to fly over the WTC site, the Cardinal edged forward in his seat straining to see the WTC site. There was no evidence of construction at all. Instead, as the helicopter approached the site, he could make out a collection of churches! There was a gothic Catholic cathedral complete with flying buttresses, a dignified and austere granite-clad synagogue, several Protestant modernist churches of steel and glass, a

Muslim mosque marked by a large dome and tall minaret tower, a Shinto shrine with magnificent wooden orange and black Torii gates, a massive Hindu temple of carved stone, a Buddhist statue, a waterfall surrounded by stone carvings of American Indian sun, animal and bird symbols as well as a statue of the Navajo Yeii Spirit, and a host of other religious symbols and shrines that he did not recognize.

What had formerly been the world center for finance and wealth was now a world center for religions and faith! What a transformation! He was mesmerized and he felt a distinct surge of joy. What an awe-inspiring sight!

And with that, Cardinal Murphy awoke with a start. He was a bit flustered and confused as he sat up erect in his chair, but he soon realized that he had fallen asleep. Checking his watch and stretching his legs, he sighed with relief upon finding that he had not been asleep too long. Then he began to smile as the dream came back to him. A world religious center in downtown New York! Wow! Then, in a throwback to his Irish youth, Sean Murphy, His Eminence and Cardinal of the Holy Roman Catholic Church, whispered to himself, "You assholes, just try to bomb that!"

CHAPTER FIVE

Ernie Flanagan closed his mobile phone and replaced it on his belt clip. It was always good to hear from Sean.

Ernie was one of the very few people who still called Cardinal Murphy by his first name, Sean. After all, they had known each other ever since that first day fifty-seven years ago when, in diapers, they shared a playpen on the floor of the Murphy's living room in Brooklyn, New York. Their mothers were best friends and lived in brick row houses across the street from each other. How could Sean and Ernie not be the best of friends?

The two lads were classmates throughout grade school and parochial Catholic high school. They were confirmed standing side by side before their joyful parents in the Catholic Church.

Sean captained the high school debate team and Ernie the chess team.

Standing six feet and three inches, Sean lettered in basketball whereas Ernie, standing five feet and six inches, lettered in wrestling.

Sean's nose was always in a book while Ernie's arm was often around a pretty girl's waist.

Sean graduated second in their high school class and Ernie was right behind him at third out of ninety-four graduates.

Sean was admitted to the Jesuit-led Georgetown University while Ernie stayed closer to home at New York University.

Sean left for Rome to attend the Pontifical North American College at the Vatican. He was ordained, served a year at the Vatican, took a commission as a Chaplain in the U. S. Army for five years, and returned to the United States for a series of pastoral and administrative assignments in the Catholic Church.

On the other hand, Ernie opted for the Peace Corps and two years in northern Africa. Afterwards, upon returning home, he surprised everyone by completing a doctorate in theology, not at a Catholic seminary, but at the protestant Alliance Theological Seminary in the picturesque town of Nyack in the lower Hudson River Valley.

Sean Murphy was now His Eminence, Sean Cardinal Murphy, of the New York Archdiocese. Ernie Flanagan was now Professor Flanagan, Chair of the Division of Bible and Christian Ministry at Nyack College, a Christian liberal arts college overlooking the Hudson River twenty miles north of New York City.

Throughout all of their travels, they remained in contact with each other. Letters, telegrams, and long-distance phone calls served them well in the 'old days.' Now, in the modern information age, email and cellular phones served to connect them. How had they ever survived without cell phones, faxes, and computers? However, with Sean's appointment to New York, two years ago, they had been meeting for lunch in the last week of each month. Well, it wasn't going to happen in July, Ernie thought to himself. And possibly not in August, either.

Too bad for he was looking forward to the mind-stretching, intellectually rigorous discussions on religion and politics interspersed with some good old Irish humor and recollections of their childhood.

Ernie turned back to the kitchen sink where he had been washing some strawberries when Sean's call came in. Now picking up five red strawberries one by one, he hulled each, and sliced the berries into a bowl of plain, whole milk organic yogurt. Next, he reached for a plastic bag of all natural granola that he liberally sprinkled onto the yogurt. He re-sealed the bag of granola and, with his stomach beginning to growl impatiently, Ernie poured all-natural, pure honey onto the feast. Satisfied, he picked up his spoon, mixed the concoction, sat down on a bar stool, and hit the television remote's mute button to turn the sound back on. He had an hour before needing to leave for a meeting in his office at Nyack College. Thereafter, he was meeting his literary agent for lunch and returning home to prepare for his fall semester of classes. Later, he would change into a business suit for an evening dinner in Manhattan where he was the keynote speaker to a collection of officers from the New York Police Department, U. S. Secret Service, and FBI. Even the Mayor would be there.

Ernie had ministered to many of the law enforcement agents who survived the 9-11 attack in New York. Long a close friend of Doug Karpiloff, the head of life safety and security at the World Trade Center, who was lost in the crashing Tower One, Ernie had dedicated many hours to Doug's memory through community service. Tonight, New York's finest and bravest were recognizing Ernie's service with a special award.

In the meantime, Ernie was content to listen to the television set on the kitchen shelf as it continued to carry news stories about Pope John Paul III with interruptions only for local traffic and weather updates. John Paul III had seemed like a good fellow with an active agenda to make the world a better place. Too bad he died so early at age sixty-three.

Originally Catholic himself, Ernie was actually Ernesto Peter Flanagan. He owed his first name to his Italian mother who insisted that her son's first name be Italian if his last name was destined to be Irish. Fortunately, his father compromised on Ernesto so that his son could shorten it to Ernie and survive his childhood in an Irish neighborhood. Ernie could still vividly recall how, as a youngster playing baseball catcher in a pickup game after school, he had learned the hard way not to break out spontaneously into fluent Italian. He never did explain his bloody lip to his mother out of respect for her and her Italian heritage, but he never spoke Italian again out of the house.

Ernie had grown up in the Catholic faith and attended Catholic schools up through high school, but, in college, he gradually grew disinterested in church matters. He rarely attended church, but in his senior year he fell passionately in love with a girl in his philosophy class. Convinced that he had met the woman of his dreams, Ernie followed her to weekly Presbyterian services and Christian youth group activities on campus.

Ernie dated the young lady throughout the school year and into the summer after college graduation. Impulsive and idealistic, both made a pact to volunteer for the Peace Corps and to re-unite two years later at the Empire State Building in the fashion of the movie "An Affair to Remember." Sadly, Ernie and his girlfriend parted ways while serving in the Peace Corps, Ernie in northern Africa and she in South America.

In northern Africa, Ernie became well acquainted with Zach Campbell, a Protestant missionary. Plain-spoken and plain-clothed, Zach was a hands-on missionary living and working alongside the African farmers. He was an indomitable Bible-toting evangelist without any pretensions. It was inevitable that Ernie would team up with Zach and it was, perhaps, only a matter of time before Ernie identified more and more with Zach's Protestant beliefs.

In particular, Ernie became familiar with Zach's Alliance Church, a scripturally-based denomination with a strong, international program of evangelism. Upon returning to the United States, he undertook and completed seminary and doctoral studies at the Alliance Church's seminary in upstate New York.

Upon ordination, Ernie spent five more years abroad in Italy, the Congo, and Malaysia where he helped establish schools and churches, guided medical teams, and even assisted in birthing three children. Those were the so-called good old days. But, even better days lay ahead.

It was in Malaysia that he met his wife, Rose. She was an attractive brunette from Indiana who had taken an elementary school job teaching English. It was, also, love at first sight for both of them. Within three months, they were married.

The happy couple returned to the United States when Northeastern University in Boston offered a faculty position to Ernie. Founded by the Young Men's Christian Alliance, better known by its acronym – the YMCA, Northeastern was a perfect fit for Ernie.

Ernie poured all of his energies into academia. In short order, he published two books of his missionary life abroad, actively advised several campus clubs, served on the admissions committee, and won the university's distinguished teaching award. The university offered him early tenure and, eventually, promotion to Department Chair and, then, to Dean. As Dean, Ernie's outgoing, friendly nature was instrumental in raising funds for capital construction campaigns and it wasn't long before the university catapulted him into the Provost's position at the young age of 50.

During this time, Rose shared Ernie's love of life and trust in God. Best of all, Rose created a happy, tranquil home that was his refuge from the travails of the world's struggles.

They were happily married and for twenty-three years raised three children together.

However, within a year after Ernie's appointment as the Provost, Rose suddenly died of a massive heart attack. Ernie, stricken with grief, was left to raise the children, two sons and a daughter, by himself. Trying to overcome his grief in the first few months, Ernie used to joke that he was the head of a Disney family – there was no mother. After all, Bambi, Snow White, the Little Mermaid, the Lion King, and Cinderella all had to survive without mothers. He thought it was so ironic that Disney, the all-American family icon, was not mother-friendly at all.

Northeastern University offered every possible concession to accommodate Ernie in his new role as a single parent, but after much careful thought, Ernie decided to step back from his demanding life at a major university. He accepted a tenured teaching position at Nyack College and happily finished raising his three children in rural upstate New York along the tranquil, majestic Hudson River.

A half dozen years had now passed and his three children were all out of the house now. The youngest son and sole daughter were both in college whereas the oldest son was working in Manhattan as a civil engineer specializing in bridge construction and maintenance.

Ernie heard little footsteps in the hallway and turned from the television to the doorway to see his one and only grandchild enter the kitchen.

"Well, good morning, Samantha! This is a cool surprise to see you this early in the morning!" Ernie jumped off of his barstool and scooped the three-year and five-month old toddler up into his arms. Samantha was a happy, talkative child with sparkling blue eyes and a huge smile. He was fortunate to be entertaining Samantha because his oldest son's wife and daughter were visiting for a week while his son was on business travel to Boston.

Samantha wasn't very talkative and buried her head in his shoulder. "Where's mommy?" Ernie inquired.

"She's upstairs getting dressed. We're going to the zoo," Samantha sleepily replied and quickly added, "I'm hungry!"

"What can I get for you?" Showing her his bowl, Ernie asked, "Want some yogurt?"

Samantha peered into the bowl and quickly made a sour face before loudly exclaiming with newfound vigor, "Nnnnnno! Cheeeeery Ohs!"

"Cheerios? But, you had those yesterday. What about all of the other alphabet letters? How about some cheery bees today? Or cheery eyes? Maybe a cup of cheery teas?" Ernie teased her with delight.

Samantha quizzically looked him in the eye and squinted intensely at him. Then, all of a sudden, she understood him and her eyes lit up. "Grampa, stop. You're silly! No bees and no teas. I want cheery oh see-real."

"Oh, you want cheerios cereal?" he correctly interpreted. "Well, okay. You sit right there and I'll cook up some Cheerios!" He put Samantha, now giggling, in a high chair at the table and found the Cheerios, milk, bowl, and spoon. Ernie prepared Samantha's breakfast with a bit of flare and pizzaz to entertain her and then retrieved his bowl to join her at the kitchen table.

"Well, well. I see grampa is quite the chef!"

Looking up, Ernie smiled and, with his mouth full, waved to Virginia, his daughter-in-law who had walked into the kitchen.

"I'm gonna get me some of that, too!" Virginia poured herself a bowl of Cheerios and joined the twosome at the kitchen table.

Virginia enjoyed escaping the city to visit her father-in-law. He reminded her so much of her husband and Ernie was a wonderful grandfather to Samantha. He had a clean-shaven, well-proportioned and handsome face with strong features, tanned high cheekbones bedecked with a few friendly freckles, and vibrant cobalt blue eyes that betrayed his sense of adventure and mischief. The creases around the edges of Ernie's eyes and mouth all curved upwards to give the look of a content and happy man who relished his blessings and had learned to overlook his woes. Virginia was, indeed, looking forward to seeing her husband age similarly.

"Did you sleep alright?" Ernie, ever the perfect host, asked Virginia. But, before she could reply, his little charge piped up.

"Yes. I dreamt about the zoo. There was a lion an' a monkey. The monkey was riding on the lion!" Samantha giggled, again. "Silly monkey." She giggled once more and then proceeded to dig her spoon into the cereal.

"Did you dream about the zoo, too?" she politely asked Ernie.

Ernie stopped eating. He had completely forgotten about his dream until Samantha asked him about it. It was a remarkable dream that, unknown to Ernie, was a harbinger of things to come in the wake of the pontiff's death. But, at the moment, the sad news of the pope's death was the farthest thing from Ernie's mind as he delighted in humoring his grand-daughter.

"No, but I did dream about a kind of animal," Ernie responded.

"What kind? A giraffe? Was it a big, yellow giraffe, grampa?"

"Actually, it was a butterfly. A great big, yellow butterfly!"

Picking up a yellow post-it note that had been lying on the kitchen table, Ernie jumped out of his chair and began to wave the post-it note while hopping around the kitchen. Samantha, laughing wildly, was thoroughly enjoying the show and Ernie was enjoying making her laugh. Even Virginia couldn't resist giggling.

"There was this yellow butterfly flying around while I was sitting in the last row of a big church. The windows were huge and full of different colors. Anyway, the butterfly kept flying around the front of the church and the men up front were trying to shoo it away. Shoo, shoo. Go away!"

"What happened next?" Samantha had to know.

Pausing for a moment to recollect his dream, Ernie continued, "Well, the butterfly flew away to the back of the church. It landed on a lady's big purple hat and then it startled a sleeping boy when it landed on his nose. Then, all of a sudden, it started flying around my head." Sitting down now next to Samantha, Ernie waved the yellow post-it note around his head, occasionally whooshing it by her head. Samantha was totally enthralled and clapped her hands approvingly. "Then what, grampa?"

"I was nervous because I didn't want to get in trouble. So I carefully waved my arms to chase it away. But, it wouldn't go away. So I got up to leave. But, you know what happened next?"

"Tell me, tell me!" Samantha pleaded.

Standing up, Ernie slapped the post-it note onto his forehead so that it stuck there and exclaimed, "It landed smackdab on my head! Nothing I could do would make it leave!" With that, Ernie started to dance around the kitchen as if trying to shake the post-it note from his head.

Both Virginia and Samantha were laughing so hard that each likely needed a change of underwear. Samantha pointed her spoon at Ernie and exclaimed, "You're so silly, grampa!"

CHAPTER SIX

Her cell phone began ringing just as she returned home to her midtown Manhattan apartment. Struggling to turn the key with her right hand while turning her front door knob with the left proved difficult enough for Cybiline Checchi without the distraction of a ringing phone. Perhaps, the cause for her aggravation was the collection of a purse, a light jacket, a Starbucks caramel macchiato – venti, skim, no foam, and a quad hit of espresso – and three morning newspapers in her arms. Then again, it could also have been the physical discomfort and nausea at returning home at seven o'clock in the morning after a raucous night out on the town.

Finally victorious, Cybiline – or Cybil and pronounced Sigh-bill by her friends – shut the door behind her with her left foot and dropped everything except her purse and coffee onto the wood floor. She got one more swig of coffee, plunked it down on a small table by the door, and began fumbling for her phone in the elegant, black Gucci knockoff purse. By this time the phone had ceased to ring, but with a quick couple of button taps Cybil ascertained that it was her editor calling.

"Shit! What the hell does he want?" Cybil reached for her coffee and dumped the purse on the table this time. She normally didn't reach the office until mid-morning and, with two days remaining before having to file her weekly column, she had planned to call in sick. And sick she was, although totally self inflicted.

Staring at the phone, Cybil was turning over in her mind whether to return the call or not when the phone began to ring again. "Hmph! Okay, okay. This better be good, Harold." And with that note of finality, Cybil flicked her black hair backwards with a quick motion of the head, pulled off her right earring, and answered the phone.

"Yeah, Harold. Whatcha' got for me?" she asked rather imperiously.

"You want me to go where? To Rome? As in Italy or New York?"

"What?! This afternoon? You've got to be shitting me! What the fuck is the rush? Can't this wait until tomorrow?"

Cybil hadn't bothered to turn on the television when she gave up trying to find her pantyhose and slipped out of Brent's pad on the lower East Side. Or was it Brad? Oh, what the heck! Who cares what his name is. She really shouldn't have gone home with the guy anyway, but he was cute and young. The double-dares from her fellow girlfriends didn't help her self control either. Anyways, she made it to Starbucks without catching the hot morning news story and, with a booming headache, she didn't even as much as glance at the newspapers' headlines.

Thankfully, Harold was there to bail her out. Over the next two minutes Harold brought Cybil up to date on the Pope's death and her next assignment. Harold needed to do a bit of sweet-talking, too; but, it didn't take much to convince Cybil that she was, after all, the tabloid's top producing, award-winning writer and that this was the top news story of a slow, boring summer with neither the Yankees nor the Mets proving worthy of a pennant. Plus, she was fluent in Italian and the former Pope's French. So Cybil agreed, although reluctantly and only after winning an upgrade to business class and an expanded expense account. In her mind, there simply wasn't anyone better to dig up juicy tidbits on whoever might be the next lucky fella' to call himself Pope.

She needed to pack quickly in order to make the midday flight out of JFK to Rome. Harold's administrative assistant at the tabloid had already found a five-star hotel and a limousine service to ferry her around Rome. She was all set, that is, except for feeling lousy, exhausted, and in dire need of a hot bath. Heading for the bedroom, she tossed the phone on the bed, finished the now-cold coffee with one gulp, and opted for a hot shower.

The hot water felt incredibly soothing. It struck Cybil that the only improvement that could be made was a good man with strong forearms running a loofah sponge over her back. Thinking ahead, Cybil admitted that while she wasn't too excited about running around with a bunch of celibate men at the Vatican, she was sure that downtown Rome would offer up the appropriate male entertainment, soothing wine, and indulgent shopping.

Exploring Rome would offer some relief from the Vatican reporting. Religious men were such Neanderthals. They were inevitably boring, hypocritical, and overly consumed with dictating rules, imposing dress codes, restricting freedom of choice, and censoring human expression.

Cybil recalled, with great distaste, her two weeks in the Appalachian foothills of eastern Ohio covering a local insurrection against a school board. The only good thing out of it all was the award for journalism that her peers presented to her later that year. Cybil, additionally, relished the proverbial black eye that she gave that bunch of religious fundamentalists seeking to include Biblical creation science in classroom instruction. Shaking her head in disbelief, Cybil recalled their seemingly archaic attacks on Darwinian evolution. What a bunch of dumbshits! Now, to top it all off, she was off to dumbshit central – the Vatican. Oh, well. If for nothing else, she might just win another award and get to enjoy 'la dolce vita' in Rome.

Feeling better, Cybil turned off the shower and reached for her towel. Just then her cell phone began to ring again. Cursing and wet, Cybil scampered across the bathroom carpet into the bedroom. Scooping up the phone while tossing her hair back, Cybil noted that the caller was Harold.

"Well, hello, again! Don't tell me that you've had second doubts and called off this escapade?" She loved to yank Harold's chain now and then.

"No? The trip's still on?" Cybil activated the speaker and placed the phone on her dresser as she peeled off her towel to dry herself.

"Of course the trip is still on. You had better make that flight!" Harold spoke with great vehemence.

"Well, why am I wasting my time on the phone instead of packing? Are you just calling to harass me or do you have something more to tell me?"

"I was so surprised that you didn't know anything about the Pope's death that I totally forgot to tell you a couple of key points!" Harold paused before continuing.

"First, I've contracted with a technician in Rome to provide some, ah, technical capabilities that will give you a bit of an edge over the other journalists there. And, second, I've got an informer for you inside the Vatican. He'll have a package with instructions waiting for you at the hotel desk when you check in. Got it?"

CHAPTER SEVEN

Despite a fitful night of sleep, Marco Spitini had awakened with anticipation. In contrast, at six o'clock that morning, Rome was still largely asleep as a light rain fell. It hardly felt like the extraordinary day he knew it would be, but then most days start just like any other day. Indeed, this would be a day where dramatic events unfold from circumstances that, at first, appear quite ordinary. Spitini reflected with satisfaction that this would be a tumultuous day with many more surprises to come that collectively would lead to the proverbial 'perfect storm' for capsizing the Catholic Church.

Arising, Spitini shuffled into the bathroom to begin his daily routine of cleaning and dressing, walking to a private chapel for prayers, stopping at his office to check calendars and emails, and ending up at the Pope's quarters around eight o'clock. Ever the punctilious and methodical man, Spitini saw no cause to alter his schedule at that point in time.

That changed upon arriving at the Apostolic Palace which houses the Pope. There was very little outdoors that, to the untrained eye, belied the day to day tranquility of the Vatican.

However, it was an entirely different matter inside the Pope's apartment on the top floor. This was to be expected as every precaution would be taken to keep details of the morning's horrific discovery confidential until the official Church announcement.

Upon reaching the main entrance to the building that houses the Pope's private chambers, Spitini paused and drew in a deep breath of air to allay any of his lingering fears. He then strode up the stone stairs and found the Swiss Guard sentries tense. He was quite sure that these young men from Switzerland did not, yet, know that the Pope had succumbed; however, the extra visitors that surely would have included the Pope's personal physician, the Vatican's Secretary of State, and the Cardinal Camerlengo early in the morning would no doubt convey to them that something was amiss.

Spitini took the elevator to the top floor and, upon stepping out into the corridor, was relieved to find far more activity indicative of a successful conclusion to last night's mission. There were a couple of medical technicians with a collapsible stretcher, several worried nuns consoling another in tears, and half a dozen plain clothed Swiss Guards and Italian police. Feigning confusion and surprise at seeing such a commotion, Monsignor Spitini stopped dead in his tracks before breaking into a swift run towards the door to the Papal chambers.

"What is the matter? Is the Pope alright? Why are you here? Can I go in?" Spitini asked in typically Italian rapid fire succession, looking terrified at one of the Pope's bodyguards whom Spitini recognized. He deftly added a nice touch of grabbing the man's muscular right arm and squeezing hard.

"Monsignor Spitini, calm yourself, please! Yes, yes, but of course, you can go in. But, ..." The bodyguards eyes trailed off towards the floor and his eyes began to well with tears. "The Pope is ...." He couldn't bring himself to say it, but his face conveyed all of the information that Spitini needed to know.

Ever the consummate actor, Spitini cried "Oh, no! It can't be!" in a high pitched tone of desperation, released his hold on the man, and darted across the threshold into the Papal study.

Over the course of the day, Spitini would learn that the nun bringing the Pope's breakfast had discovered John Paul III slumped over his desk. Unable to awaken him, she attempted to find a pulse. Not finding one, she nervously dialed the Pope's personal physician and Cardinal Isaia Biaggio, the Cardinal Camerlengo. The physician, Doctor Terzini, arrived in great haste within minutes from his Vatican clinic with the Cardinal Biaggio arriving out of breath ten minutes later to find the physician and nun both sobbing. With the help of the Pope's bodyguards, they moved the Pope's body to the bedroom, notified the Secretary of State, and began the formal process of canonically declaring the Pope dead.

In the intervening hour and a half, Cardinal Biaggio had summoned a small number of senior officials of the Roman Curia, the maze-like bureaucracy at the Vatican that functions as the Catholic Church's headquarters. In accordance with Papal edicts that lay out explicit procedures, the Camerlengo is responsible for formally establishing the Pope's demise with specific Vatican prelates in attendance. That morning, Cardinal Biaggio had stood with a small handful of men by the Pope's body and called out John Paul's Christian name of Charles Rivard three times. Hearing no reply, Cardinal Biaggio covered the Pope with a sheet and with a heavy heart declared, "The Pope is dead." The Chancellor of the Apostolic Camera, Cardinal Joseph Nubualovu, then handed the Pope's Ring of the Fisherman and a silver hammer to Cardinal Biaggio who, in turn, wielded the hammer to smash the ring. This last task is far more than a symbolic act for the ring is essential for issuing Papal edicts each of which bears the ring's imprint in a wax seal.

With the crushing of the one-of-a-kind Fisherman's Ring, the Catholic Church entered the 'interregna,' an uncertain period between Papal rule. From that moment, Cardinal Biaggio, the highest ranking official of the Vatican by virtue of his title as the Camerlengo, became the chief administrator of the Vatican. Simultaneously, the College of Cardinals consisting of over one hundred men spread across the globe, collectively assumed limited powers of the Pope. Lastly, the authority of many Cardinals heading the various Curial departments is suspended.

The papal vacancy, therefore, has a profound effect on the Vatican, but the Church's business does not entirely grind to a halt. It is, however, a time of indecision that grows more and more cumbersome over lengthy periods of interregna. It is hoped that the Cardinals speedily elect a new Pope in order to restore the usual forward momentum and authority of the Holy See. That, however, has not always been the case. Historically, the periods between Popes had gone as long as three years in one case and over a year in several others. To avoid prolonged Papal vacancies, Popes had invoked numerous rules for assembling the College of Cardinals in a conclave to elect the Pope.

The clock had now started for convening the conclave. Within fifteen to twenty days, all Cardinals under the age of 80 would gather in the Sistine Chapel to vote for a new Pope while the outside world watches for the symbolic white puffs of smoke signaling a successful election. In the meantime, the Catholic Church had to organize for a period of mourning and the Pope's funeral.

When Monsignor Spitini arrived, Cardinal Biaggio and the assembled Cardinals were leaving the bedroom upon completing the prescribed death ritual. Next, the orderlies would be called in to remove the body, John Paul's personal belongings would be gathered, and Cardinal Biaggio would begin to seal the Papal Apartments to await a new Pope. There was, however, great uncertainty in Cardinal Biaggio's mind. Was an autopsy warranted? Was this a crime scene? If so, could he truly close and seal the Papal Apartment?

As Cardinal Biaggio and the others paused, Cardinal Nubualovu was already halfway across the Papal study to return to his office where he needed to complete the official death certificate. Seeing Monsignor Spitini he halted and held out his arms to embrace Spitini. Spitini obliged him by falling into his arms and asking, "Is it true? Can John Paul truly be dead?"

"Yes, my dear Marco. John Paul is with God. May his soul rest in peace within God's Holy embrace." Now holding Monsignor Spitini's shoulders with outstretched arms, Cardinal Joseph Nubualovu offered solace to a clearly stricken Spitini.

"What should I do now?" Monsignor Spitini earnestly beseeched Cardinal Nubualovu.

"Go and pray. Pray for John Paul's soul and for the Church," Cardinal Nubualovu calmly advised him with the remaining Cardinals beginning to gather around them.

"Ahem!" Cardinal Biaggio cleared his throat to draw the attention of Spitini and Cardinal Nubualovu. "Actually, I would like to see Monsignor Spitini in my offices within an hour. I understand that he may have been the last person to speak with the Pope."

Spitini nodded and admitted that he had, indeed, been with the Pope late the night before, but that the Pope, although tired, had appeared to be in good health. "I will be at your office in an hour, Your Eminence."

With that, everyone departed. There was much to do in preparing the world for the shock of John Paul's premature death. Messages needed to be sent to every diocese, Cardinals needed to be called to Rome, the press had to be notified, and preparations for mourning had to be initiated. The sadness pervading the air did not help, but it had to be done.

Monsignor Spitini retired to St. Peter's for prayer. Feeling greatly relieved that he had succeeded in both killing the Pope and in carrying off an act of distress worthy of a Hollywood Oscar award, Spitini thankfully knelt in the pews. He set his wrist watch alarm to silently alert him in 45 minutes so that he would be on time for his meeting. Next, Spitini prayed to Allah for ten minutes and, then, began to prepare for his meeting with Cardinal Biaggio.

It was quite remarkable that Spitini could lead a double religious life in order to successfully hide as a mole at the Vatican. First, he had to persuade his discerning Catholic mentors within the very highest ranks of the Church that he was a dutiful, trustworthy Catholic priest. Second, Spitini had to learn to live with himself while leading a life filled with lies and deception. To succeed, Spitini had come to rely on the ancient Muslim tradition of taqiyya.

In Islamic tradition, taqiyya is a special privilege permitting Muslims in imminent danger to conceal their religious faith. Its use was first recorded during Mohammed's lifetime when the early Muslims were persecuted. Based on the Qur'an and other central Islamic documents, taqiyya was Islam's secret weapon. Where the West would see it as nothing more than legalized lying, Muslims viewed taqiyya as a clever exercise in deception to cozy up to their enemies, much like the camouflaged stone fish, before striking and then to hide in the fashion of a chameleon for self preservation.

Spitini had several modern examples to guide him. The infamous British shoe-bomber and al-Qa'eda agent Richard Reid effectively practiced deception to avoid suspicion by collecting empty alcohol bottles and cigarette butts to strew around his lodging. The master of deception, however, was Yasser Arafat, the former Palestinian leader. With western media cameras rolling, Arafat consistently preached peace to deceive the world. In front of Palestinians, Arafat honestly spoke of his quest to obliterate Israel.

Spitini was merely following a Muslim tradition practiced since the earliest days of Islam. Whereas his double life would later amaze and confound law enforcement analysts, Spitini was no different than many Islamic heroes through the ages and current times.

Deceptively playing the role of a penitent Catholic priest in prayer at St. Peter's Basilica, Spitini rose as his appointment neared and headed for the Apostolic Palace.

Arriving at the office of the Camerlengo, Monsignor Spitini announced himself to the administrative assistant in the outer office. Taking a seat, he awaited the Cardinal's pleasure, but within minutes was ushered into the office and another seat opposite Cardinal Biaggio at his desk. Spitini noted that others were present, too. In chairs along the outer wall of the office, Spitini recognized familiar faces to include Cardinal Joseph Nubualovu and Cardinal Narciso Maltempo of Florence. Doctor Terzini was there and Spitini was mildly surprised to spot Swiss Army Colonel Wilhelm Weissberg, Commander of the Swiss Guards, in attendance.

And so the inquisition began. Cardinal Biaggio was the only inquisitor with no one else interrupting. The questions were innocent enough with no overt suspicion of a crime. "When were you with the Pope? How did he look? What did he say? How tired was he? Did he cough or wheeze? Did he take his medications?"

All eyes were on Monsignor Spitini who began to slightly wring his hands. In answering the first question, Monsignor Spitini shifted uncomfortably in his seat and looked around the room. He noticed with a start that there was a lady standing behind him by the door! She wore a light brown business suit, a white cotton blouse, and modest leather pumps. Spitini guessed that she was in her early to mid forties and stood around five feet tall. She was very striking with shoulder length hair, a perfect tan, and an hourglass figure. She was also of Middle Eastern descent.

CHAPTER EIGHT

There wasn't anyone more surprised to be standing in the office of the Camerlengo of the Holy Roman Catholic Church than Tara Johnson. First, she had been in Rome all of 48 hours. Second, she was not Catholic. Third, she felt strangely out of place as the only woman in the group. But, here she was and she was very curious about Monsignor Spitini.

She was struck immediately by Spitini's features. Spitini's black hair, swarthy complexion and his dark glowing eyes hiding in the shadows of his thick eyebrows made for a striking first impression. Looking at Spitini's relatively calm demeanor, Tara had the sense that he was a cunning man patiently accustomed to shielding his true emotions. The round, silver rimmed spectacles atop a bold nose, his long lean cheeks, and his tight lips only reinforced her reaction. Standing perfectly erect in his black clerical robes with nothing out of place, Spitini was the very model of an Italian Catholic priest, but, although she couldn't quite put her finger on it, something was amiss. Then, in a flash of insight, Tara saw it. Spitini had some characteristics, although ever so slight, of a Persian.

Tara, or TJ as her fellow officers at Scotland Yard called her, detected signs of Persian pedigree. Years of police work gave her a sixth sense. Years as an Iraqi expatriate simply gave her a good nose for details.

Now sporting British citizenship, TJ had been an expatriate for over thirty years. But, fifteen years in Baghdad and many years thereafter in the Middle Eastern dens of London were still fresh in her memories. She remembered a happy childhood in Iraq when her father served Saddam Hussein in the country's secret police force. Unfortunately, her father was implicated in a series of failures to quell unrest in Iraq's southern Shi'ite communities and he was executed at the hands of Saddam Hussein's thugs. Quick to recognize that her family's future in Iraq was dismal with Saddam growing stronger and stronger as the de facto ruler of Iraq, TJ's mother fled Iraq in 1976 with a teenage TJ and three younger sons. With Allah's mercy and the protection of his angels, her mother packed up the kids and boarded a freighter bound for England where an uncle of hers welcomed them on the wharf with chocolates and candies.

TJ could still vividly remember him for he was a marvelous man with unfettered generosity, a perpetual smile, and the faith of a giant. TJ still believed that no other Sunni Muslim religious leader could match not only his wisdom, but also his popularity in all of London. He, too, was sadly murdered.

A young Shi'ite man who had recently emigrated to England took issue with her uncle's Sunni preaching and ambushed the cleric one morning in front of his house. TJ's uncle had angered his murderer earlier that week in preaching against Iran's totalitarian-styled leader, the Ayatollah Khomeini. Drawing a clear distinction between Sunni and Shi'ite beliefs, her uncle refused to advocate political rule for religious leaders. Clerics had a moral obligation to exercise their God-given power and talents in lobbying for rights, improved living conditions, jobs, and education free of the shadowy demands of national politics. Although clerics are inherently obligated to shape political decisions, her uncle was firm in resolve that clerics ought not to govern a nation and thereby risk compromising their religious ethics.

TJ owed much to her uncle and, although dead for over ten years, still exerted tremendous influence on TJ's Muslim faith. TJ's mother won political asylum in England, found a steady job as a housecleaning woman, and, with her uncle's assistance, put all four children through school. TJ was especially proficient in school and, to her family's absolute delight and pride, earned a degree in chemical engineering at Cambridge. From there she accepted a job with Shell and launched a career in the petroleum industry that occasionally took her back to the Middle East where she was continually reminded of her good fortune to be a woman in Europe with a topnotch education, the freedom to practice her Muslim faith, and the joys of a career. She was very fortunate in earning a good paycheck that she shared with her mother and brothers. But, the extensive travel took its toll and her interest in corporate life diminished after the initial excitement and promotions.

For no good reason other than falling madly in love with Ron Johnson, a police detective in London, TJ began new studies in law enforcement and forensics. She had married the detective, but he died nearly two years later in a terrorist bomb strike in Northern Ireland. They had had no children and TJ had not remarried. Now over fifteen years later, TJ was a successful counterterror expert and senior detective at Scotland Yard, a post that permitted TJ to combine her technical expertise, gifted intelligence, Muslim faith, and knowledge of the Middle East to protect the innocent.

She continued to visit the Middle East quite often; mostly on business, but every now and then, to visit distant relatives. She couldn't bring herself to travel there for pleasure. Remarkably, it wasn't because of her troubled childhood memories for they no longer tormented her. Rather, TJ grew more and more distressed with each visit by the rampant religious fanaticism. She had simply witnessed the callous extermination of too many innocent, peaceful people and the reckless destruction of public infrastructure and utilities that were built to improve man's lot in a harsh climate.

Although TJ understood the deep-seated roots of strife springing from man's desire to control the oil, the land, the wealth, and the citizenry, she simply could not comprehend the religious fundamentalists of the many religious faiths. Although their religious practices differed, they largely believed in the one and the same God. Did they not all trace their lineage back to Abraham? How could they, therefore, so easily justify their shameless destruction of God's creation in God's name? Why destroy what they should uphold and uplift? TJ bristled whenever she thought about it, but how dare they use God's name to needlessly kill and destroy when their true motives sprang from hearts hardened by greed, envy, and revenge?

TJ had investigated ample cases of terrorism to know that the perpetrators were all too often overcome by evil. Indeed, many terrorist cells were mere criminal organizations deceptively cloaking themselves in religious and social causes to legitimize their criminality. Preying on people's weaknesses and religious fervor, these terrorists acquired immense wealth while hypocritically recruiting the poor and uneducated to perpetrate horrendous crimes. Terrorists were adroit capitalists leveraging the economic effects of globalization to both enrich their pockets and, simultaneously, leverage the festering resentment of the poor. It didn't seem to matter whether they were Arabs, Irish, Italian, German, Indonesian, Philippino, Sri Lankan, Somalian, or whatever.

So here she was, a Muslim Iraqi in Catholic Rome. Although TJ was surprised to be at the Vatican this morning, she had long admired Pope John Paul III for his Middle Eastern peace initiatives. She did not know if a murder had been committed; but, for whatever reason, God had preordained her special assignment to Rome. She prayed that something good would come of it.

TJ had been temporarily assigned to Rome's Italian police department just this week to support the Vatican on a special assignment. TJ had not, yet, been fully briefed on the details, but she knew that her call to Rome originated with John Paul III. She was undeniably curious to learn why a Muslim woman of all people would be selected for duty at the Vatican. It wasn't uncommon for the Italian police and other international law enforcement organizations to support the Swiss Guards, but why did the Pope need a Mid East counterterror expert to augment his body guards? Now with the Pope's death, would the Vatican continue to request her services?

Upon picking up the telephone receiver in her apartment early that morning, TJ was, at first, delighted to be ordered to the Vatican. She harbored ambitions of learning more about her assignment. But, TJ was then grieved to hear of the shocking cause for calling her. TJ could not help but think that this might be a short tour of duty in Rome and that she had better hold off on her weekend shopping plans to stock her refrigerator.

Her first two days in Rome were filled with one administrative task after another, such as, signing a lease for an apartment, obtaining Italian police credentials, completing paperwork to request Vatican credentials, sitting through a newcomers orientation, and meeting several senior Italian police officers. Colonel Weissberg's invitation to join him was truly a godsend.

Listening intently to Monsignor Spitini's recollection of his late night visit with the Pope, TJ was struck by the mundane nature of it all. Nothing seemed out of the ordinary. The Monsignor appeared nervous and troubled, but that was to be expected. He offered no significant clues and there were no apparent discrepancies so she began to pin her hopes on modern technology and a visit to the Papal Apartments at the Apostolic Palace.

Fortunately, there would also be an autopsy per a secret papal edict signed by John Paul II shortly after he occupied the Apostolic Palace. The death of John Paul III would be the first instance of a papal autopsy. TJ prayed that, perhaps, it would yield a clue. She might need to stock her refrigerator after all.

CHAPTER NINE

Cybiline Checchi was surprised to make good time in reaching her midday flight. Having dripped water all over her floor in the rush to answer Harold's second phone call, she had managed to dry herself by the time Harold hung up. She returned to the bathroom to dry her hair. With time running out, Cybil opted to go easy on the makeup although, as a woman in her mid-thirties after an all-night fling, she could have used a face lift.

She found a lightweight summer outfit that was suitable for Rome, hurriedly devoured a couple of leftover sprinkle-covered chocolate donuts, grabbed her laptop case, stuck her passport into her purse, and threw together a carry-on bag. Fortunately, she kept a suitcase packed for short-notice deployments which she left with her doorman to overnight Fedex to her hotel in Rome. Cybil wasn't about to schlep a fifty pound suitcase nor risk having the airline lose it.

Her doorman earned an extra ten bucks for proving agile enough to quickly hail a cab. The tip was a bit high, but her paper was paying for everything as of the moment Harold called. What did she care?

"I need to get to JFK and I am in a hurry. I also know this city like the back of my hand, so don't take me on a costly joyride. Got that?" Cybil almost barked at the cabbie.

"Okay, lady. Okay. We go now. I will get you there fast. No problemo," the cabbie muttered. He had a real bitch on his hands and his tip was at risk big time.

The cab ride to JFK Airport on Long Island's southern shore was remarkably speedy. Many New Yorkers were out of town on holidays so the traffic was as manageable as New York traffic could ever hope to be. Cybil flipped her cell phone open and spent most of the ride calling a few friends and associates at her office to update them on her Roman whereabouts for the foreseeable future.

"Excuse me, miss! Excuse me!" Nearing the airport on the Van Wyck Expressway, the cab driver interrupted Cybil for directions. "Which airline you fly?"

Cybil momentarily put her left hand over the phone and quickly replied, "United!"

Five minutes later, the cabbie pulled his yellow sedan right up to the curb at air terminal number seven. Turning around for payment, he was greeted by Cybil's fist clenching greenbacks in his face. "Keep the change. But, I need a receipt!"

"No problem. Here is receipt." And with that, Cybil stepped out and strode into the terminal with the cabbie delighted to be free of his rider.

With no luggage to check, Cybil headed straight for the eticket boarding pass dispensers. Even the midday crowds at the airport were astonishingly depleted. She had high hopes that the line for the metal detectors would be correspondingly light, too. Cybil realized that she was on track to reach her flight's gate in record time with well over an hour to spare.

Unfortunately, a frantic lunatic appeared on the scene about a hundred feet from Cybil just as she extracted her boarding pass from the electronic contraption. The man

64

unceremoniously dropped a canvas bag onto the terminal floor, reached into it to produce a pistol and a blowtorch attached to a mini propane tank, and began shouting some unintelligible, foreign proclamations while waving the pistol in his left hand and the blowtorch in the other. Cybil could understand none of his raving except for a few mentions of "Allah!" But, she figured that it didn't much matter what the hell he said. No good was coming from whatever it was that he was shouting. For good measure, to ensure that he had everyone's attention, he fired a couple of shots into the ceiling.

Pandemonium ensued. Everyone began to run and duck for cover. Suitcases were strewn all over the place. Nearly another hundred feet behind Cybil, two New York police officers drew their pistols with one taking aim and the other running towards the gunman. Cybil, now clearly in the middle of the line of fire, darted for a gap in the nearby airline ticket counter. She nearly made it without incidence.

Hearing the police officers' demands to drop his pistol, the gun-toting fanatic turned towards the officers and got off two wild shots. Simultaneously, he ignited the blowtorch with a finger flick of a switch and lit his desert camouflage jacket on fire.

Neither of his two bullets hit a police officer. One, however, passed cleanly through Cybil's laptop in her mad dash for safety. Her hard drive had truly died.

The crouching police officer returned fire with one shot that struck its mark. The gunman rocked back as the bullet struck his shoulder. His gun flew onto the floor and the blowtorch rattled along the floor as he tumbled in a burning heap, gasping for air and in great pain. The onrushing police officer grabbed the gunman's pistol and, spotting an abandoned child's blanket, threw it onto the burning gunman in a vain attempt to extinguish the fire.

"John! John! Stand back!" His partner sternly shouted as he came up from behind with a fire extinguisher that he had pulled off of the wall. Within seconds, their target was covered in billowing white powder and the fire was out.

By this time, other New York and transit police officers arrived on the scene shouting, gesturing, and calling for medical support on their radios.

Ever the instinctive news reporter, Cybil was the first passenger to emerge from safety. Grabbing her cell phone and leaving her bags behind the airline counter, she pointed the phone towards the unfolding scene and managed to get a photograph before the fierce stares of the police warned her to keep her distance. Returning to her bags, Cybil dialed her tabloid, transmitted the photograph, and filed a quick report. This is what she lived for, but, her rapid pulse and breathing betrayed a hint of fear.

As Cybil completed her report, the emergency medical technician and ambulance appeared. The gunman appeared to be alive, but Cybil couldn't ascertain his condition with the police fanning out across the terminal lobby to canvas the area and question onlookers.

The police officer who fired the successful shot at the gunman walked up to Cybil. "Miss, are you alright? I sure was glad to see you move that fast so I could get a good shot off. It is a miracle that he did not shoot you! The good Lord was looking after you today."

"Yeah, I'm okay. But, it was just plain dumb luck that he didn't get me. Guess it's not my day to go." Holding up her laptop in one hand and its case in the other, Cybil wrinkled her nose and frowned at the police officer. "But, that shit-head Arab freak didn't do my laptop any favors." And then they both laughed, relieved to have survived another exciting day in the glamorous metropolitan city of New York.

The rest of the afternoon was spent giving the police an eyewitness statement, squeezing her new police friend for information, and filing a detailed story with her office for the evening edition while drinking a martini in the airline lounge. The flights out of Terminal 7 were cancelled for the day, but Harold's assistant booked a first class seat for Cybil on another airline departing that evening from Terminal 4. Cybil was looking forward to boarding the plane and collapsing into the seat with devoted flight attendants catering to her wining and dining needs before landing early in the Roman morning.

In comparison, Cardinal Murphy had a lackluster experience the next evening at JFK. The shooting incident on the previous day was in a different terminal and, although security was beefed up, no further incidents marred JFK's operations. He and his entourage of two priests and an administrative assistant boarded a Boeing 777 and settled in for a peaceful flight to Rome.

The Cardinal found himself seated in a first class window seat with his staff distributed in the plane's economy seating. After the hectic past two days, he was happy to relax in his seat with no plans to work during the flight.

"Hello, there. Looks like we're seat mates."

Cardinal Murphy looked up to find a white-haired, distinguished gentleman attired in a dark pin-striped suit, French blue shirt with white collar and cuffs, and a dazzling orange-red tie putting his laptop computer case on the adjoining empty seat.

"Hello to you, too," Cardinal Murphy replied.

Taking off his suit jacket and handing it to the stewardess, the gentleman sat down and took a cold iced tea from her. "Thanks, sweetheart," he said with a wink and a smile.

"Whew! I didn't think I'd make it today. The line for security was God awful." Then noting that his seat mate was wearing a clerical collar, "Oops, sorry about that slip, padre."

Cardinal Murphy smiled and politely answered back with "No offense taken."

"Thanks. Well, the line was at least a mile long. Having one of the x-ray machines break down just before I got to it didn't help either. After yesterday's shooting, the TSA folks were especially picky this morning. How about you? Do they even require a minister to go through security? I mean, why put a good Christian minister through security?" He laughed and patted Cardinal Murphy on the left arm. "Now, if you were one of those Imams it would be a different story. Not that I'm racially profiling anyone, but you've got to admit that it's pretty clear who the bad guys are. All of this political correctness in order to avoid offending the Arabs is bullshit. Oops, there I go again! Sorry about that."

He took a drink of his iced tea and stuck his case under the seat ahead of him. "Thank goodness I don't have to travel to the Middle East anymore. It's just too dicey. Americans over there just have a huge bull's eye target painted on their foreheads. It's not like we can blend in and folks over there aren't too happy with us over Iraq, Israel, Iran's nukes, or bin-Laden. Why, that fellow who shot up a terminal yesterday is a classic example of what can go wrong in their heads. Know what I mean?"

Cardinal Murphy turned and squinted at the fellow sitting next to him. "Well, yes and, then again, no. I don't condone his actions whatsoever, but at the risk of offending you, I can understand how he became mentally unhinged. The morning newspaper is reporting that he had lost his only child in a traffic accident this summer, then his job, and finally his wife when she left him to return to Jordan. Unfortunately, he was mentally unstable and in psychological counseling. It's not an affliction limited solely to Arabs, my friend. Trust me, as someone who specializes in treating human failings."

The cardinal's seat mate blinked in surprise and sat still without any comeback. Smiling at his success in quieting the fellow, Cardinal Murphy patted him on his right arm and said, "But, you're lucky today. After all, if we've got a terrorist on board today, I'm fully qualified to give you the last rites as we nosedive into the Atlantic." Murphy laughed and relaxed back into his seat, but not before his seat mate got the joke and laughed, too.

"What do you do for a living?" Cardinal Murphy inquired.

"Oh, I'm a senior VP for one of the largest defense contractors in the states. I head up the aerospace division. Business is good, but I'm getting tired of the extensive traveling. How about you?"

"Just a servant of our good Lord trying to keep the faith alive."

"Well, my mom wanted me to become a rabbi, but I wouldn't have it. There's no money in that," the business man offhandedly remarked.

Cardinal Murphy patted him on the arm again and light heartedly stated, "Well, I don't know about that. I'm a Catholic and my Church has done rather well for itself!"

Their conversation was interrupted by the flight attendant announcing take-off instructions over the intercom system. While Cardinal Murphy attentively listened, the business man turned off his cell phone, checked his Blackberry for emails one more time before shutting that down, examined his PDA, and opened his Wall Street Journal. Except for some small banter, each man was content to keep to his own affairs for the remainder of the flight. After reading a good part of a newly published biography of John Paul II and eating dinner, Cardinal Murphy relaxed with a hot cup of coffee. Reflecting on the hustle and bustle of the day, he admitted to himself having missed seeing his old friend, Ernie, for lunch that day. He hoped he would be back in New York by late August for their next regularly scheduled lunch, but the conclave to elect the next pope would take priority.

Cardinal Murphy was sure that if he had had the opportunity to see Ernie, his good friend would have cheered him up. He would have gladly traded the gent sitting next to him for Ernie's company. He was sorely in need of some good cheer for he was still in a state of disbelief regarding the pope's death. With the world around him seemingly out of control, he constantly had to remind himself that God was, indeed, in charge and that everything, therefore, would be just fine. Yet, a few good quips and some earnest debates with Ernie would go a long way to alleviating his discomfort and anxiety.

He and Ernie had some of the most free-wheeling discussions on religion, politics, society, and more. They disagreed on a good number of substantive issues and often agreed to disagree, particularly on matters of the Catholic and Protestant divide. Nevertheless, they always parted as friends and looked eagerly to their next meeting.

Points of contention typically focused on the usual flashpoints of clerical celibacy and marriage, the ordination of women, and the role of the Pope. Ernie was understandably in favor of clerical marriage. To Ernie, clerical celibacy was nothing more than a human holdover from the Middle Ages. After all, Ernie would vehemently argue, several of the apostles were married. It wasn't until many centuries later, when fearing the unwelcome influence of wives and mistresses, that the Church established celibacy. Eventually Ernie would always get around to speaking of his wife, Rose, in order to highlight the added strength he got from her love and support. Furthermore, Ernie fervently believed that he learned more about ministering from raising his kids than from any other source. It was only as a father to three wonderful, but mischievous, children that he fully comprehended God's grace to his children. Call him a rebel, but Ernie's arguments were always steeped in a mixture of strict legalism and common sense.

Cardinal Murphy would counter with strong arguments citing the institution of celibacy long before papal edict as well as the virtues of focusing exclusively on God without the competing demands of a wife and children. He would then drive home the point that the Catholic Church was one of the last staunch lines of support for the traditional family.

Well, Cardinal Murphy now realized that all of these debates would have to await his return to New York. Closing his eyes, Cardinal Murphy decided to sleep so that he would be somewhat rested and alert when the plane touched down in the morning around eight o'clock Italian time. When Cardinal Murphy awoke much later his plane was on its final approach to Leonardo da Vinci Airport. There was much to do this day and in the days ahead.

CHAPTER TEN

This was a remarkable first day of August in Rome. Despite the intense heat wave smothering Rome for weeks, the autostradas, Italy's interstate highways, were crammed with hurried cars and growling buses ferrying an all-time record number of tourists into the city. Rome's two airports, Leonardo da Vinci and Ciampino, as well as its central train station were also overflowing with an international amalgam of people excitedly hurrying to Rome or to more distant vacation spots. The influx of mourners, clerics of the Catholic Church and other religions, press corps, advance security elements for their heads of state, Italian police, and the just-plain-curious added to the August influx. Some Romans who normally vacationed in August were even induced to stay in order to welcome the intruders. Indeed, the pope's death was good for business.

Cybil was relieved to find that Rome was not shutting down entirely. She had high hopes to take every advantage of her expense account and spare time. She could almost taste the red Chianti wine, freshly made pasta drowned in mouth-watering sauces, and scrumptious Italian men. It was good to be in Rome.

Rested after sleeping away most of her first day and night in Rome, Cybil was sauntering through St. Peter's Square in the morning. No need to rush in the sweltering heat. With fresh coffee coursing through her veins and a new pair of red Prada shoes adorning her tanned feet, Cybil Checchi was on cloud nine. Her Italian language skills, although a bit rough, were coming back to her. Sbagliando s'impara! Practice makes perfect!

"So this is it!" Cybil thought to herself. Born to Catholic Italian parents, she had seen images of the Vatican from her earliest of days; but, she was the first in her immediate family to actually make the pilgrimage. She could see an informal, spontaneously-organized wake near the main entrance to St. Peter's Basilica. About fifty mourners in black were holding their rosary beads and praying by a growing mound of colorful flowers and candles. Although mindful of the somber mood at the Vatican, Cybil, nevertheless, felt exhilaration at being there. Walking up to Emperor Caligula's obelisk in the center of St. Peter's Square, Cybil halted to turn in a full circle taking it all in.

The Vatican's 108 acre complex was smaller than that of the U. S. Capitol and its amalgam of office buildings, but no less impressive. The Vatican, too, was the capital of a nation, but the Vatican had the air more of a university with church bells marking the end of classes. St. Peter's, playing the part of the administration building, seemed to preside over a collection of over-sized classroom buildings, ornate museums, plain offices, and sleepy apartments. Just like an American college campus, it, additionally, had its own grocery store, tourist bookstore, and police department. The erudite priests walking calmly, but purposefully, often with books in their arms, finished off the feel of a Jesuit university.

Cybil enjoyed it all and, for a moment, nearly felt like she was back in journalism school at Columbia University on the upper west side of Manhattan. Feeling a tap on her shoulder, she was jolted out of her daydream. She wheeled around to find a tourist holding a camera, pointing to his wife, and speaking broken, but passable Italian: "Scusi, signora. Per favore?" Pleased to be mistaken for an Italian native, Cybil smiled, took the camera, waited for husband and wife to unite at the base of the obelisk, and snapped a couple of photos before handing the camera back to the pleased couple. "Grazie. Multo grazie, Signora."

Cybil grinned, held up her wedding band-less left hand, and, with a wink, replied, "No. Signorina!" She rather enjoyed playing the tourist at the time for Cybil knew that soon enough she would be scrutinizing potential camera angles, reconnoitering favorable interview spots, and sizing up the security guards and barricades. With that she waved good bye, and headed off to find the Vatican's press office.

Thankfully, there was no throng of news hounds clamoring for press credentials at that early hour. Cybil was pleased to find that it was quite an orderly process. Within thirty minutes Cybil had her press credentials with an acceptable photograph.

Within another thirty minutes she was face to face with Moses. That is, with a Sistine Chapel fresco depicting Moses leading the Jews from Egypt to the promised land of Israel. Duly impressed by the lavish art, Cybil soaked in every detail of the Chapel, but not because of any special desire to study Michelangelo's masterpiece. As always, if it wasn't a nightclub or shop, she was all business.

The Sistine Chapel would soon be locked to tourists for it was destined to host the entire, international cast of cardinals assembled in the Papal Conclave to elect the new pontiff. Here the new pontiff would accept the cardinals' acclamation under unusually stringent security precautions guaranteeing the utmost secrecy. However, if Cybil had her way, her team would accomplish the unthinkable and breach Sistine Chapel's security.

Upon arriving at her hotel, the clerk had handed her an envelope with her name neatly printed on it. There was no return address. Once Cybil settled into her hotel suite, she opened it and found a typewritten memo with precise instructions for constructing an electronic eavesdropping device. The author was an anonymous Vatican insider who simply signed the memo 'Joshua.' The memo also provided covert means and signals for communicating with Joshua.

The specifications for the electronic gadget were highly unusual in order to avoid its detection in the Sistine Chapel where the Swiss Guards would undertake intense inspections and electronic sweeps. The device had to operate solely on batteries without a live electrical feed so its power consumption had to be exceptionally low in order to survive for at least seven days. Joshua did not think that the conclave would go longer than five days, but in the event the conclave was a prolonged affair, he would have to see about changing the battery. The hours of operation were to be programmed into the device's computer chip, but the operator had to have the capability to remotely turn it off and on, too. It, also, had to digitally store its sound recordings over the course of each day and, subsequently, transmit that recording nightly at the predetermined time of 11:00 o'clock over a kilometer in an encrypted, short burst not to exceed 5 seconds via a complicated multi-frequency formula to prevent interference or interception on any single frequency. The device, additionally, had to have an amplifier to filter out background noise thereby improving its sound quality.

As if these electronic specifications were not demanding enough, its size dimensions proved even more exacting. The eavesdropping device was to fit inside a large circular, iron hinge holding one of the large twelve narrow windows high above the marble floor of the Sistine Chapel. A thin black wire could then be unobtrusively strung along the length of the hinge to pick up the voices from far below while also permitting ease of transmission to a receiver each night. Joshua had promised to install the listening device. Unknown to Cybil, a member of Spitini's Iranian terror network was employed as a maintenance man at the Vatican and it was he who would install the device during a scheduled replacement of the hinge.

Cybil was feeling pretty good now that she had managed to get a firsthand glimpse of the Sistine Chapel. If this Joshua character could, in fact, deliver on his promises, she would have the world's top scoop. Walking with a bounce, Cybil was back to thinking about Columbia University. She had always wanted to return to the School of Journalism in order to pick up a Pulitzer Prize. Her mind racing with the possibilities, Cybil headed for St. Peter's Basilica.

TJ watched with fascination as Colonel Weissberg, commanding officer of the Papal Swiss Guards, extracted a one-inch thick folder from a tall four-drawer, green safe behind his desk. As he turned to sit, TJ noted that the tan pocket folder was sealed with a red ribbon and the folder's cover bore the papal coat of arms of John Paul III. But, it was the smaller, white file folder inside it that caused TJ to momentarily stop breathing.

That file folder bore entirely different markings and, in particular, it was the large black-ink symbol in the cover's center that startled TJ. Noting her surprise, Colonel Weissberg asked, "Do you recognize something?"

"Why, yes, as a matter of fact." Pointing with her right index finger, TJ continued, "That large symbol is a bit out of place at the Vatican, of all places, isn't it?"

Colonel Weissberg smiled at her. "Yes, it is. And that is why you're here."

What the Colonel had in his hand was the coat of arms of Iran. Approved by the late Ayatollah Khomeini, leader of the Iranian revolution, the coat of arms was a stylized rendition of the Arabic spelling of 'Allah.' It featured a central column, looking much like an obelisk that represents a sword. Above it was a seagull-looking symbol, called a 'shadda,' that denotes the doubling of the sword's power. Flanking the central sword are four crescents, two on each side, that represent the word 'Allah.' All together, the five parts of the pattern embody the five pillars of Islam.

"Colonel Weissberg, do you know how dissidents refer to that symbol?" TJ asked.

"Well, I've heard it referred to as the spider mark," he replied. "Is there another name?"

"Yes. My late uncle, a noted Muslim scholar, used a term that is popular within the community of Iranian dissidents. He called it the 'bloody fork.'"

Colonel Weissberg's eyebrows shot up. "Well, then, that name might be more appropriate. You see, I started this folder over a year ago when we were tipped off that Islamic fundamentalists were plotting to assassinate John Paul III on his trip, two years ago, to the Gulf States. The assassins never materialized so we were never sure if our hot tip was a good one or not. But, John Paul ..." and he paused looking for the right words, "..., ummm, let's just say, um, grew increasingly concerned over an Islamic threat to the Vatican after reading various confidential reports he regularly collected from his far flung Catholic dioceses."

Looking up to ensure that his office door was still closed, Colonel Weissberg continued.

"I need to tell you that you will be working expressly for the Swiss Guards. You are not to speak with the Vatican police and security forces. Do you understand?"

TJ nodded approvingly.

"Good. This is a matter related to papal security."

He looked at TJ and continued. "The Pope grew exasperated over his failure to successfully build an ecumenical partnership with Islam. He made some progress, but it fell far short of his goals. Where he sought peace, he found strife. Where he sought forgiveness, he found revenge. Where he sought attention to heavenly things, he found overzealous ambition for worldly goods and land. The Pope so much wanted to collectively mobilize all of the world's religions as a force for peace.

Instead, reports painted a grim picture where the Catholic Church was progressively more and more the target of Islamic fundamentalists, and others, bent on destroying peace. Their activities have ranged from assassination and kidnapping to intimidating parishioners and petty theft of church articles. We have also witnessed acts of defiance encompassing seemingly minor acts such as disapproving church renovation permits, cutting off electrical power to churches on Sundays, and canceling Catholic street celebrations. And, of course, the Catholic Church has been hard hit by lawsuits following scandalous revelations of priests' crimes in the United States.

In isolation, any one of these acts appears to be localized; but, the Pope was concerned that, if viewed collectively, this might be a concerted effort threatening the Catholic Church. The Pope needed a topnotch Mideast counter-terror expert to sift through the data in order to confirm or deny his suspicions. That is why you are here."

Weissberg paused momentarily before uncomfortably continuing, "However, I frankly have reservations over John Paul's concerns. I find it hard to swallow that any radical Islamic group would target the Catholic Church. The United States, yes. The United Kingdom, yes. Western capitalism, yes. But, the Church? Are the Arabs going to fly an airliner into St. Peter's? What for?"

For the next hour, Colonel Weissberg continued to hold TJ's complete attention as he recounted, in more detail, the contents of the folder. In fact, he and TJ were so engrossed in their give and take conversation that both missed the initial knock on his door. Hearing the much louder second knock, they stopped midstream and turned to face the door. "Come in," the colonel shouted firmly.

A young plainclothes officer of the Swiss Guards stepped inside the office and shut the door behind him. Handing a large sealed manila envelope to Colonel Weissberg, the officer said, "Sir, please forgive the interruption, but you asked to be notified immediately when the autopsy report arrived." Colonel Weissberg and TJ looked each other in the eye with neither able to move until the young officer had left.

Grabbing his letter opener, Colonel Weissberg rapidly slit the envelope open and began to read while motioning TJ to come around his desk to look over his shoulder.

Three minutes later he exclaimed, "Well, that's that then. Nothing abnormal. It seems that our Pope died a natural death." It was an odd mix of relief and disappointment. On one hand, neither wanted to find evidence of a papal murder; least of all Colonel Weissberg on whose watch it would be recorded for all eternity. On the other hand, both felt that the autopsy had let them down; that the culprits were very clever, indeed, and, therefore, would be exceptionally difficult to apprehend.

Looking at his watch, Colonel Weissberg said, "Tell you what. Let's lock all of this up and attend today's daily mass for John Paul III. Some time in church would do me well and, although I understand that you are a Muslim, it would be good for you to familiarize yourself with our practices as I hope you will be staying for awhile."

Cardinal Murphy was looking forward to escaping the brutal Roman heat for it was quickly taking its toll as he walked up to St. Peter's Basilica in the black cassock, red sash, and red skullcap of a Cardinal of the Holy Roman Catholic Church. The limousine ride from the airport to the Vatican had, thankfully, been air conditioned. His short fifteen minutes with the Cardinal

Camerlengo and a handful of other prelates had also taken place in cool, air conditioned climates. But, this was an entirely different matter as Rome appeared on the brink of another record setting day of humid heat.

St. Peter's Basilica was cool, much to his relief. The high, vaulted ceiling that instinctively drew one's eyes up towards heaven also trapped the rising hot air thereby permitting life to flourish below.

The third daily mass to mourn John Paul III was a beehive of activity. Nearly seventy Cardinals, just over half of the 117 members of the College of Cardinals, were arriving and filing into reserved pews. Other clerics and officials of the Vatican to include Monsignor Spitini, Colonel Weissberg and TJ, the press corps numbering Cybil among them, numerous mourners, and nosy onlookers were beginning to fill the Basilica with only standing room to be had soon by latecomers.

The Catholic Church marks the passing of a Pope with a formal nine-day period of mourning that ends with the pontiff's funeral mass and burial. This period is popularly known as 'novemdiales' – which is translated as 'nine days' – and is a term finding its roots in ancient Rome when Romans assembled to honor the dead in a service called 'novemdiale sacrum' on the ninth day of each month. Novemdiales is a time marked by a daily mass for the deceased pontiff and meetings of the Cardinals to plan the ceremonies, manage the expenses, and prepare for the conclave.

Cardinal Murphy settled comfortably into a pew and found himself sitting between Cardinal Lu Doc of Vietnam and Cardinal Valdina of Italy. He was awestruck by the beautiful pageantry of the mass. The accompanying music, wafting incense, and Latin intonations created a mysticism that was both enthralling and frightening. Meant to reinforce learning among parishioners, the traditions unfolding before him gathered believers together into a sacred dimension of worship that is a mystery to all others.

Despite the mournful poignancy surrounding the pontiff's passing, the pomp celebrated the vibrant and colorful human life in a world darkened by hardship, famine, crime, and death. To Cardinal Murphy, the Catholic Church was a safe haven for the weary gathering to rejuvenate themselves in great celebrations, for the generous valiantly offering charity and compassion to the needy, and for the children of god gathering as God's own family – loved and cherished. The sounds, fragrances, and color of the rituals deepened his love of the Catholic Church.

Cybil Checchi, sitting in some pews reserved for the press, found the ceremony overly indulgent. What a bunch of hoopla over a God that didn't exist. However, the music reminded Cybil of her mother's days as a church organist and the incense made her think of her father happily smoking his pipe at home while reading the Sunday New York Times. Her childhood memories were fond and carefree. Those were the good old days.

TJ, sitting beside Colonel Weissberg in a pew right up front, was reverently attentive and curious. Although the Catholic rituals were extraordinarily different from those of her Muslim faith, she found many similarities in the spirit of community, grief over a loss, and celebration of a life. She was discovering that the basic human motivation to gathering for worship was not all that different from religion to religion despite the vast differences in methods and music.

Sitting down at his office computer, Ernie Flanagan watched the mass in full color via streaming video on a website. Despite being half a world away, Ernie had a 'front row' seat.

This was a poignant moment for Ernie. For no particular reason, the Catholic Church had begun to pull on his heartstrings. Perhaps, his wife's death was continuing to affect him in unusual ways.

Shortly after her death, Ernie quit his prominent role at Northeastern University in order to raise his three children in the small town of Nyack. The quieting calmness of the lower Hudson Valley and his reduced workload helped Ernie and his children through the long and painful grieving period. It was good, indeed, to return to New York where he could rethink his life.

Now he was prone to wistfully recall his early walk of faith in the Catholic Church. Ernie could not help but wonder why. Was it some sort of midlife crisis? Or was it the continuation of his grieving?

In trying to rationalize this recent sentiment, he had to admit that there were elements of Protestantism that left him wanting more. For instance, Ernie was uneasy over the proliferation of Protestant church services that were often tailored to suit the individual wishes of each congregation. More than once, he patiently endured Protestant services smacking more of frivolous experimentation or extravagant entertainment than meaningful worship.

Ernie had also long been critical of the lack of solemnity in many Protestant sanctuaries. As a child he was accustomed to treating the sanctuary with extreme reverence. It was a sacred place of worship. Yet, it was all too common for Protestants to freely mingle and talk in their sanctuaries as they waited for services to begin. Women would coordinate carpool schedules for the week's youth soccer games, men would critically examine Saturday's college football games, and kids would stand on the pews or simply run amok. One Bible Church even went so far as to install basketball hoops so that the sanctuary could quickly be converted to a basketball court for youth fellowship.

Lastly, although Ernie had greatly disliked Catholic confession as a young man, he now had to reluctantly admit that the act of personally confessing to a priest was immensely satisfying. The Protestant style of confessing to general sins while standing in unison as a congregation was increasingly lacking in substance for Ernie's tastes. He increasingly grew to believe that personal confession greatly improved personal accountability.

He had even taken to personally confessing his sins to his good friend, Sean Murphy, at their monthly meetings. This regular act proved immensely satisfying and soul cleansing. Indeed, his monthly debates with Sean had reinvigorated his critical examination of Christian religious practices.

Most surprising to him, Ernie had also slipped into St. Patrick's Cathedral for Saturday evening mass on two recent occasions. What was going on?

CHAPTER ELEVEN

The day had come and gone. Following the mass, the assembled Cardinals gathered for lunch and a meeting of the general congregation of the College of Cardinals. The Cardinal Camerlengo and senior-ranking Curial clerics provided updates on the planning for the daily masses, funeral mass, and papal burial as well as for calling the conclave to elect the new pontiff. Financial reports were quickly dispensed with and a growing list of international dignitaries wishing to attend the funeral mass in less than a week was reviewed. The meeting dragged on for nearly two hours in order to respectfully answer all questions for the Cardinals who had newly arrived from abroad.

Cardinal Murphy subsequently spent an additional hour speaking privately with a small handful of American clerics studying and working at the Vatican as well as granting a short interview with Il Messaggero, a popular Italian newspaper. He had plans to dine downtown with his small accompanying staff until Cardinal Maltempo intercepted him in a corridor of the Apostolic Palace with an invitation to dine at a nearby restaurant. Although eager for a quiet, informal dinner, Cardinal Murphy graciously accepted the offer in order to avoid offending Cardinal Maltempo who many thought was a leading contender to be the next pontiff.

With his administrative assistant by his side, Cardinal Murphy dictated tasks while making his way to St. Martha's Residence at the Vatican where he would live, along with the other Cardinals, throughout the novemdiales and subsequent conclave. St. Martha's was essentially a hotel for Catholic clerics visiting the Holy See in Rome. Although not a five star hotel, it was clean, well furnished, and comfortable. And convenient. His staff had found lodging in a Vatican building associated with the Teutonic College, one of several small churches on the Vatican grounds.

Upon reaching his room, Cardinal Murphy wrapped up the list of action items for his assistant, bid him farewell, and retired to rest, wash, and dress for the evening. Around eight o'clock that evening, he emerged to meet Cardinal Maltempo and five other Cardinals in the main foyer of St. Martha's. Joining the group for dinner were Cardinal Joseph Nubualovu, the esteemed Chancellor of the Apostolic Camera; Cardinal Aldo Pellitteri of Genoa, the eldest member of the College of Cardinals at age 79; Cardinal Richard Gauthier of Montreal, Canada; Cardinal Aakar Kodavas of Mumbai, India; and Cardinal Juan Flores, the senior ranking cleric of Brasil and Archbishop of Sao Paulo. With Cardinal Murphy's arrival, the very distinguished lot exited St. Martha's Residence for a short limousine ride to the Abruzzi, a Curial restaurant favorite, near the renowned Gregorian University which happened to be Cardinal Maltempo's alma mater.

Cybiline Checchi was enjoying her campari and breadsticks when the half dozen Cardinals arrived at the restaurant. Pleased that her hotel's concierge had correctly identified a favorite restaurant of the Vatican's leadership, Cybil made a mental note to give the concierge an extra tip the next day. She studied the entering Cardinals and recognized Cardinals Murphy, Maltempo, and Nubualovu. This was, indeed, a distinguished group, she marveled to herself, as she unobtrusively photographed the group with a miniature camera in her cupped left hand.

Unfortunately, the Cardinals retired to a back room where a closed door shielded them from further public scrutiny. "Shit!" Cybil muttered under her breath, but she had to admit that it wasn't a total lost cause with other Vatican clerics around her openly talking about a wide range of subjects. Cybil was always amazed to hear how much confidential work-related information people divulged at public places. One only had to listen.

Her dinner guest arrived as the waiter delivered a large antipasto plate of roasted garlic and tomato bruschetta. Giulio Battista was the last piece of the puzzle to fall into place for he was the technician hired by Harold to support Cybil. "Good evening. Miss Checchi?" Giulio asked in perfect English, albeit with a strong Italian accent.

"Buona sera! Yes, I am Cybiline Checchi from New York," Cybil politely replied while remaining seated and motioning Giulio to sit. "Bravo, Harold!" Cybil mused as she admiringly looked Giulio over. A young athletic man, perhaps in his late twenties or early thirties, would grace her table for the evening. He had short black hair that was receding at the temples, piercing brown eyes, and a transparent beard and mustache of the short stubble style that Tom Cruise was so adept at wearing. Giulio was dressed in tight, well-worn faded jeans and a no-button, short-sleeve blue and white track-stripe polo shirt that gave every indication of sixpack abs lurking underneath.

Giulio ordered a campari and joined Cybil in nibbling on the bruschetta while engaging in small talk about the Roman heat wave, the shock of the pope's death, Italian food and fashion, and other trivial matters. Cybil would not be making the same mistake as the patrons around her talking openly about their work at the Vatican. After dinner, Giulio would lead her to his workshop to select and negotiate the prices for the electronic gear for eavesdropping, taking pictures, and listening in to official police radio transmissions. She also began to entertain thoughts of negotiating for some of Giulio's affection before returning to her hotel in the morning; but, as they say, business before pleasure. After all, 'Il tempo viene per chi sa aspettare' – all things come to those who wait.

Cocking her head and smiling sweetly, Cybil interrupted Giulio's current discourse on the planning for the pontiff's funeral, "So, tell me, what a tourist can do for fun in Rome?"

Cardinal Narciso Maltempo was a regular at the restaurant when in Rome. Which was often. The trip to Rome was a comfortable drive in his chauffeured limousine from his archdiocese in Florence, located in Tuscany 170 miles north of Rome. He found it beneficial to maintain good relations with the various Curial officials. The occasional, opportunistic photo-op with the Pope didn't hurt, either.

Florence suited Cardinal Maltempo's outgoing disposition. Home to nearly one million people in the greater metropolitan area of Florence, the city was internationally renowned and an Italian center for finance. This afforded the Cardinal national and international visibility while enjoying the pleasures of remaining in his native Italy.

He enjoyed serving God in Italy. A native, no less, of Florence, Cardinal Maltempo was accustomed to the beautiful architecture found throughout the city, the Uffizi Gallery's superior collection of fine art, the splendor of the Pitti Palace and its adjoining Boboli Gardens, the first-rate Tuscan wines, and the brilliance of the Arno River on a sunny day. He filled with pride at the sight of the Basilica di Santa Maria del Fiore, the cathedral of the Florentine Archdiocese. More popularly known as the 'Duomo,' it was the largest cathedral in all of Europe when completed over five hundred years ago. Now, only St. Peter's Basilica and just a couple of other European cathedrals could boast of exceeding its size. Nevertheless, the Duomo's architecture was capped with an inspiring, soaring dome that was unequalled in his eyes.

Florence also daily reminded him that he was following in the footsteps of some of the greatest minds and leaders in the world's history. Leonardo da Vinci was raised and instructed in the art of painting in Florence, the famous Medici family ruled the city, Niccolo Machiavelli penned his treatise of political pragmatism there, and Gucci established its famous fashion house in Florence. Florence was the birthplace of the Italian Renaissance and, to this day, remained one of the wealthiest regions of Italy. In his earlier days, he had ambitiously imagined that a Catholic pontiff from Florence would be a marvelous addition to the list of distinguished Florentines.

Cardinal Maltempo had nearly given up on his papal aspirations. At the age of seventy-six, he was nearing retirement with a much younger Pope ruling the Holy See. With the unexpected death of John Paul III, Maltempo sensed that God had opened a last opportunity for him that he could not afford to waste. If God wanted him to succeed John Paul III, he would. His exceptional qualifications clearly placed him on the list of 'papabile.' First, with over fifty faithful years of clerical service all over the world, Cardinal Maltempo was a proven leader with a comprehensive understanding of the world and the Church. Second, he was highly respected within the College of Cardinals. Lastly, Maltempo knew the Vatican's operations very well after serving there a number of times

Most recently, Cardinal Maltempo had labored as the President of Administration of the Patrimony of the Apostolic See, a post that tested his patience to the utmost. While that afforded him an expert view of the Holy See, the administrative position that often dwelled on minutiae wasn't a good fit for him. Thankfully, John Paul III had agreed to post Cardinal Maltempo back to his hometown of Florence for what appeared to be Maltempo's retirement assignment. Now it appeared that his dispatch to Florence might just lead to a resurrection of his career.

Finding everyone comfortably seated at the reserved round table and the curtain drawn for privacy, Cardinal Maltempo opened the evening's conversation by welcoming the out-of-towners to Rome and inquiring into their accommodations and travels. Additional discussions about the debilitating heat wave, Italian national elections in the fall, and other small-talk kept the Cardinals happily engaged throughout the appetizers, antipasto, and soup.

With the arrival of the main course, a large mixed grill platter adorned with fresh vegetables, the discussions turned more serious when Cardinal Maltempo invited Cardinal Nubualovu to share his experiences in finding John Paul III dead in the papal chambers two days earlier.

Cardinal Nubualovu was glad to comply and began, "Well, I am sure that Pope John Paul's death was a complete shock to all of you, as it was for us here at the Vatican. However, if truth be told, John Paul III was under medical care for pneumonia." With that, Cardinal Nubualovu launched into a lengthy narrative of the pontiff's demise. The other Cardinals listened intently to Cardinal Nubualovu's recount of that fateful morning with an occasional interruption for clarification.

Upon concluding, Cardinal Nubualovu set his fork down and refreshed himself with a glass of red Chianti. Everyone else continued to quietly eat except for Maltempo.

"I understand that Cardinal Biaggio ordered an autopsy," Cardinal Maltempo declared while closely watching Nubualovu's reaction. Frowning, Cardinal Nubualovu set his glass down and looked at his host seated alongside him as if to say, "Now why did you have to bring that up?" Everyone else, completely taken by surprise, stopped eating and turned to the African. Their stares were momentarily interrupted when Cardinal Gauthier clumsily dropped his fork with a loud clatter onto his plate.

"An autopsy?" Cardinal Murphy asked with a puzzled look. "That has never been done before, has it?"

"Well, Cardinal Biaggio thought it prudent. I, among others, fully support his decision although it is an awkward situation for us to submit the pope to a final medical examination," Cardinal Nubualovu replied in a very measured tone, but with evident discomfort at having to address the question at a public restaurant albeit in a private room.

"Awkward? I should say so!" Cardinal Gauthier stated after regaining his composure.

Cardinal Maltempo seized this opportunity to demonstrate his detailed knowledge of the inner secrets of the Vatican. "My fellow friends, the death of John Paul I after only a month in office proved, shall we say, greatly disturbing. To this day, we do not know if his death can be attributed to any sinister plot. Indeed, we were besieged by the media spinning tales of murder and conspiracy. I was serving in the Curia at that time and it simply consumed too much of our attention and proved utterly worthless. Frankly, we knew that John Paul I was in poor health. Furthermore, the workload for any new pope can be overwhelming so it should not have been too surprising to have his heart give way. However, we did have to wonder if the Catholic Church had enemies with such brazen power as to dare to murder the Pope."

Looking around at the small assembly of Cardinals and finding that he had their undivided attention, he continued, "Well, we later found out that there were such enemies when the Bulgarians sent Mehmet Ali Agca to shoot John Paul II. Our fears were well founded. The devil continues to oppose the church. After all, we rival most intelligence agencies in our knowledge of world affairs and in our global influence."

"Anyway, back to the autopsy. So the Secretary of State asked me to privately draft a document for the signature of John Paul II authorizing the Cardinal Camerlengo who, as we all know, acts as the interim director of the Catholic Church upon the pontiff's death with the power to order an autopsy. John Paul II did sign such an edict and directed that it be kept confidential. No one had found cause to order an autopsy for a pope since then. That is, until this week."

"What are you, ummmm, what d-d-do you mean? You are implying that there is cause. Didn't Joseph earlier explain that John Paul III was sick?" Cardinal Flores stammered while looking plaintively at Nubualovu.

Cardinal Nubualovu matter-of-factly replied, "We don't have any cause to suspect wrongdoing. Let me put your mind to rest. The cause for death – a breakdown in the pontiff's immune system – is well within the realm of the possible for a man suffering from a lingering bout with pneumonia. Nevertheless, we wish to forestall the media circus that has already begun in the wake of the Pope's premature death. We will likely announce the autopsy results which, by the way, are negative very soon. That should quiet the press considerably."

After an awkward silence, Cardinal Murphy inquired, "But, what if you had found an irregular cause for the Pope's death? Perhaps, some poison?"

That chilled the warm laughter over Nubualovu's light-hearted wittiness. "Yes, what if you found poison?" Cardinal Flores echoed the American's question.

Cardinal Nubualovu struggled with a reply, forming several answers with his lips, but unable to produce a reply. Maltempo jumped into the breach, "We'd probably announce it, but it would have to be treated carefully so as to assist the police investigations."

"Really?" Shouldn't we keep such a thing secret if it ever happened, God forbid?" Cardinal Flores sputtered. "Think of the media circus we would create if we announced that the Pope had been murdered. The Vatican would be one giant crime scene with police tape blocking our paths, subpoenas interrupting our schedules, and nervous clerics looking over their shoulders at night. We couldn't get any work done. 'Murder at the Vatican' would be playing in the movie theaters the following spring. No, it's one thing for John Paul II to be shot, but in surviving he became a hero and the power of God in saving him was plain for all to see. But, for someone to successfully assassinate the Pope, in a covert operation no less, would be seen as a sign of weakness. Far better for us to keep it secret whether we eventually catch the assassin or not."

Cardinal Murphy quickly countered, "The last thing we need is to extend this public perception of self-serving secrecy promulgated by the likes of Dan Brown. His novel, *The Da Vinci Code*, although clearly a true piece of fiction, caused quite a commotion in the states. Let's just say that we were pummeled, once again, in the press and had to resort to damage control and public education seminars to refute Brown's fictional assertions."

Maltempo, pleased with Murphy's reply, added, "Well, I for one, agree with Cardinal Murphy in advising against secrecy. In this day and age of rapid communications and investigative journalism, the truth would leak out eventually. Far better for us to tackle it up front in order to shape the message. Hiding a papal assassination would throw us onto the defensive and, ultimately, damage our reputation."

Maltempo then seized the opportunity to leverage this discussion for political gain. "Well, I certainly hope and pray that we do not see another Muslim assassin. Never again."

Looking around the table to find that he had, indeed, startled his peers, Maltempo continued to stake out his position for the coming papal election. "The Muslim issue in Europe is quite vexing. John Paul III, God bless him, attempted to bridge the gulf between our faiths, but I am more and more convinced that Islam defies integration. Father Serralda who has been living in North Africa for more than fifty years wrote that Muslims are perpetually at war with Christianity. Their aim is nothing short of our complete extinction. Why, I even heard that some Middle Eastern newspapers have published al-Qa'eda calls for killing two Christians for every Muslim killed by American military strikes."

The conservative Cardinal Kodavas chimed in to voice his support for Maltempo. "You're correct, my dear Narciso. We've simply squandered far too many valuable Church resources on mobilizing Islamic clerics for peace. It's time to admit the futility of any such thing. Dare we truly believe that a religion requiring its believers to turn to Mecca five times a day can produce Muslims happy to be assimilated into Europe or anywhere else, for that matter? How can we expect Muslims to accept the separation of church and state when they actively promote Iran's model of government where the mullahs alone rule? Can we really expect the Muslims to abide by the laws of established democratic governments permitting pluralism if they disavow religious freedoms? Don't forget that they believe the Old and New Testaments are corrupted!" Kodavas' voice was gradually rising when he stopped.

The cardinals were largely in agreement with some reservations, but they were clearly uncomfortable with continuing the discussion. In an attempt to enliven the somber mood that had settled over the conversation, Cardinal Aldo Pellitteri smiled and good-naturedly said, "Come, let's talk about something else. We have plenty of mourning to do so let's relax with more cheerful subjects. I, for one, will have bad dreams waking me up in the middle of the night if we prolong this talk of poisons and assassins. Why, this meat is already beginning to taste funny and

I'm losing my appetite! Besides, 'I muri hanno orecchi' – the walls have ears. We should leave such talk for the workplace."

"Funny you should mention dreams," Cardinal Murphy spoke up. I have been beset with odd dreams about the Catholic Church." With that he proceeded to describe his dreams of the World Trade Center churches and white sheep. Those stories produced some joviality as the Cardinals took turns inventing hilarious interpretations. However, with dessert and coffee now served, Cardinal Pellitteri could not resist mentioning that he, too, had been troubled by a lack of sleep due to troubling dreams.

"I actually dreamt that I was in the conclave. I remember being confused in my dream because I saw some old friends who are no longer with us – God bless their souls – sitting beside me to vote for the pope. In fact, I distinctly recall trying to get their attention to ask what they were doing there. They were dead, after all! But, they ignored me. It was like I wasn't even there. None of my attempts to get their attention worked. I was very frustrated in my dream, believe me!" Cardinals Nubualovu and Maltempo both chuckled because they knew how much their good friend Aldo hated to be ignored when he spoke.

After taking a sip of his coffee, Pellitteri continued, "So, we elect a cardinal from among us. I, of course, was disappointed that it was not me!" Pellitteri was delighted to see that his joke drew a good deal of laughter. "Okay, so I could not see who the new Pope was. Everyone had jumped up to congratulate him and they were all blocking my view. Besides, my knees ache and I wasn't too eager to stand up." Again, he smiled at the laughter and went on. "But, for some reason we all began to throw rice as if we were at a wedding. It was crazy! Rice everywhere! Everyone was dancing and jumping around. Just like at a good Italian wedding with great music and bottles of wine. Well, I noticed that after a while, the rice began to collect in a mound and pretty soon it took the shape of a huge snowball. It must have been two or three meters high and was sitting on top of a table. All of a sudden it fell off of the table and began to roll very quickly towards the group of Cardinals surrounding the newly elected Pope. They were unable to get out of its way and the rice ball crushed them. Then I woke up. In a cold sweat and feeling more tired than when I went to bed!"

Everyone looked at Pellitteri, but didn't know what to say. Maltempo was going to interject a joke, but Cardinal Flores was quick to exclaim, "I had a dream about rice, too!"

"You've got to be kidding!" Cardinal Pellitteri declared. "About rice? This is unusual."

"Yes, yes!" Cardinal Flores was clearly agitated and began to wave his hands as he talked. "We had elected a pope and he was standing on the Benediction Loggia – the balcony where new popes are introduced to the waiting throng in St. Peter's Square below – when everyone in St. Peter's Square began to throw rice. They began to celebrate. The rice was coming down like a heavy snow! Only, it began to pile up on the balcony. It got heavier and heavier until the balcony collapsed and fell far below to the Square with no survivors. I, too, awoke with a start."

The ensuing discussion struck a nerve with each of the Cardinals. They began to analyze and compare the dreams over several more cups of black coffee. Some even ordered a second dessert. The dreams were no longer joking matters. Especially for Cardinal Maltempo.

The Cardinals were so occupied with their attempts to interpret each others' dreams that they failed to notice that Maltempo was the sole Cardinal who did not volunteer a dream. He was quite content, instead, to pretend having no troubling dreams at all. However, that was the furthest thing from the truth. In his most recent nightmare, he had been elected Pope and the other Cardinals began to toss rice. In his dream, he was the one crushed by a huge rice ball.

CHAPTER TWELVE

The dining Cardinals were not alone among their peers in being beset by unusually vivid dreams filled with religious symbols. Many a member of the College of Cardinals awakened in sweat from an awkward night of sleep during the period of novemdiales. However, the Cardinals simply ascribed the dreams and uneasy sleep to a combination of the stressful preparations for the Pope's burial and the excessive August heat that sapped their strength.

Nevertheless, the Cardinals collectively managed all of the burial preparations which were considerable in number and complexity. Financial management, normally an unwelcome chore, was a relatively simple matter compared to dealing with the media horde, hosting foreign dignitaries, and supervising contractors. There was so much to do that finding time to grieve over the loss of John Paul III was easier said than done. Indeed, the daily mass for the dead pontiff was cathartic as it afforded each Cardinal some time for peaceful meditation free of the mounting administrative demands.

Thankfully, the Vatican's announcement of the pontiff's autopsy and his recent bout with pneumonia had satisfied many of the overly inquisitive news reporters. Although a good part of the media's focus remained on the near-term burial mass, the media's attention gradually shifted from John Paul III to his likely successor. With most of Europe on vacation, dormant soccer leagues, and closed legislatures the press was thankful to fill the void with speculative reporting from the Vatican.

Elsewhere in Rome, life was busy, too. Roman hotels continued to lodge record numbers of guests for the month of August. Despite the scorching heat, mourners were flocking to the Vatican. Work crews were busily assembling seating areas and barricades. Cameras with weather-proof covers were mushrooming. Security officers were besieging Colonel Weissberg with demands. Arriving foreign government dignitaries were imposing on the Cardinal Camerlengo and Curial officials.

Cardinal Murphy had been asked to assist with the planning to receive dignitaries and heads of state from North, South, and Central America. It was a tiresome duty made all the more difficult by having to deal with overly-compulsive protocol officers keen on obtaining the best services for their national leaders. Murphy's days were packed with preparations that ranged from urgent telephone calls and high priority eMails from anxious embassy officials to walking the Vatican grounds to double-check physical arrangements. Lastly, Cardinal Murphy worked with his small staff in supervising matters back at his Archdiocese in New York.

His evenings were filled with dinners in the company of other Cardinals, American clerics working at the Vatican, and visiting foreign dignitaries. Returning to his room around midnight each night, Cardinal Murphy was asleep before his head hit the pillow.

Cybil was outwardly competing with her media colleagues for interviews and stories while secretly plotting her covert electronic surveillance operation. Back in New York, Harold was content with her middle-of-the-road daily news filings knowing that her big story was forthcoming thanks to the anonymous insider's assistance.

Giulio was proving to be a technical mastermind. He diligently set about assembling the appropriate parts of the electronic listening device to meet the required technical and size specifications. Within two days he had built the contraption and tested it to Cybil's satisfaction. Although she did not understand the science behind the listening device, Giulio adeptly put it through a rigorous test plan to demonstrate its ability to eavesdrop on patrons in his electronics store. Completely satisfied, Cybil and Giulio carefully packaged it in Styrofoam pellets. Cybil then followed the explicit instructions handed to her when she checked in at the hotel. Wearing a red scarf, tan blouse and pants ensemble, and sunglasses, as directed, Cybil dropped off the package with a young man atop a Vespa moped on a small side street near the Forum. By mid-afternoon, Spitini's accomplice had replaced the window hinge and by that evening Giulio had successfully completed a final test the day before the funeral mass and a week before the conclave was scheduled to convene. Elated to find it working, Giulio later produced a bottle of red wine and two glasses from a cupboard in his apartment over his store only to turn around and find Cybil smiling and boldly standing in sexy red French lingerie.

"Where's your bedroom?" Cybil coyly inquired.

Dumbfounded, Giulio pointed to his right and happily followed a prancing Cybil down the hall.

To all appearances, Monsignor Marco Spitini, out of a job as the principal assistant to the Papal Secretary, assisted the Camerlengo, Cardinal Biaggio, with various trivial administrative chores, mostly related to official communications and press releases. However, Spitini focused his true attention on his clandestine activities.

Marco Spitini was exceptionally relieved at the public announcement of the pope's negative autopsy. The bio-regulators had worked their magic without leaving any trace of malign intentions. He was, therefore, free of any further suspicions.

In addition to contacting Cybil and subsequently having the listening device planted in the Sistine Chapel, Monsignor Spitini circulated extensively around the Vatican in order to identify the potential papal candidates for his terror network's mastermind. Spitini was pleased to find that the Italian voting bloc continued to have the strongest support, as anticipated. Three names appeared to be uppermost on the Cardinals' lists with two of those being Italians. Cardinal Narciso Maltempo, the Archbishop of Florence, and Cardinal Paolo Fassino, the Archbishop of Milan, were the two Italians. The lone non-Italian rumored to be a leading contender was Cardinal Alfredo Fernando Moratinos of Spain who held a powerful post in the Curia as the Prefect of Congregation for the Doctrine of the Faith and President of Pontifical Biblical Commission. This was the very post that Cardinal Ratzinger occupied before being elevated to Pope Benedict XVI.

Through his personal knowledge of these men while serving as the Papal Secretary's principal assistant, Monsignor Spitini had concluded that none of these three men was inclined to follow John Paul's international role and evangelical program. This was not unexpected and, in some quaint way, followed a lengthy historical pattern whereby new popes rarely fell in line with their predecessors. The difference in style and agenda of each new pope is often so very clear-cut that Italians are prone to say in their humorous ways, "After a fat pope a lean pope."

These choices also suited Spitini on another count as he had surreptitiously abused his power to acquire information that he hoped would prove embarrassing to the Catholic Church through an Iranian-inspired campaign of news leaks and propaganda-fueled innuendo.

Cardinal Maltempo lived rather lavishly by drawing on his former father's fortune that was largely built on underhanded business financing for Mussolini's regime in the early 20th century. Much like Pope Benedict XVI, any ties to the former Nazi Axis could prove troubling for any Pope.

Cardinal Fassino appeared to have no embarrassing skeletons in his closet so Spitini's accomplices would have to invent some believable tale. For instance, a strong financial supporter of Cardinal Fassino's initiatives had been acquitted in a national banking fraud scandal ten years earlier. Many felt that someone had unduly influenced a judge to acquit the prominent Italian banker. What if Spitini's network could spin a story linking Fassino to some underhanded deal exonerating the banker? With the right investigative journalist willing to compromise the truth in exchange for a fat check from Iran, Spitini was sure that Fassino would not go unscathed. Perhaps, they could even pin Fassino with other interventions on behalf of wealthy patrons of the Catholic Church.

Cardinal Moratinos was clean, too; however, one of his chief assistants had made the mistake of going out of his way several years ago to protect a Spanish priest privately accused of sexual misconduct. This had involved payoffs to parishioners and moving the offending priest in and out of churches and, occasionally, psychological counseling. Moratinos had, remarkably, been kept in the dark by his assistant. Reminiscent of the troubles plaguing the American Catholic Church, this news story could spin out of control worldwide, especially in the Middle East with the assistance of the Al Jazeera news network, with great harm to the Catholic priesthood.

Spitini, additionally, had either built damaging dossiers or had developed believable smear campaigns on a number of other Cardinals and Bishops for blackmailing or negative propaganda battles. All of this would prove very useful for supplanting the Catholic Church with the greater glory of Islam.

The negative autopsy report, planting of the electronic eavesdropping device, and raiding of confidential personnel files had notably emboldened Spitini. Perhaps, he need not flee to Iran too soon after all. Marco Spitini's Iranian masters planned to falsify his death thereby permitting him to finally live in Iran under a new identity and as a secret national hero, but his continued services over many years as a mole in the Catholic Church might prove invaluable to the Islamic cause.

Cockily, Spitini thought, "Who knows? Maybe I could even get myself elected Pope! I could use the dossiers to blackmail many in the College of Cardinals for their votes."

Although he did have to admit that his clandestine life was fraught with danger, Spitini felt Allah's angels protecting him. Everything was going to plan. Well, almost everything. Spitini and his spy network handlers had not counted on TJ's meddling. TJ had to be stopped. Stopped dead.

CHAPTER THIRTEEN

TJ had settled into an office adjoining Colonel Weissberg's office. Over the course of the novemdiales period, TJ had set about studiously poring over the voluminous file that Weissberg had earlier produced to her surprise. It was chockfull of radical Islamic terrorist incidents and other confidential reports assessing fundamentalist Islamic threats to Catholic Churches all over the world.

The work was exceedingly tedious, but necessary. Good field craft required labor intensive research and preparation. TJ spent most of her days reading, re-reading, and cross-checking the reports with each other and with additional classified documents that TJ requested through Scotland Yard, Interpol, and the Italian police forces supporting the Vatican. This enabled TJ to match the known whereabouts of terror operatives, whether Islamic fundamentalists or others, to plots and attacks against the Catholic Church.

TJ, additionally, gained access to intelligence reports detailing intercepted terrorist communications, terrorist interrogations, captured weapons and bomb caches, and terrorist groups' financial funds transfers that were very useful in assessing the veracity of the worldwide threat to the Catholic Church. TJ had rapidly accumulated so much classified material that she now outmatched Colonel Weissberg in having four large safes to his one.

Nonetheless, TJ had not, yet, come to any conclusions on the terror threat. The sheer volume of the material pre-ordained a lengthy endeavor over several months. She also needed to undertake an ambitious travel plan to personally interview sources for the Catholic reports and to meet with intelligence operatives for extensive question and answer sessions.

To handle the large amount of work, TJ had even implored Colonel Weissberg in their daily evening meetings to provide her with a couple of assistants. However, he had refused her request due to the extreme sensitivity of the subject. How would the Vatican, much less the world, react if word got out that the Swiss Guards was sponsoring a large-scale staff effort to analyze the radical Islamic terror threat? No, Colonel Weissberg reasoned that this initiative must be kept as small and discreet as possible.

Instead, Colonel Weissberg assigned one of his junior officers, Lieutenant Hans Meier, on a part-time basis to assist TJ under the proviso that she train him in counterintelligence work. The Colonel also gave TJ full access to the limited resources of the Swiss Guards and encouraged TJ to get to know as much about the Vatican and Catholic Church as possible.

Taking the Colonel's advice, TJ would take an early afternoon walk around the Vatican each day. Her Vatican credentials permitted her access to the museums and libraries, all of which she immensely enjoyed. The young men of the Swiss Guards standing watch in their colorful old-fashioned uniforms soon came to recognize TJ by sight and enjoyed engaging her in conversation whenever possible.

TJ, additionally, took the opportunity to look over the security precautions for the pope's burial mass and conclave. On one such occasion as she headed for the Sistine Chapel, TJ startled Monsignor Spitini as he rounded a corner and came face to face with her.

"Oh, buon giorno!" TJ said as both came to a full halt within an arm's length of each other. Thinking quickly, TJ added, "It's a pleasure to see you again. How have you been?" But, this time she spoke in Farsi, the native tongue of Iran.

Monsignor Spitini, clearly startled by her sudden appearance, put his two hands up before his stomach to prevent a collision, came to a stop, and managed a quick step backwards with his left foot. He was even more startled by TJ's deft use of Farsi. Looking down at the diminutive lady before him, Spitini was momentarily at a loss for words before replying, "Buon giorno, signora." Then, continuing in Italian, "Excuse me, but my Farsi is very poor despite numerous years in the Middle East."

Reaching her hand out, TJ quickly grabbed Monsignor Spitini's right hand in a handshake before he could retract it. Speaking in English now, for TJ hardly knew much more Italian than 'hello,' she replied, "Please, excuse me. My Italian is very limited. Do you speak English?"

"Yes, of course. I said that I did not understand you. Were you speaking another language?"

"Oh, yes. Yes, I guess I was." Then in a small lie, TJ continued, "You surprised me and I guess I broke out in Farsi, one of my native languages. I tend to do that. It's a reflex reaction, I suppose. So sorry." She studied him closely, but if he had something to hide, Spitini did it very well. He was a cool customer, but she noticed that Spitini did not much like her continued handshake. He looked down at their handshake, up at her, then back down at the handshake, and finally withdrew his right hand.

TJ tried the direct approach next. "Monsignor Spitini, I don't mean to be rude, but what is your heritage? I, myself, am originally from Iraq and, again, I hope I don't offend you, but you strike me as having Middle Eastern roots, too."

Monsignor Spitini chuckled and looked at a couple of Catholic clerics walking around them. Waiting for them to pass beyond earshot, the Monsignor continued, "I get that from time to time. Actually, my father left the Middle East as a young man and married an Italian bride. He did not like to speak about his origins and rarely told me much about his past. Only once did I hear him speak his native tongue, before he passed away. Except for his blood, I am about as Italian as it gets. By the way, I noticed you about a week ago in Cardinal Biaggio's office, but we were not formally introduced. Without offending you, may I inquire who you are?"

Well, he certainly is a cool customer, TJ marveled to herself. Spitini was a little stiff in his body language and the chuckle wasn't natural. He spoke in a measured tone and clearly did not relish human contact. His English was impeccable. She thought it interesting that the Monsignor appeared uncomfortable speaking until the two priests had passed by them. She made a mental note to ask Colonel Weissberg for information on Monsignor Spitini.

TJ introduced herself, saying: "I am Tara Johnson, a detective on special assignment from Scotland Yard to assist the Vatican's Swiss Guards with the security arrangements for the burial mass, conclave, and investiture of the new pontiff. I'm just another one of many, many law enforcement specialists making do in Rome for awhile."

Their remaining conversation was short lived. After trading a few trivial comments about the extreme August heat and the shock of finding John Paul dead, they parted.

TJ continued on to the Sistine Chapel where she found a couple of men in blue coveralls moving chairs for the upcoming conclave. Up above, on a tall ladder, a maintenance worker was rummaging through a leather toolkit, no doubt preparing to make repairs. Satisfied with a short visit, she left for the crypt under St. Peter's Basilica where John Paul III would be buried the next day.

Spitini was upset with himself. He gave himself a mediocre grade, at best, for maintaining a calm and natural demeanor during his chance encounter with TJ. He wasn't prepared to meet her and he noted that he had to work at improving his impromptu acting.

Arriving at his office in the Vatican Palace ten minutes later, Spitini set about making phone calls to trusted members of the Curia. Within an hour, Spitini had confirmed that TJ was, in actual fact, a Scotland Yard detective on a special assignment. Not much was known about her, but he was able to ascertain that she had requested many Vatican records on Near- and Far-Eastern dioceses as well as reports on the Pope's visit to the Middle East two years earlier. More importantly, the last monsignor with whom Spitini spoke had expressed surprise that Marco did not know about her. After all, John Paul III had requested TJ.

Why would the pontiff keep this from him? How could he have missed John Paul's request? Slightly unnerved, Spitini paced in his office contemplating how to solve the mystery surrounding TJ.

She was clearly up to something. Why would she test him by speaking Farsi? He had almost replied in Farsi before catching himself and swallowing his words. Was it truly a chance encounter? What if she was on to him? What if ... and here his heart almost stopped ... what if she knew about the eavesdropping operation? Was she not on her way to the Sistine Chapel? What if she had happened upon him in the Sistine Chapel when he was confirming that his compatriot had the listening device? Spitini was furious. He felt a sudden urge to return to the Chapel to ensure that the installation of the device was completed successfully.

He restrained his emotional impulses and continued to pace. How should he proceed? Something had to be done. He needed more information. Stopping in the middle of his office, Marco Spitini prayed to Allah for guidance. Again, the prayer calmed him and permitted him to clarify his thoughts. "All praise be to Allah!" Spitini whispered after fifteen minutes. With that he set out for the Swiss Guards.

Under the pretense of verifying security details for the following day's burial mass, Monsignor Spitini scanned the office area of the Swiss Guards looking for clues about Tara Johnson. Spotting none and not catching a glimpse of her, Spitini left, but opted to head for an exit that took him by Colonel Weissberg's office. He later thanked Allah for guiding him.

After passing the Colonel's closed door, a young Swiss Guard officer hurriedly leaving the adjoining office collided with Spitini in the hall. Caught by surprise, the officer dropped his folder onto Spitini's feet.

"Oh, scusi! Please, forgive me Monsignor! I am foolish to rush out of the office. I hope I didn't injure you!"

"No, I am fine. No need to apologize. Here, let me help you pick up your papers." Monsignor Spitini bent over along with the officer who was still apologizing to find an Arabic text with an English translation of a recent speech by the Iranian President and a United Kingdom threat assessment of Iran.

Standing up, Monsignor Spitini was even more surprised to find that the name on the door was Tara Johnson. An office immediately next to the Commander of the Swiss Guards? Her name on a fixed brass plate? A young officer of the Swiss Guards as an assistant? He was truly astounded! Tara Johnson was obviously not the run of the mill detective. Nor was she there purely on a short-term assignment to assist with August's routine security preparations. Clearly, she was playing games with him earlier in their hallway encounter. No, Spitini had to admit with a cold sweat breaking out, this lady was a threat.

Handing the papers to the young officer, Monsignor Spitini hastily left and returned to his office. He now knew what he must do. After making sure that he had no important eMails nor phone messages, Spitini left his office, exited the Vatican Palace, crossed St. Peter's Square, and headed for a nearby café.

It wasn't coffee that Spitini was after. The café was one of the hundreds of internet cafés liberally sprinkled around Rome. Exceptionally popular with the younger set and with tourists, the internet cafés offered cheap computer access to patrons. He ordered a cappuccino and promptly sat down at a terminal in the back of the café.

A bit unnerved by the afternoon's developments, Spitini looked around to ensure that no one had followed him and that no one else could see his screen. He then logged onto a Yahoo eMail account.

The email account was free and provided complete anonymity. As long as he used the account outside of his office without being observed, no one could trace the account back to him. It was a modern solution for secretly communicating with other spies.

In this case, he needed to contact his handler in order to alert him to the strong possibility that Tara Johnson was a threat to be reckoned with. Typing quickly in Italian, Spitini wrote a short note that to all appearances was a note to his father asking for help in paying the rent to his landlord. In reality, the note was asking his handler for a meeting.

Satisfied that the note was correct, Spitini sent it. Within two minutes, he received confirmation of its receipt and instructions for a rendezvous that evening. Thereupon Spitini surfed the internet for another ten minutes while sipping his cappuccino.

CHAPTER FOURTEEN

Ernie awoke with a start. "Gabriel! No! Leave me alone!" Wiping his wet face, Ernie hastily sat up in confusion not knowing if he was still dreaming or awake. Rubbing his eyes, he could make out the wall clock opposite the foot of his bed in the dim morning light filtering through a window. Ernie was unhappy to discover that he still had twenty minutes before his alarm was to ring at the usual time of 6:30 AM.

Gabriel nudged him on the right thigh and looked at him as if pleading for Ernie to get out of bed. Ernie scowled at Gabriel. "Okay, okay. You win. Go to the door and I'll be right there." Satisfied that he need not lick Ernie's face once more, Gabriel trotted out of the bedroom and down the stairway where Ernie would find Gabriel sitting by the front door waiting for his morning walk.

"Oh, Rose, how I wish you were here!" Ernie said to himself with a chortle. As a puppy, Gabriel would invariably awaken Ernie's wife each morning much to her dissatisfaction and a wet hand where Gabriel had nudged her with his wet nose. This gave Ernie an extra minute of sleep before Rose awakened him with "Ernie, YOUR dog wants to go out!" Ernie gladly obliged her, but, he had to laughingly tease Rose that Gabriel's decision to awaken her each morning indisputably proved that dogs are, indeed, a man's best friend.

Rose had wanted Ernie to find a small, cuddly dog that she could easily care for when Ernie traveled; but, if Ernie wanted a small, huggable animal running around the house he would have adopted a cat. No. Real men had real dogs that barked instead of yelping, that could sprint instead of scurrying on stubby legs, and that conducted themselves with self-assured dignity and discipline instead of jumping up on people's shins in hopes of looking cute perched atop a lap.

German shepherds were incredible dogs even if their bladders sometimes got the better of them. "Oh, well. Even humans are, at times, ruled by the most elementary bodily functions," Ernie thought to himself. Gabriel, like most pure-bred shepherds, was a highly intelligent animal with an impressive comprehension for a large vocabulary. The dog, now about nine years old, understood basic commands in English and Italian – if speaking both languages was good enough for Ernie it was good enough for his dog – as well as recognizing separate names for each of its twenty or so toys. For good measure and out of a sense of humor that only an ordained minister could have, Ernie had also instructed Gabriel in reacting to Greek and Latin commands.

Putting his feet on the floor, he stretched them and, grimacing, stood up. Hobbling to the bathroom was painful, but the morning walk with Gabriel would alleviate the discomfort from his stiff ankles. Man, he hated growing old! But, he wasn't about to quit playing pick-up basketball at lunchtime once or twice each week with his grad students and younger professors.

Within seven minutes, Ernie, attired in faded blue jeans, a dark blue NYPD t-shirt, and a blue baseball cap declaring "Life is Good!," opened the front door much to Gabriel's relief. The two of them made their morning rounds of the Nyack neighborhood on a glorious morning with the Hudson River bathed in bright morning sunlight. The pair hurried downhill with Ernie carrying the obligatory plastic bags destined for the trash barrel outside the local coffee shop where he would buy a cup of coffee for the walk home.

Seeing a picture of his buddy, Sean Cardinal Murphy, on the upper fold of the front page Ernie picked up a copy the morning's New York Times. "You feeling okay, professor?" Ron, the shopkeeper quipped knowing that Ernie rarely bought the Times.

"Well, somebody has to help keep their circulation numbers up!" Ernie shot back with a smile. "If it wasn't for the Cardinal's photo and story I wouldn't be buying it." Then with a wink, Ernie added, "Besides, the Times doesn't have a comics section. Just how can a newspaper without humor be taken seriously?"

Ernie rolled up the newspaper, waved goodbye with it and stuck it under his arm before picking up his coffee cup and walking outside to retrieve Gabriel, regally sitting outside on the sidewalk. "Come on, Gabriel! Let's go home."

Ernie was more eager than usual to return home in order to catch the pope's burial mass on television. The ritual had already concluded at the Vatican with the Times picking up a photo of his friend, Sean, kneeling in prayer alongside a long row of Cardinals clad in black cassocks. But, a Catholic cable channel was running the mass for its stateside viewers.

Reaching his house after a brisk walk uphill fueled by the rapid infusion of caffeine, Ernie let Gabriel off of the leash and headed for the kitchen to make his breakfast while watching the television broadcast. As he entered the kitchen, Ernie jumped in surprise when his phone began ringing on his belt. Looking to see who was crazy enough to be calling at that early hour, he was astonished to see that it was Sean the Cardinal himself!

"Well, good morning! Oops! I guess that's good afternoon, Sean! This is a welcome surprise. I was just thinking of you and, believe it or not, I actually bought the New York Times this morning just because it's carrying a wonderful mug shot of you on the front page!"

Hearing laughter on the other end of the line, Ernie asked, "So, my friend, how are you holding up over there? Have you wilted in the heat?" Now it was Ernie's turn to laugh.

"Naw, it's pretty nice here. Sunny and cool this morning. Might hit 80 later. So, to what pleasure do I owe this call, your Eminence?" Ernie teased his friend.

Listening to Sean Murphy, Ernie began to look puzzled. He sat down on a stool and replied, "Well, that is really weird, my friend. Frankly, I would rather have a pretty young lady dreaming about me." After Sean Murphy stopped laughing, Ernie added, "Actually, I dreamt of you, too, and we were both at the Vatican, too. How do ya' like that? Strange or what?"

CHAPTER FIFTEEN

With the burial mass completed and the pontiff sealed in his sarcophagus, life in Rome settled down considerably the following day. More shops and restaurants closed for the remainder of August after the mourners and the VIPs and their entourages departed. Even the most curious visitors were persuaded to leave by the blistering heat. The remaining journalists and tourists bravely endured the temperatures camped out in the open air at restaurants under broad white umbrellas with cold drinks or sitting by one of the myriad of splendid fountains to enjoy the refreshing coolness of the water spray.

With their preparations to eavesdrop on the conclave completed, Harold was content to give Cybil a few days off. Making the most of it, Cybil and Giulio enjoyed the respite together. Sleeping in late each morning, they would awaken and shower together. Much to Cybil's pleasure, Giulio proved particularly adept at handling a loofah sponge. That was followed by breakfast at a sleepy café with a bit of shopping and sightseeing thereafter. More sex and a nap were next with dinner preceding a night of dancing and drinking at the clubs. Then it was back to bed and, eventually, sleep.

Relieved that John Paul's body, now safely buried, was out of the coroner's reach, Monsignor Marco Spitini continued his information collection and analysis of the votes for the coming conclave, now five days away. He had very few official duties and was merely waiting to be reassigned after the investiture of the new pontiff. Among the Curial staff, Cardinals Maltempo, Fassino, and Moratinos were still rated the ones to watch. Every one secretly acknowledged that through his close associates, Maltempo was actively positioning himself for the papacy despite the official prohibition against campaigning. Fassino had placed a distant fifth to John Paul III three years earlier and was, therefore, a frontrunner. Moratinos just happened to be the non-Italian bloc's favorite. A number of other Cardinals were mentioned from time to time, but considered long shots. But, who knew for sure? After all, Karol Wojtyla of Poland was a complete surprise when elected to the papacy as John Paul II in 1978. Much to everyone's astonishment, internet gambling sites and Las Vegas were accepting bets, too; however, none of the three Cardinals favored by insiders was in the top ten odds-on favorites to win. Cardinal Biaggio led the field with 10:1 odds, but, then, the uneducated mass of bettors would be drawn to voting for the Cardinal Camerlengo who, over the past week, was the most notable of Cardinals in the press. Coming in second was Cardinal Hendrickson of Chicago who was largely supported by gamblers, many of them American, betting that the Catholic Church would finally come to its senses and yield to liberalizing reform.

On a more immediate note, Spitini was gratified to know that Tara Johnson would soon cease to be a problem. His meeting with his handler had gone well without any undue fear of detection. Spitini had succinctly shared his newfound knowledge and apprehensions over the Scotland Yard detective's activities with promises given in return that it would be taken care of. It was out of his hands.

Although too busy to explore Rome as a tourist, Cardinal Murphy attended daily mass at a different Catholic church each day beyond the confines of the Vatican. His reduced workload permitted him to spend more attention on matters back in New York and to, thankfully, rest. Preparations for the conclave to elect the new pope were largely up to Cardinal Biaggio and the Curia.

He was sleeping better, but the summer heat and sleeping in an unfamiliar bed proved discomforting. Cardinal Murphy was delighted to surprise Ernie after concluding the burial mass. Ernie's good sense of humor and joy of life boosted his spirits just when he needed it most.

It certainly was an odd coincidence, or was it a miracle, that both of them had dreamt about visiting the Vatican together. Amazingly, their dreams were very similar. In his, the Cardinal remembered welcoming Ernie to the Vatican while standing in the Sistine Chapel. It was rather remarkable because they were surrounded by a multitude of Swiss Guards in their splendid multi-colored uniforms along with brightly polished helmets and wooden pikes. He recollected wanting to leave for dinner at a restaurant, but his attempts to find a way through the crowd of guards was continually thwarted. It was a maddening, circular dream. Eventually, they ended up under an arch in the Chapel with writing over it, but he was unable to make out the letters and words. Again, his dream proved terribly frustrating as he felt the guards closing in on them while trying to read the inscription over their heads.

Later that day, after speaking with Ernie, Cardinal Murphy decided to take a look at the Sistine Chapel – partly out of curiosity over the conclave preparations and partly out of his admiration for the exquisite frescoes. Under the watchful eyes of a couple of Swiss Guards, he entered the Chapel and was immediately drawn to a series of three frescoes illustrating the Jews' rebellion against Moses in the Sinai desert after leaving Egypt. Angered and discouraged by the hardships of traveling in the wilderness, the Jews sought a new leader to replace Moses. In the end, God punishes the leaders of the revolt. They fall before Aaron, the brother of Moses, and are crushed by the enveloping earth.

The artwork simply overwhelmed Cardinal Murphy. What beautiful artistry. Only through God's inspiration could mortal hands have produced those brushstrokes. Examining the details of those three frescoes was a joy, but then his breathing suddenly stopped as his eyes darted to an inscription in the arch of the middle fresco. There was the arch in his dreams! He could hardly believe it. Only this time he could make out the letters. It read: "Let no man take the honor to himself except he that is called by God, as Aaron was."

TJ was incredibly busy. Frenetic was more like it. The twelve to fourteen hours flew by each day and she couldn't wait to get back to her office each morning in order to continue her analysis. There was simply too much information to sift through and training the young officer was taxing. Nevertheless, TJ had a hunch that John Paul III had been onto something in his apprehension over the fundamentalist Islamic terror threat to the Vatican. She couldn't quite put her finger on it, but she was confident that her sleuthing would yield fruit. In time, something would offer up an important clue.

Anxiety over security for the burial of John Paul III and the ensuing conclave had proven to be an advantage for her. Lacking much needed staff assistance, she had quietly persuaded Italian and French intelligence agencies to conduct some threat analysis of Islamic terror organizations under the guise of requiring it for immediate Vatican security estimates. She had to keep the true nature of her requests hidden from them, but her understanding of bureaucracies enabled her to creatively circumvent red tape.

The burial mass yesterday had been a success. Colonel Weissberg and his Swiss Guards, along with the Italian police, were relieved. Life looked a lot better now after concluding the rites without incidents. In fact, this was the first night in over a week that she and Colonel Weissberg did not leave their offices together. He had actually left at six o'clock for an early dinner with his wife and a full night of sleep.

The Swiss Guards office was very quiet as she headed for her apartment. Stepping outside, the August heat hit her like a blast furnace. Although born and raised in Iraq, she had grown accustomed to the weather in England so it was no surprise to feel the sweat rolling down her temples. Her pace slowed to adjust to the late night heat and to the realization that she was profoundly tired. Her neck muscles were sore from hunching over her desk all day and her right wrist was showing signs of carpal tunnel syndrome from gripping her pen too tightly.

Fortunately, it was a beautiful night with many tourists strolling across St. Peter's Square. Looking up to spot the moon and stars, she saw the stone figures atop the rounded colonnades encircling the cobble-stoned Square. They reminded TJ of guardian angels seemingly watching over the human drama below.

Her mind began to wander as she walked along the wide Via de Conciliazione stretching eastwards from the Vatican towards the Tiber River. TJ began thinking of her mother and brothers. What would they think of this crazy assignment? How long would she be in Rome before finding some time to visit them in London? Was her youngest brother, an officer in the Royal Marines, safe patrolling Iraq as a member of the peacekeeping force? Would her work make the world a safer place for him and her family?

TJ hailed a cab and gave the driver her street address. Collapsing into the back seat, TJ stared out of the window in a tired trance. She was even too tired to notice the motorcycle with its two young riders trailing the cab.

TJ was glad to see her small street. She was almost home. The taxi pulled up to the curb and TJ paid and got out. With her key in hand, TJ started to walk the thirty feet to her apartment building. Hearing the sudden roar of a motorcycle engine, TJ turned swiftly around. Her quick reflex may have saved her life. That and the unexpected pothole that jarred the shooter's arm as he squeezed the trigger.

The bullet hit her in her left thigh. Throwing herself to the ground, TJ rolled towards a parked car for cover, reached inside her light linen jacket for her Beretta pistol, and prepared to face her attackers. But, they never materialized. The motorcycle kept going and did not return.

CHAPTER SIXTEEN

"TJ! TJ! Can you hear me?"

"Ugh. Ummm … yeah." TJ groaned, licked her lips, slowly opened her eyes halfway, and began to stretch before recoiling from the pain and stiffness in her left thigh.

TJ closed her eyes and squeezed her lips together in a tight grimace, waiting for the pain to subside. She felt someone take hold of her left hand.

"You're a tough cookie. Nothing like getting shot to get you to slow down." Colonel Weissberg tried lighthearted humor to cheer her up. "Well, you're going to be just fine, but you'll probably have to keep wearing skirts with low hems to hide your new scar."

"Oh, haha. That could only be Wilhelm." Opening her eyes, again, TJ peered out at Wilhelm Weissberg and attempted a smile. "Yup, just like I thought. Nobody else is as good a smartass as you."

"Well, you know what they say. It takes one to know one."

"Yeah, oh well. However, it sure is good to see you. Sorry to ruin your first early night at home."

"No problem. By now, my wife is accustomed to calls in the middle of the night. Too bad criminals don't sleep."

"So, what did the doctor do to me? And when can I get out of here?" TJ asked. Shortly after arriving at the hospital, she had passed out from blood loss. Up until then, while lying on the sidewalk, she was able to punch the speed dial button on her cell phone for the Swiss Guards' main line. Her conversation was punctuated by short breaths and groans from the pain, but the young man on the other end of the line got the message. A small group of young Italians returning from a night out on the town had then happened upon her. Fortunately, one of them was an emergency medical technician who set about wrapping his shirt around her thigh and elevating her feet to stem the blood flow while his girlfriend sat with TJ's head nestled in her lap. The Swiss Guards, in the meantime, had called for an ambulance which arrived ten minutes later with TJ's head beginning to swim.

She maintained consciousness for the entire trip to the hospital, all the while cursing under her breath about letting her guard down. The late hours and summer heat had taken their toll on her alertness during the cab ride, but all of her instincts and quick reflexes kicked back in as she reacted to the loud motorcycle and striking bullet. Nevertheless, relieved to see the hospital's emergency room doors swing open for her, TJ capitulated to her blood loss.

"The doctor says you'll be fine. Thankfully, the bullet passed cleanly through your leg without striking the bone or any major nerves. You were in surgery for less than an hour and you've been sleeping here for about three hours. The doctor patched you up and pumped some blood back into you. They want to keep you for a couple of days, but you'll probably be up and walking by this afternoon." Wilhelm squeezed her hand and offered her a cup of water.

TJ reached for the straw in the cup and gingerly drank. "Thanks. I don't like hospitals. Can you get me out of here today?"

Weissberg chuckled while putting the cup back on the nightstand. "As a matter of fact, I had a feeling you'd say that. I've already made arrangements to have you transferred this afternoon to our little infirmary at the Vatican. Doctor Terzini and the Sisters are looking forward to spoiling you."

TJ was surprised by this generosity. Not knowing what to say, she grinned and merely stammered, "Thanks!"

"In the meantime, an Italian policeman is on duty outside your door and Hans will be over to help you this afternoon. By the way, I'm assigning Hans full-time to assist you from here on out. Oh! I almost forgot! A good friend and colleague from the Italian police will be coming by the Vatican after you are settled to talk with you and to file your report." He studied her face and continued, "So, since you're awake, how about telling me what happened?"

"Glad to." TJ proceeded to recount the evening's trip home; but, she had very little that was useful for the police. Besides, TJ was embarrassed to admit that she had not noticed anything out of the ordinary from the moment she left her office to the time she stepped out of her taxi.

Colonel Weissberg listened intently to TJ and, occasionally, interrupted with a question for clarification. After she wrapped up her narrative, he sat looking at TJ while rubbing his chin, deep in thought. "Well, my dear, this does not smell like a typical mugging by Italian thugs. I think that this was a hit. Either your enemies have followed you to Rome or you've stirred up a hornet's nest by digging into the Pope's files. Either way, you need to lay low. You were very lucky tonight."

TJ nodded in agreement, but then added, "Wilhelm, luck had nothing to do with it. I can't help but feel that fate brought me to the Vatican. As I was walking through St. Peter's Square, the carved saints looking down from the top of the colonnade reminded me of guardian angels. Did you know that we Muslims believe in angels, too? Then, after I called your office to report that I had been hit I found a silver crucifix under my left leg when I inspected the wound. Check my jacket pocket over there. It should be in there."

Colonel Weissberg reached for her light linen jacket by the nightstand and readily found the crucifix in its pocket.

"Wilhelm, God was looking after me. These were professionals taking aim at me. It was simply nothing short of a miracle that I'm here talking to you right now. Besides, there is now no doubt in my mind that I'm getting too close to the truth at the Vatican. John Paul was, indeed, onto something."

CHAPTER SEVENTEEN

Marco Spitini was seething. "What complete idiots! I've pulled off the assassination of the century and the so-called professionals can't silence a woman by plugging her with a couple of bullets! I am risking my neck here, at the Vatican and they back me up with rookies! Dim-wits! Assholes!"

News of the botched attempt on TJ's life had quickly spread through the Vatican. Although Spitini knew that his team had tried to whack her, everyone else, now over a day later, believed that it was a mugging gone bad. Priests and nuns were shocked at the rare violence. Typically, youngsters on vespa mopeds would drive up behind unsuspecting tourists to snatch purses and cameras right off of the tourists' arms before dashing off. Many a tourist's shoulder was dislocated, but they were never shot. What was happening to Rome? Soon, it would be dangerous like New York City! Mama Mia!

Spitini looked up from his computer monitor at the internet café. He had just sent an email updating his handler on TJ's health. Marco would rather have reached his hands through the wires to wring some necks. "What idiots!" Marco exclaimed silently to himself. To ascertain Tara's true condition, he had taken some risks. Risks that he would rather not have had to endure. For instance, knowing that Doctor Terzini promptly returned to the clinic at 1:30 after lunch each afternoon, he had planted himself outside the Vatican Palace to seemingly bump into the doctor by accident. Spitini was not at all pleased to be reacting to unwelcome events. The plan was falling apart!

Within a few minutes, the reply message appeared in his in-box. Clicking it open, Spitini read that he should be very circumspect and patient in order to avoid drawing attention to himself. Under no circumstances was he to come anywhere close to Tara Johnson. The author, also, directed Spitini to refrain from contacting the team until the conclave opened. If Spitini was discovered, the entire operation would be in jeopardy. Let everyone think it was just an attempted burglary gone ugly. Lastly, another hit on TJ was impossible in the near future, but, perhaps, later. Especially if she traveled to the Middle East anytime soon.

No apology! No mention of thanks or regard for his personal safety! The nerve! Spitini continued to fume. Did they think he had spent the better part of his life in the Catholic Church for the sake of Islam to be surrounded by a bunch of buffoons! Did they not know how much he had sacrificed for their cause?

It took immense self-control not to throw his coffee cup across the room and to begin smashing keyboards. Hitting the delete key with great force, Marco killed the message and then logged off before heading for the exit and his office.

Marco was so very angry that, as he left, he had not noticed a young Persian man at the coffee bar among the tourists and Italians. This fellow waited for five additional minutes and then walked out of the café to his motorcycle. Yousef Sami didn't like what he saw in Spitini's frowning face and gruff behavior. It was very unlike Spitini, the cold, aloof master of self control. He would be reporting back to Spitini's handler within the hour that he feared Spitini might be unraveling. One more problem to add to the list.

"Well, are you comfortable?" Colonel Weissberg inquired.

Looking up at her unexpected visitor, TJ smiled and replied, "You didn't tell me that this was a five-star hotel!"

"This is one of our best kept secrets!" Then, looking at Doctor Terzini, Weissberg added, "If the good doctor gets fresh with you, just let Hans know!" Weissberg and Terzini both laughed and shook hands.

Pulling up a chair by TJ's bed, Colonel Weissberg spent the next half hour talking with TJ about her investigation.

"I'm sorry to have to run, but I have an appointment with the Cardinal Camerlengo to review the security measures for the conclave. He also wants to know more about your condition and your work here," the Colonel declared as their deliberations wound down.

Seeing him standing up to leave, TJ quickly said, "Wilhelm, I need a favor. Can you give me one more minute?"

"Of course. But just one minute. The Cardinal does not like to be kept waiting."

"Sure. Sure. Actually it's something for you to bring up with Cardinal Biaggio, but it is very sensitive. Look, I've been thinking very hard about this. I'm operating on a hunch, but it's very important to my investigation." Pausing for Colonel Weissberg's reaction, TJ concluded it was safe to continue. "I respectfully request that you find everything you can on someone of interest. That includes having the police secretly check into his background – family history, education, friends, spending habits, recent travels, and so forth. I would also, very much, like you put this person under observation."

Colonel Weissberg looked a little surprised, but he was still listening. "Okay, I give up. Who are you talking about?" he asked.

TJ looked Weissberg straight in the eyes and whispered, "Monsignor Marco Spitini." This time she got a reaction out of Wilhelm.

CHAPTER EIGHTEEN

Amazingly, the following three days were uneventful. Preparations for the conclave went ahead without any problems, but as the seminal event neared, the Vatican, once again, was a busy spectacle. The legions of reporters, photographers, and tourists descended upon the Vatican where the entire leadership of the Holy Roman Catholic Church had now assembled to elevate one of their own to the papacy.

True, not every pope in the Church's long history had come from the ranks of the Cardinals. Certainly, the very first bishop of Rome, St. Peter, was nothing more than a plain fisherman before Jesus, chose him as an apostle and as the rock upon which to build the Church.

Thereafter, bishops of Rome had included a number of surprises. History records that a presbyter named Fabian was elected Pope by a miraculous event during his visit to Rome in the year 236. His visit coincided with the papal election and it so happened that a dove settled upon Fabian's head at a propitious moment. Seeing a parallel with the descent of the Holy Spirit, the surrounding clerics unanimously placed Fabian on the papal throne.

In 903, feuding priests and monarchs compromised by selecting a parish priest. Gregory VII, universally regarded as one of the Church's greatest popes despite being regarded as a plain and humble man, was picked from the ranks as a mere subdeacon in 1073. In several instances, European monarchs pressured the Roman clerics to elect their favorites, whether cardinals, bishops, or not. One dictator of Rome, on his deathbed, even obtained the election of his son as pope. Not surprisingly, bribes, electioneering, and threats were not unheard of throughout the Church's history in electing pontiffs.

In more recent times, however, rules and procedures enforced by Papal edicts have secured a more orderly transition. Electing popes from among the Cardinals, although not the express rule, has certainly been the norm. It is also a practice that endears itself to the many cardinals of the Curia in Rome who desire a pontiff familiar with the Curial practices. No need to upset the proverbial apple cart, after all.

Although membership in the College of Cardinals is not a requirement for election as pope, only Cardinals have the right to vote. The only requirement is for the pontiff-elect to be a baptized male Catholic Christian. If the elected person is not a bishop, he must first be ordained as a Roman Catholic Bishop by the Dean of the College of Cardinals. If not a priest, he must first be ordained as a priest, then as a bishop. Only then may a person be invested as the Supreme Pontiff of the Holy Roman Catholic Church, the Patriarch of the West, the Bishop of Rome, Vicar of Jesus Christ, and the Sovereign of the Vatican.

The explicit rules promulgated by the Popes had to be followed with strict obedience. And so, on the eve of the conclave, every Cardinal had gathered in St. Martha' Residence adjacent to St. Peter's Basilica. St. Martha's now resembled a fully-booked hotel with over a hundred Cardinals ensconced in its guest suites and single rooms.

The Cardinals were busy late in the evening of August 12 preparing for the opening rites of the conclave the next day. Some were congregating in the dining hall discussing various Church matters. Others were laying out their scarlet choir dress, a cardinal's most lavish and ornamental attire, in preparation for the coming day's formal events. Still others were reading the Bible or praying. One or two had even managed to fall asleep.

Cardinal Murphy was visiting Cardinal Aakar Kodavas of Mumbai, India, in the Indian's suite. They had hit it off right away for both men found that they enjoyed a good story ending in a laugh, a precious commodity with serious matters at hand. Furthermore, Cardinal Kodavas, at age seventy-five, had already participated in two conclaves so he gladly imparted his experiences to Cardinal Murphy.

"..., well, my dear friend, I pray that the next pope lives a long, happy life so that this conclave is my last. It would be good for the Church and it would be good for me. I'm not getting any younger and these sojourns to Rome wear me out," Kodavas said. He paused while looking at his watch. "In that case, this might be both your first and your last conclave, my friend."

Cardinal Murphy nodded and asked, "Do you mind if I play the role of a party pooper and call it a night?"

Kodavas sighed. "Pray for guidance, my friend. We must seek God's will in our vote tomorrow. That, above all else, is the secret to surviving the pressure of the conclave."

Eyeing Murphy, Kodavas followed this with, "Do you know that I have a guardian angel who appears to me in my dreams from time to time? Do angels visit you, too?"

Startled by this question, Murphy stopped reaching for his Bible on the coffee table and looked over at Kodavas.

Kodavas didn't wait for an answer. "I have always been fascinated with the stories in our Holy Bible where angels visit mankind. Add to that the tales of visions and dreams. They are all splendid stories. God surely has a sense of drama. I am most fascinated by it all."

Kodavas' voice trailed off and he looked wistfully skyward. Then, snapping out of it, he refocused on Murphy. "In the Book of Numbers, you'll recall that the Holy Bible records God's words to Aaron and Miriam: 'When there are prophets among you, I the Lord make myself known to them in visions; I speak to them in dreams.' Well, I don't count myself as a prophet, but I have learned to listen to my dreams and you should, too."

Murphy looked at him quizzically, but, again, he did not get a word in before Kodavas continued.

"I understand from Cardinal Pelliterri that God has been speaking to you in your dreams, Sean. You must pray for God's guidance so that you can correctly interpret them. Don't forget that you are not alone among the Cardinals in being visited by remarkable dreams. I daresay that dreams have come upon many of us in both of my past conclaves. But, I feel different this time. The dreams are far more vivid and I am having greater difficulty making sense of them. Some think it is the discomfort of the unbearable heat here in Rome, but, I am well accustomed to the heat at home in India. No, there is great unease among many of us who are veterans of the conclave. We must pay heed, my friend."

Kodavas paused to look at his fellow Cardinal. Murphy took the opportunity. "Why would I, a Roman Catholic Cardinal, dream of welcoming men and women of other faiths?"

Kodavas sat silent so Murphy continued. "It is only through Christ that we find God."

After a prolonged silence, Cardinal Kodavas replied. "Sean, we do not know when men and women come to know Christ. Must it be while on earth as humans? Furthermore, God will make the final determination. We are here to serve man and to guide them. We don't have the responsibility of deciding who enters heaven."

Murphy nodded. "Yes, yes. Who knows? Those who do not know Christ on earth may have another opportunity after leaving the world we know."

Two hours later with the clock approaching midnight, both men were in deep discussion comparing and evaluating their dreams. Finally, as the church bells tolled midnight, both men recognized that they had better go to bed. The next day would come upon them fast.

Returning to his suite and easily falling asleep quickly, Cardinal Murphy was frustrated by a circular, never-ending dream where he was urgently seeking his familiar inscribed arch in the Sistine Chapel during the conclave. After what seemed an interminable amount of time, he finally found it hidden behind a bank of tri-pod mounted news cameras recording the cardinals' votes. Shocked to find the conclave's secrecy violated, he spent the remainder of his dream unsuccessfully trying to oust the reporters and pulling the electrical cables from the cameras.

The next morning did, in fact, arrive too early. Cardinal Murphy was tired after his vexing dream in the Sistine Chapel, but the anticipation of his first conclave had a similar rousing effect on him as it does each year on young American children awakening on Christmas morning to attack their pile of presents under the Christmas tree.

After breakfast in the dining room of St. Martha's, Cardinal Murphy and his fellow peers walked to St. Peter's Basilica for the mid-morning *Pro Eligendo Papa* Mass which is translated as the 'mass for the electing of the Pope.' Rather than begin the conclave that morning, the Cardinals had, following the funeral, decided to begin the conclave that afternoon. So rather than proceeding to the Apostolic Palace, they retired to St. Martha's for lunch and a short rest period. It wasn't until two o'clock that the Cardinals headed for the Pauline Chapel inside the Apostolic Palace.

There, Cardinal Murphy felt like he was having an out-of-body experience for he had great difficulty believing that he was actually attending the opening formalities of a conclave. He found himself wishing to take photos, but that, along with any electronic recording, was strictly prohibited on the threat of excommunication, His pulse accelerated when, Austrian Cardinal Meissner, the Dean of the College of Cardinals, entered the Chapel to address the host of cardinals with a welcome and last-minute instructions. Concluding with a prayer, Cardinal Meissner, with the assistance of four priests, began to line up the cardinals for the procession into the Sistine Chapel. This was it! He could feel the hairs on the back of his neck bristling with excitement.

Satisfied that the cardinals were in the proper order, Meissner began singing. Invoking the Holy Spirit in a cherished tradition, the Cardinals all joined him in singing the Veni Creator Spiritus in Latin and solemnly walking in a distinguished procession into the Sistine Chapel. There, the Cardinals filed into the rows of chairs behind small desks, still singing. Behind them a number of junior clerical assistants, the secretary of the College of Cardinals, the Master of Papal Liturgical Celebrations with two masters of ceremonies, other Church officials, and two physicians filed in as well. When everyone was correctly positioned at his chair, the Dean of the College of Cardinals signaled the Cardinals to end the hymn.

More formalities remained. Looking approvingly at his peers by the altar atop the raised platform under the eastern wall of the Sistine Chapel, Cardinal Meissner began reading an oath of secrecy: "We, the Cardinal electors … promise, pledge, and swear that whichever of us by divine disposition is elected Roman Pontiff will commit himself faithfully … we promise and swear to observe with the greatest fidelity and with all persons, clerical or lay, secrecy regarding everything that in any way relates to the election ... and never to lend support or favor to any interference, opposition, or any other form of intervention, whereby secular authorities of whatever order and degree or any group of people or individuals might wish to intervene in the election of the Roman Pontiff."

Cardinal Meissner then motioned with his hands for the cardinals to sit while simultaneously nodding at Cardinal Pellitteri, standing nearby in the first row along the north wall of the Sistine Chapel. Pellitteri turned and calmly walked up to Cardinal Meissner, placed his right hand on the Holy Bible which lay open at the Gospels, and spoke, "I Aldo Pellitteri, do so promise, pledge and swear. So help me God and these Holy Gospels which I touch with my hand."

Over roughly the next hour, each of the Cardinals stepped forward to personally recite the oath before their peers. At this point, Cardinal Murphy looked up with expectation at Goffredo Cammarata, the Master of Papal Liturgical Celebrations, who, upon taking a deep breath, vigorously declared, "Extra omnes!" The Latin words translate to 'Everyone out!' and with that, nearly everyone other than the cardinals, stood and walked out. The Swiss Guards standing watch outside the chapel's main entrance subsequently closed and locked the door.

With the church bells announcing four o'clock, Goffredo Cammarata began speaking. The assembled cardinals had selected him to give the *de eligendo pontifice* lecture in which he addressed the gravity of the decision facing the cardinals and a number of key challenges and opportunities for the cardinals to weigh in their decision making. A quarter of an hour later, Cammarata concluded and left.

Cardinal Meissner rose. "In keeping with the rules of the Universi Dominici Gregis, we will vote only once this afternoon. If we do not elect a pope, we will reconvene tomorrow morning. But, before we proceed, are there any remaining questions or doubts among you about this august body's task set before us by the almighty God?" Hearing none, he continued, "We will now draw the names of the three scrutineers, the three infirmarii, and the three revisers from among our peers in the College of Cardinals. May the Lord guide my hand and give strength to those so selected. Amen."

Cardinal Murphy recalled that the scrutineers are responsible for distributing, collecting and counting the paper ballots, the infirmarii are in charge of collecting the ballots from ill cardinals in the Vatican infirmary, and the three revisers are responsible for validating the election count. Looking around, he proudly observed his colleagues attentively following the extensive, formal procedures.

Hearing his name called out as one of the three infirmarii, Cardinal Murphy rose and joined his two compatriots at the dais. They included his earlier dinner partner, Cardinal Gauthier of Canada, and Cardinal Henderson of New Zealand. Once they were organized, the scrutineers began to distribute the rectangular paper ballots that were simply inscribed with the words, *"Eligo in summum pontificem."* This translates to 'I elect as supreme pontiff.' A blank space was provided for each cardinal to write a name. One of the scrutineers provided a single ballot to Cardinal Murphy for the infirmarii to take to the lone cardinal who was too ill to attend the functions in the Sistine Chapel. With each cardinal personally casting their ballots at the dais in the meantime, Cardinal Murphy and his two other designated infirmarii would cast their votes and that of the ill cardinal upon returning.

"My fellow cardinals, shall we proceed?" Murphy asked his two colleagues. Each nodded affirmatively. With Cardinal Murphy leading the way, the three infirmarii walked down the open middle of the Sistine Chapel, through the marble transenna dividing the chapel in two, and to the large door. Hearing

Cardinal Murphy's three knocks, the Swiss Guards opened the door and permitted the three cardinals to proceed.

The three cardinals walked slowly but purposefully towards the infirmarii. A monsignor and Swiss Guardsman, waiting outside for them, escorted the infirmarii. Not a word was spoken.

Doctor Terzini met them at the door upon arriving at the infirmary and led the party to a private room. Terzini advised them, "Cardinal Roger Francis Maria, the English Archbishop of Westminster, has been battling cancer for over a year. I have been treating him daily since his arrival a week ago, but he, unfortunately, is growing weaker each day. The funeral mass was very hard on him so I admitted him to the clinic for rest and round-the-clock medical care. I pray that he survives the conclave to welcome the new pope." Having proffered this information, Doctor Terzini opened the door and stood back while the three cardinals entered the room. He shut the door behind them.

"Cardinal Roger Maria, we have come to ask you to vote for the supreme pontiff of the Holy Roman Catholic Church," Cardinal Murphy formally announced as the three visitors approached the right side of the bed. Although he was reclining against some pillows which were propping him up in bed and his reading glasses rested on his nose, Cardinal Maria did not move. His eyes were closed. With a pang of anxiety, Cardinal Murphy moved closer and gently placed his right hand on Maria's left shoulder. There was no reaction. Looking up at his two colleagues, Cardinal Murphy saw that they, too, were perplexed and uneasy.

All of a sudden, Cardinal Maria grabbed Cardinal Murphy's right wrist in a tight grasp, sat straight up in his bed, opened his eyes, and stared directly into Murphy's eyes. Murphy winced in pain as he stepped back half a step in utter surprise. "Wha ....?" Murphy didn't get to finish his exclamation.

"You must be careful! God's hand is moving and we cannot stop it!" Shaking uncontrollably now, Cardinal Maria nearly shouted, "Do you understand? Do you?"

Cardinal Murphy tried to embrace Cardinal Maria to calm him, but the Englishman would have nothing of it. Pushing Murphy's head away with his left hand while still tightly gripping Murphy's wrist in his right hand, Maria loudly exclaimed, "Stop! Listen to me! Listen!" Then, in a hoarse whisper, "The angel of God appeared to me in a dream. He descended in a pillar of cloud and stood at the foot of my bed. When I asked him if he had come to take me to heaven, he told me that it was not, yet, my time to go. He, first, needed me to communicate a message to the College of Cardinals."

Cardinal Maria appeared to be fully awake. His eyes were now darting between Cardinal Murphy and the other two cardinals. He was clearly agitated, but his shaking stopped. Still holding on to the New Yorker, Maria, once again, whispered, "The angel said, 'Hear my words, Roger Francis Maria! Hear my words! God seeks another. The cardinals are to put down their pens and listen. It will be revealed to them. If they do not elect God's chosen pope, the plagues of Egypt will befall them one by one until they obey God's will.' The plagues of Egypt! I cannot vote. We cannot vote. Do you understand?"

Cardinal Maria stared at Murphy, then grimaced in pain, and collapsed. With Maria's grip now released, Murphy clutched Maria's shoulders and, over his left shoulder, shouted, "Doctor Terzini!"

CHAPTER NINETEEN

"I'm afraid that he may only have hours, perhaps days at best, ahead of him," Doctor Terzini somberly reported. "I don't know what came over him, but I've sedated him so that he will sleep through the night."

Terzini picked up the syringe and studied the electronic flat panel display on the wall above the bed that was monitoring Cardinal Maria's medical vital signs. "I'll have a Sister sit with him tonight. The best we can do is to keep the Cardinal comfortable in his last moments. In the morning, I will have a priest give him the last rites.

Turning around to look at the three infirmarii, the mournful physician added, "I am so sorry that you will not be collecting Cardinal Maria's vote. Please, convey this to Cardinal Meissner with my regards." Tossing the syringe into a medical waste container, Terzini opened the door and led the cardinals into the hallway.

"Thank you, Doctor Terzini," Cardinal Henderson said as he reached out and shook the doctor's hand. Cardinals Gauthier and Murphy echoed the thanks as they all shook hands with

Terzini and set out to return to the Sistine Chapel with the blank ballot.

Not wishing to break the secrecy of the conclave, all three remained silent alongside their two escorts, but upon hearing the door close behind them in the Sistine Chapel, the three halted to confer amongst themselves. The incident had rattled them. Not only were they grief-stricken over finding a fellow Cardinal near death, but his ominous warning struck a chilling chord in each of them.

Cardinal Murphy was the first to speak. "We're duty-bound to return the blank ballot and to provide Doctor Terzini's medical evaluation to Cardinal Meissner."

"Yes, but explaining Cardinal Maria's outburst will be more difficult. We do not know if he was hallucinating. He could have been under the influence of the drugs," Henderson pronounced with a shrug of his shoulders.

"He certainly did not behave rationally. In fact, he scared the living daylights out of me!" Cardinal Gauthier chimed in. "Would it be wise to inform the entire College of Maria's outburst?"

The three looked questioningly at each other. Murphy spoke first. "Let's let Cardinal Meissner decide. We should report the full account to him. Agreed?"

Gauthier and Henderson nodded in agreement and, flanking Murphy, followed him through the gate in the transenna, up the middle of the seats facing inwards under the watchful eyes of the sitting cardinals, and up to the Dean of the College of Cardinals standing on the raised platform.

"Welcome back, my fellow cardinals," Meissner declared. "Please, give the ballot to the scrutineers." He pointed to the long table to his right. "Then I need you to vote. Everyone else has cast their ballots."

"Cardinal Meissner, we need to confer with you, first," Cardinal Murphy quietly but firmly announced. "Unfortunately, we have distressing news to share with you. Cardinal Maria is not well and is unable to fulfill his obligation as a cardinal elector. There are, additionally, rather unusual circumstances that require your decision." Holding the ballot up for Meissner to see, Murphy proceeded to disclose the details of their visit to the infirmary.

Cardinal Meissner listened intently while striking a penitent pose of looking down at his clasped hands. When Cardinal Murphy concluded his account, the veteran Dean looked up at Gauthier and Henderson. "Do you have anything to add to the account? Is Cardinal Murphy accurate in all counts?"

"Yes. Completely!" Gauthier remarked with Henderson nodding in agreement and adding, "We are very troubled by Cardinal Maria's mental condition. It was truly bizarre."

"Yes, very odd. It is remarkable that all three of you are fluent in English and, so, fully competent to have understood Maria's quick outburst," Meissner replied thoughtfully. Looking out at the seated cardinals, Meissner added, "The cardinals are restless to conclude the vote. Let me propose that we proceed with your votes and with the tally as your new information has no impact on the vote at this point. If we return tomorrow morning, I will disclose the account of your visit to the infirmary. In the meantime, I plan to ask for prayers for Cardinal Maria after informing the College that Cardinal Maria is unconscious and near death and that, therefore, he is unable to cast his ballot."

Seeing no dissension among the three infirmarii, he motioned for them to turn in the ballot and began speaking to the assembled cardinals. "Fellow cardinals, I need to ask for you to pray for one of our brothers. God is calling Cardinal Maria. Our three infirmarii were delayed by a distressing downturn in Cardinal Maria's health that has left him heavily sedated and sleeping in Doctor Terzini's care. Clearly, Cardinal Maria is unable to vote. Again, I ask for your prayers."

The Sistine Chapel filled with the sound of chattering cardinals and creaking wooden chairs. Cardinal Meissner allowed this to continue for another ten minutes during which time Cardinals Murphy, Gauthier, and Henderson slid their ballots into the large chalice with each declaring, "I call as my witness Christ the Lord, who will be my judge, that my vote is given to the one before God I think should be elected."

Watching the infirmarii return to their seats, Meissner announced, "My fellow Cardinals! I must now ask for your silence so that we may count and validate the ballots." With that, a scrutineer picked up the chalice, shook it, opened it, and began to extract the ballots one by one. Only after confirming that the number of ballots matched the number of cardinal electors, did the three scrutineers record and announce the name on each ballot.

Next, the three revisers checked the ballots and the scrutineers' count. Finding everything correct, they handed the final tally to Cardinal Meissner.

"I have the final vote tally. 116 votes have been cast by 116 eligible cardinal electors. The following Cardinals received votes: Cardinal Moratinos, 32 votes. Cardinal Maltempo, 24 votes. Cardinal Biaggio, 17 votes. Cardinal Meyer, 16 votes. Cardinal Fassino, 16 votes. Cardinal Suarez, 6 votes. Cardinal Ahidju, 5 votes. Therefore, no cardinal received the required two thirds vote. We will re-convene tomorrow morning at eight o'clock."

As the cardinals rose to leave, black smoke from the Sistine Chapel signaled that the world would have to wait for its new pope.

CHAPTER TWENTY

"We've got it! It worked!"

"Did you hear that, Harold? No? We got the recording! Look, I've got to go. I'll call you once we've listened to it. Bye!" Cybil dashed over and hugged Giulio. "Play it! I want to hear it."

"Uno minuto, per favore. I have to decompress and decrypt the file." Despite having a scantily clad, sexy American woman hanging onto his shoulder, Giulio was completely focused on the computer screen. "There. Okay, here we go." Giulio busily manipulated the wireless mouse and within seconds, he and Cybil were listening to the Veni Creator Spiritus over the computer's speakers.

"Wow! The sound is much better than I had anticipated. Giulio, you are amazing!" Cybil gave Giulio a wet kiss on his cheek and plopped herself into a highback brown office chair next to him. "I don't think that the old geezers are going to break into Motown, but it's kinda' cute, isn't it? Singing in Latin probably reminds the boys about the good ol' days when they ruled the Roman Empire. Well, fellas, a lot has changed."

Cybil grabbed a notepad, took a sip of Giulio's coffee, and settled into her chair for a long night of work.

Back at the Vatican, the residents of St. Martha's were mostly asleep. Forbidden to communicate with the outside world, the cardinals had no access to television, radio, email, newspapers, magazines, and even the internet. They were alone with their Holy Bibles, fellow colleagues, thoughts, and God.

In room after room, many cardinals were busily dreaming. Some were reviewing the day's activities in their sleep. Others were dreaming of their homes, childhood memories, and worries. And some were being visited by angels in their dreams.

On the fourth floor, Cardinal Murphy's dream placed him on a dirt road walking in a procession with the College of Cardinals. As he rounded a bend in the road, a broad, green valley opened up below them. Looking ahead, Murphy could make out a large, wooden structure sitting in a meadow. He squinted, but could not make it.

As the cardinals marched, others joined them on the road. The first group to join them included Buddhist monks. Then, at an intersection, Greek Orthodox Christians filtered into their ranks. As the road dipped towards the structure, Tibetan monks rose from benches to join the procession. Numerous other religious groups kept joining the parade: Muslim clerics in turbans, Hindus, and a variety of protestant ministers. There was even an American medicine man in an elaborate feathered head-dress. Murphy marveled at the colorful assemblage of religious garb as the procession wound along the hillside.

Nearing the structure, Murphy could finally make it out. It was a giant wooden ark! At least a hundred yards long and four stories high, the ark was nestled among a grove of apple trees. A long gangway extended from an opening two stories high down to the meadow.

The head of the procession far ahead was now beginning to walk up into the ark. As the column entered the ark, the procession began to sing. He couldn't believe it, but everyone was singing the song from the old Coca-Cola television advertisement: "I'd like to teach the world to sing, to sing in perfect harmony ...." Murphy was expecting something more akin to the Veni Creator Spiritus, but, then, this tune was appropriate for this international, ecumenical procession. No one was turned away.

Cardinal Murphy finally reached the gangplank. Stepping onto it, he looked up at the opening. Had it not been for the long line marching up behind him, Murphy would have come to a complete halt. For there, under a Christian cross, stood John Paul III welcoming everyone, regardless of religious affiliation."

On the second floor of St. Martha's, Cardinal Maltempo fancied himself at the rudder on an ancient, wooden fishing boat on the Sea of Galilee. The sail was set and the crew of four men was looking ahead to the approaching shore. They had, apparently, been very successful that day as the boat was fully laden with fish.

One of the other crewmen turned around to Maltempo and pointed to the starboard side, directing Maltempo to bear more to the right. Narciso recognized the man as Moratinos. Looking around the boat with more attention, he recognized Biaggio leaning against the mast. However, the fourth was a stranger. Maltempo eyed him carefully, trying to comprehend why he was part of their distinguished crew. The man looked more like a fisherman than the others. Perhaps, he was the skipper?

The stranger was a sturdy man of medium height with a large chest, wide shoulders, and muscular arms. He had the dark hair of an Italian, but the lighter skin and blue eyes of a northern European. Maltempo guessed that the stranger was in his fifties or, perhaps, late forties. Giving up on trying to place the stranger, Maltempo was about to ask the fellow who he was when the crew suddenly sprang into action. They lowered the sail and put a couple of oars into the water.

With a mere hundred feet left to the shore, Maltempo spotted a lone man waiting for them. Instinctively, Maltempo realized that it was Jesus. He didn't know how and why he knew this, but he did. There stood Jesus in his beard, long hair, simple brown robe, and sandals with a walking stick in his right hand. Awestruck, even in his dream, Maltempo froze. He wanted to wave, to jump out of the boat and swim ashore, and to fall at Jesus' feet, but Narciso could not move. Seeing this, the other men began shouting at Maltempo to correct his steering.

"But, it's Jesus! Look, it is Jesus waiting on the shore for us!" Narciso shouted to the men. Regaining control of his muscles, Narciso now began to vigorously point to Jesus. At this, the men stopped rowing and stared in disbelief towards the nearing shore.

As all four men turned their attention shoreward, the boat began to run aground in the shallow water ten feet from Jesus. Narciso began scrambling out of the boat fully intending to wade up to Jesus. "Here am I, Jesus!" Narciso yelled excitedly.

But, he suddenly stopped at hearing Jesus shout back. "Narciso, stay with the boat. You are needed at the rudder while the men pull the boat ashore. This is not your time." Then pointing to the stranger, Jesus spoke, saying, "You! Follow me."

The stranger in the dream was astonished to hear Jesus calling him. Replying, he stammered, "Me? Are you really pointing at me? Surely, you wish one of these cardinals to follow you? I am just a plain fisherman." No one was more shocked than Narciso Maltempo to be told to stay with the boat. Indeed, all of the cardinals were stunned that Jesus did not call them.

Pointing, again, at the stranger, Jesus firmly declared, "No. The others will come ashore with the boat to feed my people with the fish. I need you to come with me."

"Me?" the stranger questioned, pointing at his chest.

"Yes, Ernesto, come ashore and walk with me."

CHAPTER TWENTY-ONE

The cardinals began boarding the buses at 7:30 the following morning for the short ride from St. Martha's residence to the Sistine Chapel. They could have easily walked the short distance, but the bus ride helped to maintain secrecy. This time, the cardinals filed directly into the Sistine Chapel without the previous day's opening ceremonies. Their oaths were still valid, but new scrutineers, infirmarii, and revisers would be selected for the day.

Once all cardinal electors were accounted for, Cardinal Meissner opened the conclave with a prayer that included Cardinal Maria, and administrative announcements. His last announcement concerned Cardinal Maria.

"My fellow brethren, Doctor Terzini informs me that Cardinal Maria had a peaceful night. He awoke briefly this morning and requested that the last rites be given to him. Monsignor Merino of the Curial staff was honored to serve the Cardinal in that capacity. Cardinal Maria expressed his thanks to all of us for our prayers, but, Cardinal Maria is heavily medicated and is sleeping again. He is, therefore, unable to vote and we do not expect to need the three infirmarii today. We should all continue to pray for God to lay his healing hands on Cardinal Maria to grant him peace and freedom from pain."

Meissner paused, cleared his throat, and uncomfortably tugged on his sleeves in weighing his next words. "I must also bring to your attention certain events that transpired yesterday during the infirmariis' visit to Cardinal Maria. Remember that Cardinal Maria is in very poor health and his mental condition is questionable under heavy medication for his considerable physical pain. Nevertheless, it is my duty to convey the infirmariis' report to you this morning. May God grant each of us the power of discernment and wisdom to decide for ourselves what to make of yesterday's events that I will now relay to you."

The Sistine Chapel was utterly silent as each cardinal fixed his undivided attention on the Dean of the College of Cardinals. Meissner cleared his throat once more and then proceeded to summarize Cardinal Murphy's account of the visit to the infirmary.

"So, you now understand why this matter is of special concern to us. As men of God, we have learned to heed God's Word in whatever form it may come to us. We are well acquainted with the mystical. With the unexplainable. It is, therefore, entirely possible that an angel visited Cardinal Maria to pass a critical message to us. If so, we should consider a pause in our voting."

Meissner let this last point sink in before proceeding. "However, per papal edict, we are to continue voting with a minimal degree of debate and discussion in order to conclude two votes each morning and two votes each afternoon until we elect a pontiff. We, additionally, offer the caution that Cardinal Maria may not be of sound mind."

Cardinal Hightower of New Orleans asked, "Has anyone else in this chapel received a visit from an angel with a similar message? Would we not expect God to declare such a message to more than one of us, and a sick cardinal at that, if the message was, in fact, so very important to our deliberations?"

A murmur swept through the Sistine Chapel at Hightower's comments. Several cardinals spoke up in agreement with Hightower essentially stating that while God guides the cardinals by way of the Holy Spirit, He grants the cardinals great latitude in selecting a specific person. After all, if God personally chose each pontiff, how could you justify the selection of so many deficient, even scandalous, popes throughout the Church's history? No, God must be understood in more flexible terms where God guides and man votes.

Meissner studied the assembled cardinals for a couple of minutes thereby permitting discussion. Finally, he declared, "May I have your attention?" Looking around the room for the cardinals' attention, Meissner continued speaking, "Did any other cardinal have a similar dream that would shed light on Cardinal Maria's outburst?"

There was silence as the cardinals all looked around the chapel at each other. No one spoke up; however, just the slightest perspiration began to form on Cardinal Maltempo's brow. He wondered to himself if his dream had anything to do with Cardinal Maria's vision and whether his dream was, in fact, anything more than a dream. He felt that the whole affair was silly, but, nevertheless, he was wrestling with himself and nearly raised his hand to speak when Cardinal Meissner decided to proceed with the morning's first vote. Feeling that he had lost his chance to address his colleagues, Maltempo remained silent. The die was cast and the vote would proceed.

The rest of the morning continued without interference. Cardinal Meissner and his assistants conducted an exceptionally orderly conclave with two ballots cast by the time the cardinals left for lunch and a short rest at St. Martha's Residence.

The balloting had focused on three cardinals. In the day's first ballot, the theological conservatives began to swing their votes to two Italians – Maltempo and Biaggio – while those adhering to the international, ecumenical agenda of John Paul III supported Moratinos. It was beginning to shape up as a battle between perspectives, that is, whether to look inward in shoring up and reforming the theological foundations of the Church in order to resist relativism and secularization or to look outward at the world in order to promote justice by attacking health, housing, economic, racial, and religious problems.

At the end of the tally, Cardinal Moratinos held a slim lead with 50 votes from, largely, the social-leaning block of electors. Cardinal Maltempo counted 37 supporters and Cardinal Biaggio had 29 votes. Therefore, no candidate had secured the necessary 79 votes, two-thirds of cardinal electors, much less half, and the conclave proceeded to the morning's second ballot – the third of the conclave.

Emboldened by the fact that the votes cast for the two Italian conservatives totaled more than Moratinos' fifty supporters, the inward-looking cardinals began to line up behind their leading candidate, Maltempo.

Therefore, at the conclusion of the morning's final balloting, Moratinos' drive began to stall. Moratinos – 52 votes; Maltempo – 45 votes; Biaggio – 19 votes.

Lunch and the rest period were marked by a number of private discussions between the cardinals. The conservatives continued to rally behind Maltempo. They saw him as a stronger candidate than Biaggio. Whereas Biaggio was viewed narrowly as a Curial official, the cardinals judged Maltempo's current service in the Florentine archdiocese coupled with his prior role in the Curia as more comprehensive and supportive of the many diocesan needs.

Over the last three years under John Paul III, they had seen their liturgy weakened, declining financial budgets for biblical evangelism in favor of mounting financial support to fight disease, abortion, and other social issues around the world.

They had, as well, witnessed John Paul's setbacks in ecumenical outreach to Islam and the growing secularization of traditional Catholic nations as the West's crusade for globalization swept the world.

Sensing that they would eventually carry the day, the conservatives continued to swing from Biaggio to Maltempo. They, additionally, began courting Moratinos' supporters. Encouragingly, they only needed to peel fifteen electors from Moratinos to achieve the needed 79 votes.

Moratinos' supporters rightly perceived the upper hand of the conservative block. Seeing their future at stake, the Curial officials in Moratinos' corner permitted themselves to be courted by the conservatives for key assignments at the Holy See in Rome. They reasoned that despite having a conservative pontiff, they could exert great leverage in continuing John Paul's agenda through key posts in Rome.

Thus, as the cardinal electors re-assembled for the afternoon ballots, the die had been cast. It was only a matter of time before Moratinos would fade from the scene. The Church was destined to have an Italian pontiff once again.

The first ballot confirmed the movement in support. A few cardinals stood firm in their support of Biaggio in hopes of wringing concessions, but Maltempo surged ahead of Moratinos for the first time. At the end of the afternoon's first ballot, the vote stood at 69 for Maltempo, 40 for Moratinos, and 7 for Biaggio. Black smoke streamed from the Sistine Chapel's smokestack one more time, but the upcoming fifth ballot of the conclave would be a mere formality.

Indeed, it was. Everyone saw it coming and the social reformers capitulated. Maltempo secured 96 votes, well over the needed 79 ballots to secure the necessary two-thirds of the College of Cardinals.

A wave of applause swept through the Sistine Chapel. The difficult interregna period was at an end. With great relief, they had a leader and an agenda again. Lastly, they could return home to tend to the swelling work awaiting them.

Cardinal Meissner rose and asked the junior cardinal deacon to call for the Secretary of the College of Cardinals and for the Master of Papal Liturgical Celebrations. He then began to walk over to Narciso Maltempo.

Narciso had watched the day's votes with great satisfaction. Finally, he had realized his youthful papal ambitions. He would serve his remaining days leading the church he so dearly loved. His doubts from earlier in the morning had deserted him in the afternoon as victory emerged.

Nevertheless, his bouts with his troubling dreams had played havoc with his sleep and appetite. Over the last two weeks, he had barely slept and had lost over ten pounds from his medium frame of 170 pounds. Narciso was, additionally, dehydrated from the Roman heat wave. So, as he rose to meet Cardinal Meissner, his light-headedness was not entirely due to the exhilaration he was feeling.

Cardinal Meissner stopped in front of Narciso Maltempo and, in Italian, asked, "Do you accept your canonical election as Supreme Pontiff?"

Narciso took a deep breath. He felt a little dizzy. Perhaps, he had stood up too quickly so he steadied himself against his small desk. He momentarily closed his eyes. Another deep breath and he felt better. Opening his eyes, he looked straight at Meissner who was expectantly waiting for Maltempo's affirmative reply.

Maltempo began to open his mouth and form the first syllable of the Italian word 'accepto' meaning I accept. But, at that moment his jaw locked. Try as hard as he could, Maltempo could not speak! His heart raced. He felt flush and small beads of sweat erupted from his forehead. His jaw!

He felt a surge of fear and, suddenly, recalled his upsetting dream from last night. He heard a sharp, piercing sound in his ears and, then, the voice from his dream: "Narciso, stay with the boat. This is not your time."

With Meissner reaching out to hold him and the entire College of Cardinals looking on curiously, Maltempo completely realized with a shudder that he was following his own will, not God's will. He was fighting God! This was entirely too much for him, particularly in his weakened state.

Friends would later tell Maltempo that he over-reacted; that, in his poor condition, he mistakenly permitted the power of a dream to reverse the reality of his God-given election. The cardinals, all led by the Holy Spirit, had settled on him. How could he decline elevation to the papal throne?

Maltempo abruptly pushed Meissner back and began waving his arms across his face. "No! No! I do not accept. God wants another," he shrilly declared, able to inexplicably speak again. Then Narciso Maltempo's world went black and he collapsed into Meissner's arms.

CHAPTER TWENTY-TWO

The orderly conclave instantly descended into pandemonium. Dodging cardinals, the two attending physicians rushed forward to assist Cardinal Meissner who was struggling to hold his unwieldy patient. Upon breaching the wall of cardinals surrounding the unconscious Maltempo, the physicians laid Narciso on the floor and took his vital signs. Much to their relief, he was still breathing; but, Maltempo did not respond to any attempts to rouse him.

Cardinal Murphy, sitting near the physicians, had the quickness of mind to snatch the stretcher and follow the physicians.

"Grazie!" Doctor Leone thanked Cardinal Murphy.

"Let me help you!" Cardinal Murphy responded before helping the physicians transfer Maltempo from the hard floor to the stretcher. Within minutes, the dazed cardinals had cleared a path for the physicians who wasted little time in carrying their patient out of the Sistine Chapel to the infirmary.

"Fellow Cardinals, please return to your seats! Fellow Cardinals, return to your seats, per favore!" Cardinal Meissner shouted, waving his arms, in an attempt to restore order. "I beg you to be seated!"

It took several minutes of patient coaxing, but the cardinals eventually took their posts again. Meissner, looking over them from the dais, was a bit perplexed as to how best to proceed when it struck him that a prayer for Maltempo was in order. That would also quiet the room and give everyone, to especially include himself, time to calm down.

"Let us pray for Narciso! We must ask for God's compassion on Narciso! Let us also beg for God's guidance at this troubling instant of time!" Meissner exclaimed before leading his colleagues in prayer.

Nearly ten minutes later, Meissner concluded the prayer. "Amen." Feeling a bit calmer now, Meissner declared, "My fellow Cardinals, it is now nearly six o'clock. We should retire to St. Martha's for dinner, rest, and prayer. I will look into Cardinal Maltempo's medical condition tonight and we can, then, confer on how best to proceed. But, I believe that we should shelve formal discussion until we have rested."

Meissner paused. Wringing his hands, he simply wanted to leave the Sistine Chapel for calmer surroundings where he could think and confer with senior members of the College of Cardinals. The day had ended in catastrophe and cool heads had to prevail.

"Please, God, give me the wisdom and strength to prevail!" Meissner was thinking to himself when he realized that someone was shouting to him. Turning to his left to better hear, Meissner asked, "What was that? Can you repeat that?"

"Si. Cardinal Meissner, what color should the smoke be? We can't leave before sending the signal!"

Meissner was dumbstruck. He stared blankly at his assistant master of ceremonies, Monsignor Terrazza, as he wrestled with the answer. Then, finally regaining his composure,

Meissner nervously declared, "Black. Black smoke. We have no pope."

Cybil lay awake beside Giulio in bed. She had had difficulty falling asleep after bringing Giulio to a wild climax in bed. Giulio, on the other hand, was already asleep when she returned to the warm bed from the bathroom. Her mind was racing and, no matter how hard she tried, she could not relax. She was extremely frustrated because she needed the sleep so that she and Giulio could be back at work in less than five hours to download the second day's voice recording. She'd be a wreck without some sleep, but there was simply too much racing through her mind.

She told herself that the day had been very successful. After listening to the recording of the first day from midnight to roughly four o'clock that morning, Cybil and Giulio had composed a written summary report before breakfast. Although the first day of the conclave had been confined to the afternoon, it had some newsworthy items.

For one thing, Cybil had the list of initial candidates. That, alone, would put some money in her pocket. Under the guise of an inside tip and her prowess in investigative reporting, Cybil sold the list of names to a good friend running a gambling operation in New York's Little Italy.

Second, Cybil had the scoop on discovering that one cardinal, in the infirmary, was deathly ill. She would spend the latter half of the morning and early afternoon interviewing Curial staff about Cardinal Maria and 'googling' to acquire background information and photos on the ill cardinal. She, additionally, deployed a photographer to snap some photos of the infirmary's exterior. Happily, he reported back that he had captured the attending physician, Doctor Terzini, on digital film, too. By four o'clock, Cybil had composed a short sensationalistic story on Cardinal Maria that she sent to Harold via email along with the earlier summary report and the afternoon's digital photographs. Harold promised her to publish it in the morning.

Giulio, in the meantime, had successfully uploaded the audio file and summary report to Joshua's secure website server and had transcribed the entire conclave's discussions. By the time Cybil looked up from her keyboard at four o'clock, she was pleasantly startled to find Giulio mischievously smiling and standing naked in the doorway with a bottle of champagne and two glasses hiding his more interesting anatomical parts.

Now two hours later, Cybil desperately wanted to sleep. But, there was one more thing keeping her awake. She realized that she was falling in love with Giulio. Propping herself up with her left arm on a pillow, Cybil began to run her right hand through sleeping Giulio's hair. Cybil truly enjoyed working with him and began to list his exceptional qualities. He was a hard worker, he didn't need much instruction, he took the initiative, he shared his ideas, he interjected humor to break up the monotony or to dampen the high pressured atmosphere, he was technologically gifted and intelligent, he spoke five languages, he ran a profitable shop, and … well, he was simply the perfect partner in crime – so to speak, of course! But, those were only his professional qualities. In addition to all of that, Giulio could cook – in the kitchen and in bed! Cybil smiled and kissed Giulio's forehead. He was everything she had ever wanted. Could this truly be love?

Cybil had never slept with one man for an entire week. Much less spent as much time with any one man. Relationships got in the way of her jet-setting lifestyle and Cybil wasn't one to become vulnerable by opening herself up to anyone else. Before you know it, you're always calling the guy to let him know where you're going and what time you'll be back, you're fretting about what to get him for birthday, Christmas, and anniversary presents, eating dinners at the in-laws, watching your mother show him your baby pictures, and, worst of all, washing his dirty laundry and socks. Men were terribly messy. No, a real relationship wasn't in the cards for her.

Maybe some day a rich, older man would get lucky enough to plunk a big diamond ring on her finger. Cybil had always wanted a millionaire who was a compulsive workaholic so that she could enjoy a nice mansion at the Hamptons on Long Island by herself and the pool boy and the neighbor's husband.

Nevertheless, here she was entangled in an affair with a virile, intelligent, and exciting Italian in the grand city of Rome. Could she be happy in Rome? Would it offer the excitement of New York? Perhaps, she could use it as a springboard to explore Europe. A life of freelance writing? Lord knows, the Europeans have ample scandals she could write about. Then, back to the fundamental question: was this truly love?

Marco Spitini was relieved to find the audio file and report. He enjoyed the skullduggery of playing the anonymous Joshua. Smiling, he recalled how he had picked that code name. Drawing on the Old Testament, he had carefully selected the name of a spy. Moses had selected Joshua to lead the initial forays into the promised land after the long, circuitous march from Egypt through the barren wilderness of the Sinai Peninsula.

Sitting at a computer terminal in, yet, another downtown café, Spitini meticulously studied the report. He was very pleased to find that he was, once again, correct in identifying Maltempo, Fassino, and Moratinos as the leading candidates. Totaling the votes, he was now supremely confident that the conservative block of cardinal electors would carry the conclave thereby turning the Catholic Church away from John Paul's internationally activist program. Moratinos' early lead did not, therefore, bother him much.

He correctly reasoned that Biaggio's support was lukewarm, at best, and would likely evaporate in Maltempo's favor. That was good news for Spitini if he remained in the

Catholic Church instead of heading to Iran because it was Maltempo who had actively advocated Spitini's posting to the Vatican as John Paul's secretary. Yes, Maltempo might be inclined to place Spitini in a key Curial position and then, one day, to raise Spitini to the exalted rank of bishop! Bishop Spitini – that sounded good! An undercover bishop in the Catholic Church! Think of the damage he could do!

Regardless of his immediate future, Spitini gleefully admitted that it was only a matter of time before an Italian regained the papacy and turned the Church's attention and finances to internal matters. The era of international activism was coming to an end for the time being. In its vain attempt to corral its present subjects before they fell victim to globalization and its associated economic secularization, the Church would abandon its missionary zeal elsewhere. Spitini cheerfully rejoiced that Islam would be all too happy to take the field and fill the void.

Sipping his coffee, Spitini closed the document, exited the website, and sent a short, terse email to his Iranian handler stating that everything was going to plan. Victory was at hand. Spitini felt a rush of self satisfaction at this. All of his work and calculated risks were paying off. Over twenty years of self-sacrifice and kow-towing to Catholic elders was yielding fruit. Perhaps, now the boys might give him the recognition and honor he deserved! Spitini was a happy man as he left and returned to the Vatican.

Yousef Sami did not like what he saw. Not at all! Peering over the computer monitor while continuing to watch Spitini, he noticed that someone else was trailing Spitini, too! A young man, probably in his early thirties. Definitely a European for he was very light-skinned with blonde hair and blue eyes. Yousef had seen the fellow earlier, but now, seeing him again, in the café he was sure of it. Spitini had picked up a tail. Worse, yet, Spitini did not even appear to have realized it!

The boys would not be pleased with his report later that night. This could only mean one thing. Spitini was compromised. They would have to take care of it. Or take care of him.

CHAPTER TWENTY-THREE

Barely able to contain their thoughts and emotions aboard the buses in the company of the drivers, the cardinals let loose upon returning to St. Martha's Residence. Cardinal Meissner and a select group retired to Meissner's suite, but the others all seemed to gather in the main entryway and the adjoining dining room without any indications of retiring to their rooms.

Many of the initial comments focused on Maltempo's reaction to his election.

"What was Maltempo thinking?"

"How could he decline the papacy?"

"Was he out of his mind?"

"Did you see how his face contorted and turned scarlet red when he tried to speak? He must have had a heart attack or stroke!"

"And, then he collapsed! A man in his mid-seventies has to be more careful and mindful of his health!"

"Would he live?"

"And what about Roger Maria? Was he still alive?"

After venting on matters of physical and mental health concerns, the cardinals then moved on to the business point of view. Both, the conservative and socially-conscious blocks needed new candidates. But, who? Among conservatives, who could match Maltempo's comprehensive experience spanning both the Curia and local church leadership? It had to be someone who could retain the cardinals that the conservatives peeled off of Moratinos in the afternoon. That would likely be extremely difficult. Sure, they had the majority, but two thirds were needed!

In contrast, the socially-conscious block needed to find a compromise candidate who was a middle-of-the-road nominee acceptable to the conservatives. Moratinos would not do. After all, with a clear majority on the conservative side of the ledger, the College would never elect an international activist cut of the same cloth as John Paul III. At best, the more outward looking block could only hope for a compromise candidate who could, over the long run, minimize the conservatives through key Curial appointments and the elevation of supporters to the College of Cardinals.

The entire establishment was in an uproar, but it was only going to get worse. After a half hour of this loud haranguing, it was inevitable that one of the men would have to use a bathroom. None less than Cardinal Aldo Pellitteri, the eldest among them, excused himself from a cluster of cardinals and headed to the bathroom located under the main stairway on the ground floor. All was well until he flushed.

Running as best as a 78-year old man can, Aldo Pellitteri hurried back to the entryway shouting, "It's red! This can't be! The water is red! Dark red like blood! Cardinal Maria's warning is true!"

At this the blood drained from every cardinal's face.

When Moses returned to Egypt after his miraculous encounter with God, in a burning bush, instructing him to free the Jews from Pharaoh's ruthless grip, Moses found that Pharaoh's heart was hardened. Pharaoh would not yield to the single Creator and free the Jews. In fact, Pharaoh ordered that heavier work be laid on the Jews. So much so, that the Jews were enraged with Moses for angering Pharaoh. Seeing Moses agonize over his predicament, God instructed Moses to perform magic in Pharaoh's court to demonstrate God's power; but, Pharaoh was not impressed and his heart remained hardened.

God next instructed Moses to meet Pharaoh on the banks of the mighty Nile River with a threat to bring a series of plagues upon Egypt until Pharaoh relented and freed the Jews. With Pharaoh refusing to let God's people go, God first struck Egypt with a series of plagues. The first was to turn the Nile River's water into blood. The fish died and stank. The Egyptians could not drink the water and had to dig wells to find water.

Pharaoh's heart remained hardened. In response, God covered Egypt with frogs. Subsequent plagues, in order, included gnats throughout the land of Egypt, swarms of flies, a deadly pestilence destroying the livestock, festering boils on humans and animals, thunder and hail, devouring locusts, three days of darkness, and death to every firstborn. Only then did Pharaoh relent and free the Jews.

"Come see for yourselves! Here in the bathroom! Turn on the water and see!" Aldo shouted as he headed back to the bathroom.

With the cardinals crowding around him, Pellitteri turned on every sink and flushed every toilet. The water was, in fact, deep red. And it stank horribly!

With the bathroom too small to hold over a hundred men, those outside the bathroom headed for the kitchen where they asked the kitchen staff to turn on the faucets. The water there was deep red, too! A few who went to their rooms reported back that the water in their personal bathrooms was dark red, as well. And it stank!

The assembled College of Cardinals was in a full blown uproar with no chance of calming down any time soon. Sending hotel staff around the Vatican to check the water, they were distressed to hear the reports that all of the water at the Vatican was a dark red and it stank!

"Cardinal Maria's dream is coming true! God has struck us with the Egyptian plague!"

Cardinal Murphy inched over to one of the running faucets in the kitchen. A man of ordinary common sense, he filled a glass with the running water and studied it. "This is iron rust in the water. It is not blood." Then turning to the chef, "Please, call the Roman water authority and inquire into any pipe breaks. I think we have a broken water main!"

After an interminable wait of ten minutes surrounded by anxious cardinals and kitchen staff, Cardinal Murphy had his answer. The water main feeding the Vatican and much of its surrounding neighborhoods had broken. The gigantic pipe was, in fact, built of cast iron and the break was in an area of red clay. The combination of the iron rust and clay was the culprit for the red water and rotting odor. The operator at the water authority advised everyone to refrain from drinking or bathing in the water until repairs were to be made sometime the next day. Thereafter, she advised everyone to boil their drinking water until tests could verify its safety for human consumption.

The scientific, common sense explanation for the mishap slowly appeased the cardinals, but great apprehension continued to persist. The cardinals were up very late that night recounting the day's catastrophic events and planning for the conclave's third day. The lights were on long past midnight, before each cardinal finally succumbed to weariness. The only good news of the evening came from Doctor Terzini who reported that both

Narciso Maltempo and Roger Maria were alive. However, neither was conscious. Maria was still heavily sedated and on death's doorstep whereas Maltempo was in a coma after appearing to have suffered a stroke. Medical tests over the next few days would, hopefully, determine the extent of the stroke's damage and Maltempo's potential for recovery.

Cybil and Giulio were spending the night listening intently to the recording of the second day. A large pot of coffee sat on the table as the bleary-eyed couple took notes. Knowing that no white smoke appeared above the Sistine Chapel that day, Cybil and Giulio were expecting an uneventful audio file. At about seven o'clock that morning, they discovered how wrong they were.

CHAPTER TWENTY-FOUR

"Holy cow! This is hot shit!" Cybil exclaimed excitedly as the audio recording unveiled Maltempo's rejection of the papacy and his astonishing physical collapse. "This is incredible!"

Giulio was shaking his head in disbelief and saying, "Le disgrazie non vanno mai sole." Cybil, having regained her fluency in Italian, correctly understood him to say "Troubles never come alone.'

"Si, Giulio. What a mess they have on their hands! But, their troubles are my profit. This will make great copy!" Cybil could already see her name on the Pulitzer Prize. What a scoop!

"That's all, Cybil. That's it for day number two. You have a great story here. Harold will be excited." Giulio looked over her with a big smile and gave her a kiss on the forehead.

Cybil leaned forward in her chair and stretched out her arms until her elbows rested on Giulio's broad shoulders. Wrapping her forearms behind his neck, Cybil continued to lean forward until their noses touched. Then, looking deep into

Giulio's eyes, Cybil softly said, "Thanks, Giulio. I couldn't have done this without you. Really, you're marvelous."

Giulio responded with a kiss while firmly grasping her slim waist. "Grazie. Multo grazie. You are wonderful, too!"

Just as the two of them began to entertain thoughts of a victory romp in the sheets, Cybil's phone began to ring. Jumping at the startlingly loud ring, Cybil sighed and gave Giulio one more quick kiss before releasing her hold on him and snatching the phone from the table. Flipping it open to see who it was, Cybil smiled. "It's Harold."

"Hiya' Harold! What's up?" Cybil snapped into the phone as only a New Yorker can.

"Yup, I've just finished listening to the recording. You won't believe it, Harold! Lady luck is smiling at us. This is pure gold!" Cybil's speech was accelerating as her excitement surged. "Look, I can't tell you what we've got over the open phone line, but it's real good. Reeeeaalllll good! Can you say Pulitzer?"

"No, I haven't written the report, yet. Geez, Harold! I just finished listening to it. Besides, it's just after seven o'clock over here and a woman has to eat, too, ya' know!"

"Okay, okay. I promise. I'll hop to it right away. I should have it done within the hour and I'll call you before I leave for the Vatican to see what you think. Say, did you run my story about Roger Maria? I haven't even had the time to check our paper's website to look for it. You did? Great! Thanks, Harold!"

"Okay. Got it. I'll give your thanks to Giulio!" Cybil looked over at Giulio and blew him a kiss.

"Tata for now! Ciao!" Cybil hung up and put the phone back by the computer monitor. "Okay. Full steam ahead." Picking up her laptop, Cybil grinned with sparkling eyes and said, "I'll start the report if you find us breakfast!"

Matters at St. Martha's Residence were just as frenetic, but far less jovial. There were a lot of groggy cardinals sitting around the breakfast tables uneasily contemplating yesterday's disastrous series of events. Not a soul had slept well and each time any of them got up in the middle of the night to use the bathroom, he was welcomed by the foul stench of the red, rotting water. Fortunately, the staff had reacted quickly to provide bottled water for each cardinal or else they could not have shaven, brushed their teeth, and washed their faces.

Very few of them felt much like talking. There would be plenty of time for that in the Sistine Chapel later that morning. Poor old Meissner! How would he regain the upper hand and restore calm order to the conclave? He had a tough job ahead of him. No matter. In the end, each cardinal concluded, in his thoughts, that God was, after all, in charge and everything would work out for the good of it all. All glory be to God! They took comfort in knowing that there would, indeed, be a happy conclusion to all of this. But, if only they could divine what that might be!

Aldo Pellitteri, ever the good-humored Italian, tried to cheer up the five cardinals sitting glumly at his table. "Eat! My friends, eat! The pastries looked delicious and, despite the foul water, our expert kitchen staff has found enough bottled water to brew delicious coffee." Smiling, Aldo proclaimed, "L'appetito vien mangiado! Appetite comes with eating! So, eat! These troubles will soon disappear and we will have a pope. We must keep the faith, my brothers."

He was greeted with a couple of smiles, but not much more. "Aldo, what about Maria's dream? Pharaoh's plagues? The water stinks and looks like blood. Could this truly be the wrath of God?" Cardinal Vicenzo D'Aquanni worriedly asked.

"I must admit that I, too, was not myself last night when I flushed the toilet and found dark red water filling the bowl. Frankly, after Narciso's episode I was on edge. But, thanks to

Sean Murphy and his calm reasoning we now have a perfectly rational explanation for the whole water mess. A broken water main! That's it. A broken water main!" Having raised the cheerfulness factor at his table, Aldo Pellitteri happily bit into his pastry and gulped his coffee.

"I think you're right, Aldo." Cardinal Gauthier, sitting opposite Aldo, declared. "Really, the plagues of Egypt? Here in Rome? Why, the second plague consists of the frogs climbing out of the Nile to overrun Egypt. That's impossible here in Rome! Why, there is no appreciable frog population here and, even if there were, they couldn't just jump over the stone embankments and walls, could they?!" Chuckling now and looking around at the other cardinals, Gauthier went on to say, "No. It's all just happenstance. We must keep calm and permit the Holy Spirit to continue guiding us through this confusing time. God is good!"

Hearing the conversation at Pellitteri's table led to similar discussions at the surrounding tables, so that by the conclusion of breakfast, the cardinals were feeling in better spirits.

"The buses have arrived! You may begin boarding now!" Monsignor Terrazza announced from the doorway. "It's a beautiful, sunny day for a ride to the Sistine Chapel!"

Buoyed by Aldo's inspired good humor, the cardinals quickly finished their coffees and rose to board the buses. The three idling tour buses already had their air conditioning running at maximum levels with the morning temperatures already approaching record numbers. The short walk across the baking cobblestones was long enough and the cardinals thankfully sank into the soft bus seats.

The three bus engines roared to life and began to move forwards. For a moment, that is. For all three came to a sudden, complete halt.

CHAPTER TWENTY-FIVE

Frogs! Or, rather, frog pieces and parts! Raining down on them from the heavens! Frog guts, frog legs, and frog heads! Even plastic frog toys to include a Sesame Street hand puppet of Kermit the Frog pelted the three buses.

It was pure bedlam in each of the buses. The cardinals were in utter, absolute shock. Some froze, unable to move or say a word; perhaps, hoping that this was all just a bed dream. Others began shouting, fearful that the buses' rooftops or windows might be damaged thereby exposing them to the green froggy slime. With the world's media photographers busily clicking away, the Catholic Church's leadership sat in their buses under a thick, gooey blanket of frog parts.

Overhead, three small helicopters hovered a mere hundred feet above each bus. They had arrived on the scene out of nowhere as the buses began to move and had discharged their frog loads from massive buckets slung underneath. The choppers continued to hover until they verified that they had hit their marks. As they left, a fourth helicopter flew over the unfolding drama and released a bucket load of weighted clear plastic spheres, measuring about twelve inches in diameter onto the courtyard in front of the lead bus. As the spheres hit the buses and cobblestones, the plastic cracked and released hundreds of cards, t-shirts, and metal buttons.

With the fourth helicopter departing the scene, the media hounds rushed forward to pick up the materials. The Swiss Guards were too busy moving towards the buses to care and the cardinals were looking on through smeared bus windows.

"It's Greenpeace! Greenpeace did this!" Shouts went up from the reporters as the photographers edged closer to the buses for more pictures. Francisco Marino, Cybil's photographer, was reaching for his second camera and looking forward to the price his pictures would fetch from her. In his mind, this was like manna falling from the skies. His favorite photo that he luckily managed to snap was that of a cardinal anxiously looking out a window of the middle bus with both hands high on the window as if he were trying to get out. Best of all, the better part of a frog's head was glued to the window right in front of the Cardinal's open, gaping mouth. He would take this to the bank!

Francisco grabbed a card that was fluttering along the cobblestones in the wind and quickly read it. On the card was a picture of a speckled frog and a short message. Apparently, Greenpeace was protesting the Catholic Church's obstruction of environmental initiatives to protect the natural habitats of frogs succumbing to a waterborne fungus in Central and South America. Thinking quickly on his feet, he photographed the card and stuck it in his satchel for Cybil.

Monsignor Spitini looked on with amusement although he was careful to act the part of a Catholic monsignor by frowning and shaking his fist at the helicopters. Spitini couldn't help but rejoice at the Church's embarrassment. He was sure that the pictures would be circulating around the world on the internet before the hour was up. Sometimes, globalization could be put to good use, he cynically thought to himself.

He contemplated running forward to the buses in order to pretend to assist the cardinals, but the Swiss Guards had matters well in hand. Technically, he wasn't supposed to have any contact with the cardinals anyway, so Spitini was happy to watch. Besides, he knew that his terror network's plans for the day would add to the cardinals' misery. This was going to be a good day for Islam.

The Swiss Guards were uncertain what to do with the cardinals. The buses couldn't offload the clerics at St. Martha's because the cardinals would have had to walk across the frog slime covering the immediate area around the buses. Fortunately, Colonel Weissberg appeared at that moment and, taking charge, waved the buses on while barking orders to the drivers to proceed to the Sistine Chapel. Weissberg had the common sense and clarity of mind to realize that there was no sense in hosing the buses down since the foul water was not much better than the rotting frog parts. Hopefully, on the short drive around St. Peter's Basilica to the Sistine Chapel, the buses would shed most of the frog parts. Furthermore, he knew that he couldn't keep the cardinals on the buses much longer. Nor did he want to provide the media with any more photographs.

Once the buses had departed, he began shouting orders to his men to push back the reporters and to gather up the Greenpeace paraphernalia. Watching his men, he spoke hurriedly into his police radio, "Sergeant Sebastian, call the Italian police. I want to know where those helicopters came from and where they land. I want those pilots in handcuffs!"

"What a mess," Weissberg muttered to himself. "What next?"

CHAPTER TWENTY-SIX

The buses slowly wound their way through the Vatican compound and pulled up by the Sistine Chapel to disgorge the indignant cardinals. No longer apprehensive over their recent plight, the cardinals' mood had shifted during the short ride to raw anger over the audacity of the attackers. Unaccustomed to being ignominiously treated like the corporate executives of a logging or petroleum company, the cardinals were not, at that moment, in a forgiving disposition towards the environmental scoundrels who had dropped rotting frog parts on their buses.

Not eager to please the press, the cardinals were determined to disembark from the buses in a calm, dignified manner and, then, to solemnly march into the chapel. They nearly made it.

A large cloud of gnats quickly surrounded the buses and cardinals. Drawn by the putrid flesh encasing the buses on a hot day, the gnats quickly multiplied. As if that wasn't enough, many of the unruly gnats followed the cardinals into the Sistine Chapel.

The few photographers who had managed to run behind the buses arrived to find new photo opportunities. The cardinals were making a spectacle of themselves in wildly swatting at the gnats. It was, by no means, a regal procession.

Cybil's photographer, Francisco, was exceptionally fleet of foot and arrived on the scene to capture the third busload of cardinals swatting their way forward. Francisco had another winning photo when he zoomed in on Cardinal Moratinos with a telescopic lens to snap a photo of him completely covered from scarlet skull cap to his chin in gnats. Ecstatic, the photographer kept shooting until his digital camera's picture card was full. He then picked up his phone and called Cybil.

The cardinals entering the Sistine Chapel had hoped to disengage from the swarming gnats, but hopelessly fought a losing rear-guard battle. Although the vast number of gnats was left feasting on the frog innards, a substantial number had followed the fleeing cardinals before the doors closed to seal the chapel. Thereafter, only with much swatting, waving, and ducking were the cardinals finally able to alleviate their discomfort.

Cardinal Meissner's initial impulse was to call for a recess of the College of Cardinals, but returning to the foul smelling, gnat infested buses was out of the question. Orchestrating an exodus on foot was another option, but there remained the question of whether the gnats would find them again. Besides, the main entrance to St. Martha's was likely inundated with gnats feasting on the frog entrails lying on the cobbestone courtyard. Meissner wouldn't even entertain entering through the service entrance for that would be far too undignified – especially with the paparazzi aiming their cameras at them anew.

To say that Meissner faced a raucous and infuriated assembly was an understatement to the n-th degree. Many cardinals continued to swat at gnats, whether real or imagined. Bickering over the conditions was rampant and the two physicians were moving around administering ointment for insect bites. Lastly, a few cardinals simply sat staring blankly at the floor, clearly despondent over the upsetting start to the day.

Cardinal Murphy sat stoically while taking in the evolving drama. Although the morning's events, on the heels of Maltempo's breakdown, were admittedly distressing, the American was disquieted by his colleagues' over-reaction. He simply had not pictured his first conclave descending into chaos.

Yes, Maltempo's fit was upsetting; but, then again, weren't they fortunate that Maltempo refused the papacy before falling into a coma? Where would they be if he had collapsed after accepting the election?

Yes, the water was foul. But, wasn't there a rational explanation? Hadn't the staff at St. Martha's reacted with speed to acquire and distribute bottled water?

Yes, Greenpeace's ambush was embarrassing to the security forces; but, wouldn't the world condemn such a despicable atrocity? The villains would be apprehended and justice would be victorious.

Yes, the swarming gnats were disconcerting; but, again, wasn't there a perfectly rational explanation? Gnats would naturally encircle the rotting frog flesh on a hot day.

"We must get a grip on ourselves," Murphy muttered to himself. The commotion was not showing much signs of subsiding and Meissner appeared content to confer with his assistants rather than addressing the assembly. Rather, everyone was free to move about and talk.

Across from Cardinal Murphy, Cardinal Gauthier privately fretted. Alternately swatting at the annoying gnats and biting his finger nails, Gauthier, too, was exasperated with his colleagues. However, his perspective markedly differed from that of Murphy.

Gauthier was alarmed that God's hand was moving against the cardinals. Terrifyingly, the plagues levied against the Egyptian Pharaoh were unfolding, one by one! Didn't everyone see this?

No, the water was not transformed into blood as was the Nile River; but, it looked like blood and stank!

No, frogs did not spring forth from the river in biblical fashion; but, frogs now, undeniably, covered their buses. Greenpeace was nothing more than God's modern tool for bringing the second biblical plague to life.

No, Moses was not there to strike the earth thereby turning the dust of the earth to gnats throughout the land; but, in keeping with the biblical order of the plagues, gnats appeared!

No, Gauthier admitted that this was far more than a series of coincidental mishaps! Would a swarm of flies strike next? Why didn't Meissner acknowledge this, too? The madness had to stop now! But, how?

Gauthier continued mulling over the current state of affairs. For whatever reason, God's hand was moving against the College of Cardinals; but, they had been warned. Maria's outburst had, thus far, proven true. Whether he was of sound mind or afflicted by hallucinations was now immaterial for they had elected one of their own only to find themselves beset by the first three biblical plagues of Egypt. Perhaps, Maltempo's declaration just before he fainted offered a clue. Had he not shouted, 'God wants another?' Had Roger Maria's angel also visited Narciso? If so, it was vital for Narciso to regain consciousness so that they might learn more of God's will.

Murphy and Gauthier pointed up the two diametrically opposed arguments circulating around the chapel. They were foremost in Meissner's mind, too, as he finally reached a decision to open the floor for debate. The balloting would be postponed.

Turning towards the cardinals and walking forward to the edge of the dais, Meissner raised his hands to win everyone's attention.   The men in scarlet began to quiet and turned their attention to Meissner. Seeing a glimpse of order returning for the first time that morning, Meissner breathed a sigh of relief and began to speak. Unfortunately, he didn't get more than a word out before the cardinals were plunged into semi-darkness.

Several miles outside Rome, a bright flash of light followed by a rumbling boom signaled a fresh calamity. A key power station serving the Vatican and parts of Rome exploded with violent brilliance. A second strike, timed perfectly thirty seconds later, toppled the wires of a Vatican transformer station. Power to the Vatican was immediately cut with little hope for a speedy restoration of services.

Spitini's band of brethren had conducted two precision strikes with timed bombs against the local power infrastructure. It could not have come at a worse time for the assembled cardinals. First, the few air conditioned spots of the Vatican, to especially include the Sistine Chapel and St. Martha's Residence, were now at the mercy of the heat wave. Second, this day was a holiday with many employees of the power company on vacation. Rome was fairly deserted on the fifteenth of August, popularly known as Ferragosto, each year.

Seeing his office lighting fade to black, Spitini grinned widely. What a day! His team had finally come through! Perhaps, their slip up in failing to eliminate Tara was, after all, an isolated incident that they could later correct. Regardless, Spitini was overjoyed at the continuing public humiliation of the Holy See.

Now the world could see how weak the Catholic Church had become. They couldn't even protect a mere 108 acres where their entire church leadership was meeting in secrecy, much less guard their global turf from encroaching secularization.

176

This attack was far more than an attempt to embarrass the Catholic Church. Eager to have the cardinals conclude the election, Spitini's compatriots had targeted the electrical power. Without lights, air conditioned lodging, and power for other sundry office gadgets, it was hoped that the cardinals would curtail their prolonged debates.

Allah's hand was moving in grand fashion. Who could doubt it now? The environmentalists' ambush was a happy twist of fate preceding the terrorist attack. Spitini was absolutely thrilled.

"Well, no need to sit in the dark," Spitini declared out loud. Locking the door behind him, Spitini left his office and headed for the taxi stand. He would need to go further than usual to find an internet café with power so that he could read Cybil's daily report.

TJ and Wilhelm Weissberg looked at each other in alarm. They were comfortably sitting in Weissberg's office after the call came in from the Italian police that they had tracked the helicopters and subsequently nabbed the Greenpeace activists at a farm just outside Rome. Their joy was short lived as Weissberg's windowless office went dark before the emergency generator kicked in to restore lighting. When the boom of the Vatican bomb echoed across the rooftops, they both knew that something serious was awry.

Weissberg was the first to jump up out of his chair. TJ, still nursing a sore thigh, followed him into the hall leaning on a cane. Now a ball of energy, Weissberg was already shouting orders to dispatch men across the Vatican.

"Get the Sistine Chapel guards on the radio! Call the security forces, too. I want a situation report!" With his desk sergeant quickly reacting, Weissberg pointed at another man and sharply commanded him, "Franz! Call the Italian police to report a possible bomb explosion!"

"SC, this is base, over."

"Base, SC here, over."

"SC, what is your status, over."

"The lights went out, but the emergency lights are now on. We heard a boom immediately after the power went out, but don't know if it was an explosion. The cardinals are still inside. Everyone appears safe here, over."

Sergeant Weil looked up at Colonel Weissberg for further instructions. Neither of the two men looking at each other had experienced anything like this at the normally peaceful Vatican.

"Sergeant Weil, get more men, with sidearms over to the Sistine Chapel and St. Martha's Residence. Find the buses and put an armed guard on each. Then close the museums and shops; without power there is no sense keeping the tourists there anyway. After the guards lock up the museums, have them conduct a search for bombs – search for odd objects! Lastly, wake up the men who are off duty. Have them report within fifteen minutes and give them sidearms, too." Pausing to take a gulp of air after that staccato series of orders, Weissberg looked at Weil to see if he had, in fact, digested all of that. "Got all of that?"

With Sergeant Weil nodding affirmatively and picking up his radio, Weissberg turned to Franz Weghofer who was hanging up the phone and asked, "Well?"

Franz promptly replied, "The police are dispatching men to the Vatican now. Probably a dozen; more if we need them. They'll report here, first. A bomb squad is on its way, too. A good part of Rome has lost its power, too.

"Good. Franz, keep me posted. I also ...."

Sergeant Weil's base radio came alive and interrupted Colonel Weissberg. "Base, this is Lieutenant Hartig. We have a fire at the transformer station near the helipad. Looks like an explosion. Everything is 'kaput.' I've called the fire station. Over."

"Sergeant Weil, tell Hartig that I'm on my way. I'll be on my radio." Then, turning to TJ, "TJ, will you stay here and help? If that was a bomb, I could use your expert experience in terror response. Consider yourself deputized!"

Weissberg ran out the door while TJ grabbed a chair by Sergeant Weil's desk.

"Rompicazzo! Vaffanculo!" Giulio bellowed from his seat at the computer terminal. Cybil, putting on make-up in the bathroom, echoed his sentiments, "Shit! Kiss my ass!"

"Who turned off the lights?" Cybil cried at Giulio.

"Not me! I was in the middle of uploading the audio file to the website!" Giulio smacked the side of the monitor in disgust and stood up. He walked across the room to look out of the window. "Looks like the whole neighborhood is out of power. The traffic lights aren't working. But, I'll go check the fuse box to be sure it's not just us." Giulio, clearly exasperated, left for the basement.

Cybil strode over to the window to complete her make-up. She had a half hour to meet her photographer at the Vatican. He sounded very excited about his photos.

Cybil's phone rang. "Now what?"

Dashing over to the computer, Cybil scooped up her phone and flipped it open. It was Francisco, her photographer. "Hello, Francisco! What's up?"

Cybil stood up straight and her eyes almost popped out of her head. "An explosion? They think it was a bomb?"

"Holy cow! Yes, yes! I'll get over there right away!"

"What was that?"

"The helipad? Got it. I'll see you there. I'm on my way!"

Giulio returned to find Cybil hurriedly slipping on her shoes. "The power is definitely out. Damn!"

"Giulio, I've got to go now. Francisco just called again. The transformer station at the Vatican is burning. It looks like a bomb." Then, reaching into her bag, Cybil pulled out her hotel key and lightly tossed it towards Giulio. "Go to my hotel room. Maybe they've got power there. Take my laptop; it's got the report and audio file on the hard drive. Call me if you have any problems!"

Cybil was out the door within two minutes and looking for a taxi to the Vatican.

Francisco stuck his phone back onto his belt and wiped the heavy sweat from his brow. He then picked up a camera and focusing on the firemen battling the small blaze near the Vatican's helipad, Francisco snapped a couple more photographs. He then turned his zoom lens on Colonel Weissberg who had just arrived on the scene.

Francisco had not expected to be so busy at the Vatican. A veteran paparazzi, he had accepted this job with grave reservations, but Harold had offered too much money for Francisco to turn the job down. Otherwise, Francisco would be happily snapping photos of bare breasted movie starlets bathing at the French Riviera and drunken soccer stars at wild late-night parties. He had hoped that the conclave would be short so that he could flee Rome's hot, sticky weather for the pleasant Riviera; but, his stay in Rome was surprisingly exciting and financially rewarding.

Cardinal Meissner stopped dead in his tracks and froze. He could not believe it! Nothing was going right. He grew doubly concerned when the sound of the explosion rattled the windows of the Sistine Chapel. Amazingly, the cardinals remained seated and quiet. A few seconds later, the lights slowly flickered on as the emergency generator started up. An audible sigh of relief swept across the cardinals.

"Please, go find out what happened to the lights and what that explosion was," Meissner asked his assistant, Monsignor Terrazza. Then turning back to the College of Cardinals, Meissner began to speak.

"My fellow colleagues, thank you for remaining calm. Like you, I am concerned about the explosion and momentary loss of lights. I've asked Monsignor Terrazza to look into it with the Swiss Guards. I also regret the misfortunes we have suffered this morning. The devil is at work in attempting to thwart God's will, even here at the Holy See. We also suffered a grave setback with Cardinal Maltempo's breakdown yesterday. Fortunately, he is alive and in the finest medical care. Nevertheless, we must now start our search for a pontiff anew and under very trying circumstances. No one can blame you for being deeply concerned over our state of affairs. Nevertheless, knowing that God is with us, we must remain calm and of one mind in fulfilling our God-given task to elect a new pontiff. Therefore, I propose that we postpone balloting in order to open the College of Cardinals to discussions. Is there any objection?"

There was no objection. In fact, they all remained silent while watching Monsignor Terrazza return to the dais and whisper in Meissner's ear. Meissner nodded. "The guards are looking into the explosion. They do not, yet, know what has happened; but, they advise us to stay here where we are safe." Cardinal Meissner reached for a bottle of water and took a sip before continuing, "The floor is now open for discussion."

"Now this is more like it," Cardinal Murphy thought to himself as he listened to the deliberations. "Rationality has returned!"

Over the next hour, the College of Cardinals lived up to its reputation as the principal leadership of the Catholic Church. The cardinals conducted themselves in a very thoughtful and dignified manner. The analysis of the past events ranged from the views privately expressed by Cardinal Murphy to those of

Cardinal Gauthier. The two major factions, the conservatives and social-justice advocates, also took the opportunity to express their views on the direction of the Church. It was, all in all, a comprehensive discussion.

The news that a bomb had destroyed the Vatican's transformer station proved disturbing and led to a conspiracy debate on whether an outside group was orchestrating the various mishaps. Although that was cause for thought among many of the cardinals, most did not seriously entertain the notion that someone could cause Maltempo's breakdown, destroy a water main, pay off Greenpeace to launch frogs at the buses, herd gnats towards the Vatican, and, finally, bomb the Vatican.

In addition to the discomfort of operating on reduced lighting from the emergency generators, the Sistine Chapel was becoming uncomfortably hot with the outside heat in Rome over 40 degrees centigrade under a blazing hot sun.

Under pressure from several cardinals to do something about the heat, Meissner ordered the twelve windows high atop the walls to be opened in hopes that a cross-breeze might materialize to ventilate the chapel. However, there was some lingering apprehension over a possible return of the gnats, so one window on each of the northern and southern sides of the chapel were opened. Relieved to find no horde of gnats poised to plunge onto them, Meissner ordered the remaining windows opened. Initially, the maneuver seemed to work as a breeze did turn up. However, the series of misfortunes plaguing the cardinals was to continue.

At first, no one noticed a few flies filtering through the windows into the chapel. But, within ten minutes a large swarm of flies, carried by the light breeze into the chapel, descended upon the cardinals. Cardinal Gauthier and his like-minded group of cardinals didn't know whether to jump up in victory or to cry in exasperation. The fourth biblical plague had appeared on the scene to vindicate Gauthier's argument!

CHAPTER TWENTY-SEVEN

In no time, the Cardinals had elected to table their discussions and to flee the Sistine Chapel. Agreeing to reconvene in the Sistine Chapel the next morning, they rapidly decamped their fly-infested seats and boarded the cleaned buses. Returning to St. Martha's at nearly noontime, they assembled in the dining room to talk over lunch before retiring to their rooms for an afternoon of rest, informal conversations, and prayer.

The cardinals were exceptionally pleased to find that the water was, once again, clear and clean. Despite the holiday, Roman officials had somehow managed to repair the broken water main. Perhaps, their luck was turning, after all. However, St. Martha's had no generators to provide backup electrical power. Unable to cook, the staff was left to serve cold sandwiches and fruits for lunch while nervously watching the refrigerated food begin to spoil.

Food, however, was one of the last things on the minds of the cardinals. With the fourth biblical plague of Egypt materializing, Cardinal Gauthier was the center of their attention. Arguing persuasively, the Canadian cardinal was drawing more and more believers to his side of the argument. Even Cardinal Murphy had to admit to himself that the sequence of catastrophes was statistically too improbable to ignore any more. Murphy and his colleagues found it impossible to dismiss Gauthier's line of reasoning for they were men of faith accustomed to seeing God's will in everyday matters and defenders of the Word fervently believing in the authenticity of the biblical accounts.

Nevertheless, the heat at St. Martha's soon began to take its toll and, at Cardinal Meissner's behest, the cardinal electors withdrew to their rooms. The staff scurried around to each of the rooms with bottled water and all of the remaining ice, but, without air conditioning, St. Martha's continued to swelter in the heat. Not even the open windows alleviated the discomfort because there was hardly any breeze at St. Martha's, snugly tucked in between large buildings on the south side of St. Peter's Basilica.

Giulio, however, was enjoying cool air. He was overjoyed to find electrical power at Cybil's downtown hotel when he arrived there mid-morning. Setting up shop at a desk in the sitting room of Cybil's expansive fifth floor suite, Giulio transmitted the summary report to Harold in New York and uploaded the audio report with the file to Joshua's website. Satisfied at having completed his mission, he ordered breakfast from room service and inspected Cybil's lodging. He happily spotted the wet bar with a refrigerator and microwave as well as a large television in the sitting room. Additionally, the expansive suite included a large bedroom with a king-sized bed and a small balcony. The marble bathroom was not all that large, but Cybil had not crammed makeup and toiletries in every available shelf. He could make it work. 'Well,' he thought, 'if power is not restored anytime soon, I could make myself quite comfortable here.'

Spitini arrived at a downtown café within minutes after Giulio had completed the file transfer. Sitting down with a cup of coffee, Spitini logged onto the website and eagerly read the report. He was both overjoyed and disturbed by what he read. On the one hand, he was thrilled that the College of Cardinals was in clear confusion following Maltempo's breakdown. However, on the other hand, Spitini was anxious over Maltempo and the future direction of the papal election. Maltempo's election would have sealed the Church's fate. Spitini could have retired to Iran as a hero victorious in all of his estimates and actions. His handler and fellow team of terrorist brethren would have to admit to Spitini's genius and render the appropriate honors. They would have to match Spitini's uncanny success by finally redressing their botched attempt at Tara's life.

Well, regardless of Maltempo's maddening declination of the papacy, Spitini felt sure that the Church was tottering on the edge of a deep, dark abyss. With firsthand knowledge of the environmentalists' morning assault on the buses and his brethren's successful strikes against the two power facilities on the heels of a disastrous second day of the conclave, the College of Cardinals would be in disarray. And publicly disgraced as well. Surfing the internet, Spitini gleefully discovered countless photos of the slimed buses and gnat-covered cardinals. Pictures of the bomb attacks would surely be posted soon, too. In fact, that story would likely be the evening headline in Rome.

Thinking through the various sequels to Maltempo's failed election in his usual cold, scrupulous method, Spitini deduced that the inwardly-focused conservatives still held a majority of votes. They would likely still carry the day, perhaps, winning new converts to their side after the disgraceful collapse of internal security and orderly calm of the conclave. Now, more than ever, the conservatives could drive their point home that more attention was needed on internal matters. They would argue that they had had enough of the ecumenical programs draining their coffers and valuable Church attention. It was time to return to patching up the very foundation of the Church. However, Spitini was anxious about the conservatives finding another candidate who could draw two thirds of the vote as easily as Maltempo. If the conclave's deliberations lengthened to a week, the conservatives might have to settle for a compromise candidate. Especially in the blistering heat for no one would wish to prolong the conclave under those conditions. Then again, the thought occurred to Spitini that, perhaps, a compromise candidate would prove even better for the Islamic cause. A compromise candidate would probably be an Italian to appease the conservatives and he would probably be hamstrung while caught in the middle of both powerful factions.

Concluding his analysis of the conclave, Spitini returned to the work at hand. He dashed off a short cryptic note to his Iranian handler, the professor, with a short analysis of the conclave and congratulations on the successful attacks. Spitini then surfed the internet again and exited the café for a slow walk in the hot sun and, eventually, a return to the Vatican. Unnoticed by Spitini, a middle-aged Italian man, observing him from a restaurant table across the street, laid money under the coffee cup on the table and rose to follow Spitini.

"These pictures are tremendous!" Cybil exclaimed and hugged Francisco. "Absolutely fantastic! Harold will flip when he sees these!"

Francisco grinned and shrugged his shoulders as if to say, 'Ah it's nothing much. Just another day at the office.'

With the fire extinguished at the Vatican's transformer station, Cybil was ready to move on. "Let's grab some coffee somewhere nearby and you can tell me all about the morning. It will make fantastic copy; but, I don't have much time because I've really got to hustle if we want your photos and the story in tomorrow morning's edition back in New York." With that,

Cybil and Francisco left the helipad and began the short, hot walk across the far western end of the walled compound toward St. Peter's Basilica.

Upon reaching a café and ordering coffee and pastries, Cybil furiously scribbled on her notepad while Francisco recounted the morning's bus ambush, attack of the gnats, and fire. Her pulse raced with excitement. Coupled with her inside knowledge of Maltempo's collapse, Cybil was piecing a truly sensationalistic story together in her mind. Visions of rising to her peers' applause upon being named a Pulitzer Prize winner, once again, danced in her head.

By noon, Cybil had joined Giulio in her hotel suite to hammer out the story for tomorrow's morning edition. An hour later, she called Harold to alert him to her email. "Harold, you won't believe the photos that Francisco took! He's incredible! Magnifico!" She smiled at Giulio and blew him a kiss. "Take a look at the story I just sent to you. I dare you to tell me that I won't win a Pulitzer for investigative reporting this year! Ciao, baby!"

She hung up and with a large grin jumped onto Giulio's lap and began kissing him all over his face. Sliding down his lap onto the floor, she grabbed his belt and jokingly said, "Well, I'll be! Look here at this belt buckle. It says that 'If you're this close to read the buckle, please undo me.' Guess I've gotta be the bad girl!" With that, she handily opened the buckle and then Giulio's pants. Within a minute, Cybil was merrily perched atop her workhorse of a man for the remainder of the afternoon.

"Wilhelm, can you give me a lift to the bomb site? I would like to see it for myself," TJ inquired.

"Yes, of course," he replied. Weissberg was standing at the sergeant's desk drinking cold bottled water. He was drenched in sweat and continually wiped the sweat from his face with a towel. "It was hot enough without the fire. What a day!" After taking another big gulp of water, Weissberg continued, "The police bomb squad is out there now so you can ask them about it. Come on, let's go!" Turning to Sergeant Weil, Weissberg commanded, "See if you can get more information on the other explosion at the power station!"

Weissberg and TJ strode down the hall and out to Weissberg's white Fiat. Walking around to the driver's door, Weissberg said, "Hop in, it's open!"

As they were driving up the hill behind St. Peter's Basilica, TJ remarked, "Wilhelm, I don't like this. I'm afraid the Vatican is under attack."

She looked over at him to see him nod. "I wouldn't be surprised if the bombers were also behind the morning ambush of the buses. The pilots that the police apprehended won't know anything, but it's entirely possible that someone secretly funded and planned that escapade to coincide with the bombs later in the morning."

Weissberg pulled the car over and stopped the engine. They had reached the safety cordon around the helipad. Still wiping the sweat from his eyes, he asked, "What do you recommend?"

TJ stared out of the window at the police bomb squad rummaging through the burnt debris. "Let me bring in a few experts. I have some ideas about augmenting your capabilities in the short term. If we are dealing with a terrorist group and if it is connected to radical Islam, we are dealing with a very, very serious matter."

"I've increased the security at the Vatican and I have recommended that the museums and shops remain closed for a couple of days. But, my force of Swiss Guards is small. The Italian police are, thankfully, reinforcing us; but, the Vatican will be watching the expenditures closely. I don't have much room to maneuver."

"Don't worry about it. The guys I want to bring here operate on a different source of funding. You'll never get a bill and, if they nab the bad guys, you get the credit. Nobody will know that they're here."

"Sounds good. How soon can they get here?"

"If all goes well, within twenty-four hours; give or take depending upon the red tape." She then looked over at Wilhelm and calmly stated, "You know, if the bus ambush and this bomb attack was coordinated, we may be dealing with an insider." She let that sink in before continuing, "I've learned from years of experience to dismiss coincidence. In matters of perfect timing, more often than not, someone got a hold of the timetable. We may have an internal problem."

Weissberg stammered, "At the Vatican?"

"I'm only saying we may have a problem. This is one of the last places where you might expect traitorous behavior, but it happens all of the time. Just ask the CIA. Anyway, I'll look into it very discreetly and, in the meantime, we'll keep our eyes on Monsignor Spitini." With Weissberg sitting dumbfounded in the car, TJ opened her door, stuck her cane out, and limped over to the bomb squad.

The ringing phone woke Cybil out of a deep sleep. Confused and still half asleep, Cybil thrashed around in bed looking for the source of the disturbing noise without success. The ringing stopped and Cybil threw herself back onto her pillow for more sleep. Unfortunately, the phone began to ring again. Now more awake, Cybil recognized her phone and instinctively groped for it on her bedside table. Realizing that she was on the other side of the bed, she stretched over Giulio's bare chest to reach the phone in time. "Yeah, hello." Cybil mumbled into the receiver. "Who is it?"

"Oh, hi Harold. No, no. Everything is fine. You caught me napping before another long night of work." She was now sitting in bed and rubbing her eyes. Giulio had awakened, too, and was softly caressing her bare back.

"What's that? You like the story and the photos? Terrific!"

"Look, remember mums the word on Maltempo. We can't share anything from the hidden recorder. But, I'm going to pay a visit to the hospital to snoop around and we've got the inside scoop once the conclave ends. Okay?"

"Yeah, everything is going well. Giulio and Francisco are super and I can't complain about the hotel. Tell your secretary, Ginger, that I'll bring her back something for taking care of me."

"Yup, talk to ya' later, Harold. Ciao for now!"

Cybil flipped her phone closed and squinted at the alarm clock. Six o'clock. A couple more hours before she had to get up for dinner and work. Putting the phone on the near bedside table, Cybil turned over to snuggle in Giulio's arms and quickly fell asleep.

The cardinals appeared back in the dining room around seven in the evening. They were disappointed to find a selection of fruits, cheeses, and breads for dinner in place of the roast beef listed on the weekly menu. Gauthier, on the other hand, grew more animated at finding that the dinner meat had spoiled in the powerless freezer.

"It's the fifth plague! Okay, I admit that there is no pestilence killing breathing, walking livestock, but the spoiled meat has the same effect. The livestock is ruined and we can't eat it!"

Murphy happened to be standing by Gauthier's side. "Look, Richard, I think you've gone too far this time. Your earlier arguments are far more convincing, but ruined meat in the freezer is hardly a deadly pestilence wiping out a nation's livestock. Come on, let's relax and eat."

Gauthier was offended by Murphy's casual remarks. "May God help us all!" Gauthier responded and continued unabated with his examination of the spoiled beef. But, most of the other cardinals wouldn't have much of his arguments either. Several didn't even come down for dinner, electing instead to pray and fast in their rooms. It was a hot, quiet evening at St. Martha's Residence.

Cardinal Murphy was mentally and physically exhausted by the time he reached his suite. He quickly prepared for bed and managed to find enough energy to pray before falling onto the mattress. It wasn't long before he was asleep.

In the very early hours of the morning, Cardinal Murphy began to dream. It resembled Narciso Maltempo's last dream aboard the fishing boat. Only Murphy was at the rudder in his dream with a crew manned by the three Italians Maltempo, Fassino, and Biaggio. There was also a stranger with his back to Murphy.

As the boat neared the shore, the crew recognized Jesus and excitedly called to him. Jesus acknowledged their greetings by waving to them. He then called and pointed to the stranger in the bow of the boat. The stranger was astonished to hear Jesus calling him. Replying, he stammered, "Me? Are you really pointing at me? Surely, you wish one of these learned men to follow you. I am just a plain fisherman." The three Italian cardinals were stunned that Jesus did not call them and began to talk among themselves.

Pointing, again, at the stranger, Jesus firmly declared, "I need you to come with me. You will be the rock upon which my Church is rebuilt."

"Me? Are you sure? Don't you want Maltempo?" the stranger questioned.

"I asked Maltempo to stay with the boat, but he didn't listen. Ernesto, I want you to come ashore and walk with me. I will make you a fisher of men," Jesus declared.

"Ernie, is that you?" Cardinal Murphy shouted.

The stranger turned around. His good friend, Ernie, looked him in the eye and replied, "Sean! I didn't realize that was you at the rudder."

At this last line, Cardinal Murphy awoke with a start five minutes before his alarm was to ring at seven o'clock. He was wide awake. And terrified. Now what?

CHAPTER TWENTY-EIGHT

Cardinal Murphy was the last cardinal to board the bus. With a pit seemingly the size of a grapefruit in his stomach, he had elected to skip breakfast and had come downstairs only at the last moment. Although this day would be one of the most memorable in his life, he was dreading it for there was a very good chance that his reputation would be in tatters before the day was over.

Utterly focused on the dilemma of his dream, he was caught by surprise at the sight that welcomed him on the bus. Approximately one out of every four cardinals had a nasty heat rash on his face. Boils! They had boils! Over the previous afternoon and night the extreme heat had, indeed, been blistering.

Cardinal Murphy could not help but feel that Cardinal Gauthier had won new believers. He, too, was becoming a believer. It was just possible that, perhaps, some variation of the biblical plagues had, in fact, struck the College of Cardinals as foretold by Cardinal Maria. If that was true, then God was miraculously intervening in the conclave. Recalling the words of Roger Maria and Narciso Maltempo, Murphy realized that, if this was the case, God was calling on the cardinal electors to sidestep one of their own for an outsider. His dream no longer seemed so outlandish, but would the cardinals believe him? Could he himself dare to believe it?

If there were any lingering doubts among any of the cardinals regarding Gauthier's analysis of the past events, they were swept away by the storm that hit after they disembarked from the buses. With the Swiss Guards closing the doors of the Sistine Chapel, the first rain in three weeks began to fall on Rome. Within moments, it was pouring and flashes of lightning lit the morning sky. Within minutes, hail the size of golf balls pelted the Vatican. The seventh biblical plague had materialized!

The cardinals sat still in horror listening to the hail rocketing off of the roof and to the crack of thunder overhead. Gauthier no longer had to preach for everyone was now a believer. Recalling Roger Maria's words sent chills through them. There was no doubt that God was directly warning them. Yet, if not Maltempo as pope, then who? How were they to identify the pontiff God had chosen?

The hail was damaging cars and trees. The wind tore through the narrow roads of the Vatican, driving wave after wave of soaking rain along the cobblestones. It was, therefore, not a surprise to have hail break one of the windows in the Sistine Chapel. The small falling glass shards rattling onto the chapel's floor were immediately followed by a thin streak of lightning that pierced the narrow opening in the glass pane to strike the metal hinge housing Giulio's listening device. That single bolt of lightning was powerful enough to destroy the electronic circuits without any chance of future repair.

With the help of the Swiss Guards, Monsignor Terrazza located plastic sheeting and, climbing atop a tall ladder he installed a makeshift patch over the broken glass. Watching from below, the cardinals remained silent in what seemed a surreal situation.

With the storm seeming to subside, Cardinal Gauthier stood and began to speak. He spoke eloquently and calmly about the mishaps that had befallen the College of Cardinals. Yes, the first seven plagues that struck Pharaoh had now found them. The probability of any other explanation was absurd. As men of faith and biblical understanding, Cardinal Gauthier convincingly argued that the College of Cardinals must admit that a miracle was unfolding around them. God had chosen to intervene in the conclave, not through the Holy Spirit, but personally. They, therefore, were obliged as God's faithful servants to yield or risk the pains of the remaining plagues.

Upon sitting down, the conclave's order disintegrated. Although the cardinals now agreed with Gauthier, they remained at a loss about how to proceed. How were they to identify the future pontiff? Were they doomed to suffer the next plague, one by one, until they got it right? How would God reveal his choice to them? It seemed all so impossible and they were rightly frustrated and at a loss.

That is when Cardinal Murphy assembled his courage, made up his mind, and stood to address the College of Cardinals. Unfortunately, he tried in vain to be heard. Then, walking up the middle of the seated cardinals and shouting near the top of his lungs while waving his arms above his head, Cardinal Murphy finally won his colleagues' attention.

"My fellow cardinals, I believe I know who God has chosen. I believe that the person was also revealed to Cardinal Maltempo and that that is why he declared that the papacy was not his but meant for another."

At this pronouncement, the College of Cardinals was silenced. Everyone was intently watching him and listening for his next words.

"Roger Maria was visited by an angel. He had dreams. For that matter, many of us have had troubling, vivid dreams over the last week or two. You are well aware of that. Only, we remained mystified by the dreams. No one could rationally explain the dreams. Is that not so?"

Looking around pleadingly at the cardinals, Murphy continued to gather his courage while his knees felt like they were going to buckle at any moment.

"I had a dream last night. I believe that God revealed his choice to me."

Murphy took a deep breath. And then another. His pulse was racing and he could barely believe what he was about to say.

"God revealed his choice to me because I am probably the only one among you who knows the outsider. I can hardly believe it myself."

Several cardinals spoke up to question his assertions. "Who is it? How do you know that God revealed his choice to you? What if it's just a dream? Shouldn't we wait for Maltempo to regain his consciousness in order to corroborate your dream?"

These cardinals had struck upon the very heart of Murphy's doubts. He had been struggling with the very answers to these questions ever since awakening after the dream. Now, standing before his peers on questionable grounds, he was no longer at a loss for an answer. It struck him almost out of the blue. It was the only possible answer.

His dream had to be corroborated by others. If he and Maltempo had both seen Ernie in their dreams, perhaps, others had, too. Praying fervently that his gut feeling was a good one, Murphy began to recount his dream aboard the fishing boat. But, he deliberately neglected to identify the stranger called by Jesus. Instead, Cardinal Murphy asked, "Has anyone else here had a similar dream?"

There was complete silence in the chapel. Only the creaking of chairs and rustling of clothes and papers as cardinals turned and shifted to look around. With his knees seeming to shake and his head growing dizzy, Murphy looked about in hope; but, no hands shot up. No one spoke up. 'Well, so much for that,' he thought to himself and took a step forward to return in shame to his chair.

At that instant, Cardinal Pellitteri stood and declared that he had had the identical dream. Then Cardinal Juarez of Spain. Then Cardinal Kamolvisit of Thailand. Even Cardinal Meissner. Others rose one by one until ten cardinals were standing.

Regaining his composure and staying on the dais, Cardinal Murphy next declared, "If these ten cardinals, indeed, had the same dream as myself, they likely saw the same stranger aboard their fishing boats. Now, as far as I know, none of us have shared this dream with each other. Is that correct?"

The ten standing cardinals all nodded affirmatively.

""Then I propose that we each take a sheet of paper and privately write a description of the stranger in our dreams. If the descriptions are comparable to the College's satisfaction, I will identify the stranger who is a personal friend of mine, a man raised as a Catholic, an ordained minister, and a stalwart Christian of the finest mold. We can then call him to the Holy See and determine if he is the stranger in our dreams and if we believe that he is God's choice to lead our Church."

No one disagreed and a few even shouted their concurrences.

"Very well then." Picking up a piece of paper and a pen from the desk set reserved for the scrutineers, Murphy began writing while continuing to talk.

"Here are the key descriptive elements for the eleven of us to describe. Approximate age, height, and weight. Race. The color of his hair and eyes. Any distinguishing features, such as tattoos, missing limbs or fingers, or birthmark. Clothing. And, lastly, whether you heard Jesus call his name." Murphy read the list of elements a second time to ensure that the other ten had the complete list.

"While we write, I would ask that Monsignor Terrazza draw three other names to select scrutineers for scrutinizing our eleven descriptions."

Monsignor Terrazza was flabbergasted, but complied. Within three minutes, three cardinals had mustered atop the dais as scrutineers. With the other nine cardinals now busily writing, Cardinal Murphy turned to Cardinal Meissner with a request before both of these men began to write their descriptions. "Can you ask Monsignor Terrazza to print a photograph from the internet? If we agree on their descriptions of the stranger in their dreams, I would like to show you and all of them a photograph of the man I recognized in my dream to see if it is the same man you saw."

Meissner nodded affirmatively and called Terrazza over.

"Monsignor Terrazza, would you, please, pull a photograph off of the internet?" Handing a slip of paper to the monsignor, Cardinal Murphy continued, "Go to the website on this paper and find a photograph of the professor whose name I have also written down."

Monsignor Terrazza exited the chapel and returned ten minutes later with a photograph in a file folder that he handed to Cardinal Murphy.

Monsignor Terrazza then gathered the sheets of paper as each cardinal completed his assignment and handed them to the scrutineers. With all eyes keenly watching them and Murphy's heart pounding, the scrutineers carefully studied the descriptions. After what seemed like an eternity, the scrutineers looked up. The one in the middle, Cardinal Moratinos, spoke for them all in saying, "We have found uncommon similarities in all of the descriptions. However, it is not for the three of us to make this decision. It is for the College of Cardinals. We will, therefore, now read each description in its entirety."

The three scrutineers took turns reading each description aloud. With minor variations or occasional omissions, the eleven cardinals had, in fact, closely agreed in describing an older man in his fifties or early sixties, of medium height and weight. A muscular man with broad shoulders. Light skin of a Caucasian. All agreed on dark or black hair. A full head of hair, in fact. Nine remembered seeing blue eyes while two remembered green eyes. No one recollected any distinguishing features such as scars or tattoos. The stranger was wearing a brown robe and leather sandals in all eleven dreams. Eight remembered the name as Ernesto, but one thought it was Eduardo and another Earnest. The eleventh cardinal could not remember a name.

Cardinal Meissner spoke up and instructed Cardinal Murphy and the other nine cardinals to approach the raised platform. Once all eleven men had assembled, Murphy showed them the photograph of Professor Ernesto Flanagan. They were astounded and quickly agreed that the man in the photo, in fact, looked amazingly like the stranger in their dreams.

The College of Cardinals was awestruck. Eleven of their own had sworn that they had had identical dreams. Moreover, they had independently more or less identified the single stranger whom Jesus called to the shore. Struggling to understand the significance of this, the cardinals were each asking themselves the same questions: "Could this stranger truly be destined to lead the Catholic Church? Could this really be happening? Is God actually intervening so very directly and forcefully? Picking up on the religious significance of the number twelve, was Maltempo the twelfth cardinal with the identical dream? Why a stranger as pope and not one of them? Could they truly accept all of this as a matter of faith? And, lastly, just, who was this stranger in the eleven dreams?"

Cardinal Murphy sensed it was time to answer that last question now that his dream had been matched by at least ten other cardinals. "The stranger you seek is …." Murphy stopped to correct himself. "The man that God has by all appearances called to lead the Catholic Church is Ernesto Flanagan. He was baptized and confirmed in the Catholic Church so he meets the qualifications for elevation to the papacy. He is, additionally, an ordained minister with a doctor of divinity degree who is living in New York State, not far from my residence."

Murphy stopped for a moment because his next few words would be hard for the cardinals to accept. Bracing himself, he continued, "However, there are some irregularities that I must make you aware of. Although still technically a catholic, Ernesto is a protestant minister teaching at a non-denominational Christian college."

The shock reverberated among the assembled cardinals.

Moratinos spoke for all of them when he uncontrollably exclaimed, "A protestant minister? Protestant?! Don't tell me that he is a Freemason, too!"

Murphy kept going in order to prevent the conclave from disintegrating into chaos. "Ernesto is one of the finest Christians I have ever known. I have known him for my entire life and I can personally vouch for his character and Christian credentials. However, my appraisal is irrelevant for we have all agreed that God has likely chosen Ernesto. Only God's appraisal counts. We have no right to limit God's selection with rules of our own human making. The bottom line is that we must call Ernesto to Rome and thoughtfully, even prayerfully, consider him. Each cardinal who has seen him in a dream should also verify that Ernesto is, indeed, the stranger called to the shore by Jesus. Thereafter, each of us is free to follow matters of faith in casting our ballot. May we trust in God sufficiently to do His Will."

Cardinal Meissner stepped forward and announced, "Brothers, we all recognize this as a difficult and uncertain task. We find ourselves facing great uncertainty with little definite information to guide us other than our faith. We know through the Word that God has talked to mankind through dreams and visions from the earliest of all times. We know that St. Paul, who was martyred here in Rome, came to know Jesus Christ through a

miraculous vision while traveling to Syria. Jesus called Paul as an apostle in a most dramatic and personal manner. Yet, we are practical men who have lived and worked in this world where observable facts, physical laws, and rules too often dictate our actions. We are, perhaps, too used to smaller, insignificant events lacking the great drama of Paul's vision. We are men of faith who are led by the Holy Spirit, yet we feel uncomfortable at the thought of God visibly and personally intervening in our lives in so dramatic a fashion. My fellow cardinals, we are witnessing a miracle of great dramatic significance. By definition, this miracle defies the world's laws of physics and bounded rationality. God is shouting at us and we should do well to listen for God is all powerful and, therefore, free to do as he wills. If He wishes to intervene, He will howsoever He chooses. We cannot box Him in for to limit Him is to limit his power. I am confident that we are on the right path although the light is dim and our steps unsure. Nevertheless, in due time, God will light the path ahead when He so chooses. Let us unite in faith over this miracle set before us by our Lord, the Holy Spirit, and our Savior Jesus Christ to do His Will."

Meissner's speech had a profound sobering impact on the assembled cardinals. Although racked with misgivings, they could not argue with Meissner's line of reasoning.

Meissner concluded by saying, "Therefore, I recommend that we unanimously agree to send Monsignor Terrazza and the commander of our Swiss Guards aboard the pontiff's private airplane to invite Ernesto Flanagan to the Vatican. Once he is here, we may question him in order to determine his character and fitness for leading the Holy See. In the meantime, we should remain cloistered in prayer and open our hearts and our minds to God and the Holy Spirit."

Cardinal Murphy quickly added, "I should also like to send one of my assistants here in Rome, Monsignor Campbell, with Monsignor Terrazza to serve as an escort and guide in New

York. Also, Cardinal Meissner, I would like to have special permission to call Dr. Flanagan to invite him to the Vatican and to alert him to Monsignor Terrazza's arrival. None of us should rightly expect Ernesto to accept our invitation to Rome on such short notice; however, a call from me, as his friend, will likely prove persuasive. Of course, I will not explain the reason for our request nor should Monsignor Terrazza have to bear the burden of justifying our invitation to Dr. Flanagan. Furthermore, I would not inform Monsignor Campbell nor Colonel Weissberg of our reasons for summoning Dr. Flanagan. Once Ernesto arrives here, we should collectively inform Ernesto while seated in this chapel of our reasons for calling him to the Holy See. Does this meet with your approval?"

Without seeing any dissent, Cardinal Meissner asked Monsignor Terrazza to request Colonel Weissberg's attendance and to alert the aircrew to begin travel preparations.

Fifteen minutes later, Colonel Weissberg entered the conclave. Another five minutes thereafter, he left with a mission, but also with many questions.

TJ smiled at Wilhelm as he returned from the Sistine Chapel. "So, what gives? I heard that your presence was required at the conclave," TJ asked thinking that the cardinals had wanted a security update.

"I don't know what to make of it, TJ," Weissberg replied quizzically with a shrug of his shoulders. "They're sending me to New York City to pick up a guest and bring him to Rome."

"New York?!" TJ exclaimed.

"We're flying in a couple of hours. On one of the papal airplanes, no less." Weissberg looked to his left at one of his sergeants, "Sergeant Hoffman, can you please locate Major Steinman and ask him to come see me immediately?"

Then turning back to TJ, "Major Steinman, as my deputy, will be in charge until my return. But, if you need me for some emergency, you can reach me on the plane through the communications system. I think my cellular phone might work in New York, too."

He looked at her thoughtfully and then asked, "TJ, the cardinals want a thorough background check on the fellow I'm picking up in New York. Can you run an 'Ernesto Flanagan' of New York through your system? He's an American."

"Of course. Is there anything special I should be looking for?" TJ asked.

"Not that I know of. He's supposedly not a criminal. Cardinal Murphy of New York told me that Flanagan is a longtime personal friend of his. Flanagan is in his fifties, holds a doctorate in divinity, and teaches at Nyack College a few miles north of the city. He's a former vice president or something similar from Northeastern University in Boston and is widely published and known in Christian circles. That's about all I know of him. But, the cardinals want a complete background check. Criminal record, traffic fines, drug problems, love affairs, financial position, organizational memberships, psychological and medical health, family, friends, relatives, and so forth. And they want it pronto. Multo pronto, in fact!"

"Well, I'll try, but they're asking for a bit much!"

"Give it your best shot. Hire a private detective in New York if you need to. Cardinal Murphy said that money is not a concern."

"Heck, if that's the case, I'll fly first-class to New York and take care of it myself from a huge suite at the Waldorf!" TJ winked at Weissberg and they both laughed. It felt good to laugh again. Why did life have to be so complicated?

"Francisco? Good. You've heard about the bomb at the power station outside of Rome? Yes?"

"Can you get out there to take some photos?"

"Excellent. When you have them, just email them to me. I'm staying put at the hotel today to write. I think I can spin a tale of terrorism and conspiracy that will make Harold salivate, but I need a good shot of that power station. Say, while you're out there, can you snoop around and see if any of the police are talking about it?"

"Great! Ciao, Francisco!"

Cybil flipped the phone shut and looked at Giulio. He was relaxing with a cup of coffee and the daily *L'Osservatore Romano* – *The Roman Observer* – which is the quasi-official Vatican newspaper. He could afford the break for they had already completed and forwarded the audio file and its associated summary report.

Cybil was delighted to hear that the illicit recording of the conclave's third day continued to portray a College of Cardinals in downright confusion after Maltempo's breakdown. The cardinals' concerns over the biblical plagues were proving to be very interesting for it was giving Cybil a brilliant idea for an article. She had already dreamt up possible headlines: 'God Strikes the Vatican.' Or 'Cardinals Test God's Will.' Or, her favorite, "God Be-Devils Cardinals.'

Cybil had found an on-line Bible to research the ancient plagues suffered by Pharaoh at the hands of God's servant, Moses. Remarkably, it was the first time since her teenage parochial school days that Cybil had read scripture. The story of the plagues made for good reading, but Cybil readily dismissed it as another fairy tale with little modern day relevance to the coincidental events unfolding at the Vatican. Indeed, the cardinals' fascination with the plagues was just more evidence to support her belief that religious men were Neanderthals. However, it would make a great story in New York where it would catch the eye of the city's Jewish and Christian communities. Sales at the deli shops and supermarkets could be brisk.

With a little bit of artistic imagination and Francisco's photos of the frog-smeared buses and the gnat-covered Cardinal, Cybil was sure that she could craft a whale of a story for the front page of her paper regardless of whether the livestock pestilence or locusts materialized.

Walking out onto the balcony, she watched the rain. Earlier it had been pouring in a deafening thunder storm, but now the rain was a calm summer shower muffling the traffic noise below. Cybil realized that this was the first time that it had rained in Rome during her two weeks abroad. The temperature was much cooler, too. All in all, it was a rainy, sleepy morning. Plus, Cybil was homesick.

Giulio came up behind her and put his arms around her. He gave her a kiss on her neck and held her. Cybil relaxed in his embrace and, continuing to watch the summer shower, she wondered if Giulio might consider moving to New York.

CHAPTER TWENTY-NINE

With a few cardinals nervously looking for devouring locusts, the College of Cardinals boarded the buses around noon after agreeing to suspend the conclave for the day. Returning to St. Martha's in the light rain and cooler air, the cardinals were eagerly looking forward to some needed rest and time for reflection. The cardinal electors had collectively embarked on a course that none of them had ever envisioned.

Upon entering St. Martha's, Cardinal Meissner reassuringly put his right hand on Murphy's shoulder. "Thank you for speaking up this morning, Sean. In reflecting on it during our bus ride, I realized just how much you must have been wrestling with your competing elements of faith and logical, common sense. I know how much you risked in speaking. Thank you."

Murphy couldn't help but hug Meissner. "Thank you. That means a lot to me. Thank you."

Then, they both strode over to the head of the Residence's staff to request use of her phone. Murphy first alerted Monsignor

Campbell to prepare for a round trip flight to New York and then placed a long distance call to Nyack, New York.

Ernie was, once again, in his kitchen when Sean Murphy's call came in. Putting down his coffee and dog leash after his morning jaunt with Gabriel, Ernie took the call.

"Hello! This is Ernie," he cheerfully spoke into the receiver.

"Sean! What a surprise? I didn't think that you could call me until you elected a new pope? Or is the American news behind the times?"

"No pope? Well, I hope that you don't get into trouble calling me. Is everything alright?"

"It is? That's good. So what's up?"

"You want me to come to Rome? You're kidding, right?"

Ernie sat down, now completely perplexed. "Sean, why do you need me at the Vatican? You're joking around, right?"

Ernie listened to his friend Sean for the next five minutes unable to bring himself to interrupt. Then he asked, "For how long do you need me there?"

"You don't know?! Sean, you know that this sounds nuts, right?"

It took another ten minutes of cajoling and personal assurances for Sean Murphy to convince Ernie to come to Rome aboard the pontiff's airplane.

"Sean, I don't know what to make of this. It will be hard to just up and leave, but if it's that important to you I will do my best. Look, when did you say the plane was leaving Rome?"

"In two hours? Well, they'll land about seven or eight hours later, and then they've got an hour or two, depending on traffic, to reach Nyack. That would put your guys here around five o'clock in the evening. With any luck, we could all be back on the plane by eight and in Rome the following morning."

"Say, what are the names of the gents you are sending?"

He picked up a pen and post-it notes. "Terrazza, Campbell, and Weissberg. Okay, I am writing their names down. Say, what number can I reach you at in the meantime? Okay, I got it."

"Alright then, my friend. I'll see about packing. I do look forward to seeing you, but this is one of the wackiest things I've ever heard of. I sure hope you know what you are doing!"

"Right. Okay. See you tomorrow. Bye for now."

Ernie hung up. He had lost his appetite for breakfast. What in the world did Sean have in mind? Why couldn't Sean tell him what was going on? How long would he be in Rome? This was just plain crazy!

And then, more practical matters came to mind. Who would take care of his dog, Gabriel? Were his neighbors at home to ask about collecting his mail and newspapers? What about his appointments?

CHAPTER THIRTY

Ernie noted with satisfaction that he had accomplished more by noontime than most people do all day. Good friends of his, just down the street, would take Gabriel in. Manny Durso said he'd look after the house and his son would take care of collecting the newspapers and mail each day after school. Ernie's secretary at Nyack College had rescheduled or cancelled his appointments for a week. A half hour at the computer was all he needed to read and reply to his emails. The thermostat was reset to minimize the air conditioning and a number of lights now had timers controlling their lighting cycles. A load of underwear and socks was in the dryer and the water faucets to the clothes washer were turned off. Ernie had even taken advantage of the cool morning to mow his yard.

His three children weren't sure what to make of his sudden trip to Rome, but he had promised Sean not to divulge the true reason for traveling to anyone, to include his children. He refused to lie, so Ernie simply informed them that an important consulting opportunity had come up, but that he had agreed to a non-disclosure clause prohibiting him from discussing it. All three wished him well and promptly gave him ideas for things to bring back for them. 'Kids will be kids,' he thought to himself, 'no matter how old or young they are.'

Now standing in his kitchen, Ernie was mentally reviewing his list of tasks to ensure that he did not forget any. A few came to mind, notably packing, but Ernie decided that lunch had to come first. His appetite had returned in the flurry of activity; but, he needed a rest. And a cold beer. He wasn't interested in leftovers nor in slapping a sandwich together, so he picked up the phone and called Rudy's Pizzaria to order a small three-cheese and chicken pizza with corn meal crust and all-natural ingredients.

While waiting for the delivery, Ernie first loaded his dishwasher and put away the pots and pans drying in the rack atop his kitchen counter and then began to tidy up the living room for his guests. Fortunately, he didn't use that room much, so a bit of dusting and a quick run through with the vacuum to pick up Gabriel's hairs just about did it.

Giving up on the timely delivery of his pizza after forty minutes, Ernie finally grabbed that Sam Adams from his fridge, but no sooner had he plunked himself into his kitchen chair than the doorbell rang to announce his pizza. Returning to his chair minutes later, he set the pizza box down onto his table and, then laughingly, exclaimed out loud, "An ad for three NASCAR drivers on the top of the box and Rudy's still can't drive the pizza to me on time! Go figure!"

The pizza didn't stand a chance. Nor did the beer. Over lunch, Ernie had given up trying to deduce what Sean's motives were for calling him and sending the papal airplane to pick him up. He simply could not find a suitable explanation so his mind returned to his travel preparations. Settling on assembling some books and papers to work on in preparation for his fall courses, Ernie threw the empty pizza box in the trash, dropped the beer bottle in the recycling bin, and walked down the hall toward his study.

Ernie picked up his laptop case and began eyeing his desk while running his right hand through his thick, dark brown hair. It looked very 'professorial,' that is, it was cluttered. Yet, Ernie swore he knew where everything was and, more than once, defended himself by asking, 'If a cluttered desk is a sign of a cluttered mind, then what is an empty desk a sign of?'

The doorbell rang as Ernie was stuffing the laptop into its case. He wasn't expecting anyone, but, it was about time for the mailman to make his daily stop. Maybe he had a package for Ernie. Walking expectantly to the door, Ernie swung it wide open without first checking who might be on the other side. Perhaps, he should have.

A reporter and photographer were waiting in ambush for Ernie. No sooner had Ernie opened the door than he was blinded by the rapid bright camera flashes and rapid-fire questioning from the reporter.

"Dr. Flanagan! Sheila Butts of the New York Daily News! Is it true that you are going to the Vatican? Why is the Holy See sending the pope's airplane to New York? How come a professor from Nyack College gets a ride on the pope's airplane? Just who will you see in Rome? Can we get your comments?"

Ernie immediately stepped back into the safety of his hallway, but Sheila simply responded with two steps forward. The camera man, a whole half foot taller than the diminutive reporter, hovered over her right shoulder while continuing to photograph Ernie.

Ernie finally came to his senses when he saw two strangers crowding into his home. "Stop! Get out! Just who do you think you are?" Ernie bellowed at them while sternly pointing towards the front of his house. "I will call the police if you do not leave my property! Now, get out!"

He grasped Sheila's right arm and firmly, but not violently, turned her towards the open doorway while putting his right hand up in front of the camera lens. Gabriel suddenly appeared in the hallway to lend his support by barking loudly. "I don't know why you're here, but there's nothing to see and nothing to say."

At the sight of Gabriel, Sheila offered no resistance and the photographer was backing up quickly; however, Sheila continued with her verbal barrage. "Dr. Flanagan! Dr. Flanagan! Please, let's be civil. My editor is willing to pay you for an interview!"

Ernie had reached the porch at this point. "Pay me? For what?"

"You tell me!" Sheila quickly shot back.

"Look, lady! I don't have time for this. Get off my property or I'll call the police!" Gabriel was now barking from the door and Ernie was reaching for the cell phone on his belt, but Sheila and her companion obligingly retreated towards the sidewalk.

Ernie watched with some satisfaction, but he was baffled at finding the New York Daily News on his doorstep. He was amazed that the tabloid knew of his trip. How did they know?

Sheila and her photographer apparently were planning on camping out on the sidewalk. Sheila slid her van's side door open and reached into a cooler for a soda can while her camera man began changing out his camera's picture card. Ernie watched with great annoyance and then went inside to call Sean. His guests, now somewhere over the Atlantic, should know about the welcoming party.

He dialed the number that Sean had left, waited, and then in perfect Italian asked the lady for Sean Cardinal Murphy of New York.

"Sean, look, I don't know what's going on, but I thought you and the folks on the plane bound for JFK should know that there is a welcoming party from the press waiting in my front yard. The New York Daily News. Any idea how they got involved?"

Ernie listened to Sean and replied, "A reporter, named Sheila Butts, and her sidekick companion with a camera."

"Yes, thanks. I'm about ready. I just need to pack. Are you sure you can't tell me what this is all about?"

Ernie frowned. "Okay, well I guess I'll see you tomorrow. Take care." Looking out a front window, Ernie saw that Sheila was still out there. But, she now had company. A van with Fox News markings had just pulled up behind Sheila's van.

CHAPTER THIRTY-ONE

"Hiya' Harold! So, did Sheila have any luck with this Flanagan guy? Did he crack under pressure and let it slip why he's coming to Rome?"

"No? Well, it figures. And she probably won't get any more from Weissberg and the priests when they arrive in Nyack. Once again, it's all up to me to find out what's going on. We'll be downloading the recording for day number four in a few hours so I might find out. Otherwise, I could try asking this Joshua person for help."

Cybil paused to listen to Harold relaying Sheila's description of Flanagan. When Harold finished, Cybil remarked, "He sounds like a regular joe to me even if the pope's plane is on its way to fetch him."

"What did you say? Oh. Okay. Hey Harold! In the meantime, can you have somebody in New York do a background look-see on Flanagan for me?"

"Okay, thanks. Give Sheila my regards. Ciao!"

Cybil hung up the phone and turned her attention to Giulio. "Well, Giulio, we've got nothing on Flanagan, yet."

"You will, don't worry. What do you say about going out for dinner? I feel like a big plate of pasta and seafood," Giulio proclaimed while rubbing his muscular stomach and yawning. "We've got at least three hours before we get to work on the recording."

"Sounds good. Throw in a bottle of Chianti and you've got a date," Cybil teased with a smirk and a wink.

"Major Steinman! You're putting in a late night! How can I help you?" TJ looked up from her desk where, once again, she was hunched over reports.

Werner Steinman walked in and sat down beside TJ's desk. He had a small cardboard box on his lap. "We've got a couple of problems and I need your help."

"Of course." Her curiosity piqued, TJ put down her reading glasses and sat up.

"First, Cardinal Meissner, the Dean of the College of Cardinals, called. You know of the plane we're sending to New York?"

"Yes. Colonel Weissberg informed me before leaving."

"Yes, very good. Well, it seems that we have a security leak. A reporter and photographer showed up at Dr. Flanagan's home in the last hour. They were asking a lot of questions about the papal airplane and Dr. Flanagan's plans for Rome."

"Oh, my! No one outside the Vatican knew about that!" TJ was astonished at the press' uncanny ability to ferret out information.

"But, the second problem may be more interesting to you. I can really use your help," Major Steinman matter of factly stated. He, then, reached into the small box and pulled out a small, burnt electronic device. Holding it up for TJ to see, Steinman quietly asked, "Do you know what this is?"

"You bet! It looks like a listening device to me," TJ replied in growing interest. Leaning forward to take it from him, TJ asked, "Where did you find it?"

"We found this in the Sistine Chapel an hour ago when making repairs to a window that the hail storm broke this morning. It was inside the hollow space of a large iron hinge. We're not sure, but we think that the morning lightning hit it after the window glass cracked from the hail."

TJ almost jumped up out of her chair in excitement. "The Sistine Chapel?!"

She closely examined the device. It was incredibly small with a thin black wire. This was not something she had seen in any store. "This was custom-made," TJ observed. "Very nice handiwork. Someone knew what he was doing." Then looking back up at Steinman, "Did you get any prints or serial numbers?"

"No prints, but there is a serial number on the amplifier." He handed her a small slip of paper with the serial number.

TJ set the paper down alongside the listening device and paused to think while drumming her fingers on her desk. Steinman patiently watched her and waited. After a minute, TJ laid her hands flat on the desk and exclaimed, "Major Steinman, can you show me which window it was? I may be on to something."

"Of course. Is now a good time for you?"

The Alitalia Airlines' executive jet from Leonardo da Vinci Airport in Rome was entering U. S. airspace at about two o'clock eastern standard time on August 16. Colonel Weissberg yawned and stretched with one of the flight attendants gently shaking his arm to wake him.

"I'm sorry to disturb you, sir, but we have a call for you from the Holy See. You can pick it up on the phone to your right. Channel 1."

"Yes, thank you. Where are we?"

"We are over the United States and we will be landing in about an hour. Can I get you something to drink? Perhaps, coffee?"

Weissberg nodded. "Yes, thank you. A cup of coffee sounds good. Black, please."

Looking out the window, Colonel Weissberg could make out the hills and lakes of the northeastern state of Maine. He had to yawn and stretch, again, after stealing a nap. Looking behind him, Weissberg saw that the two priests and Swiss Sergeant Weil were still sleeping.

He picked up the phone. "Hello. This is Colonel Weissberg."

"Colonel, this is Werner. I'm sorry to disturb you, but Cardinal Meissner asked me to call you about a potential news leak."

"Leak? Where?" Weissberg nervously asked. He nodded at the flight attendant who had just set a cup of coffee in his armrest.

"A reporter and photographer appeared at Dr. Flanagan's home early this afternoon. A woman named Sheila Butts from the New York Daily News – one of those sensationalistic newspapers. She knows about the papal airplane flying to New York to bring him to Rome," Major Steinman bluntly informed him.

"What? You've got to be shitting me? How did they find out?" Weissberg was no longer in need of the caffeine to wake up.

"We don't know how they found out. The reporter wouldn't tell Dr. Flanagan. But, he is very concerned. Anyway, Cardinal Meissner thought it was best for you to know before you land. You will probably find the press waiting for you at Dr. Flanagan's home and, possibly, when you land in New York."

"Yes, of course. I appreciate your call, Werner. Thank you. I'm assuming you're already looking into the source of the leak?"

"Yes, sir. I have also spoken with TJ to see if she can support   us."

"Very good. TJ is excellent," Weissberg declared. "Anything else, Werner?"

"Yes, sir. TJ would like to speak with you for a moment, but I have other news, too. This is distressing news, but we found a listening device in the Sistine Chapel." Steinman stopped knowing that Weissberg would explode at this news.

He did, waking up his three companions. "A listening device? Werner, that's impossible! We inspected and re-inspected that place every day! What is going on?"

"Wilhelm, it's okay. I think I know how it got there," TJ calmly spoke on the phone this time. "The Italian police are on their way right now to pick up one of the maintenance men for questioning."

"TJ, are you on top of this?" Weissberg asked.

"Yes, Wilhelm. Remember that special team I asked you for permission to bring to Rome?"

"Yes, yes. What about it?"

"They're arriving in the morning. They will be able to help with the electronic forensics so we can track the device back to its builder. I'm meeting them at Leonardo da Vinci while Major Steinman interrogates the maintenance worker. I also think I know how the press found out about Dr. Flanagan, but I can't share that with you on this phone. Make sure you get some sleep on the return flight home because you'll be busy when you get back."

Hearing the doorbell, Vahid jumped up from his comfortable perch on the sofa and headed for the door. Vahid was surprised to be greeted there by three policemen.

"Vahid Nosrati?" The senior police officer held up his credentials and took a step forward into the doorway to prevent Vahid from slamming the door shut.

Vahid was caught by total surprise. He knew instantly that he had made a grave error in thinking that his girlfriend was the one ringing the doorbell. Vahid froze and blinked, wanting to run but knowing that flight would be futile. Indeed, a pair of policemen was positioned outside to catch anyone jumping from the second story apartment.

"Are you Vahid Nosrati?" The police officer inquired, again.

"Si. I am Vahid."

The police officer was now standing inside the apartment with his two fellow officers in the doorway. Looking around the room, the senior police officer asked, "Are you alone?"

"Yes. Why?"

"Can I see your identification card, please?" Then looking back at Vahid, Sergeant Gaudio coolly said, "Vahid Nosrati, you are wanted for questioning. I have orders to bring you to the police station."

"For what?" Vahid innocently pleaded. "Am I under arrest? What about my rights?"

Sergeant Gaudio remained calm and stared at Vahid. "You have no rights. You are not an Italian citizen. Let me see your identification."

Vahid dug into his back pocket and withdrew a wallet. He pulled out his identification and handed it to Sergeant Gaudio.

Sergeant Gaudio pointed towards the door and said, "This way."

Sandwiched between Italian police officers, Vahid nervously left his apartment. He knew that his scheduled cellular call to Masoud would alert his compatriots, but could they do anything for him?

Much later that night, Masoud Sadeqi knew something was amiss when Vahid failed to call. He was worried for Vahid's safety, but, more importantly, Masoud was alarmed over the security of his entire network and its operations at the Vatican.

Masoud was a naturally cautious man who only undertook calculated risks. After spending over twenty years building his terror team while covertly masquerading as a university professor, Masoud wasn't about to over-react. He was content to do what he did best: wait, watch, and listen. There was always time for Plan B.

CHAPTER THIRTY-TWO

A small band of reporters and photographers, tipped off by their brethren in Rome, welcomed the papal delegation as it deplaned shortly after four o'clock in the afternoon at JFK Airport. The group of two priests and two Swiss Guardsmen moved swiftly through a customs checkpoint at a small, private terminal and, without responding to the media, climbed into a black stretch limousine.

"Remind me to thank your Cardinal Murphy for arranging this limousine," Monsignor Terrazza said to Monsignor Campbell. Terrazza and his three traveling companions were relieved to take cover behind the black-tinted windows shielding them from the cameras.

"His eminence, the Cardinal, would have it no other way," Campbell politely responded and took a seat behind the driver to assist with directions, if needed. "Is everyone comfortably seated?" Campbell inquired. "There are bottles of water, sodas, and light snacks for the ride. Please, feel free to help yourselves as we have a lengthy commute through the city during rush hour. Nyack is about ten miles north of the city on the opposite shore of the Hudson River. It will probably take us over an hour, perhaps, even two." Seeing Weissberg wince at hearing that he would be seated in a car for a couple more hours, Campbell smiled and apologized, "Sorry, Colonel!"

Monsignor Campbell motioned to the driver to proceed. The limousine, followed by a convoy of media vans, slowly made its way out of JFK and north on the Van Wyck Expressway. Campbell peered out of the front window for a few minutes and satisfied that the driver knew where he was going, Campbell closed the window separating the driver from the guests. Monsignor Terrazza then picked up a mobile phone and called the Vatican with a situation update during an uneventful, slow ride to Nyack, New York.

Slightly unnerved by Sheila, Ernie walked around the house to ensure that the windows and doors were locked. He quickly finished stuffing course materials into his laptop case and then set about packing upstairs in his bedroom. Sean said to be sure to bring a couple of his good business suits, preferably the dark gray suits. Not knowing how long he would be in Rome, Ernie packed for a one week business trip assuming that the Vatican could handle his laundry for a more extended stay.

Peering out of an upstairs bedroom window, Ernie kept a watch on the media gang. He was pleased to find that they were keeping to the sidewalk, but he was even more pleased to see a Nyack police car pull up. Sergeant Manny Durso, his next door neighbor, stepped authoritatively out of the sedan and began to question Sheila and her cohorts. Ernie realized that Manny's wife, Melissa, must have alerted her husband to the neighborhood's trespassers.

Ernie got downstairs to the front door just in time to meet Manny on the porch. "Hi, Manny! Boy, am I glad to see you!" Ernie extended his hand to shake and, with his left hand, clapped Manny on his right shoulder.

"Melissa called to say that you might need help. She saw the news vans out front and got worried about you. Everything alright?" Manny inquired.

"So far so good!" Closing the door behind them, Ernie confided in Manny that he was, in fact, nervous after Sheila had ambushed him. Ernie let on that he was even more apprehensive over the appearance of the additional Fox News van.

"Is there anything I can do to help, you know, like rough them up or haul them off in a paddy wagon?" Manny jokingly asked with a grin.

Ernie thought for a minute and then replied, "Yes, Manny, there is. Thank you for asking." Knowing that Manny and Melissa were devout Catholics, Ernie continued, "Look, a couple of Catholic priests from the Vatican and their Swiss Guardsmen are due to arrive around five or six o'clock to pick me up. I know I told you I was going to Rome, so please forgive me for not saying anything about the folks from the Holy See; but, I didn't want to make a big deal out of it."

Manny whistled. "The Vatican! I didn't know you rated that high, professor."

"Trust me, Manny, I don't. Frankly, between you, me, and a fencepost, I don't know why I'm going to Rome. But, apparently, the press thinks it's a big to-do. Say, if the Daily News puts my mug on its cover, can you keep a copy for me?"

"Sure thing. Heck, I'll keep a copy for myself and have you autograph it. Then I can finally say that I know someone famous!" Manny laughed.

"Yeah, right. You're a joker alright. How does Melissa put up with you?" Ernie returned the favor.

"Beats me! I think she's just hanging around to cash in on that juicy policeman's life insurance policy," Manny quipped.

"Well, you're a lucky fellow, Manny. And tell Melissa that I'm very thankful for alerting you."

Pausing a moment to regroup, Ernie continued by saying, "Anyway, Manny there is something you can do for me. I'm worried about my guests from the Holy See. I don't want Sheila and her merry band of camera men to ambush them and chase them up to my front door. Is there any chance that one of Nyack's finest can stand guard for a couple of hours?"

"Heck, yes, Ernie. I get off duty in an hour and will personally see to it then. In the meantime, I'll have Officer Sawyer swing by. Jack will keep the press in line."

"Hey, thanks a million, Manny. I owe you one. I really appreciate it." Ernie shook Manny's hand vigorously and smiled, greatly relieved for the police backup.

As Manny headed out the door, he bellowed over his shoulder, "Say, Ernie, just bring me back a souvenir from Rome. Maybe something for Melissa. Her birthday is next month."

"Manny, you got a deal! See ya' later!"

Officer Jack Sawyer arrived ten minutes later much to Sheila Butts' consternation. Ernie grinned to himself and patted Gabriel, now visibly positioned in the large bay window of the front living room. "Good boy, Gabriel. Good boy."

Welcomed by the flashing bulbs of cameras, the black limousine pulled into Ernie's driveway at 5:40 that evening. Manny Durso successfully kept the journalists at bay as the limo's passengers exited and walked up to Ernie's front porch. Seeing an additional three news vans coming up the street, Manny called for backup before shouting yet another warning at the aggressive reporters and photographers.

Ernie was relieved to see Monsignor Campbell whom he recognized from his monthly forays into the city to visit Sean. "Hey, Monsignor Campbell! I'm glad you're here. Come on in!" Ushering his four guests into the living room, Ernie calmed Gabriel and ordered the dog to continue its watch in the window.

"Dr. Flanagan, let me make the introductions," Campbell announced once all were assembled in the living room. Ernie shook hands with Monsignor Terrazza, Colonel Weissberg, and Sergeant Weil, in that order, and, unsuccessfully, offered them refreshments.

"Is there any chance that you can tell me why the Holy See is sending me to Rome?" Ernie hoped that he could squeeze some information out of his guests.

Monsignor Terrazza wasn't about to admit that he, alone among the four, knew the cause for the invitation to Rome so he gladly let Monsignor Campbell talk for the group.

"I'm afraid that I don't know the reasons for your trip to the Vatican, either, Dr. Flanagan. Sorry I can't help you. All I know is that Cardinal Murphy asked us to escort you to the Vatican."

Ernie was disappointed, but had expected as much. "Well, okay, then. I suppose that I am ready to go." Ernie pointed at his two suitcases and briefcase next to a sitting chair.

"What about your dog?" Sergeant Weil asked.

"Oh, Sergeant Durso of the local police force and my next-door neighbor, will fetch Gabriel and take him to a neighbor. It's all pre-arranged."

Sergeant Weil nodded and, having moved over to the suitcases, picked them up. "Very good. I'll take these to the limousine and will wait for you all."

Ernie walked through his house one more time to make sure that he had not forgotten anything. Checking his jacket pocket for the passport, he returned to the living room and announced that he was ready.

To the shouts of news reporters clamoring for answers to their questions, the four men left the house to join Sergeant Weil in the limousine. Ernie walked over to Manny to thank him once more and to hand over the house key. Then he jumped into the limousine that had pulled up alongside the two men. Finally, they were off!

At about the same time, but in Rome, Giulio gave up trying to locate the listening device's burst transmission. It simply wasn't there! Thoroughly frustrated, he returned empty handed to Cybil's hotel suite.

"Nothing? Absolutely nothing? Are you sure?" Cybil was puzzled. They had been so very fortunate all along that she never seriously considered a total technological failure. "Isn't there something that you can do to fix it?"

"I tried everything, my dear precious Cybil! Trust me. But, there never was any signal. Nothing at all."

So much for possibly discovering who this Dr. Flanagan might be, never mind, having the inside scoop on the next pope. With Giulio carefully keeping his distance, he watched an irate Cybil cuss and rant for the next fifteen minutes. When she began to run out of steam, Giulio gingerly approached her and began rubbing her shoulders.

"Well, maybe our guy Joshua can find out what went wrong. Otherwise, it's back to the beat at the Vatican with all of the other journalists. Shit!"

CHAPTER THIRTY-THREE

Ernie enjoyed his first flight aboard an executive jet, but he was eager to get it over with so that he might discover the reason for the call to Rome. Nevertheless, after some discussions Ernie was sound asleep somewhere over the Atlantic. Although he rarely managed to sleep aboard an airplane, Ernie was completely exhausted after the intensely nerve wracking day preparing for his trip.

Ernie fell deep asleep and, towards the end of his sleep, he dreamt of his arrival at the Vatican. In the dream, Ernie walked into the Sistine Chapel and stood in awe of the splendor of the chapel. Ernie looked around at the beautiful architecture and art as the chapel began to fill with tourists. Feeling hemmed in, Ernie searched for the exit. He was caught in a frustrating dream where he could not escape the bustling crowd. All of a sudden, the tourists all began to move towards one wall. Ernie was swept up in the crowd despite desperately trying to break out. The crowd began pointing at the wall whereupon Ernie looked up to see an arch inscribed with the words, "Let no man take the honor to himself except he that is called by God, as

Aaron was." At that instant, a bright light shone on him and blinded him.

Ernie awoke with a start and found himself blinded and bathed in bright sunlight! The plane had banked slightly as it neared Rome thereby allowing the rising sun to strike Ernie squarely in the face. Ernie instinctively raised his left hand to block the sun and grimaced until the plane leveled off. With the sun out of his eyes, Ernie opened them and stretched his legs.

Seeing Ernie awaken, the flight attendant smiled and brought him coffee. Ernie was especially happy to hear the flight attendant announce the descent into the Leonardo da Vinci Airport. Sitting up in the leather seat and sipping his coffee, he excitedly watched the Italian countryside rise up to greet the plane on its descent into Rome.

The others had not slept much on the return flight. A couple of in-flight movies were available on small television screens and, otherwise, the passengers occupied themselves with reading and light banter.

Monsignor Terrazza spent a good part of the first hour speaking with and studying Ernie. Terrazza was very pleased to hear Ernie speaking fluent Italian and to learn that half of Ernie's heritage was Italian. Terrazza also found Ernie to be a very likeable and disarming gentleman with a broad variety of interests and hobbies. However, Terrazza couldn't bring himself to view Ernie as papal material.

Terrazza was expecting someone more distinguished in appearance. Perhaps, a little taller, too. Ernie simply didn't carry himself regally. Ernie very much looked the part of a small college professor and not much like a pope. Plus, Ernie's home proved disappointing to Terrazza. For whatever reason, he had pictured a more grandiose house looking across a large lawn or formal gardens at the Hudson River. Moreover, Terrazza shuddered at spying formica counter tops and a worn linoleum floor in the kitchen. Nevertheless, in the end, Terrazza admitted to himself that he liked Ernie.

TJ was already at the airport, but she was waiting for another flight scheduled to land a half hour ahead of the papal jet. She was standing in a private office where the team would be bypassing customs. TJ was nursing her third cup of coffee after stealing a mere three hours of sleep in her newly occupied Swiss Guard apartment at the Vatican.

The interrogation of Vahid Nosrati had yielded nothing although there was no doubt that he was the maintenance worker TJ had spied at work on the very window where the listening device was found. Vahid stubbornly claimed his innocence despite having the Vatican maintenance records proving that he had handcrafted a replacement iron hinge.

TJ, however, recognized body language and eye movement that belied his words. For example, at the critical moment of telling a lie, Vahid would look aside instead of looking her in the eye. He also shifted nervously in his chair and cleared his throat whenever TJ inserted Farsi phrases into her Italian and English. TJ hoped to eventually break him, but that would have to wait until she returned to Rome with the team of specialists.

The special investigative team that TJ had requested was deplaning and due to meet her at any moment. The team, composed of three men, was part of a covert European Union-sponsored task force for combating terrorism. TJ had worked with this particular team on several occasions and knew them to be exceptionally proficient.

Geoff Corson, the Brit on the team, was a technology expert who would be perfect for conducting a forensic analysis of the listening device found in the Sistine Chapel. Jan Rasnicki of Poland was a foreign intelligence officer specializing in radical Islamic terror organizations. The third man, Manfred

Eitzenberger of Germany, was a cryptology mastermind who spoke nine foreign languages, to include Farsi and Arabic.

TJ was happy to see them as they cleared customs. Corson spotted TJ first. "Well, good day to you my lady!" Corson merrily chirped as he gave TJ a hug. "How is your leg?"

With the other two men surrounding her now, TJ smiled and said, "Just a flesh wound after another boring day in the office. Come on, now. The four-wheeled chariot is waiting outside."

The papal jet landed within minutes after TJ had left the airport. To avoid the press, the five passengers walked directly across twenty feet of tarmac to a waiting limousine. A light rain was falling and the Roman delegation was delighted to find that the temperatures had cooled considerably since their departure.

Unaware of their escape, Cybil and Francisco waited another hour along with ten other reporters inside the terminal before giving up and returning to Rome.

Marco Spitini was frowning at a downtown internet café near the Roman Forum. There was no daily summary report nor an audio file from Cybil. He found this particularly distressing as it was essential to discover who Dr. Ernesto Flanagan was and what the College of Cardinals was up to.

Spitini opened his website and it was only then that he found himself truly wishing for a quick end to the operation. There, on his screen, was a coded message from his mentor, Masoud, informing him that the police had apprehended Vahid. So that's why there was no information from Cybil! Someone had discovered the listening device planted in the iron hinge!

Spitini began to curse under his breath and he could feel his blood pressure go sky high. Damn amateurs! Couldn't Masoud find better help that could match Spitini's genius?

CHAPTER THIRTY-FOUR

"Welcome to Rome! Did you have a good flight?" Cardinal Murphy hugged Ernie.

"Hello there! Yes, it was a good flight, but, as always, the safe landing was the best part," Ernie cheerfully remarked. "I even called my three kids from the plane as we were taxiing to the terminal." Then, putting on a more serious face, Ernie asked, "So, are you finally going to tell me what's going on?"

Murphy smiled. "Yes, I suppose I will have to, Ernie. I suppose I will have to." They were standing in Cardinal Biaggio's office in the Apostolic Palace. "Take a seat, Ernie."

"Sean, I've been sitting all the way across the Atlantic. It feels good to be standing."

"That might be the case, but trust me. You'll want to sit down for this."

Ernie nervously cocked his head to the left and eyed his old friend.

"In fact, I want you to sit down because I'm too old to have to pick you up off of the floor."

Monsignor Terrazza appeared at that moment with a nun carrying a tray of coffee and pastries. "Forgive me for interrupting, your eminence, but I have your coffee and something to hold you until you can eat a proper meal." The nun set the tray down on the desk and poured coffee into the two cups.

"Thank you, Sister," Cardinal Murphy kindly said and waited for Terrazza and the nun to leave. The door closed.

"You still like your coffee black?" Murphy asked, handing a cup to Ernie who had taken a seat at a small coffee table.

"Yes, but the last thing I need is a jolt of caffeine. Sean, you're stalling. Come on now, out with it."

Sean Murphy looked to his right at a crucifix on the wall. He had carefully thought through how to break the news to Ernie, but it all seemed so silly now. Just how should he reveal the reason for bringing Ernie to Rome?

Then, in a flash, it came to him. Start at the beginning he told himself. Just start at the beginning.

"Ernie, how have you been sleeping? Any troubling dreams?"

"Why, yes. Why do you ask?"

Sean smiled. "I thought you might. Do you mind telling me about your dreams?"

"Okay, but I'm not sure what you're getting at. What do my dreams have to do with my trip to Rome?"

"Trust me. So, go ahead."

For the next fifteen minutes, Ernie recounted several of his dreams to include the one on the airplane to Rome.

"Thanks for sharing your dreams, Ernie. I've been having dreams, too." Sean proceeded to share all but his final dream with Ernie.

"I like the one where you fly into the World Trade Center site to find the collection of churches," Ernie remarked. "Hearing your dream, it hit me that the reporters have counted the victims every which way except by religion. I mean, we know how many men versus women. We know the age breakdown. Of course, it was widely reported how many nationalities were represented. The victims were also listed by employer. But, to the best of my knowledge no one thought to examine their religious affiliations. I wonder how many fellow Muslims the terrorist hijackers murdered."

The room fell silent. "I wish I could make sense of the dreams, Sean. We could use someone like Joseph to interpret our dreams."

Ernie was referring to Joseph, the biblical son of Jacob, who correctly interpreted several dreams while captive in Egypt. Upon correctly deciphering Pharaoh's dreams, Pharaoh set Joseph free and appointed him to a high position. Joseph, subsequently, collected the crops for seven years in anticipation of seven years of famine thereby saving Pharaoh's kingdom.

"Well, that's why I've asked for you, Ernie. Will you be my Joseph?"

"Sean, I'm not a clairvoyant! I don't even understand my own dreams, much less yours."

"Give yourself a chance. Look, there's another dream I need to tell you about. But, first, let me relate a series of misfortunes as background."

He continued. "Let me just say that what I'm about to tell you is very sensitive, confidential information that I trust you will take to your grave."

For the better part of the next hour, Sean Murphy told Ernie about his visit to Cardinal Maria, the election of one of their own, that cardinal's refusal and collapse, and the subsequent misfortunes befalling the College of Cardinals.

Murphy then described the fishing boat dream. However, Sean did not share that the stranger on the boat was Ernie.

"Ernie, we independently wrote down our descriptions of the stranger on the boat and we found an uncanny match across all of our dreams. Believe it or not, most of us even remember the name of the stranger that Jesus was calling in our dreams. Can you believe that?"

"That is remarkable! Your dreams really matched?" Ernie excitedly asked.

Sean nodded yes. "Ernie, what do you think it all means?"

Caught up in the moment, Ernie began to analyze the events and the fishing boat dream. He concluded by saying, "Although your mishaps were not identical to the biblical plagues, the similarities and, especially, the sequence is simply too unique to be coincidental. I would agree that you have witnessed miraculous events. God is, indeed, at work in the College of Cardinals. The fishing boat dream appears to be the keystone in the arch, so to speak. You know, the stone block in the upper center of the arch that holds it all together. All of the plague-like misfortunes are simply the other blocks in the arch leading up to the keystone. Without those events, the fishing boat dream would just be another dream. Of course, the fact that a dozen of you would have the identical dream is quite amazing, too. If I were a betting man, I would say that the stranger in your dreams is God's choice for the papacy."

"Excellent!" Sean Murphy smiled and clapped his hands. "I was hoping you would discern the meaning of the dreams!"

Ernie was visibly puzzled. "But, Sean, isn't all of that obvious? I mean, we're talking about something that is seemingly mystical and coincidental, although the odds are fairly big against a rational explanation. Anybody else, like those who don't put their faith in Christ, wouldn't believe us no matter how plain it might be to us. So, you didn't need me to interpret the dream. You guys already knew what it all meant. This is not ...."

Ernie stopped speaking all of a sudden. He looked hard at his good friend, Sean, and sat upright. His lips started to move, but he uttered no words. His heart seemed to jump up into his throat. Ernie's pulse began to race and he felt his face flush. The hairs on the back of his neck stood up in fright.

Cardinal Murphy knew Ernie well enough to know that the only way to break the news to his friend was for Ernie to figure it out on his own. There was no need to tell Ernie like he had originally planned. It was far more effective to let Ernie deduce it all. Clearly, Ernie had done just that.

Ernie gulped, took a deep breath, and asked, "Who is the stranger?"

Sean did not answer. Instead, he smiled and patiently waited.

Ernie slowly raised his right hand, looked Sean straight in the eyes, and pointed at his own chest.

Sean nodded his head.

"Me?" Ernie whispered in disbelief.

Sean just nodded his head, again.

Ernie dropped his right arm and just sat there in his chair staring at Sean. Then, all of a sudden, Ernie erupted.

"No way! Forget about it."

He got up and, wildly waving his arms, started pacing.

"I'm not a Catholic cardinal, much less a bishop or a priest, for that matter."

Ernie paused to look at Sean in exasperation.

"You're crazy! Sean, tell me that this is a bad joke. I promise that I won't kill you for pulling a stunt like this, but, please, tell me that this is just a big joke!"

Sean did not nod agreeably.

"Ernie, I would never pull a joke like this on you."

"Forget about it!" Ernie resumed his pacing.

"Ernie, I'm very serious. The College of Cardinals wants to meet you to positively identify you as the stranger in the fishing boat dream."

"No!"

"Ernie, God has chosen you for some inexplicable reason."

"Cut the crap, Sean. I'm not qualified."

"Well, let's think about that. According to papal edict, all one needs to be is Catholic. And, unless, I am mistaken, you were confirmed in the Catholic Church and you have not been excommunicated despite serving God as a protestant minister. Think of it as a bureaucratic snafu in your favor."

Sean apprehensively watched his friend taking a turn for the worse.

"In fact, Ernie, you've been moving back to the Catholic Church. You've been attending Mass. I'm taking your confessions. I dare you to deny that!"

Ernie had returned to his frozen state staring in utter disbelief out a window.

"Ernie, my fellow cardinals and I are still wrestling with this, too. I suspect that the cardinals are going to ask you some hard questions in order to learn more about you. They will examine their hearts and, in faithful obedience to the Holy Spirit, will ultimately decide the matter. But, it's hard to say no to God. Several have tried. Tell me, Ernie, how many have won that argument against God?"

CHAPTER THIRTY-FIVE

"... and guide us in understanding your Will for no one can receive anything except what has been given us from heaven. Thank you for baptizing us through water and your spirit so that we might have the hope of faithfully serving you here on earth and, one day, in your kingdom of heaven. This we pray in the name of Jesus Christ, our Lord and savior. Amen."

Sean Cardinal Murphy did not have to coax Ernie into praying. It was the natural thing for both men to do at that difficult time. With Monsignor Terrazza standing guard outside the office door, both men were guaranteed of having as much uninterrupted time as they needed. But, the cardinal had not anticipated spending the better part of an hour bent over in his chair with an arm on Ernie's shoulder.

Upon concluding the prayer, both men breathed deeply and stood up. Cardinal Murphy remained apprehensive over Ernie's mental state and he fervently hoped that the prayer would achieve its intended goal of calming his friend. Looking now at Ernie, Sean Murphy was trying to discern Ernie's thoughts, but it was proving difficult with Ernie continuing to look at the floor.

Finally, Ernie looked up at his friend and smiled. It was a weak smile, but a smile, nevertheless. Smiling back with immense relief, Sean put his right arm around Ernie's shoulders.

"Are you alright?" Sean asked.

"Yeah. I think I'll be fine. But, I just don't know what to make of all of this. Despite the dreams, it all seems rather outlandish," Ernie replied meekly. "So, what do we do now?"

"Well, that's a good question. The College of Cardinals has greatly strayed from the rules governing the conduct of the conclave. We're now doing our best to adapt the rules to the new circumstances, but it is a day to day affair. We're slowly learning that our rules are too constraining and cumbersome to meet God's unforeseen demands."

The clock chimes let both men know that it was two o'clock in the afternoon. "Ernie, I need to introduce you to a committee of cardinals this afternoon. Ten cardinals to be exact."

"Are these the other ten cardinals who shared your fishing boat dream?"

"Yes, that's right, Ernie. If we're going to pursue this matter any further, it just makes sense to, first, verify that you are, indeed, the stranger in their dreams. They've seen a photograph of you from the Nyack College web site, but it's crucial for them to meet you."

Ernie nodded in agreement and Cardinal Murphy continued. "These cardinals have not only been instructed to identify you, but, also, to question you in order to learn more about you. They will report back to the College of Cardinals and, only then, will the assembled cardinals decide whether to admit you to the conclave or not. Clearly, if the ten cardinals do not recognize you, the case is closed and there are no grounds to impose on the College of Cardinals. I might also add that I'm very apprehensive over this."

"Sean, for all of our sake, I hope they don't recognize me. That would end this craziness. I mean, I can understand why you might see me in your dreams since you know me, but there is no earthly reason why they should see me in their dreams."

"Precisely, Ernie. There is no earthly reason."

Murphy let that sink in before proceeding.

"If the cardinals report back that you do look like the fellow in their dreams and that you merit further consideration, we will ask you to address the College of Cardinals tomorrow morning. And that's just the beginning, Ernie. I can't say I know what will transpire, but we're essentially going to open up the floor for questions and answers. I simply don't know any other way of satisfying the cardinals. I don't even know how long the cardinals will want to question you. I suppose it could last more than a day."

"Okay. I guess we'll all just feel our way through this like a bunch of blind men. I just hope that we get it right."

Murphy smiled and calmly quoted scripture from the New Testament, "For we walk by faith, not by sight."

Turning to face Sean, Ernie smiled and said, "Okay, you win. Let's get going, but, please, give me a bathroom break first!"

With a hearty laugh, both men walked across the office to the door and, with Monsignor Terrazza and a Swiss Guardsman in tow, walked down the hall to a bathroom. Upon returning to the office, Cardinal Murphy dispatched Monsignor Terrazza to fetch the committee of cardinals.

Sean and Ernie waited pensively in the office counting the minutes. Cardinal Murphy paced between the desk and door while Ernie sat in an armchair staring at the floor and wringing his hands in nervous anticipation. The knock at the door fifteen minutes later caused both men to stop and look up at the door and, then, at each other. Ernie rose to stand by the desk while his friend walked to the door.

"Yes, please, come in!" Cardinal Murphy warmly greeted the cardinals as he opened the door.

One by one the cardinals filed in and stood in the center of the office. Upon admitting the tenth one, Cardinal Murphy closed the door and moved to the front of the group of cardinals facing Ernie.

"Please, my esteemed colleagues, permit me to introduce Dr. Ernesto Flanagan to you." Cardinal Murphy motioned Ernie to step forward and then introduced each cardinal by name. Ernie calmly shook hands with each man and unsuccessfully attempted to remember their names. He did, however, recognize Cardinal Meissner's name and was surprised that the Dean of the College of Cardinals, himself, was one of the ten cardinals visited by the fishing boat dream.

It was Cardinal Meissner who spoke first, saying, in English, "Thank you for agreeing to come to the Vatican to meet with us. We have heard much about you from Cardinal Murphy and we have been most anxious to meet you for reasons that I am sure Cardinal Murphy has now explained to you."

Seeing Ernie nod affirmatively, Meissner continued, "Dr. Flanagan, the set of circumstances that brings you to Rome at our invitation is, shall we say, exceptionally awkward. I can only imagine how you are feeling at this very moment. I can assure you that we, too, are very uncomfortable. Fortunately, as Christian leaders of the faith, you and I share the conviction that we must remain open to God's leadership wherever He may take us."

Replying in English, Ernie quickly gathered his wits.

"Cardinal Meissner, thank you for your kind words of assurance. You are absolutely correct in ascertaining my frame of mind. Cardinal Murphy's telephone call inviting me to Rome caught me off guard and, I must admit, the secrecy surrounding the cause for his call was unnerving. His revelation as to the reason for calling me to the Vatican has taken me by complete surprise from which I have not, yet, recovered. I am suffering a bit from jet lag, as well, so please forgive me if I am not quite myself."

Ernie gazed at the collection of cardinals standing attentively before him. He paused and blinked as the full weight of the moment struck him. It was simply incomprehensible to him that one day he could be walking his dog in the small town of Nyack and the next day addressing the senior leaders of the Catholic Church in the Apostolic Palace.

Ernie continued by saying, "I am struck by the serious nature of this moment. Frankly, it is inconceivable to me that you would seriously entertain any thoughts of considering me for the papacy. Nevertheless, I, too, am struck by the seemingly miraculous chain of events at the Vatican and the dreams you have all seen. I agree with you that we must be careful in permitting God to lead us, but I pray and sincerely hope that I am not the man in your dreams, much less a serious contender for the papacy. There must be another reason to explain it all so that I may return to my home soon."

"Perhaps, perhaps. We must truly be careful in proceeding. Would you mind sitting with us so that we may learn more of you? I'm afraid that Cardinal Murphy has the advantage over us of knowing you." Cardinal Meissner motioned towards the group of chairs to proffer a seat to Ernie.

"Yes, yes. Of course. I am at your service, Cardinal Meissner."

After everyone was comfortably seated, Cardinal Meissner opened the discussion. "Doctor Flanagan, would you, please, begin by telling us a bit about your life story. Tell us about your family, your work, your hopes and goals, and, of course, your faith."

Ernie looked at Cardinal Meissner with surprise. "That's a tall order, isn't it?" Looking over at his friend Sean and rubbing the palms of his hands along his trousers to wipe off the accumulated perspiration, Ernie hesitated and cleared his throat.

"I don't mean to bore you with a lot of detail, but shall I just start with my childhood and parents?"

"Yes, please. That would be perfect. Take your time. We are in no hurry."

The remainder of the afternoon seemed to pass quickly. After Ernie's chronological review of his life the discussion quickly moved on to matters of Christian faith. It wasn't very long before the cardinals began to zero in on Ernie's reasons for leaving the Catholic faith to attend a Protestant seminary.

That was the one question for which Ernie had prepared the most. "Please, don't take offense; but, I had anticipated this issue to be your first question. After all, my current Protestant credentials would, in all likelihood, rule out any further consideration of myself for the papacy."

"You are entirely correct, Doctor Flanagan. However, you were raised a Catholic. You were confirmed as a Catholic. And Cardinal Murphy tells us that you have recently returned to attend Catholic Mass. Your papers may state that you are Protestant, but I am struck by how Catholic you truly are. And of course, we have this matter where events of Biblical proportion have brought you to our attention. Frankly, at this point, we are stepping beyond our stated rules and acting on faith alone. So, no, you are hardly disqualified. Besides, many a person has walked a complicated and unpredictable path of faith. Please, continue."

Ernie smiled and, over the ensuing half hour elaborated on his Protestant conversion. This led to a lengthy question and answer period with all of the cardinals taking part. The dialogue then moved on to Ernie's experiences as a missionary and university provost as the cardinals assessed his leadership capacity.

At six o'clock, Cardinal Meissner stood up to signal the end of the questioning. "Doctor Flanagan, thank you for agreeing to come to the Vatican so that we might meet you. We all recognize that these are the most extraordinary conditions. It would be logical and reasonable to end this here and now. You are neither a cardinal nor a bishop. You are not even a practicing Catholic. Nevertheless, after seeing you face to face, I am struck by your resemblance to the man in my dream. I am, additionally, comforted at finding you to be an active, man of Christian faith. I cannot speak for my fellow cardinals, but I don't foresee an early departure for you, Dr. Flanagan."

After the cardinals had left the office, Ernie was by himself for nearly a half hour. Although physically drained, he was unable to sit and, with his mind racing, stood by a large window gazing out at the light rain falling onto the courtyard. Ernie could not help thinking that this was all a horribly wrong dream. He was ready to tell his good friend, Sean, that he had had enough and wanted to leave immediately for the airport to return home. The more he thought about it, the more attractive that option looked to him, but Sean Murphy's arrival temporarily reined in any further thoughts of escape.

"Well, my friend, I hope you don't mind hanging around for at least another day," Sean Murphy announced as he came in through the doorway. "We conferred and all agreed that you bore a marked resemblance to the stranger in their dreams. The cardinals are also relieved to find that you are a strong Christian and a capable administrator. They are, however, very concerned over your Protestant background. I'm not even sure myself how we can explain your consideration, much less potential election, to the world. If you think we're flabbergasted about the turn of events, just wait until our faithful parishioners hear of this. We're lucky that this is not a democracy or else a vote of no-confidence would likely remove every Cardinal."

Murphy looked up at a wall clock. "The bottom line is that Cardinal Meissner will recommend that the College of

Cardinals admit you to the conclave tomorrow for further questioning."

"You mean interrogation, don't you?" Ernie shot back.

"Now, now. You're neither a criminal suspect nor a murder witness testifying on the stand. Admittedly, the questioning may be hard and direct, but that is completely reasonable given the momentous decision that is at hand. Don't forget that we're all just as nervous and uncertain about all of this as you are."

"Fair enough. Sorry, I'm tired and still in a state of disbelief, my friend," Ernie replied. "So, what's next?"

"Monsignor Terrazza and Sergeant Weil of the Swiss Guards will drive you to the Hotel Intercontinental in the heart of Rome. We are still without electricity here at the Vatican so we have a top-notch suite reserved for you at the hotel. A Swiss Guard will stay in an adjoining room in case you need anything. If I were you, I'd take a long, hot shower to relax, have room service bring you a big Italian dinner like your mother used to cook, and fall into bed. We will probably pick you up around eight o'clock in the morning so that you are here when the conclave convenes an hour later. The committee will report to the assembled cardinals and we will then decide whether to proceed. If we do, I'll escort you into the Sistine Chapel."

"That sounds good. I could use all of the above. Especially the sleep. Maybe this will all make more sense in the morning."

"Don't count on it, Ernie. I've been trying to make sense of it for a couple of days and I can't say that it does, yet. Come. Let's go find that limousine so you can get some well deserved rest. I'll be praying for you, my friend. I'll be praying for all of us."

Monsignor Marco Spitini warily eyed Dr. Flanagan walking out of the Apostolic Palace and up to a waiting limousine. Cardinal Murphy and Monsignor Terrazza flanked the American and, behind them, a Swiss Guard Sergeant in plainclothes completed the entourage. If only he knew who this Flanagan character was, Spitini uneasily thought to himself.

Spitini was inclined to believe that Flanagan was a counterterror specialist and, therefore, a dangerous threat. It surely was more than a mere coincidence that Flanagan had been summoned to the Holy See following the discovery of the listening device and Vahid's subsequent arrest. Spitini's theory was reinforced when Sergeant Weil stepped inside the limousine with Dr. Flanagan. 'Yes, he's a security expert alright. I'll have to notify the team to add Flanagan to the list with TJ,' Spitini reflected before leaving for downtown Rome.

"Wilhelm, this Doctor Flanagan is a true renaissance man. On the outside, he has simple tastes, but on the inside he appears to be quite the intellectual. He's well traveled, has raised successful children, is highly respected by his students and university colleagues, and is widely published on religious and social issues. He rose to the top of a highly respected American university; one, by the way, that was founded by the Young Men's Christian Association in the very early part of the twentieth century. Furthermore, he was a standout athlete in his younger years and continues to keep fit by playing sports, kayaking, hiking, piloting air gliders, and, believe it or not, skydiving!" TJ placed the file on Colonel Weissberg's desk and sat down. "Most importantly, the cardinals will be relieved to hear that Doctor Flanagan has no criminal record, no bad debts, and no medical problems. He pays his taxes and votes. He even served on several community boards and ran, albeit unsuccessfully, for the town's school board. He probably lost because he ran as a Republican in democrat-leaning New York. All in all, he's a model citizen."

Picking up the file and browsing through it, Weissberg thanked TJ, "You sure work fast! This is exceptionally comprehensive on such short order. How'd you do it?"

"I've got my means, but I'm not telling. My sources are still working on the file, but that's probably 80 per cent complete."

TJ's assistant, Lieutenant Hans Meier, entered the office at that instant, carrying a book box. TJ quickly added, "But, there's more."

"More? More what? What do you mean?" Colonel Weissberg was confused as Lieutenant Meier carefully put the box down on the floor beside his Colonel. Weissberg looked at Meier and, then, TJ before bending over to rummage through the box.

"As I said, Doctor Flanagan is widely published. I managed to collect a copy of everything he has published. In the box, you'll find journal and magazine articles, editorials, and three books. Hans even managed to print the syllabus of every course that the professor teaches," TJ proudly announced.

Picking up a book from the box, Weissberg began to thumb through the pages. "I like this title. 'Immutable Truths in Changing Times: How to keep core values but adapt the strategy.' Published by a national American publisher, no less. Very impressive."

"I also discovered that he has published two articles critical of the Catholic Church's ecumenical programs. It appears that he thinks the Church should improve its relations with the other Christian churches that it has spawned over the centuries. He feels that Catholics are missing out on a valuable chance to mobilize a wider Christian coalition for worldwide evangelization in the face of Islamic aggression."

"That should go over well with the cardinals," Weissberg chuckled. "Well, let's get this over to Cardinal Meissner. Hans, can you take care of it? Also, don't forget to make sure we keep a copy of everything."

"TJ, thank you very much for all of this. By the way, how is your team doing? Are they responsible for any of this, too?"

"They helped a little bit with Flanagan's file, but not much. I've got them working hard on tracking the amplifier and other odds and ends, such as our friend Spitini. The apartment is just a ten minute walk from here if you ever want to pay them a visit. I'll let you know as soon as we discover anything."

"Good. Very good, TJ. Don't forget that you're coming over for dinner tonight. My wife, Helga, is cooking a family favorite and is looking forward to seeing you, again. You have to take a break from your long nights at the office!"

CHAPTER THIRTY-SIX

"Good morning, Ernie! How does the world look to you today, my good friend?" Sean Murphy loudly asked as he shook Ernie's hand. "You did eat breakfast, right?"

"Top of the morning to you, too, Sean! I'm happy to report that I slept like a baby. In fact, I don't even remember dreaming!" Ernie happily replied with a wink of the eye as he stepped out of the limousine. Then turning around, Ernie closed the door, waved at the driver, and shouted, "Grazie! Arrivederci, Vicenzo!"

"He's got a terrific sense of humor. Did you know that Vicenzo has a son working in Manhattan? On Wall Street! And a daughter leaving next week to attend NYU? Sean, you need to invite them to one of your masses at St. Patrick's!" Ernie was giving every indication of feeling better.

"No, I didn't know that. It sure is a small world. You know, you're amazing at how quickly you get to know people."

"It never hurts to make friends, Sean. I can use every one of them, especially on a day like this when your fellow cardinals will grill me. Who knows, maybe I'll need Vicenzo to make a quick getaway before the inquisition burns me at the stake as a Protestant heretic parading as a pontiff."

Acknowledging his friend's humor, Cardinal Murphy jokingly replied, "We don't burn anyone at the stake anymore. Now we use gas grills with mesquite and a bucket of barbecue sauce. We can't afford to leave any charred remains for the police to find so we dispose of the evidence by devouring our victims!"

"Touché, my friend! Okay, lead on!" Ernie actually had eaten very little for breakfast because his stomach was full of the proverbial butterflies at the thought of meeting the entire College of Cardinals. The humor was merely an attempt to boost his own morale and to screen his apprehensions.

As they entered the Apostolic Palace, Monsignor Terrazza and a Swiss Guard greeted them and led the way towards the Camerlengo's office where Ernie had met with the committee of cardinals. Approximately two hour later, they were escorting Ernie towards the Sistine Chapel. Cardinal Murphy began speaking, "Ernie, I'll be at your side during the entire day except for lunch. I have to join the cardinals for lunch, but we've set up lunch for you back in the office. Monsignor Campbell will take care of everything."

"Lunch? Are you fattening me before setting me on the spit?" Ernie continued to joke, but Cardinal Murphy wasn't having any more of it and ignored Ernie.

"We're heading to the Sistine Chapel where the College of Cardinals is assembling to meet you. There will be armed Swiss Guards at the door who will permit us to enter."

Ernie nodded, but did not answer. Cardinal Murphy continued, "Once we enter the chapel, we will walk up the center to a raised platform where we will meet Cardinal Meissner, the Dean of the College of Cardinals. He will probably make some introductions and yield the floor to you, as we discussed yesterday. Just be yourself and talk from your heart, Ernie, and everything will be fine."

After a short walk, they arrived at the doors to the Sistine Chapel.

"Ernie, are you still okay?" Murphy asked.

"Not really, but let's get on with this," Ernie nervously responded with the full gravity of the moment settling upon him.

The Swiss Guards opened the door and the two friends stepped inside. The interior lighting was dim with the Sistine Chapel still operating under emergency lighting following the bomb attacks, but Cardinal Murphy and Ernie could plainly see the cardinals gathered at the far end of the chapel, just beyond the transenna, a small wall that divides the Sistine Chapel in two. Cardinal Murphy, leading Ernie, set out for the far end of the chapel, but suddenly came to a complete halt.

All of the lights had turned off! The chapel had been plunged into near darkness save from the faint light streaming in from the windows high above them.

Startled, Cardinal Murphy stood still while waiting for his eyes to slowly begin to adjust to the dark. Could this be yet another mishap striking the conclave?

"What's going on, Sean?"

Before Cardinal Murphy could answer him, the lights began to flicker and, after a few seconds, turned completely on. They were no longer limited to the emergency lighting. The Sistine Chapel's electrical power was working again!

"The power is back on! We have electricity, again!" Cardinal Murphy excitedly exclaimed. Indeed, at the very moment that he and Ernie had entered the Sistine Chapel, the power company's crews had restored electricity to the Vatican after completing repairs.

"It's a miracle!" Murphy whispered, dumbfounded, by the positive turn of events after initially suspecting another disaster. The other cardinals were, likewise, elated and happily chattering.

First, the water main had been repaired. Then, the August heat wave finally broke. Now, electrical power was restored!

Ernie was elated to see the cardinals in a festive mood as he and Murphy walked up to the raised platform where a grinning Cardinal Meissner welcomed him. "Welcome to the Vatican, Doctor Flanagan! You sure know how to make an entry. Isn't it miraculous how the electricity was restored as you entered?"

Standing alongside Cardinal Meissner and looking out at the august body of cardinals, Ernie was overcome with awe and a deep sense of reverence. He was a mix of emotions for on one hand he was tense and, on the other hand, he was excited to be standing in the midst of a conclave.

Cardinal Meissner was about to introduce Ernie when he stopped. Meissner smiled and waited for Ernie who was now whispering a prayer to himself, "Lord God, may the words of my mouth and the meditation of my heart be pleasing in your sight, O Lord, my rock and my redeemer. Please, allow my mouth to speak words of wisdom; the utterance from my heart to give understanding. Hear my prayer, O God; listen to the words of my mouth. Through Jesus Christ, my savior, I pray. Amen."

"Amen." Cardinal Meissner echoed Ernie. Then, looking at the cardinals, Meissner proceeded to introduce Ernie. "Fellow cardinals, I have the honor of introducing Dr. Ernesto Flanagan to you this morning. This is a momentous occasion for us to welcome the doctor into our midst as we deliberate and pray. As you know, ten of us briefly met Doctor Flanagan yesterday afternoon and ascertained that he is, in fact, the very man we saw in our dreams. The challenge we now face is to understand God's will and the purpose in knowing Doctor Flanagan. If we are to have any hope of correctly interpreting the events and dreams of the past few days, we must come to an understanding of who Doctor Flanagan is. Indeed, the critical element here is Doctor Flanagan; why has God led us to him?"

Turning to look at Ernie, Meissner now said, "Doctor Flanagan, I would like to invite you to take the floor and to speak extemporaneously about yourself. Thereafter, if you will permit us, I should like to ask you to take questions from the College of Cardinals."

Ernie nodded and replied, "Yes, certainly, Cardinal Meissner."

"Very good. Thank you, Doctor Flanagan." Pointing to a chair, Cardinal Meissner added, "Please, feel free to be seated. There is also a glass and pitcher of water on the small table. You will also find a pad of paper and pen in case you would like to make notes to yourself. Lastly, all of our discussions are strictly confidential. Will you pledge on your honor as a Christian standing before God to keep all that is said here to yourself?"

Ernie took a deep breath and gazed out at the cardinals. "Yes, so help me God, I pledge to keep our discussions confidential and to reveal them to no one." Still in a state of disbelief, Ernie had concluded that all he could do was to simply be himself. He had nothing to lose. In fact, his wish was to leave empty handed. The last thing he wanted was to prolong the affair, much less be further considered as a viable candidate for the papacy. So, if he came across poorly, so much the better.

"Good morning. I am honored to be invited to meet you on such a historic, momentous occasion as the conclave in the history of the Catholic Church. To find myself in the Sistine Chapel surrounded by such a distinguished body of faithful servants of the Lord is a true honor. I shall never forget this moment and I, therefore, pledge that I will truthfully and completely answer all of your questions. Although I fully understand the reasons for finding myself here, I cannot help but feel that there is some other equally plausible reason for explaining the circumstances surrounding my call to the Vatican. I am struggling with all of this and I must, truthfully, admit that I am neither qualified nor interested in being considered to lead the Catholic Church."

With that introduction, Ernie launched into his life story. For approximately forty-five minutes, the cardinals listened attentively to Ernie. They were pleased to find a humble man of sincere and deep faith who was well organized in his thoughts, well spoken in his words, personable, and confident in his delivery.

Upon concluding his remarks, Ernie thanked the cardinals, again, and sat down. He was thankful to drink the cold water for his throat was dry and he discovered that his shirt was wet from perspiration.

Ernie expected to field a few questions, but fully expected to be dismissed soon. After all, he made no effort to hide his reasons for leaving the Catholic Church and studying at a Protestant, non-denominational seminary. Soon, he was convinced, he would be checking out of his hotel room and returning home to New York. It was just a matter of time.

Ernie couldn't have been more wrong. The questions came at him quickly. At times, several cardinals would speak up simultaneously and, at times, he had to field rapidly fired follow-up questions. After only an hour of this questioning, Ernie could feel the sweat on his brow and wished he had brought a spare shirt.

The questions that morning focused on Ernie's books and articles. He was surprised to discover that the cardinals had amassed and read his publications, but he was pleased to explain his arguments. In some instances, particularly for his early journal articles, he had to ask the cardinals for a copy in order to recall specific segments and excerpts. Ernie even pulled out his pocket-sized Holy Bible to look up and cite biblical verses.

In the end, Ernie surprised himself at the vigor with which he threw himself into the arguments. However, he found it impossible to resist the cardinals' challenges to his beliefs, to the causes for which he had given his life, and to the arguments of faith with which he had wrestled over a lifetime. Swept up in the moment, Ernie no longer faced the College of Cardinals with trepidation. Free of any aspirations to the papal throne, he was free to argue his points as he wished. Whether his arguments won any converts was of no concern to him. He was free to focus solely on the substance and elegance of the arguments. In summary, Ernie truly relished jousting with such a distinguished body of Christian scholars.

As the bells rang twelve times to signal lunch, the cardinals were so absorbed in the arguments that no one wanted to break for the midday meal. So Cardinal Meissner arranged for lunches to be brought to them and for a small break.

Cardinal Murphy and his colleagues were equally surprised at Ernie's spirited and well-reasoned arguments. In fact, Cardinal Murphy believed that his monthly lunches debating theology, contemporary religious issues, and church management had, in fact, prepared Ernie for this day.

Although the amount of agreement and disagreement varied over the course of the day, few in the room could argue that Ernie's positions were poorly conceived, inadequately documented, and feebly argued. The cardinals found Ernie to be their equal in matters of faith, church management, and communications skills.

Ernie endeared himself to several of the Italian cardinals, largely from the conservative faction, by injecting Italian proverbs, recalling lessons from his Italian mother, and adding a touch of earthy humor to his arguments. Ernie's predisposition towards conservative views on pre-marital sex, abortion, and homosexuality also found approval in the conservative wing of the College of Cardinals. Although Ernie merrily felt that his critique of the Catholic Church was ensuring his eventual dismissal from Rome, his critical evaluation of the Catholic

Church's failures found favor among the conservative cardinals wishing to reform the church.

His understanding and recollection of events from his missionary days abroad in the Pacific Rim, Africa, and Europe also found favor with a wider collection of cardinals. His exceptional background in international missionary work, his perceptive understanding of diverse cultures, and his support of ecumenical programs won the support of many in the liberal wing of the College of Cardinals.

Nevertheless, many of his views on reforming the Catholic Church, particularly his positions on ordaining women as ministers and permitting priests to marry, drew sharp counterpoints from the cardinals. Ernie proved equally adept at winning agreement and at drawing disapproval.

Whether from mental exhaustion or from a lack of further substantive issues, the discussions began to dwindle by five o'clock in the afternoon. Ernie had gone through three pitchers of water and his voice had grown hoarse. Sensing this, Cardinal Meissner rose and asked Ernie for his closing arguments.

"Doctor Flanagan, I think that it is time to conclude our deliberations for the day. I would like to thank you for your spirited and well-reasoned arguments and for allowing us to get to know you better. But, before we close, I would like to take the liberty as the Dean of the College of Cardinals to ask the final question. Will you permit me this honor?"

Ernie nodded and said, "Si. But, of course."

"Thank you, Doctor Flanagan. If you had had the opportunity to have an audience with Pope John Paul III, what would have been three key points you would like to have made to him?"

Cardinal Meissner sat down, folded his hands in his lap, and unassumingly waited for Ernie's answer. Ernie drank the last of the water in his glass, scribbled some notes on a pad of paper, and slowly rose to address the College of Cardinals. Ernie's monthly get-togethers with his good friend, Sean Cardinal Murphy, would now prove exceptionally beneficial because Ernie knew all too well what 'hot button' issues were on the cardinals' minds.

Ernie began slowly. "I would like to thank you for inviting me. I am, of course, still in complete surprise at finding myself here under these circumstances; but, no matter how you proceed, I want to let you know that this is a special honor. To deliberate key Christian concepts and issues before this eminent assembly of noble and learned men of faith in the grand Sistine Chapel is something I will never forget. You have truly humbled me.

You know that I was born and raised a Catholic. You are, also, aware that those same Catholic credentials are now in doubt after my many years as an ordained Protestant minister. Nevertheless, we share common roots and are all traveling on a circuitous path lit only by God. In his light we are all Christians.

All too often we overlook our key, common bonds: belief in one benevolent and all powerful God, faith in our savior Jesus Christ who reigned perfect in the flesh and gave his life for us so that we might live in eternal communion with God, and trust in the Holy Spirit that guides us this very day.

In focusing on our differences we often engender mistrust and strife. Protestants and Catholics have fought bitter wars over the centuries. Northern Ireland is but one example of still festering wounds. The twentieth century's holocaust and today's confrontations with Islam further highlight the ongoing battles between religions for mankind's soul.

So, my first point to John Paul III would have been that the religions must make peace in order for nations to make peace. In that sense, I would have supported his ecumenical outreach. It was an outreach that built on the second John Paul's ecumenical initiatives and on the Polish Pope's sincere attempts to find common ground for common peace and justice."

Ernie paused and studied the cardinals before continuing.

"We must be mindful not to squander the potential for achieving peace by letting matters that are seemingly substantive, but which in truth are not, separate us. The world focuses on our petty differences and thereby subverts our matters of faith for achieving its political and economic goals. Once again, possessions triumph over spirit.

This is especially egregious when religious leaders assume the leadership of nations and go on to fill the world with messages of hate, selfishness, and pride. When they foster revenge and war instead of preaching godly messages of peace, charity, humility, and faith in order to counter the brokenness of the world with God's unending love.

Today, we see religious leaders in the Middle East destabilizing our hope for peace by inspiring their citizens to kill infidels under the pretense of serving God. Only in uniting as a single force under God, can the world's religions counter this evil and achieve God's purposes. In joining ourselves, we separate ourselves from dishonest men and women abusing religions for worldly goals."

He paused to take a sip of water.

"This leads to my second point. Namely, that the Catholic Church has the opportunity to mobilize Christianity, of whatever denomination, to oppose the violent, radical sects of Islam. Indeed, the Jews, many other religions, and even parts of Islam would join us in that common cause.

Already we see that the Catholic Church is becoming an important communicator of what Islamic faith is to Europe and to the world. The European press is already reporting on a re-birth of Christianity as a reaction to the threat of radical Islam. Editors already write of a diabolical Catholic plot to capitalize on the growing Islamophobia to scare secular Europe back into your pews.

You must not let the world's media and politicians frame the debate. You have the chance to take hold of the debate by demonstrating leadership and mobilizing the faithful."

The cardinals sat quietly listening.

"The Catholic Church calls itself the mother church. Indeed, there is an inscription in the original basilica of the Roman Catholic Church – I believe it is the Lateran Basilica in Rome – that reads, in Latin, 'Omnium urbis et orbis ecclesiarum mater et caput,' or, in English, 'Mother and head of all churches of the city and the earth.'

Indeed, the Catholic Church has spawned many churches much as a mother gives birth to many children. No matter how much my fellow Protestants may argue, these churches are the offspring of the Catholic Church with the same genetic make-up, with the same roots to Jesus and, ultimately to Abraham. We may profess differences in theology and ceremonial practices, but, in the end, we are bound by numerous common beliefs.

A mother recognizes that her children will never look exactly like her, much less act exactly like her. Nevertheless, a mother takes pride in raising her children, in passing her heritage along to her children, and in loving her children's individuality. A mother's children are her heirs.

I ask that you are careful to avoid letting the world paint you as a bad mother. How many Protestant and Catholic believers quarrel because each believes his church to be the one and only true church? This is why my Italian mother would attend my protestant church services, but then cross the street to attend Catholic services. Despite worshipping the same God and adhering to the same essential tenets of faith, my service never was good enough for my Catholic mother."

Thinking of his mother, Ernie's eyes grew misty.

"Now, I would argue that Christians collectively should mobilize all people of faith, to include Muslims."

He paused to underscore his next point.

"I must admit that I have strong reservations about Islam."

He let that sink in.

"In stark contrast to Judaism and Christianity which base their faith on a long list of distinguished prophets over many centuries, Islam reshapes religious faith based on one prophet's life alone.

I have also long taken issue with a number of Islamic practices and beliefs. The suicide bombers, the atrocious attacks on the World Trade Center and Pentagon, and the global Islamic radicals' persecution of so-called infidels torments us all.

We are left wondering if Muslims join us in believing in a loving God we learn to know or if they believe that God is a distant authoritarian ruler whom we'll never comprehend? Do they respect human life? Can we trust them?"

Ernie looked around at the assembled cardinals as if he were looking for an answer.

"On that latter count, the Islamic concept of 'taqiyya' permitting Muslims to lie stands out against the Judeo-Christian practice of honesty. We are told that a light must shine in the darkness. A light cannot remain hidden under a basket. We take oaths attesting to our honesty on the Bible; yet, Muslims pride themselves in deception. Where our believers die as martyrs at the point of a weapon for failing to renounce Christ, radical Muslims appear all to eager to die as martyrs carrying a suicidal weapon that simultaneously kills as many infidels as possible. We die for honesty whereas the radical Muslim terrorists kill by deceiving."

He was growing weary. Were his arguments making any sense or was he beginning to babble?

"In many ways, it would be natural for us to join the growing international chorus for confronting Islam militarily and economically. You may also recall that even Martin Luther viewed Islam as a violent Satanic movement that will never be converted.

Yet, the Bible is replete with examples of God and Jesus inviting citizens of many nations, believers of diverse religious factions, disreputable sinners, and complete human failures into God's kingdom, albeit by submitting to God's commandments summarized so eloquently by Jesus in proclaiming that we should love God with all of our heart, soul, and mind and, subsequently, to love our neighbors as we love ourselves. Moreover, one may argue that Jesus declared the kingdom of God and never meant to confine that to any one collection of people in a particular church.

As God reaches out to us sinners through his abounding grace and mercy, so we must reach out to fellow sinners. No matter how costly to our church coffers and no matter how impossible matters may appear. That applies equally to sinners within our churches and to sinners beyond, such as the radical Muslim terrorists."

He paused. He noted some frowns.

"So, my third and final point to John Paul III would have been to adapt the Church's strategy, but not its core values, in its ecumenical outreach and internal reformation.

The Catholic Church can ill afford confusing its core values with its strategies for serving God. Times change and the Church, like any organization, has to change with the times in order to effectively communicate God's message of love and hope to a broken world that neither knows nor understands God. The same can be said for any Christian faith, whether Protestant or Greek Orthodox.

Don't change your core values. Rather, change your strategy. This requires you to abandon the security that comes from doing something merely because you've always done it like that.

The Catholic Church took the right step forward in the 1960's when the Second Vatican Council promulgated changes that caused you to engage the worldly culture as a people of God rather than as a city of God set high on a hill and, thus, unattainable by any but the most saintly parishioners and priests.

For example, the Second Vatican Council replaced the Latin at Catholic Mass with the language of the people thereby giving more people access to their Catholic religion. Did the Mass change? No, just the language. You still conducted Mass in the same manner and you continued to worship God through Jesus Christ and under the leadership of the Holy Spirit. In other words, you kept your core values, but changed your strategy to reach the broken world, to make God more accessible.

Despite permitting the world to paint you as an ultra-conservative, tradition-bound institution, you and I know that the Catholic Church has changed dramatically over the centuries and continues to change even today.

The Catholic Church gave birth to new Catholic Orders whenever confronted with social upheaval and threats. You founded the Benedictines when Barbarians assaulted Rome in the fifth century. The Dominican and Franciscan Orders were your response to the large-scale social changes brought about by the appearance of metropolitan cities. Martin Luther's Protestant Reformation witnessed the emergence of your Jesuit Order.

Even we Protestants adapt to social change. The proliferation of Protestant denominations is nothing more than an ongoing adaptation to society.

We must grapple with the challenges facing Christianity by standing firm in our faith. We must draw on our common ground rather than distinguish ourselves based on differences in theology and practice. We must mobilize as a force for peace in this world and for mankind's reconciliation with our heavenly Father. And, finally, we must adapt our strategy while remaining true to our core Christian values that you and I share. Call me a Protestant or call me a Catholic. It's your choice. But, we can all agree that I am a Christian and that I believe in the catholic, all-embracing, church of Christian believers.

If the Catholic Church or, for that matter, any major religion can achieve success in the above three issues, the world will be a better place and God's kingdom will be served."

Ernie's voice was now nearly shot. He dearly wanted a cup of hot tea. He wanted a bed. He wanted to be left alone. He had reached the point at which he no longer cared what the outcome might be as long as there was an end to it all.

Ernie shifted uncomfortably on his feet as he recognized how tired he was. He looked over at Sean and then at Cardinal Meissner. Collecting himself, he proceeded to thank the College of Cardinals.

"Again, thank you for bestowing this honor upon me. I pray that you now know that I am hardly the Protestant infidel some of you might have expected to see standing before you today. We may disagree on several points as was demonstrated during our daylong discussions; however, we share many beliefs and my Catholic roots run deep.

Lastly, I do not seek the papal office. I would discourage you from considering me any further, but I must let God's Will be done. If I am, indeed, elected, I am very reluctant to accept. I cannot help but think that there is some other reason for the unusual events and visions.

You face a seemingly insurmountable question in discerning God's Will as you move forward in this papal conclave. But, you are men who have practiced deep faith for many, many years so none of us should ever doubt that you, through the Holy Spirit, can identify God's Will despite the cacophony of noise, inharmonious contradictions, and apparent coincidences. In the end, no matter what your collective decision might be, the world will scrutinize your decision. No doubt, all of you will revisit your decision over and over in the years ahead. I do not envy you and I pray for you. I pray for us all."

Sean Murphy almost jumped out of his chair to applaud Ernie, but the Cardinal in him held back. Many other Cardinals would have likely joined him. After days of tribulation, indecision, and trials, Ernie's inspirational address lifted their spirits considerably. Here was a man who could have just as easily been an Army General exhorting his troops to victory.

The next five minutes were a flurry of activity. Cardinal Meissner thanked Ernie and Cardinal Murphy led Ernie through the ranks of the cardinals to the chapel's doorway. The Swiss Guards then escorted Ernie to the waiting limousine. Thankfully, Vicenzo, the driver, recognized Ernie's tired state of mind and drove without talking.

CHAPTER THIRTY-SEVEN

Ernie sat on the balcony of his hotel suite gazing out over the city of Rome. He was recovering from the day of intense questioning with a glass of Campari. His feet were up on a small, low table. Empty dishes lay on a cart off to the side. Despite having no appetite when he arrived at his hotel suite, he had ordered dinner from room service only to discover that he was starving.

It was a pleasant evening in Rome, but his internal body clock was still attuned to the eastern standard time zone in the United States so it felt more like mid afternoon. The jet lag added considerably to his discomfort. Indeed, the jet lag, in conjunction with the highly unusual state of affairs, combined to make Ernie feel like he was living a fairy tale. It all felt so surreal.

'This can't be happening to me,' Ernie was thinking to himself.

'I don't want to live the rest of my life here. I want to go home to New York.'

'I want to go on morning walks with Gabriel.'

'I want to babysit Samantha and all of my other grandchildren that will surely arrive.'

'I want to teach the new college course that I organized for the fall semester.'

'I want to bicycle along the river road hugging the western shore of the Hudson River between Nyack and Piermont.'

'I want to go out to dinner with my friends.'

Ernie took a drink of his Campari and continued to mull over his position. 'Heck, I don't want to lead the Catholic Church. It's an impossible task tackling the inertia of the bureaucracy. I'm just asking for a bruising in the political infighting that's sure to occur. I ran from the Catholic Church to the protestant seminary as fast as I could.'

'Okay, I've been inching back to the Catholic Church, but ....'

He stood up and placed his hands on the balcony's railing. 'I'm not cut out to lead the Catholic Church! I had my hands full with the little bit of missionary work I did earlier in my life and with the small Nyack congregation I led for three years. I'm not qualified to make multi-billion dollar budget decisions. Who am I to approve the appointments of cardinals and bishops? If anyone should be the pope, it's Sean! I'm just a simple guy with simple skills.'

Ernie's soul searching continued for an hour until, just after eight o'clock, he convinced himself that he simply would not accept the papacy if the College of Cardinals elected him. Basta! That was that. He didn't want the job and they couldn't make him take it.

Ernie made a monumental decision. He was going to leave and return home to Nyack. He had had enough of this silliness. He was convinced that despite all of the talk about dreams and biblical plagues, the cardinals would never elect anyone not in their ranks. Having settled on that decision, Ernie rose, entered the suite, and walked down the short hallway to the study. Sitting down in a soft leather chair at the executive desk, Ernie called up the internet and checked the flights leaving Rome that night for New York. He found a British Airways flight departing that night at 11:00 for London with a connecting flight the next morning to JFK. Pleased, Ernie booked himself a ticket.

Packing was a simple task because he had never fully unpacked. Within the hour, Ernie stood with his luggage at the front of the hotel, much to the consternation of Sergeant Weil who was frantically calling the Vatican for instructions. A minute later, he was in the back seat of a taxi headed for the Leonardo da Vinci Airport. Looking out of the windows at Rome, Ernie felt guilty for running off in the night without telling Sean, but he was sure that Sean would understand. The College of Cardinals would surely come to their senses!

Driving out of Rome, even in the relatively quiet month of August, was an arduous undertaking. Traffic was never accommodating. So Ernie wasn't too bothered by the high volume of cars on the road with him and the stop and go of the traffic.

He was beginning to relax at the thought of walking into his home when he felt himself lurching forward into the front passenger seat. A black sedan had come to a sudden stop directly in front of his taxi. Sandwiched between two cars on the left and right, the cab driver could not swerve and hit his brakes as hard as he could while sounding his horn. None of that, however, helped. The taxi rear ended the sedan and came to a complete stop. Fortunately, the light blue utility van behind the taxi did not hit them from behind. Or so Ernie thought.

Speaking on walkie-talkies with the black sedan's driver, the driver of the van knew in advance of the sudden stop. The van drove up behind and tapped the taxi's rear bumper thereby solidly boxing the taxi in with no place to go. No sooner had the van stopped, than two men jumped out of the van and rushed up on either side of the taxi. Reaching the taxi in a matter of seconds, the men tore open the taxi's rear doors and pulled a dazed Ernie out onto the road. A pistol shoved into Ernie's ribs convinced him to move with the two men to the van. They pushed him into the van and jumped in on top of Ernie as the van backed up and drove away.

Sergeant Weil, following Ernie in another taxi, watched helplessly as Ernie was kidnapped. Weil's taxi was stuck behind other cars. Jumping out of his taxi, he was too slow and too far back to come to Ernie's aid. Watching the van driving away, he grabbed his cell phone and placed an emergency call to the Vatican.

CHAPTER THIRTY-EIGHT

"Lie down on your stomach! Hands behind you!"

Ernie was nearly paralyzed in fear, but complied with the instructions as best as he could while getting shoved and hit. His attackers jumped into the van on top of him as the van sped off to the right. Ernie was gasping for air when his attackers slipped a pillow case over his head and secured his hands with plastic ties. "Stay where you are! Do not move and nothing will happen to you," the attacker straddling Ernie's waist barked at him in English.

The van continued moving along, but pulled into a deserted lot ten minutes later. The kidnappers tugged the van's side door open and gruffly pulled Ernie out. Standing uneasily between two men firmly holding his upper arms, Ernie took a deep breath in preparation for loudly shouting for help. But, his attackers were too quick for him and shoved him into a sedan.

"Bend over! Be quiet!" Hands grabbed the pillow sack and yanked Ernie's head forward and down so that he was doubled up in the middle of the car's back seat. His assailants continued to hold the pillow sack and rested their elbows on

Ernie's shoulder blades. No one spoke except for the man in the front passenger seat who seemed to be giving driving directions in Arabic or some similar language.

Ernie ached all over and his arms were throbbing in pain at the reduced blood flow, but he was trying, albeit without success, to track the turns and to listen for key sounds that he might use to later identify the route. The drive was painfully long and Ernie had no sense of his whereabouts. With daylight disappearing after nearly an hour on the road, the car slowed and pulled into a warehouse.

With the driver turning the engine off, the kidnappers got out and pulled Ernie out of the car while threatening Ernie to remain silent and cooperative. The kidnappers hauled Ernie down a hallway and pushed him through a doorway into a large, bare room.

"Sit on the floor!" Someone kicked Ernie in the back of his right knee knocking him to the ground. Ernie fell heavily onto his right side, unable to break his fall as his hands remained tied behind his back. One of his assailants promptly sat on him, straddling Ernie's chest while another knife wielding assailant cut and stripped Ernie of all of his clothes and shoes, except for his underpants. Next, they cut the plastic hand ties and shackled Ernie's ankles and wrists in metal handcuffs. Lastly, the terrorists clamped a large headset over Ernie's ears.

Ernie winced in pain as loud rock music deafened him. However, he was thankful that no one was striking or shoving him anymore. Ernie was content to lie on the concrete floor and let the blood rush back into his arms.

Ernie prayed for God to spare his life. It wasn't easy to concentrate with the loud music blaring in his ears, but Ernie stubbornly persisted and managed to recite the Lord's Prayer in his mind. Over and over.

CHAPTER THIRTY-NINE

Ernie did not sleep for the remainder of the night. Under the watchful eyes of his captors, Ernie sat up and, with his head bowed, prayed. He simply didn't know what else to do. He was scared, hurt, and confused.

At seven o'clock in the morning, Ernie was taken by surprise when Masoud Sadeqi removed the headset. Ernie sat up straight, not knowing what would happen next. Would he be pulled to his feet or hit? Was his life in imminent danger?

"Doctor Flanagan, why are you in Rome?" Masoud asked in perfect English.

Unfortunately, Ernie's ears were ringing after a barrage of loud rock music. He could hear a voice, but could not make out the words.

"Doctor Flanagan, why are you in Rome?" Masoud asked, again.

"What?" Ernie shouted hoarsely, his lips dry. "I can't hear you. My ears are deaf from the music."

Masoud, sitting behind Ernie, motioned to one of last night's assailants. "Give him some water."

Rahman picked up a bottle of water and lifting the pillow case above Ernie's mouth put the bottle to Ernie's lips. "It's water. Drink!" Rahman shouted at Ernie.

With water beginning to spill over his chest, Ernie took a couple of big gulps before Rahman withdrew the water and let the hood drop. Ernie figured that if they wanted to kill him, they would resort to a weapon other than poison. The water felt good and the ringing in his ears slowly began to subside.

Masoud patiently watched his prisoner. After five minutes, Masoud repeated his earlier question, "Doctor Flanagan, why are you in Rome?"

Ernie, now hearing Masoud, replied with a question, "Who wants to know?"

"You don't need to know, Doctor Flanagan. Your life is in my hands. At any time, I can inflict terrible pain on you. I might even kill you. That's all you need to know. So, Doctor Flanagan, why are you in Rome?"

"Is that where I am? Am I still in Rome?"

Masoud motioned to Rahman, again. This time Rahman kicked Ernie in the unprotected groin. Ernie gasped for air and instinctively closed his thighs while rolling onto his side. Rahman violently pulled him back up and put a rope noose around Ernie's neck. He cinched it tight around Ernie's neck, but did not cut off Ernie's air.

"Doctor Flanagan, if you value your life, you will cooperate. I don't want to kill you, but if you're of no value to me, then I have no other choice. Why are you in Rome?"

Ernie, still in pain, was weighing his options. It occurred to him that he was probably a dead man anyway, but he refused to give up hope. Then, again, maybe this was just a bunch of opportunistic thugs looking to exchange him for a suitcase of money. Regardless, Ernie realized that he had nothing to hide. He was, after all, not a prisoner of war or a spy pledged to withhold all secrets to the point of death.

"Okay. Okay. I'll talk. Look, I don't know what you want, but I'm sure that someone will pay the ransom for me. You don't want to kill me."

"Doctor Flanagan, I need to know why you're in Rome so I can set the appropriate price for your head. Are you worth more dead or alive?"

Fair enough, Ernie thought. I've got the guy talking and nobody is kicking me in the balls. So far so good. Let's see how far I can push it.

"A friend asked me to visit. One of the Cardinals made me an offer that I couldn't refuse."

Masoud motioned to Rahman who placed his right foot between Ernie's shoulder blades and tugged at the rope to rapidly tighten the noose. Ernie gasped for air and grimaced in pain. Rahman firmly held him in check for nearly a half minute before releasing him and loosening the noose.

Ernie coughed and spluttered as he began to breath.

"Let's try direct answers, Doctor Flanagan. I don't care for you to waste my time," Masoud sternly admonished Ernie. "Who are you and what are you doing in Rome?"

It took Ernie a minute, but he finally replied, "You won't believe this, but so help me God, the cardinals are considering electing me as pope." Ernie had decided that his life was in God's hands, not theirs. Therefore, he might as well tell the truth. Perhaps, it would set him free.

"Doctor Flanagan, I'm not amused with your jokes!" Masoud impatiently bellowed at Ernie.

Without planting his foot against Ernie's back, Rahman viciously pulled on the rope knocking Ernie backwards onto the concrete floor. Rahman then began to slowly drag Ernie across the floor while another of last night's assailants, Yahya, kicked Ernie in the ribs.

Ernie thought that his life was coming to an end. In addition to the severe pain from the kick and the tight noose, the rough concrete was now tearing his back and arms open. Once again, Ernie was struggling to take in air for what seemed like an eternity. In reality, it was about a half minute.

Rahman eventually loosened the noose and, kicking a bloodied Ernie in the thighs, ordered him to sit up.

With great effort, Ernie managed to sit up in sharp pain. He was coughing and, although in severe pain and mental anguish, Ernie was determined not to satisfy his tormentors by howling in pain.

"Doctor Flanagan, I thought you learned your lesson. I don't have a sense of humor!" Masoud was incensed. Who did this asshole think he was? These Americans were always so damn arrogant!

Masoud now began to shout at Ernie. "You're a police officer, aren't you, Doctor Flanagan? Or maybe a counterterror expert? The Vatican hired you to hunt us down, didn't it? You arrogant bastard! So the hunter is now the prey caught in the trap!"

Ernie was confused, but he quickly understood that his interrogator was looking for a specific answer. At that point, he figured that the truth didn't matter much. His interrogator wouldn't accept the truth. Ernie simply said, "No. You're wrong."

"Doctor Flanagan, I'm rarely wrong. And certainly not this time. We have New York newspaper photos of you accepting an honorary award from the New York Police Department. On your right is the Director of the Secret Service and sitting to your left is the FBI's Deputy Director for Counterterrorism. You want us to think that they give awards to just anyone? We have other articles covering your extensive work with the police. Are the newspapers lying? You're much more than a simple minister. No, I dare say you are much more than that, Doctor Flanagan. I think the minister and professor titles are just a cover for your covert work."

"You're wrong. I don't lie. I am not a police officer. I am a minister who ...."

Ernie was cut short by another kick to the ribs.

Masoud looked with disdain at Ernie. What a weakling! This man was nothing more than a western pagan whore hiring himself out to the highest bidders. Masoud nodded to Rahman. He then spit on Ernie and left the room with Rahman removing the noose from Ernie's neck.

Yahya followed Masoud out into the hallway. Once the door was closed, Masoud turned around and took a hold of Yahya's right arm. "Keep him alive for the time being, but see what information you can get out of him. Maybe we can get more information out of him before we kill him. Give him some water, but no food."

Yahya nodded and Masoud continued, "This is getting out of hand. We're going to have to clean up the mess and tie off the loose ends. Tell Yousef to take care of Spitini and the American reporter."

CHAPTER FORTY

"TJ, can you join me in my office?" Colonel Weissberg briefly stuck his head into TJ's office as he returned to his office from St. Martha's Residence.

TJ grabbed a pad of paper and, with her leg free of pain, walked briskly into Weissberg's office. She was careful exiting her office because the Swiss Guards' center of operations was, once again, a hub of commotion following the report of Ernie's kidnapping.

"Close the door, TJ." Weissberg was standing next to his desk, head down and rubbing his temples in frustration. "This place is getting wilder and wilder by the day. Who would have thought that the Vatican, normally a peaceful holy site, would be this exciting?"

Both had been up all night on the 18th. The call from Weissberg's officer reporting Ernie's departure, with luggage in hand, from the hotel and, then, his kidnapping came in as TJ was putting in another late night. Weissberg had returned back to his office after the first call. It was now early morning on the 19th, around seven o'clock, which would have been the time TJ normally arrived at her office. Weissberg was especially hard hit after his roundtrip flight to New York. He had not had much sleep for the past 48 hours.

"Can you believe that they're upset with me for letting Flanagan leave the hotel? What did they want me to do? Lock him in his hotel room? Arrest him upon leaving the hotel? He's a free citizen! Flanagan can come and go as he wishes. How can we stop him? Damn!"

Weissberg, now standing erect and waving his hands in the air as he spoke, was particularly irritated because, under the assumption that Ernie was headed to the airport, Weissberg had dispatched a couple of officers and Monsignor Campbell to the airport to talk him out of leaving. "Plus, we tried to call Flanagan on his cell phone, but the son-of-a-bitch evidently turned it off!"

Weissberg lowered his hands, placed them on his hips, and began to pace in front of his desk. TJ let him vent and patiently waited for new instructions which, she correctly assumed, would be forthcoming after he settled down. She knew that 'they' were the cardinals whom Weissberg had just been to see at St. Martha's Residence.

Weissberg finally came to a halt and looked at TJ. "Guess what the scarlet-hatted gentlemen had to say?" He didn't wait for an answer and continued, "They said that Flanagan was the single-most important person for the Vatican! The most important! They said there was no option but to find him alive. It was a matter of the very highest priority!"

TJ was surprised. The most important person? Really?

Seeing her surprise, Weissberg exclaimed, "See? You're just as surprised! So I ask the dear Cardinal Meissner what he's talking about? After all, I was part of the delegation to New York and this Flanagan guy doesn't look that important. TJ, he's a normal guy. He's just a small-town college professor. He's not a college president, not a politician, not a millionaire, or anything else from what I can tell. He's just a likeable fellow and friend of Cardinal Murphy!"

"How did Cardinal Meissner reply to your question about Flanagan? Did he tell you why this man is so important?"

"He refused to tell me! Can you believe that? Now they're keeping secrets from security! I just about blew my top! Meissner said that he absolutely could not confide in me. Sure, he apologized, but a lot of help that is! So, now I'm in a tight spot! Think about it! I have to go to the Italian police and tell them that the Vatican needs all of their top resources because this Flanagan guy is the most important man in the world, only I can't tell them why! Heaven help us!"

Weissberg felt better after getting that off of his chest. Now looking at the accumulated papers on his desk, Weissberg sighed. "Well, I'll call the Italian police and see what we can do about persuading them to throw everything they have into finding and rescuing Doctor Flanagan."

After meeting with Colonel Weissberg in Cardinal Meissner's suite at St. Martha's Residence, Meissner and Murphy attempted to chart their next moves. They were nearly panic-stricken over Ernie's kidnapping. Just when they had seemed to turn the corner to put their string of misfortunes behind them, another crisis struck. They wondered if the string of bad luck would ever end. Murphy was, understandably, doubly troubled as he worried over his best friend's life. He felt horrible over his responsibility in bringing Ernie to Rome and, thereby, endangering him.

"Sean, we must trust that everything will be fine and that Doctor Flanagan will be found unharmed. I expect that his kidnappers will contact us soon with a ransom demand that we will gladly pay for his release."

"I certainly hope so. I can't imagine who would want to harm Ernie other than a bunch of thugs who thought he was rich merely because he had a top suite at the Hotel Intercontinental."

"Colonel Weissberg assured me that he would press the Italian police for all of their support. Believe it or not, the Italian police have incredible experience in tracking down criminals after years of chasing the Red Brigade terrorists. They'll find your friend. However, in the meantime, I suggest that we inform our fellow colleagues. I don't wish to interrupt their deliberations after meeting Doctor Flanagan yesterday, but we must share this news."

"I understand. I agree with you." Cardinal Murphy solemnly concurred. "I will, also, have to call Ernie's children to notify them. I will ask them to stay in the U. S. until we know more. Monsignor Campbell will work with the three of them."

"Keep the faith, my friend," Meissner reassured him. "While the police search for Doctor Flanagan, everyone will remain at St. Martha's for the day reading Doctor Flanagan's books and articles. I've divided the cardinals into groups and each group is responsible for reporting tomorrow morning when we reconvene the conclave in the Sistine Chapel. I, also, suspect that several will ask to speak with you regarding Doctor Flanagan's qualifications and your extensive knowledge of him. That will help keep your mind off of the troubling circumstances."

"Hey, sleepy head. Time to wake up!" Cybil nudged Giulio in the ribs and planted a kiss on his forehead. Giulio stretched and opened his eyes to look at Cybil who was sitting on the edge of the bed in her hotel suite. "I've already showered and dressed. Room service is bringing breakfast up any minute now."

Cybil was excited about playing the part of a tourist. Harold had told her to take a couple of days off. With the listening device's failure and Spitini's inability to plant another device, Harold was considering bringing Cybil home to New York. He reasoned that Cybil had enough material for some sensational follow-up articles and that not much more would come of extending her costly stay in Rome. So Harold instructed Cybil to take a couple of well-earned days off while he thought about it.

Cybil had some thinking to do, too. A couple of days along the Amalfi coast and a jaunt out to the island of Capri would be just what she needed to clear her mind. With Harold pressuring her to return to New York, the time had arrived to make a decision on Giulio and Rome.

Marco Spitini excitedly re-read Masoud's coded email. He was going to Iran! Finally! Masoud congratulated Spitini on his great success and wrote that the nation's leaders were preparing to welcome him as a hero of Islam. Indeed, a sumptuous villa was waiting for him in the mountains outside of Tehran!

The instructions were short, but, in essence, Spitini was to meet a contact one block from Rome's railroad station in the early evening of the next day. Spitini was to wear regular clothes without any sign of being a Catholic Monsignor. Further instructions would then follow.

Elated, Spitini quickly typed a reply message confirming his agreement. On his way out of the café, he bought a second coffee and a large apple pastry to celebrate.

Watching from his sidewalk seat under a green, red, and white umbrella across the street, Yousef smiled and ordered a second cup of coffee, too.

CHAPTER FORTY-ONE

The first day was tough. After his initial interrogation and beating by Masoud, Yaya and Rahman had continued the torture for another couple of hours. Thankfully, the night in captivity passed without any further incidents.

Exhausted and with considerable back pain from being dragged across the rough concrete floor, he lay uncomfortably on his left side in a fetal position. The headset still blared rock music into his ears, but, fortunately, his captors had turned down the volume from deafening to moderately loud. Unable to hear or see a thing, Ernie alternated between consciousness and sleep.

Now in his second day of captivity, Rahman and Yaya picked up where they had left off. They seemed to delight in inflicting pain and in taunting Ernie. They wouldn't accept the truth. Or, perhaps, they didn't want to know the truth. They had made up their minds that Ernie wasn't really a professor, but a covert law enforcement agent.

Today, Rahman and Yaya had switched tactics. After the first hour, they began to question Ernie about the Cardinals. What were they doing? What were they discussing? Had they elected a pope? How close were they to electing a pope? Who was the leading candidate?

By noon, the two interrogators were thoroughly frustrated at Ernie's ignorance. They had beaten Ernie, choked him, dragged him across the floor, and threatened him with death. Rahman had even gone so far as to hold an unloaded pistol by Ernie's head. They laughed whenever Ernie winced at the click of the pulled trigger. However, Rahman and Yaya finally quit the torture in order to obey Masoud's guidance requiring them to keep Ernie alive. For the time being anyway.

For the remainder of the afternoon and evening, Ernie's thoughts roamed across a wide variety of subjects. He thought of his children, envisioned meeting his wife and parents in heaven, and desperately wished to have his hood torn off to reveal the Italian police rescue squad. In striving to remain hopeful, Ernie reviewed his preparations for the fall semester of courses he would teach at Nyack College. He also spent a good deal of time recounting his day among the cardinals at the conclave. Ernie was pleased that he had remained true to his self throughout the conclave's discussions and he had, in point of fact, greatly enjoyed the mental sparring. Nevertheless, he was solidly convinced that the cardinals would now come to their senses and dismiss him. He sourly reflected that it likely did not matter much because his chances of ending up with a bullet in the head were evidently strong.

He gave up trying to understand his captors and their motives. Life simply had failed to make much sense from the moment Sean called him to notify Ernie that the papal airplane was en route with a delegation to bring him to the Holy See. Perhaps, if he was rescued, someone might be able to explain it all to him.

Ernie surprised himself by praying for his captors. Praying for his captors to release him was easy, as was praying for the Italian police to rescue him. However, Ernie prayed that

God would be merciful and save the kidnappers' souls from complete evil entrapment. Visions of John Paul II visiting his imprisoned assassin, Mehmet Ali Agca, came to mind.

In further attempting to hold back his despair, Ernie fervently prayed with thanksgiving for the life that he had enjoyed. He thanked God for the love and mercy God had shown him. He thanked God for his parents, his wife, and his children. He thanked God for the wonderful opportunities to serve God on earth.

Somewhere in the early evening of his second day as a prisoner, Ernie finally fell deep asleep for several hours. Dreaming, Ernie found himself standing on the shores of a large lake with his dog, Gabriel, sitting by his side. The red sun was just then rising over the water horizon ahead of him, but it was already unbearably hot in the rocky desert surrounding the lake's marshes. With Gabriel trotting alongside him, Ernie then began to walk along the lake's marshy shoreline in search of the area's inhabitants.

Rounding a tree-lined bend in the shoreline, Ernie spied a large group of people a hundred yards from him milling about on a spit of land jutting into the lake. They appeared agitated and several were arguing with each other and wildly waving their arms in various directions. As he drew nearer, he recognized the Catholic cardinals in their scarlet choir dress. Seeing Sean Murphy, Ernie walked over to inquire what the cardinals were up to. Shouldn't they be in Rome? Sean appeared to be flabbergasted at seeing Ernie, but quickly confided that the cardinals had left Rome in disarray after finding that God had struck them with several ancient, biblical plagues. Trying to make amends, they were attempting to return to the Holy Land and Jerusalem; but, they were stymied at not being able to replicate Moses' act of parting the sea. Murphy asked Ernie for ideas, but Ernie was stumped for a solution. Nevertheless, Ernie took a seat on a large, flat boulder and watched the cardinals with growing curiosity.

The colorful collection of cardinals was divided into numerous small groups with each trying to part the sea. One group was waving their hands and long staffs over the water. Another was reciting biblical verses in unison and yet another was holding hands in a large circle while kneeling on their knees in prayer. One other group was furiously thumbing through their Bibles in a vain attempt to find a secret code to unlock the mystery of the parting of the Red Sea. Three gregarious cardinals were taking up a collection in order to raise enough money to charter a ferry.

Ernie watched with fascination, but, after a while he grew bored and began petting Gabriel. At that moment Gabriel jumped up and barked at a seagull that had landed nearby. A second later, Gabriel lurched after the bird, but was too slow to catch it. Returning to an amused Ernie, Gabriel miraculously spotted a foot-long dry branch which Gabriel picked up with its teeth in hopes that Ernie would play fetch with him. Sitting down at Ernie's feet, Gabriel dropped the branch and barked at Ernie.

Ernie picked up the stick and tossed it. Gabriel took after it and happily returned with its tail wagging wildly. Ernie threw the stick a second time with Gabriel returning with it again. "Good boy, Gabriel!" Ernie remembered saying.

Picking up the stick a third time, Ernie threw it towards the lake knowing that Gabriel would enjoy the cooling water. With Gabriel sprinting into the water, the stick arched high in the blue sky and fell into a cluster of reeds just ahead of the dog. No sooner had the splash subsided than the water began to bubble. Gabriel halted, looked at the strange effervescent water, turned and retreated to the safety of the beach by Ernie's feet.

The bubbling now drew the cardinals' attention. With everyone now staring at the peculiar event, the water grew shallow. Within a minute, the water had retreated to expose a muddy sandbar. Ernie and the cardinals watched in utter amazement as the lake's falling water level collected in vast, shallow pools. A network of muddy high ground now crisscrossed the lake and offered passage to the far shoreline.

Before he knew what was happening, the cardinals had jumped onto the pathway. Murphy excitedly ran over to Ernie, hugged him, and pulled him off of his perch atop the boulder and into the moving crowd. It was a slow march. The elderly cardinals had a difficult time plodding through the mud in their finest clerical robes and the mud devoured many a scarlet slipper.

Following them far out into the lake, Ernie tripped on a rock. As he fell into the mud, a bullet whistled by his head. Turning to look towards the shore, he caught sight of a half dozen men sporting rifles giving chase. Shouting a warning to his compatriots, Ernie picked himself up and goaded the weary, out of shape cardinals until they all reached the dry, rocky shoreline.

Stopping to catch his breath, Ernie looked back over his shoulder at the rapidly advancing thugs. However, Ernie was startled to find a tidal wave bearing down on the pursuing assailants. Within a minute, the wave swallowed them. Some flailed in the rushing water, but all drowned.

Abruptly awakening from his vivid dream, Ernie was overcome with an overwhelming sense of anguish. Through the dream, Ernie finally realized that he, much like Moses, had been fighting against his all-powerful God. Moses had very reluctantly followed God's instructions to approach the Egyptian pharaoh with demands to free the Jews. Although a former member of pharaoh's household and a noted military commander, Moses felt inadequate to answer God's call. First, Moses had abandoned his fellow Jews when he had had to run for his life many years earlier after killing an Egyptian soldier. Second, Moses suffered from a speech impediment, thought by many to be a stutter, which he felt precluded him from confronting pharaoh, much less authoritatively addressing the Jews. Lastly, Moses had a wife and children whom he loathed to leave. Only after repeated negotiations following a startling appearance in a burning bush, was God able to convince the reluctant Moses to pick up a wooden staff and head to Egypt as the anointed leader of the Jews.

Ernie now realized that his fears and misgivings over the surprising call to assume the leadership at the Vatican were much like those Moses faced. Convicted by his dream, Ernie pledged, if ever he was rescued, to serve God in whatever capacity God selected for him. Ernie's personal misgivings over his qualifications, his youthful flight from the Catholic Church, and his wish to remain in Nyack at home among his family and friends were selfish barriers Ernie had erected to rationalize his current flight from God.

"TJ, are you ready for good news? Hold on to your knickers, but we tracked the amplifier's serial number to a small electronics shop in Rome!" Geoff Corson was beaming as he relayed the good news to TJ in her office

"That's terrific! Come on in! Close the door and tell me more!" It was early in the evening, but TJ remarkably felt a surge of energy after another dreary day reading through reports.

Sitting down in a chair by her desk, Geoff pulled out a file and handed it to TJ. "There's the documentation. A Giulio Battista was the last known owner of the amplifier. His shop isn't far from here. From the looks of his webpage, it's a small electronics shop specializing in radio gear and spying devices! How about that? Anyway, the chap looks like a young Italian. What do you say we go snooping?"

"By all means, but just snooping, Geoff. Let's leave the heavy handed investigating to the local police and Swiss Guards. Go snoop around his shop and call me. I'll alert Colonel Weissberg, in the meantime."

But, before TJ could get up to find Weissberg, she and Geoff were surprised to hear the Colonel looking for her. "TJ! TJ!" Weissberg banged on her office door twice before quickly opening it. "TJ! Good news! The Italian police found Doctor Flanagan!"

CHAPTER FORTY-TWO

"Flanagan is being held in a warehouse in the harbor of Civitavecchia!" Weissberg was nearly out of breath in his excitement. "It's incredible, but it only took them two days to find him!"

"Slow down, Wilhelm. Take a deep breath. Where is this Civitavecchia and have the police rescued Flanagan?"

"No, no. He's still being held by his kidnappers. The police counterterror squad is watching the warehouse, but has not, yet, moved in to rescue Flanagan. Apparently, he's alive and under guard, but, the police don't want to put him at risk in an assault on the warehouse. It looks like the kidnappers are heavily armed, but no one is quite sure, yet."

"Is Civitavecchia in Rome?" TJ had not mastered Italian geography, yet.

"Oh, sorry. I forgot that part. No, Civitavecchia is an ancient town northwest of Rome on the coast. It's about an hour's drive from here. It used to be Rome's seaport, but now it is principally a port for cruise ships and for ferries to Corsica and Sardinia."

"How did they find him?" TJ asked.

"Good question. Come on, let's go downtown to the police command center. My car is outside."

"Yes, I'm coming!" Then, turning to Geoff Corson, TJ said, "Keep me posted. I'll fill the Colonel in on your findings on our drive downtown." TJ picked up a notebook and her cell phone before dashing off after Weissberg.

TJ and Colonel Weissberg arrived at the Italian police headquarters a half hour later and were quickly admitted into the secure command center. The deputy police chief and two of his senior officers welcomed them and offered them a couple of chairs in a small, glass-enclosed office off in the wing of the command center. After the welcoming formalities, one of the senior police officers proceeded to brief TJ and the Colonel.

"After you alerted us to Doctor Flanagan's kidnapping, we initiated several electronic investigations to locate his possible whereabouts. First, we examined video footage from our traffic surveillance cameras in Rome. We were very excited to find video of a light-blue utility van and a black sedan traveling together in the vicinity of the kidnapping shortly after the reported time of the incident. Unfortunately, the kidnappers changed vehicles. We actually found the utility van, which had been stolen from a construction company, in an abandoned lot. Someone had hosed down the inside of the van so we didn't get any forensic evidence either."

TJ and Weissberg nodded. TJ instinctively knew that they were dealing with professionals, possibly terrorists. This was not a bunch of criminal thugs looking for a large ransom. The Italian deputy police chief seemed to read TJ's mind for he added, "This is a level of sophistication that is reminiscent of the Red Brigades terrorists' kidnapping of Aldo Moro, one of our prime ministers, in 1978. They boxed his car in and kidnapped him, much like these criminals did with your Doctor Flanagan.

Anyway, we found Moro shot to death and stuffed in the trunk of a car two months later."

The senior police officer then continued, "We have a very good relationship with the electrical power company and the telephone industry. In the hope that the kidnappers would take Doctor Flanagan to a deserted facility, we began scanning electrical power consumption and cellular phone transmissions. We started examining areas of Rome and then, in concentric rings, we looked at the regions around Rome. It sounds like a lot of work, but nowadays computers can do this very quickly. We found twenty facilities where electrical power consumption increased dramatically within a day of Doctor Flanagan's kidnapping. Next, we scoured cellular telephone transmissions in and around the same areas where power consumption increased. That narrowed the list to four areas of interest. Then, we examined the traffic surveillance cameras for these four areas and, lo and behold, we found a sedan in Civitavecchia that shows up in Rome's surveillance cameras near the deserted lot where we found the utility van."

The police officer produced a photograph of the sedan. The photo had been magnified so one could plainly see the driver, a passenger in the front seat, and two men in the back seat. There, between the two men in the back seat, one could make out another passenger bent forward at the waist.

"We dispatched our undercover counterterror team to Civitavecchia early this afternoon. They covertly set up listening devices around a warehouse in the harbor of Civitavecchia. By late afternoon, they had intercepted conversations by the kidnappers that positively placed Doctor Flanagan in the warehouse."

Colonel Weissberg and TJ were impressed. Again, anticipating their question, the deputy police chief spoke up. "We are moving police elements into surrounding buildings and we are continuing to monitor the warehouse. We are not one hundred percent positive how many criminals are in the warehouse or in which room we can find Doctor Flanagan. Our information is still too imprecise to risk an assault. However, we appear to have some time to act because the conversations we have intercepted don't indicate any imminent danger to Doctor Flanagan. They are not torturing him. In fact, the terrorists are debating what to do about him. However, if they do intend to harm him, we will move in quickly. My men on the ground are positioning themselves and refining the plans."

Cardinals Meissner and Murphy had just completed dinner when Colonel Weissberg's call announcing the good news about Ernie arrived. The news was a true godsend after the deliberations over Ernie in the conclave because, at the end of that day, the cardinals had voted to resume balloting the following morning. The cardinals collectively agreed that balloting had been satisfactorily suspended for several days to permit them to regroup, but that they were now sufficiently confident to proceed anew.

Both Meissner and Murphy privately agreed that the following day's balloting would likely yield a momentous result. The conclave was very likely going to elect Ernie.

True, there were grave reservations about Ernie's qualifications and the meaning of the Cardinals' dreams. Many would vote for another candidate. However, for reasons based on faith and practicality, momentum was building for Ernie's election.

On account of faith, the cardinals were reluctant to oppose the miraculous intervention of God. Not only were the cardinals taken aback by the seemingly miraculous dreams and series of catastrophes, but the men noted that life had improved since Cardinal Murphy's revelation of his dream. The unfortunate mishaps reminiscent of the biblical plagues had come to an abrupt end. Plus, the heat wave had broken, the water main was repaired, and electrical power had been restored. This was far too much of coincidence for men of deep faith to ignore or to dismiss.

On account of more practical matters, Ernie was the compromise candidate sought by many after Maltempo's collapse. Ernie's outspoken support of the Church's ecumenical and missionary programs appealed to the social-minded Cardinals opposing Maltempo. Likewise, Ernie's firm words about reforming the Church's strategy while strengthening its core values pleased the conservatives. Lastly, neither camp viewed Ernie as a strong pope. The more cynical among them deduced that Ernie's lack of experience would lead to his dependence on them.

With a cold sweat breaking out over both men, Cardinals Meissner and Murphy were quick to realize that if the cardinals were, indeed, going to elect Ernie Flanagan, it was essential to rescue him. What would happen if no one could produce Ernie to accept the election?

Elsewhere in Rome, Marco Spitini was making his way to the railroad station. In accordance with his instructions, he was not wearing any clerical clothes and he had not packed a suitcase. Stepping out of the taxi, Spitini looked over his shoulder to see if anyone was tailing him and began walking towards his rendezvous.

Reaching the building, he hesitated before entering the front door. He was surprised to find a couple of young men holding hands leaving the building. Spitini was not expecting to begin his exodus to Iran at a cheap hotel that evidently catered to homosexuals.

He looked up at the hotel's metal sign over the door. No, there was no mistake. It was the right hotel. Warily, he walked up the two steps and into the front foyer. He avoided eye contact with the clerk and briskly walked towards the dirty staircase.

Climbing four flights of stairs, Spitini arrived at the door to room 410. Standing outside the door, Spitini straightened his jacket and ran his right hand over his hair. Eager to move on, Spitini knocked.

Yousef opened the door and ushered Spitini into the dimly lit, shabbily furnished room. "Come in, Marco. Come in. I'm very honored to finally meet you." Yousef closed the door and moved alongside Spitini.

"Thank you. I am looking forward to setting out for ...."

Spitini suddenly stopped speaking and looked down in horror at his stomach. "What are you doing?" Spitini stammered as he attempted to back away from Yousef.

A larger and stronger man, Yousef firmly grabbed Spitini's belt and pulled his victim closer while plunging the switchblade deeper into Spitini's gut. He felt Spitini shudder and begin to struggle so Yousef yanked up on the knife and then pulled it hard to his left thereby irreparably cutting Spitini's intestines. Having doomed Spitini to die, Yousef pulled the blade out and let Spitini drop to his knees cupping his stomach with both hands.

Spitini looked pleadingly up at Yousef. "Why? Why?"

Yousef looked down at Spitini and sneered, "Why? You arrogant little bastard! Why? Because you are a liability. We can't have the police arresting you. With you dead, no one will ever know what happened to the pope. You were never leaving Rome. Never. You're going to die in disgrace as just another priest who fancied boys." Spitini was going into shock as Yousef moved behind him. Yousef planted his left knee firmly in the middle of Spitini's back, grabbed Spitini's hair in his left hand, pulled Spitini's head up and back, and efficiently slit Spitini's throat. Letting go of the hair, he let Marco Spitini slump onto the floor gurgling for air and losing massive amounts of blood.

Yousef watched Marco Spitini die. In an attempt to make the murder look like a lover's quarrel and theft, he tore up the room and, then, rifled through Spitini's pockets to find Marco's wallet. Yousef removed all of the cash, slid Spitini's watch off of his wrist, and yanked the gold crucifix from Spitini's neck. He quickly washed the items, his hands, and knife in a small washbasin and left with satisfaction, thinking, 'One down, two to go.'

CHAPTER FORTY-THREE

On the same night that witnessed Spitini's demise and Ernie's discovery, Cybil and Giulio contentedly walked into the front foyer of Cybil's hotel lovingly holding hands. The young man at the desk smiled, welcomed them back to the hotel, and handed Cybil her mail. "Grazie!" Cybil cheerfully responded and headed towards the elevators with her right arm now around Giulio's waist and his left arm slung over her bare shoulders.

The two days along the Amalfi Coast had been glorious. Confident that she truly loved Giulio, Cybil had come around to deciding that she would stay in Rome. She had nervously broached the subject to Giulio last night as they lounged on the balcony of a small hotel overlooking the Mediterranean Sea and, much to her delight, found that he wanted her to stay. It was much too early to talk about marriage, but Cybil knew in her gut that this relationship was meant to last a lifetime. She had found her great love. In Italy, of all places!

Feeling like a giddy teenager with a crush, Cybil was anxious to tell her parents and friends. Harold would likely be furious to lose his star reporter, but Cybil still hoped to write free lance pieces for the Daily News from Europe. She was excited.

The happy couple kissed in the elevator and, hand in hand, walked down the hotel corridor to Cybil's suite. "Well, my dear, here we are!" Cybil announced as she opened the door.

"Si. Here we are!" Giulio replied as he followed her into the darkened suite, closed the door, and flicked the lights on. Those were the last words he ever spoke.

Four pistol shots, fired from a pistol outfitted with a silencer, found their marks. The first two hit Giulio in the chest, killing him before he hit the floor. The third bullet hit Cybil in her left shoulder just above her heart and the fourth bullet, fired as she was falling, hit her in the head and sheared off most of her left ear. She fell alongside Giulio with blood streaming from her head.

Yousef calmly stepped over his two victims, opened the door, and quietly left the suite. He pulled his fedora low and took the elevator to the parking garage in order to avoid the guests and staff in the foyer. A minute later he had vanished.

Shortly after the assassin had left, the bell hop arrived at Cybil's suite with the luggage. Hearing no response to his knock on the door, he gingerly unlocked the door and stuck his head inside to call for Cybil's permission to enter. He froze the instant he saw the two bloodied bodies lying on the floor. Gasping, he dropped the bags and ran for the elevator to alert the manager downstairs in the foyer.

CHAPTER FORTY-FOUR

"We need to kill him and close up shop, Masoud!" Rahman firmly declared. "Yousef took care of Spitini and the American journalist last night. Let's get rid of Flanagan and be done with it. Vahid doesn't know anything so if we lay low, all of this will blow over. We've done our job at the Vatican."

"Yes, but maybe we can make this look like a mafia operation and exchange Flanagan for a large ransom," Ali Golbarian proposed.

"The hell with that. Why should we risk getting caught? No, I agree with Rahman. Let's drown the bastard in the harbor and be done with it," Mehrzad, yet another one of Masoud's thugs, asserted.

Masoud patiently listened to his team argue over Flanagan's fate. He, too, was tiring of Flanagan on the morning of Ernie's third day in captivity. He never expected Flanagan to provide any details about the Vatican's suspicions and investigation and, therefore, Masoud did not pursue the torture and interrogation of Flanagan. Rather, Masoud wanted to send a warning shot across the path of TJ and her associates in retribution for arresting Vahid. An elegant kidnapping would go a long way to display his outfit's superb professional skills and Flanagan's eventual death would clearly demonstrate that he meant business. Masoud very much wanted to even the score with the self-important western authorities and he took special delight at the thought of killing Americans, the very vermin of the earth. It was time for Muslims to show their ferocity and strength.

Focusing anew on his compatriot's arguments, Masoud held up his hand to signal silence. "Flanagan has to die. Rahman is correct about needing to clean up loose ends, but Flanagan's death holds a special significance. We must exact our revenge for Vahid's imprisonment. We must let the Italian authorities know that they are dealing with a cunning and powerful organization. Flanagan is a necessary sacrifice in our holy war against the west. Who better to kill than an American?"

Masoud paused to reassure himself that his warring partners were in full agreement. "We'll throw him to the fish tonight. Since we're in Italy, let's use the methods of the Mafia. Okay?" Masoud laughed and his fellow terrorists joined him.

"Let's get everything packed up. Rahman, you get the honors tonight. Carry the doctor to the side door and toss him into the water. Tie some weights to his feet to make sure he sinks and stays there." Masoud had picked a warehouse that was built directly on the edge of the harbor. A twenty-foot wide warehouse door opened directly onto the harbor where the water was over twenty-five feet deep.

Rahman grinned broadly and swapped a high five with Yahya before asking, "When?"

"Ten o'clock. Yahya, you help him. You, too, Ali. Mehrzad, I want you and the other two to sterilize everything inside. Wash this place down and make sure that nobody dropped anything. I want to leave this dump as fast as we can. We'll head south along the coast and split up. Everyone should lay low for the rest of the month. Go on summer holiday. We'll regroup next month. In the meantime, I'll send an anonymous note to the police letting them know where they can find their Doctor Flanagan. Is that clear?"

The counterterror squad leader looked up at his colleagues after listening to the terrorists' deliberations. "It's showtime, guys! We've got twelve hours to put a plan in place. Any ideas?"

His chief communications officer raised his right hand slightly. "Yes. I think I've got a dandy of an idea with minimal risk to Flanagan. You're going to like this one, guys!"

CHAPTER FORTY-FIVE

"Fellow Cardinals, we have all agreed to resume balloting this morning. I believe that yesterday's deliberations over Doctor Flanagan's qualifications and over our continued appraisal of the earlier events have proven advantageous despite having to digress from standard conclave procedures. Before we select the three scrutineers, the three infirmarii, and the three revisers, I must ask if any of you have any questions or reservations about proceeding."

Cardinal Kodavas stood. "Ahem. Fellow Cardinals, our discussions have been, shall we say, intense. I just wish to make one final point."

Cardinal Meissner nodded his approval and Cardinal Kodavas continued.

"Jesus Christ chose twelve common men as the original apostles. There was not a single rabbi. Not a single Pharisee. Not a single so-called learned man."

A few Cardinals shifted uneasily in their seats.

"And they were all Jews."

More uneasily shifted in their seats. A few coughed.

"Let's listen to our God. Let's let him make the choice free of our rules. Open your hearts and let the Holy Spirit guide you."

With that, Cardinal Kodavas sat down.

Cardinal Meissner tensely waited for ten seconds. There were no further comments and no objections. He relaxed and continued with the protocol. First, nine names were drawn for the positions of scrutineers, infirmarii, and revisers. Next, the ballots were distributed   Finally, the cardinals, in order of seniority, marched to the raised platform and deposited their ballots in a large chalice resting on an altar. Each cardinal recited the oath: "I call as my witness Christ the Lord who will be my judge, that my vote is given to the one who before God I think should be elected."

Cardinal Murphy looked at his friend's name written on his ballot. He could hardly believe that he was casting his vote for Ernie, but, as a matter of faith, he could not write any other name on the ballot. He was so nervous that his hands actually trembled when he folded the ballot in half. Bending his head down, he looked to calm himself through prayer while waiting for his turn to approach the altar.

When his turn arrived, Sean Cardinal Murphy rose and walked to the altar where he cast his ballot for a fellow American. He returned to his seat and expectantly joined his colleagues in observing the conclusion of the balloting.

The tension in the room was running high among all of the cardinals. Every one of them was battling an internal mix of trusting faith and analytical reasoning. No matter how hard they evaluated the facts, no matter how meticulously they reviewed Doctor Flanagan's record, and no matter how difficult they found it to find conclusive evidence to support their conclusions, they were all driven to act purely on faith. They had taken the leap of faith where facts had left off.

The world would never understand their act of faith. It would make no sense to the outside world. To the media hounds and politicians waiting outside for a white smoke signal, the cardinals' dreams were pure fiction and their seeming biblical misfortunes were nothing more than a mixture of coincidences and criminal acts.

Indeed, what else could one expect of the world? Without knowledge of God, the world had no underlying basis permitting it to make sense of the seemingly senseless.

For those men in the Sistine Chapel, the whole affair was simply a miracle. For whatever reason, God had elected to directly intervene in the conclave. Although each man struggled mightily with this admission, none of them wished to counter the moving hand of God.

It was, therefore, with tremendous relief and thanksgiving that the assembled cardinals heard the third scrutineer announce the name of Ernesto Flanagan on one hundred of the ballots. It wasn't unanimous after all, but the vote was decisive. Now if only they could rescue him and convince him to accept.

CHAPTER FORTY-SIX

As the cardinals were casting their ballots and Masoud was plotting Ernie's murder, Geoff Corson anxiously looked across the desk at TJ. "Well, my dear, do you want the good news or the bad news first?"

TJ knew Geoff well enough to know that something was awry. "Okay, give me the good news first."

TJ frowned. She wasn't in the best of moods.

"We found Giulio Battista," Geoff announced matter of factly.

"Well, I like that news. How bad is the bad news?"

"Let's just say that I'm glad you're sitting down, old gal," Geoff replied. He drummed his fingers on her desk not wishing to share the news, but he continued, "Giulio Battista is lying in the morgue with two bullets in his chest."

"Damn!" TJ rarely cussed, so this mere, one word defamatory remark clearly signaled her displeasure.

Geoff shrugged his shoulders. "Sorry, dear. He returned to his girlfriend's hotel suite last night. Somewhere in the short span of time between entering the room and the bell hop arriving with the luggage, someone had neatly planted two bullets in him. He didn't stand a chance."

"Who did it?" TJ shot back quizzically.

"Good question. The hotel cameras show Giulio and his girlfriend entering the suite and, a minute later, a person with the body build of a man leaving. I saw the video. No chance of seeing the assassin's face."

"Assassin? Why do you use that word?" TJ perked up.

"Call it a hunch. The hit man evidently ransacked the suite and made off with some valuables so you might think that this was a burglary gone wrong. However, he was clearly waiting to ambush the couple. He dropped them as soon as they entered with nice, clean shots. This fellow carries a Beretta and knows how to use it. A good marksman. No, he was waiting for them. The rest of the stuff in the room was just window dressing to throw us off of the mark."

"Interesting. Most interesting. It sounds like our man Giulio served his purpose and, once the eavesdropping device was found, he was no longer needed. He might even have been hiding from his colleagues if he was avoiding his shop and shacking up with some dame. So, who's the girl?"

"Believe it or not, she's alive. She took one in the shoulder just above the heart. A couple of inches lower and she'd be toast, too. The second bullet hit her in the head and sheared off her left ear. It must have been a bloody mess. The bloody head wound probably saved her life, though. The killer must've taken one look at her head and figured she was dead."

"Geoff, for crying out loud, who's the girl?" TJ was slightly irritated to have to ask twice.

"Oh, sorry, dear. Right. Some American journalist named Cybiline Checchi. She's out cold in a hospital after losing so much blood, but the doc actually thinks she might make it."

"Checchi? Did you say Checchi?" TJ asked, taken aback.

"Yes. Do you know her?"

"You bet I do. You bet I do! She was seen meeting on two occasions with someone I've had tailed. So she and Giulio were shacking up?"

Before Corson could answer, he and TJ were interrupted by Major Steinman standing in the office doorway.

"Forgive me, TJ, but I have some news for you."

"Yes, what is it?" TJ inquired while waving the Major into her office. She noted that Steinman looked nervous.

"It's Monsignor Spitini. He's dead. Murdered downtown last night in a cheap hotel. The cleaning lady found him this morning."

Cardinal Meissner relaxed after the three revisers verified the vote in accordance with protocol. However, he now had new concerns. The cardinals now wished to see Doctor Flanagan in order to put the question of acceptance to him. Meissner looked down the center aisle and met the eyes of Cardinal Murphy. Neither had a good answer, but both had agreed that, in the event of Ernie's election, they had no choice but to reveal the truth about Ernie's condition.

Taking a deep breath, Cardinal Meissner took the proverbial plunge and, to the uttermost consternation of the cardinals, revealed Ernie's precarious situation at the hands of kidnappers. Although the cardinals were clearly exasperated and concerned, Meissner was taken aback by the seeming calmness of their response. The conclave did not dissolve into chaos as it had under earlier misfortunes.

Aldo Pellitteri, the oldest cardinal of the lot, stood up and spoke for the entire College of Cardinals in saying, "My fellow brethren, we need not worry. After leading us this far, God will not desert us. We have every hope that Doctor Ernesto Flanagan will join us here soon and grant us the joy of accepting the papacy as God has preordained. Come, let us pray the remainder of the day."

CHAPTER FORTY-SEVEN

The remainder of the day was a day of preparation and planning. And prayer. All eyes were on ten o'clock that night. Unaware that he was central to all of it, Ernie continued to lie on the bare concrete floor of the warehouse in Civitavecchia. He was weak from a lack of food, suffering from stiffness and soreness in his back and four limbs, and temporarily deaf from the loud rock music playing into his ears twenty-four hours a day.

Hoping to see Ernie safely rescued, TJ and Colonel Weissberg both traveled to Civitavecchia that afternoon to monitor the police operation from a mobile command post near the harbor. Meanwhile, the cardinals prayed throughout the day in the Sistine Chapel and, then, collectively retired for dinner and prayer throughout the evening at St. Martha's Residence.

As ten o'clock neared, Rahman pushed a wheelbarrow alongside Ernie. He slapped Ernie on the right upper arm to get Ernie's attention and then removed the headset from Ernie. Rahman and Ali then pulled Ernie up to his feet, shuffled Ernie in front of the wheelbarrow, and pushed Ernie down into the wheelbarrow.

Yahya appeared in the doorway with a heavy, metal chain running through a large cinder block and asked, "Ready?"

Rahman grunted, "Yeah. Let's go. Ali, keep your pistol to his head."

Ernie's ears were ringing from the loud music. Unable to hear his captors, Ernie didn't bother to ask what they were doing. He knew that he was in a wheelbarrow, but he didn't know what to make of it. Should he be relieved to be moving? After all, if they wanted to kill him, wouldn't they just kill him where he lay? Then again, if they were simply moving him, why was he in a wheelbarrow instead of a car?

Masoud opened the double-doors and peered out at the harbor. He flicked the warehouse's outdoor lights off and continued to patiently scan the harbor. After five minutes, he waved his men forward. Yahya walked to the edge of the concrete floor and looked around. Seeing nothing of concern, he slowly set the cinder block and chain down.

"Okay. Don't take too long, Rahman," Masoud ordered.

As Ernie was wheeled up into the open doorway, he instantly felt the light breeze. The ringing in his ears had begun to subside so he could hear Masoud. He apprehensively hoped for the best.

Rahman and Ali hoisted Ernie onto his feet. Thereupon, Yahya hastily attached the chain-wrapped cinder block to Ernie's ankle shackles and nodded to Rahman.

"Hey, doctor police man. Can you hear me?" Rahman whispered into Ernie's right ear.

"Yes, I hear you," Ernie hoarsely whispered in return.

"Good. I want you to know what we're doing. Do you have any idea?" Rahman taunted Ernie with glee.

"Setting me free?" Ernie hopefully replied.

"No, sir. We're going to kill you, doctor police man. I'm going to feed you to the fish. New York mafia style. We want

306

you to feel at home." Rahman laughed and pulled the hood from Ernie's head.

Ernie instantly felt an ice cold sweat break out all over. He was surprised to suddenly be looking into the faces of his captors and killers. Quickly looking around to his left he saw the black water.

Before Ernie could think of his next action, Ali grabbed Ernie's shoulders in preparation for pushing Ernie while Yahya lifted the cinder block in preparation for tossing it into the water. Instinctively, Ernie took a deep breath of air, but he was unprepared for Rahman's punch. Rahman hit Ernie as hard as he could in the stomach thereby cruelly knocking the air out of Ernie just as he felt himself falling into the harbor.

The water quickly closed over his head as Ernie sank. The salt water caused excruciating pain in the open wounds in his back. Ernie kicked his feet as forcefully as he could in a vain attempt to free himself of the dead weight holding him under water. He could not see a thing in the black water and he was rapidly running out of his short supply of air. So this was it, Ernie thought to himself. So much for dying peacefully as an old man in his sleep. Worst of all, he didn't even know who his captors were or why they wished to kill him.

Masoud and his men watched Ernie disappear from sight with great satisfaction. Rahman spit into the water and grinned. They waited a minute and then closed the doors and headed for their cars.

Out of sight in the depths of the water, Ernie gave up struggling and committed himself to dying.

CHAPTER FORTY-EIGHT

The Italian counterterror squad leader barked orders into his radio and the Italian police descended on the warehouse. A large, armored truck suddenly appeared and battered the warehouse's main door down. Stun grenades exploded and tear gas streamed through the warehouse. Within a minute, Rahman and Mehrzad were dead and the other terrorists were apprehended.

Out in the water, Ernie was totally unaware of the attack on the warehouse. His lungs were burning and about to explode as he gave up hope and silently prayed to himself with clenched teeth. Then, out of nowhere, Ernie felt human hands! Within seconds, a scuba regulator was set in his mouth and Ernie was enjoying beautiful, life-giving oxygen! Next, Ernie was free of the cinder block and floating to the surface.

Five police divers gently guided Ernie through the water to an inflatable motor boat in the harbor. Another two officers pulled Ernie out of the water, set him on the floor of the boat, and swiftly cut his shackles. With an emergency medical technician administering medical care, the boat raced to a nearby pier where

Colonel Weissberg and TJ impatiently waited alongside an ambulance to welcome Ernie back to freedom.

With Meissner's permission to leave St. Martha's Residence, Murphy headed to the hospital to see Ernie. Despite staying up all night in anticipation of hearing the news about Ernie's rescue, Murphy displayed surprising alacrity at two o'clock in the morning as he anxiously jumped out of the limousine and nearly ran up the ramp to the side entrance reserved for senior Catholic clerics. Doctor Terzini was waiting for him just inside the door and guided him to Ernie's room where two Italian police guards admitted them.

"Sean! What are you doing out of bed in the middle of the night?" Ernie smiled and began to kick off the covers in an attempt to get out of the bed.

"Stay right there! Don't dare get out of bed, my friend!" Murphy loudly exclaimed. Briskly walking the half dozen steps to the bed and mindful of the nurses tending to Ernie's injuries and the intravenous line running into Ernie's arm, Murphy resisted throwing his arms around his good friend to hug him. "Man, it's good to see you! Praise the Lord for saving you!"

"Yes, praise the Lord for saving me; in more ways than one, Sean. In more ways than one."

Murphy's arrival had interrupted a couple of nurses who were changing the temporary bandages on Ernie's neck and back that the medical technician had applied in the ambulance.

"That's quite a bruise you have around your neck!" Murphy looked over the shoulder of one of the nurses to inspect Ernie's condition.

"Shoot, that's nothing." Stretching out his wrists, Ernie displayed his badly bruised and cut wrists. "My ankles don't look much better, but they're a prettier shade of purple," Ernie joked. "But, the worst part of it all, is my back. Here take a look before these wonderful nurses re-apply the bandages." Ernie gingerly leaned slightly forward and twisted to his right to give Sean a better view. "It probably looks worse than it hurts, but I guess that I won't be sleeping on my back for a while!"

"Ouch! That looks like it hurts, my friend. It looks like they dragged you over a bed of nails!"

"Nah, just some rough concrete floor. I guess I'm lucky they didn't do more to me. But, I figured that I was a goner in the harbor."

The two friends spent the next half-hour joyfully visiting. With the medical staff hovering around Ernie, neither of them brought up any mention of the conclave. Instead, Murphy kept the focus on light-hearted banter and Ernie's medical care. Ernie informed Murphy that the physician wanted to keep him at the hospital for at least two days, unless the medical tests and x-rays revealed anything disturbing. Ernie had suffered only superficial injuries without any apparent broken bones, but he was severely dehydrated, malnourished, and suffering from the onset of infection in the cuts and scrapes along his back. Ernie promised not to run from the hospital. Although he despised lying around a hospital, Ernie admitted that he looked forward to a couple of days under medical care.

Sleep came easily to Ernie after Murphy's departure. A nurse awakened him six hours later for medical tests and a light breakfast. Thereafter, Ernie fell asleep again to awaken in the early afternoon. Feeling stronger and mentally alert, Ernie devoured his lunch and settled down to read the Holy Bible.

"Excuse me, Doctor Flanagan. Would you mind if I interrupted and visited?"

Startled to hear a British accent, Ernie looked up from reading to see a slim, attractive Middle Eastern woman standing in the doorway. Behind her, Ernie recognized Colonel Weissberg and he spotted another man in an Italian police uniform. "Yes, come in. Whom do I have the pleasure of meeting?"

"Thank you, Doctor Flanagan." Walking into the room and up to Ernie, she continued, "I am Tara Johnson, but you can call me TJ. I am a detective from Scotland Yard on special assignment to the Vatican." Turning slightly to her left, TJ introduced her two companions, "I am pleased to introduce Police Chief Carlopoli of Rome and I believe that you already know Colonel Weissberg, the commander of the Vatican's Swiss Guards."

"Yes, good to see you again, Colonel." Ernie shook hands with Weissberg and then with Chief Carlopoli, "It's a pleasure to meet you, sir. I believe that I am indebted to you and your men for rescuing me."

Pleased for the compliment, Carlopoli smiled and replied, "Thank you, Doctor Flanagan. My men deserve all of the credit."

"Why don't the three of you pull up those chairs against the wall? I could use a bit of company. My two sons and daughter are on their way from New York, but, in the meantime, I'm all yours," Ernie cheerfully announced and pointed to the chairs.

Ernie waited for them to pull over the chairs and sit. "So, what can I do for you? I suspect you would like to know more about the kidnapping."

"Yes, that's right; but, we've also got a lot to share with you," Colonel Weissberg declared. "But, first, I'm going to yield to my good friend, Paolo, to ask you questions about your kidnappers. Then, TJ will fill you in on some events that have transpired at the Vatican."

Over the next forty-five minutes, the four engaged in an intense discussion of the kidnapping. Ernie wasn't able to provide many details, but did cause a stir when he revealed that Masoud thought that he was a counterterror expert called in by the Vatican.

"Actually, that would be me," TJ laughingly said. "They tried to kill me, too."

"Oh? Well, I'm glad they didn't!" Ernie exclaimed. "Looks like they're not very successful terrorists. O for two is not a record to brag about!"

"Ah, well, there you're wrong, Doctor Flanagan," TJ announced. "They are, actually, two for five which I understand is an excellent batting record in your American baseball game."

"Two for five? Well, you do have some interesting information to share. How about it?" Ernie looked eagerly at TJ.

The next phase of their discussions took well over an hour. In that time, TJ disclosed the murders of Giulio and Spitini, as well as the attempts on Cybiline and herself. Over the course of the previous day, helped by the taped recordings of the terrorists' conversations in Civitavecchia, TJ had also put many of the pieces together. Cybil had also awakened that morning thereby giving TJ additional information. Masoud and his band of terrorists had freely discussed bombing the power plant and the Vatican's transformer station, as well as letting it slip that Spitini and Vahid had planted the listening device, built by Giulio Battista, in the Sistine Chapel. TJ, therefore, knew that Spitini was part of Masoud's outfit, but as of yet, TJ did not fully understand that relationship. Nor did she suspect that Spitini had murdered John Paul III. Perhaps, the police interrogations of Masoud and his fellow surviving terrorists would reveal more.

"So, tell me, who is Cybiline Checchi? Did you say that she is an American journalist?" Ernie asked.

"Yes, that's right. From your hometown. Brooklyn, New York. She works for the New York Daily News."

"The Daily News? The reporter who ambushed me at home was from that tabloid!"

"Checchi probably had something to do with that," TJ speculated.

"How is this woman doing? You said she was shot along with her boyfriend?" Ernie asked.

"Checchi is recuperating in a room one floor below this room. We had her transferred here late yesterday after her surgery. A couple police are guarding her room as we know that Masoud's principal assassin is still at large. For the time being, that is," Colonel Weissberg interjected.

"Well, that's pretty much the whole story," TJ concluded.

"Can I visit her tomorrow?" Ernie asked.

TJ shrugged her shoulders. "That's fine with me, but you'll probably need to check with the physician. She's pretty weak and very distraught over her boyfriend's death. It might not be the best time."

"Ah, but there you're wrong, detective. Where you police deal with broken laws, we pastors deal with broken souls. She probably needs a pastor by her side more than anything at this moment."

CHAPTER FORTY-NINE

"Hello. Excuse me, but do you mind if I come in?" Ernie softly asked as he stuck his head through the partially open door into Cybil's hospital room. After visiting with his three children over the past three days at the hospital, Ernie had begun to impatiently roam the hospital halls when he remembered to look in on Cybil. With one of his police escorts alongside him, Ernie found her room easily by merely looking for the police guards in the hallway.

Cybil was resting, but awake. She was connected to several electronic monitors and an intravenous line, but she managed to lift her head and look in his direction. Ernie carefully walked in and sat down beside her in a chair.

One quick look at Cybil was all Ernie needed to know that she was both in great physical and spiritual pain. He gently took her left hand in both of his. "Hi, Cybiline. I'm Doctor Ernie Flanagan. Believe it or not, we're both from Brooklyn! Do ya' think that the medical staff is up to having two New York patients in this joint?" Ernie joked, hoping to take her mind off of her pain.

Cybil was taken aback. "Flanagan? The Doctor Flanagan from Nyack?" Cybil whispered in a rasping, slow voice.

"The one and only Flanagan. But, please, call me Ernie."

"Call me Cybil. Like cyber, not sibling."

"Cybil, it is! That's a unique pronunciation. I like it!"

"Yeah. Me, too."

Ernie looked at Cybil. She was very pale from her lost blood. A large bandage covered most of her skull and more bandages protected her left shoulder and chest. Her left hand felt cold and weak. Her eyes and her nose were very red; probably from crying, Ernie deduced, from the used facial tissue littering her floor. Worse, her eyes looked like those of someone who had given up. Someone who no longer had something to live for.

"I'm not a medical doctor, Cybil. I'm a minister. I thought that you might like a minister to talk to."

"Thanks, but no thanks. It just doesn't matter anymore," Cybil declared. "I don't care anymore if I die. I'm probably going to jail anyway. I've totally screwed up my life. I can't fix it. It's hopeless."

"There, there. Keep your chin up young lady. It's hard to keep a New Yorker down. The world isn't going to end and neither are you. Why, I just about met my maker a couple of nights ago, but I'm still here through the grace of God. God is watching over you at this instant, too. If he can save me, he can surely save you. Trust me."

Ernie watched Cybil, but she couldn't bring herself to reply as tears began to well up in her eyes. "It's Giulio, isn't it?" Ernie asked. "I heard that your friend didn't make it. I'm so very sorry."

Cybil started to sob and spluttered, "I should be the one killed. Giulio shouldn't even have been at my hotel. They were after me."

Ernie caressed her hand and listened.

"I loved him! And now I have nothing!"

315

Ernie stayed by Cybil's bedside for a couple of hours. Throughout that time, he mostly listened as a close friend and, occasionally, he ministered to her. Ernie was heartbroken at her condition, but, by listening to her confession, he also knew that her lifestyle had been reckless and destructive. She lived from day to day in any number of wanton relationships with men, she drank excessively, and she aggressively pursued fame and fortune at any cost. Life was bound to come to a screeching halt some day. Now with her life in tatters, Ernie prayed that God would enable him to lend Cybil a hand in reassembling the pieces. He found himself wanting to help restore her to God for he sensed that she was a woman of valuable skills that could serve God's purposes. Now, he only had to persuade Cybil to believe in herself.

Sensing that Cybil was finally drifting off to sleep, Ernie got up to go. As he released her hand to turn towards the door, he was surprised to find Cybil firmly take a hold of his right hand.

"Ernie, thanks for visiting. I've messed up my life, but you're right. I can fix it. When I was a little girl, my mom always used to tell me that things looked better in the morning."

"That's my girl! Now you're talking sense."

Cybil smiled. A weak smile, but a smile, nevertheless. "Can I ask you for a favor, Ernie? Before you leave, would you say a prayer for me?"

Now it was Ernie's turn to have tears well up in his eyes. "Sure thing, Cybil. I would be honored."

Ernie stood by her bedside. Keeping his hand on Cybil's forehead and continuing to hold her left hand, the two New Yorkers prayed together.

Ernie left Cybil asleep and returned to his room to find Sean Murphy waiting for him. "Well, look at what the cat dragged in! It's good to see you!" Ernie walked over and gave

Sean a hug. "Are you taking me out of here? Please get me out of here before I go nuts. Please!"

"Actually, yes," Murphy replied. "The doctor has agreed to place you in my custody, providing you let Doctor Terzini at the Vatican clinic change your dressings daily." Murphy held up one of Ernie's bags. "I brought your clothes. Whaddaya' say?"

"I say give me my clothes and wait outside for five minutes!"

"Deal! I'll be right outside," Murphy replied and walked out.

True to his word, Ernie emerged five minutes later with a large smile. "Say, any chance that we can stop to eat? The lunch was okay, but it wasn't much."

"Listen to you! Beaten and bruised and left to drown two days ago, and now you're up and around looking for food. How do you do it?" Murphy laughed. "Come on. This way to the limo, my friend."

The two friends reached the limousine and climbed in. A couple of police officers riding motorcycles pulled in front of the limousine as it exited the parking lot.

Ernie was comfortably wedged on his side into the back seat. Looking up at Murphy, Ernie asked, "Where to, Sean?"

"Good question, Ernie. Where do you want to go?"

CHAPTER FIFTY

Ernie and Sean arrived at the Hotel Intercontinental late that afternoon. To Ernie's pleasant surprise, the Vatican had asked the hotel staff to hold the suite open for Ernie. Not wishing to draw attention to himself as a cardinal out on the town during the conclave, Murphy had agreed to join Ernie for an early dinner only under the condition of eating in the suite. The Vatican had found rooms at the Intercontinental for Ernie's two sons and daughter and they, therefore, joined the two good friends for dinner.

Despite favoring red wines, Cardinal Murphy had insisted that they open a bottle of white wine that evening and so they settled on eating fish for the main course. The meal proved far more sumptuous than Ernie had enjoyed at the hospital and, for that matter, than Sean had tasted at St. Martha's Residence. Afterwards, they all comfortably settled into chairs on the balcony with hot coffee and dessert as the sun sank lower and lower on the western horizon where New York was still enjoying a sunny afternoon. The two friends used the occasion to make up for their canceled July lunch date and, so, the conversation was far-ranging and, as usual, good humored and contentious much to the delight of Ernie's children.

At nine o'clock, Sean decided he needed to return to the Vatican. Mindful of Ernie's wounds, Sean carefully gave Ernie a big hug, wished him a good night's sleep, and promised to have Doctor Terzini visit him in the morning and to send the limousine for Ernie and his sons and daughter at one o'clock the next day. After Ernie watched the limousine driving onto the street from his balcony, he went inside to visit with his children. Finally, as the clock struck midnight, everyone decided to call it a night, but not before agreeing to have breakfast together. Alone, again, Ernie put out a suit to wear the next day and quickly repacked his suitcases.

The next morning proceeded as planned. Doctor Terzini arrived to check Ernie's wounds and to apply fresh bandages. With his three children arriving in good spirits for breakfast despite the gray skies and light rain, Ernie persuaded the physician to stay and join them for breakfast. Doctor Terzini, normally a reserved man, seemed to relax and enjoy the light-hearted family banter.

As he was leaving after breakfast, Terzini informed Ernie that Cardinal Maltempo had awakened from his coma during the previous day. Miraculously, Maltempo had minimal physical damage to his motor skills from the stroke. In fact, Maltempo had insisted on joining his brethren in the conclave that day.

Regretfully, Cardinal Roger Maria had died in his sleep last night. Terzini assured Ernie that it was simply a matter of time, but it was Terzini's choice of words that resounded with Ernie. Terzini had smiled and calmly stated, "The good Lord has gathered his loyal and faithful servant, Cardinal Maria, unto Himself and rewarded him for a job well done."

Later that morning, little Samantha and her mother surprised Ernie much to Ernie's eldest son's delight. After a hug for her dad at the door, Samantha bolted across the room to hug Ernie and to give him a wrapped present. Ernie laughed hysterically when he opened the gift for Samantha had given him a glorious, framed print of a bright yellow butterfly!

The remainder of the morning was spent with his family recollecting family stories and memories of his wife. A light lunch rejuvenated everyone, but Ernie's family grew quiet as Colonel Weissberg knocked on the suite's door at one o'clock to signal the arrival of the Vatican's limousine.

Five minutes later, with his suitcases stowed in the limousine's trunk, Ernie, Colonel Weissberg, Monsignor Campbell, and Monsignor Terrazza were moving through Rome's traffic in between motorcycle police escorts to the front and rear of the vehicle, as well as a black van carrying armed members of the Italian special weapons assault team that had rescued Ernie three days earlier.

To Ernie, the limousine ride seemed to take forever, but it wasn't long before the caravan pulled up behind St. Peter's Basilica. As Ernie exited the limousine, the clouds parted to reveal bright rays of sunshine streaming earthward. Looking skyward, Ernie smiled and, with a flock of white pigeons flying overhead, declared, "God is good!"

Looking back to his traveling companions, Ernie shook hands with Monsignor Campbell and Colonel Weissberg. He then nodded to Monsignor Terrazza who proceeded to guide Ernie inside through a series of chambers and hallways to the main inner entrance to the Sistine Chapel.

No sooner had the Swiss Guards knocked loudly three times on the massive doors than the doors swung open. Ernie hesitated, took a deep breath and, again, nodded at Monsignor Terrazza. Trying to assume a dignified appearance in spite of his bandages and sore limbs, Ernie deliberately walked into the

Sistine Chapel with Monsignor Terrazza leading the way, between the standing cardinals, up to the raised platform.

Ernie smiled when he saw his good friend, Sean Cardinal Murphy. However, a mere ten steps from the raised platform, Ernie abruptly halted when a weak voice called out in Italian. "Ernesto! That's him! That is certainly him!"

Turning to his right, Ernie was surprised to find an elderly cardinal in a wheelchair excitedly pointing at him. "Ernesto, may God bless you and forgive me!" Instantly knowing that he had the pleasure of meeting Cardinal Maltempo, Ernie turned to his right and went down on one knee by Maltempo's side. "Cardinal Maltempo, I am honored to finally meet you. Alas, we are all sinners in need of God's forgiveness. Praise God for miraculously restoring your health!" Ernie gingerly took hold of Maltempo's right hand and kissed it. Rising, Ernie left the speechless Maltempo and approached Cardinal Meissner on the dais.

"Good morning, Cardinal Meissner!" Ernie shook the cardinal's hand and joined him, face to face, on the platform.

"Good morning, Doctor Flanagan," Meissner responded. "How are you today?"

"By the grace of God I am alive, Cardinal Meissner. Although I am walking forward with great uncertainty, God is leading me and all of you are at my side. That's all I need."

Beaming, Meissner nodded and looked to his right at the expectant cardinals. Turning back to Ernie, Meissner now spoke loudly, in Italian, with firm conviction so that his colleagues could clearly hear him. "Ernesto Flanagan, the cardinal electors of the Holy Roman Catholic Church acting in faith as servants of our Lord and Savior, Jesus Christ, and guided by the Holy Spirit are in agreement that God has selected you as Vicar of Christ and Successor of Peter. Do you accept your canonical election as Supreme Pontiff?"

Ernie's heart raced and he felt himself shiver. It was only with the greatest difficulty that he turned to face the cardinals awaiting his reply. Gazing at the cardinals in their finest choir dress garments, Ernie felt strangely out of place in his business suit and minister's collar. Ernie licked his dry lips and folded his hands behind him in an attempt to hide his trembling fingers. He then began to speak.

"Our God is good and merciful. He gives us strength to overcome the despair of finding ourselves less than capable for the tasks he lays before us. Indeed, God calls us to be the comforters, not the comfortable, of the broken world in which we live.

He calls all of us to step, in faith, beyond our limitations and beyond our knowledge into uncharted waters. He calls us to walk to Him, as Peter did, across the dark depths and the tumultuous waves keeping our eyes fixed on Him, not understanding, but trusting, that He will not let us sink and drown.

It is folly to deny His will although the world does its best to distract us and to confuse us. The instant we take our eyes off of him, we sink and are lost. By God's grace, we do not sink and drown if our lives remain fixed on Him. By God's grace, He offers us the hope of eternal life above the dark depths and foaming waves crashing around us.

I lost sight of God's will. I fell into despair at my limitations. Evil then took a hold of me and nearly killed me. But, as I sank in the water, drawing ever nearer to hell, my eyes looked up to heaven and my soul sought God. It was then that God proved to be my savior. If it wasn't for God, I would not be standing here among you. In more ways than one. I still feel less than capable of adequately fulfilling the task that you are asking me to accept. I lack the knowledge. I lack the experience.

Nevertheless, I will no longer run from God. I must follow the example that all of you have set in prayerfully recognizing and subjecting yourselves to God's will in spite of not fully understanding God's will.

Therefore, with many reservations but with all of the hope and courage that a simple man can have, I accept the election. Accepto!"

The Sistine Chapel instantaneously broke out into wild applause and jubilation. The cardinals all pressed forward towards Ernie. Cardinal Meissner knelt before him, placed the new Ring of the Fisherman on Ernie's ring finger and kissed his hand, but Ernie would have none of that. He pulled Meissner to his feet and simply hugged the cardinal. Then, with each cardinal approaching him one by one, Ernie hugged them and would not permit them to genuflect.

By the time Cardinal Murphy reached the front, Ernie was happily in tears. "Sean, stand here by me. Look at the two of us Brooklyn boys. Who would have ever thought it would come to this?"

As the celebration wound down, Cardinal Meissner got Ernie's attention and asked, "By what name do you wish to be called?"

Ernie wiped away the last tear and grinned widely. Looking Meissner in the eyes, Ernie authoritatively declared, "Jonah Paul the First!"

At this the cardinals erupted in cheers and more applause that lasted for several minutes. After several attempts, Cardinal Meissner finally was able to get everyone's attention.

"My fellow brethren, we must first conduct a mass. As we all know, Jonah Paul the First is neither an ordained priest nor a bishop of the Holy Roman Catholic Church. We, therefore, must conduct a mass before we announce the pontiff's election. Please, return to your seats!"

With order restored, Cardinal Meissner led the College of Cardinals in a mass within the Sistine Chapel to ordain Ernie as a priest and bishop. The solemn ceremony, lasting well over an hour, was exactly what Ernie needed to calm himself and to properly reflect on the significance of the unfolding events.

At the conclusion of the ceremony, white smoke and ringing church bells announced to the world that a new pontiff was poised to minister to it. The cardinals could hear the crowd in St. Peter's Square cheer.

Ernie was led to the adjoining Room of Tears where the papal garments awaited him. The white silk cassock, white skull cap, and red shoulder cape were lying on a large chair.

Ernie eyed the white papal robe. Although he had incredibly accepted the pontiff's post, Ernie was not willing to don the elaborate garments. He stared at the immaculate, hand-crafted clothes for several minutes, hardly believing that he was now the Catholic Pope. "This isn't right," he calmly said to himself. Turning, he walked back to the door and asked Monsignor Terrazza, standing just outside the entrance, to bring Cardinal Murphy.

Two minutes later, Sean Murphy arrived. "What is it, Ernie? Uh, sorry. Your Holiness."

Ernie squinted at him with one eye and wagged his finger. "Look, if you have to stick to protocol, do it in public. But, when it's just the two of us, you had better be calling me Ernie! This is hard enough for me without feeling that I lost our personal friendship. Okay?"

"Of course, Ernie. Sorry about that."

Exasperated, Ernie pointed at the papal garments. "Sean, I can't wear these extravagant robes! They're too much for the simpleton in me. I'll never feel like myself. I'll never be able to comfortably move among the very people to whom I need to minister. Everyone will be in too much awe of me in this elaborate outfit. I know that I'm likely breaking with a tradition here, but this won't do. If I'm the Pope, I should be able to

THE FLANAGAN OPTION

Your Opinion is Requested

I value your opinion of this novel
and would like for you to provide me with your review.

Please, email your comments to me at
DrBBowman@Gmail.com

Did you enjoy this novel?
How did the novel affect you?
Are the characters believable?
Is the plot development plausible?
What do you think of my writing style?
What do you think of the level of mystery and suspense?
d the novel cause you to consider matters of faith and religion?
Would you recommend this book to your friends?

If you provide me with your name and address
I will send you a free, autographed copy of the novel
t is picked up for publication by a major publishing house.

Thanks!
Bruce

decide what I would like to wear. Please, find something else for me to wear. Something more fitting for the ministry I envision!"

"Okay, okay. Ernie, I give up. What on earth do you have in mind?"

An hour later, a cardinal, framed by the center window of St. Peter's Basilica, was standing on the balcony of the Hall of the Benedictions to introduce the new pontiff to the world. With the media transmitting the event to the world, the cardinal declared: "I announce to you a great joy. We have a pope! His Most Eminent and Reverend Lord, Lord Ernesto Bisho Flanagan of the Holy Roman Church who has chosen for himse the name of Jonah Paul I."

After a flurry of hugs from his family and with TJ Colonel Weissberg looking on, Ernie stepped onto the bal for the world to see its new pontiff, a stranger from the far s of America who had safely reached the shoreline of Eur answer Christ's call.

Standing now in full view of the swelling crowd a cameras, Ernie blinked in the bright sunlight and wave plain, white monk's tunic and sandals.

Di

if